795

D1457368

Tizard

Sir Henry Tizard in Canada, 1947

TIZARD

RONALD W. CLARK

THE M.I.T. PRESS
Massachusetts Institute of Technology
Cambridge, Massachusetts

Copyright © 1965
by The Massachusetts Institute of Technology
All rights reserved

Library of Congress Catalog Card Numbers 65–12911
Printed in Great Britain

94/.5
6 8 059

Q
143
T5
C6
68059

HARVARD
UNIVERSITY
LIBRARY
MAR 4 1966

Acknowledgements

The author wishes to thank: Lady Tizard and Professor J. P. M. Tizard for giving him access to Sir Henry Tizard's papers and allowing him to quote from them; Sir Donald MacDougall for allowing him to consult Lord Cherwell's Papers in Nuffield College; Sir Solly Zuckerman for writing the Foreword.

He also wishes to thank the Controller of Her Majesty's Stationery Office for permission to quote from Crown Copyright material; and the following for permission to quote private letters or documents; Bennett Archambault; the late Lord Beaverbrook; Dr. R. B. Bourdillon; Dr. Vannevar Bush; Sir James Chadwick; Sir John Cockcroft; Sir Winston Churchill; Air Chief Marshal Lord Dowding; Air Vice-Marshal MacNeece Foster; Sir Roy Fedden; Dr. Otto Frisch; Sir Harold Hartley; Professor A. V. Hill; Sir Cyril Hinshelwood; General Lord Ismay; Professor R. V. Jones; Brigadier Charles Lindemann; Dr. C. J. Mackenzie; Sir Mark Oliphant; Dr. Rudolf Peierls; Sir Harry Ricardo; Sir Edgar Sengier; Lord Swinton; Sir George Thomson; Mrs. John Watson.

He also wishes to thank for permission to quote printed copyright material: George Allen & Unwin Ltd. for the extract from 'The Department of Scientific and Industrial Research' by Sir Harry Melville; The Cambridge University Press for the extract from 'One Story of Radar' by Dr. A. P. Rowe; Frederick Muller Ltd. for the extract from 'Jet' by Air Commodore Sir Frank Whittle; Cassell & Co. Ltd. for the extracts from 'The Second World War' by Winston Churchill; William Collins & Co. Ltd. for the extract from 'Triumph in the West, 1943–1946', by Sir Arthur Bryant. 'The Spectator' for the extract by Oliver Stewart. R. E. Threlfall for the extract from 'The Gentle Art'; Angus & Robertson Ltd. for the extract from 'Woomera' by Ivan Southall. In addition he is grateful for the chance of reading before publication, the proofs of: 'Design and Development of

Weapons: Studies in Government and Industrial Organisation'
by M. M. Postan, D. Hay and J. D. Scott, (H.M.S.O.).

The author wishes to make it clear that any opinions in
'Tizard', and responsibility for the facts given, are entirely his
own unless the reverse is obvious. But he has been given great
help by many of Sir Henry's friends, and would like to thank the
following in particular:

J. E. Adamson; Professor Sir Edward Appleton; Lord Birken-
head; Professor P. M. S. Blackett; Dr. B. K. Blount; Sir Frederick
Brundrett; T. S. R. Boase; Dr. E. G. Bowen; the late Lord
Brabazon; Air Commodore Sir Vernon Brown; Dr. W. A. S.
Butement; Sir John Cockcroft; Lt. Col. H. L. Cooper; Sir
Harold Roxbee-Cox; Sir Maurice Dean; Dr. B. G. Dickins;
Dr. H. J. T. Ellingham; the late Wing Commander Grenfell;
Dr. Noble Frankland; Dr. D. H. Hammick; Professor A. V. Hill;
G. R. D. Hogg; L. A. Jackets; Douglas Johnson; Professor R. V.
Jones; Air Marshal Sir Philip Joubert de la Ferté; Dr. Alexander
King; G. C. Lowry; R. G. MacNeill; the late Marshal of the
Royal Air Force Lord Newall; Air Vice-Marshal Sir Walter
Pretty; Air Vice-Marshal R. L. Ragg; Dr. A. P. Rowe; Dr. L. E.
Sutton; Lawrence Tanner; Sir George Thomson; R. E. Threlfall;
Dr. Barnes Wallis; Sir Charles Wright; L. L. Whyte; Sir Solly
Zuckerman.

Special thanks are due to Sir Harold Hartley for generously
giving the author the benefit of his researches for his Obituary
Notice of Sir Henry published by the Chemical Society; to Sir
William Farren for the use of his bibliography of Sir Henry's
writings published in the *Biographical Memoirs of Fellows of the Royal
Society*; and to Denys Forrest for reading the manuscript and
making numerous helpful suggestions.

Contents

Illustrations

Foreword
by Sir Solly Zuckerman

It is only five years since Sir Henry Tizard died. But to many his name already seems to conjure up little more than a picture of some kind of personal struggle for power in places where scientific advice bears on the formulation of national policy. Sir Charles Snow, who dramatized the clash of Sir Henry Tizard with Lord Cherwell, could hardly have anticipated this outcome of his colourful account of the relations and characters of these two distinguished scientists – even if he correctly foresaw the debate which it stimulated about the channels whereby informed advice should be directed towards those who are responsible for government in a scientific and technological age.

Ronald Clark has now given us a complete picture of Tizard, based upon a study of some five hundred files of private papers which he left, and which had not been consulted before, as well as the diaries and unfinished autobiography which Sir Charles Snow studied. In addition Ronald Clark has had access to Lord Cherwell's archives, which had already been used by Lord Birkenhead in the biography he wrote. On top of all this he was able to consult a mass of private letters and documents belonging to various people whose paths had crossed Sir Henry's. The result is a volume which undoubtedly becomes part of the history of our times.

Tizard's greatest single achievement was the encouragement he gave to the development of the chain of radar stations which assured the R.A.F.'s victory in the Battle of Britain. None of the scientific ideas behind radar was his, but without his support, backed by the prestige gained through many years of intimate and successful co-operation with members of the Air Staff, it is doubtful if our defences would have held in those vital days of 1940. Tizard's own place in history is secure for this contribution alone.

But there were other contributions – all admirably told by Ronald Clark. He describes the events leading to the setting-up in 1934 of the famous Committee of Air Defence, in whose deliberations distinguished scientists, serving officers, and politicians played a part, and which foundered in 1936 because of the clash between Lindemann, later to become Lord Cherwell, and the rest of the Committee, led by Tizard. Fortunately, this first phase of the Committee's existence had not passed before the foundations of radar were securely laid. Clark describes the later reconstitution of the Committee without Lindemann, and the next eighteen months during which a radar system proper was built. He then tells of the eclipse of Tizard and his committees, and of the increasing dominance of Lord Cherwell, Sir Winston Churchill's chief wartime adviser on scientific and technical matters. Ronald Clark also gives us a clear account of Tizard's return to Whitehall after the war, and of many other events which uniquely illustrate phases in the evolving system within which science and politics converge.

The picture which is painted of Tizard will prove eminently true to those who knew him well. Tizard's achievements were great. He was a scientist who immediately won the confidence of the scientific establishment. He commanded loyalty even when his judgment was at fault. For Tizard was not always right. He was sceptical about the likelihood that scientific knowledge of the atom could be harnessed for military purposes; he felt that 'unnecessary excitement' was being generated by the belief – correct though it proved to be – that the navigation of German aircraft was being assisted by radio beams. There is the suggestion that he held that the invasion of Normandy in the summer of 1944 would be bound to prove a disaster. Events have also told against his vision of the institutional ways whereby science can best help the State. And as Ronald Clark shows, some of his views, as well as those of his staunchest allies, were in the latter part of his public career too often coloured by a violent antipathy to Cherwell, who emerges from Ronald Clark's book not quite as black as on other occasions when his name has been mentioned in the same breath as Tizard's.

In spite of all this Tizard is correctly revealed by Ronald

Clark's book as a beacon of a particular kind in the history of England – as a man who more often than not pointed the right way, and as a person who could be relied upon to fight to keep it open.

5th October, 1964.

Foreword to the American Edition
by
Vannevar Bush

Much has been written about the disagreements between allies during a great war. Little has been written about the deep friendships which appear among comrades in arms of different nations, even among comrades whose efforts, behind the lines, are devoted to placing advanced weapons in the hands of fighting men. It is especially fitting that an edition of a book on Henry Tizard should appear in the United States for he exemplified strongly the mutual respect and friendship which developed between scientists and engineers of the United States and their counterparts in the United Kingdom.

It was primarily due to the skill, patience, and geniality of Tizard that interchange between Britain and the United States, on the development of weapons, was put into effect and made fully operative, long before the United States entered the war. There is no doubt that this collaboration resulted in a more effective war effort and contributed significantly to ultimate victory. In so doing he made a host of American friends who will welcome this volume.

It was not easy to do. There were stuffy admirals and generals on both sides of the ocean. There was a widespread conviction on both sides of technical superiority, and there was doubt as to the others guardianship of secrets. The partnership between scientists and military men, which later in the war produced striking results, had not then developed. The civilian scientific effort in the United States had barely begun. The maze of complex loose organization on both sides had not crystallized into effective form.

Through this confusion, Henry Tizard threaded his way with a sure step. He fully attained his objective, and left no bitterness behind. We, in the United States, hail his memory with gratitude and affection.

8 September, 1964

Author's Preface

Sir Henry Tizard's life is a record of one man's influence on defence science between 1914 and 1951, a period which saw it transformed to the decisive factor in a nation's survival. Although this transformation was in great measure due to the efforts of Sir Henry himself, he never became entirely reconciled to the new situation he had done so much to create. Thus he was inclined to agree that if scientists 'became politicians they would act like politicians' – yet at the same time he believed that 'such phrases as "back-room boys" are deplorable'. And he saw only the opening stages of the continuing debate about the exact place which they might best occupy between Parliament and quiet back-room.

Within the bounds of his job, he had the quality of the well-cut diamond which looks slightly different from whichever angle it is viewed. Thus to the student of aviation, he was the man who had established the science of test-flying and, in a later period, helped fashion radar into a tool which the R.A.F. could use in battle. To his close personal friends he was the man full of good stories, deploring in them the frailties of Whitehall and the follies of the Services with a mixture of regret and kindly understanding. To the professional scientist he was one of the few who knew just which Civil Service button might be pressed, at what moment, by whom, with the greatest effect. Only those who made close contact with him fully appreciated his prickliness, his toughness, the unpredictable and in some ways surprising streak of individual non-conformity which made it so difficult to fit him into any of the pigeon-holes for which he had at first seemed suitable. These qualities, and his ability to rub men up the wrong way – an ability which he rarely exercised by accident – influenced the views which his contemporaries formed of him. All agreed that he was of the first rank; only his position in the rank was sometimes debated.

His faith in what science could achieve enabled him to concentrate all thought, all energy, all ambition, on the public good.

But this concentration left remarkably little time for private affairs, for personal enthusiasms, for that appreciation of the arts which is the reward of most questioning minds. His interest in literature was of the conventional kind and he drew great pleasure from his wide reading of Johnson and Kipling, Dickens and Stevenson. He had considerable knowledge of the goldsmiths' and silversmiths' crafts, but his interest in most of the arts was slight and in the rest non-existent. He had a good eye for country; indeed, inside the scientist there may well have lurked the topographer. And behind the curtain which he was apt to draw down in front of his public affairs, there lay a happy family life.

In person, Tizard was of medium height, wiry rather than strong, of a build always trimmed to the bone. He wore well, indefatigable through the years, and one of his few weaknesses was to worry disproportionately about his minor ailments; only the records prove that these were not, as observers may sometimes have suspected, raised to the usefulness of diplomatic illness. His voice was clear, clipped, and of an extraordinary variety. It could, as in some of his broadcasts, be crisp almost to the point of heartlessness, recounting even personal stories of old friends with a detachment that concealed his own feelings. It could also, when he warmed to an audience, make him a most effective after-dinner speaker. Here his success was perhaps unexpected, for he was suspicious of showmanship; he distrusted all forms of self-advertisement and for this reason disliked more than one able scientist, more than one fine airman. His tastes in dress, drink, and food were restrained. He had a good knowledge of wine yet drank little – although one of his few extravagant enjoyments was champagne in a pint tankard – and smoked a pipe moderately.

Wherever possible, Sir Henry Tizard operated with the anonymity of a scientific Hankey. Yet he was frequently in the eye of the storm; there were many storms, and it would have been impossible to track their courses with any accuracy but for the exceptional co-operation which I have been given in the use of documents. Lady Tizard and Professor J. P. M. Tizard have allowed me to make unrestricted use not only of Sir Henry's diaries and unfinished autobiography, but also of his correspondence and papers, personal and official – more than 500 files of them in all, none previously consulted. Lord Cherwell's extensive archives were also made available to me; and much similar material was also provided from other sources.

I have supplemented this documentary evidence, written by the men involved, at the time of critical events, by conversation with many of Sir Henry's friends to whom I am greatly indebted. Oral witness is sometimes questioned, but its value is stressed by no less a historian than Trevelyan. 'The conversations of veterans must, of course, be listened to with critical vigilance as well as with respect', he says in his preface to 'Garibaldi and the Thousand' ' . . . but their impressions throw light on the spirit, opinions, and mutual relations of the men and parties with whom they worked. And even in matters of detail, particularly in military affairs, they often enable the puzzled historian to reconcile or choose between conflicting statements in books, or to understand some incident otherwise unintelligible.' For that reason, if for no other, I am most grateful to those who have given up valuable time to help me. Their views have not always agreed. Indeed, it would be remarkable if they had. But it is therefore only fair to say that any opinions expressed here, implicit or explicit, are my own unless the reverse is obvious.

' . . . for much of my working life I have been intimately concerned with that peculiar business called war, which is as old as agriculture, which is subject to the most violent booms and slumps, the cause of which we do not understand, and in which the incentive to succeed is greater than any profit or ideological incentive in civilian life.'

Sir Henry Tizard in *The Passing World*

CHAPTER ONE

Early Years

Henry Thomas Tizard was born on Sunday, 23 August, 1885, at 10 Kingswood Villas, Gillingham, Kent. The houses, with their walled gardens reaching back to a network of narrow streets, today look towards the buildings on the slightly higher ground nearby. Eighty years ago open fields stretched in far closer and from the crest of a neighbouring ridge one could see the Medway, with grey ironclads anchored off the recently enlarged dockyards. Moving heavily downstream, low in the water with their cargoes of Kentish corn, fruit, bricks, and tiles, there passed a constant traffic of russet-sailed barges, navigating the reaches below Rochester Bridge and tacking down the main channel to Sheerness, the Thames estuary, and the open sea. Much local life depended on the river, and concern with the fortunes of ships and sailors was equalled only by that for the hop-fields which pressed in towards the outskirts of the town. The papers reported 'Hop Intelligence' and 'Foreign Hop Intelligence' as well as postings to and from the Chatham Dockyard and the Garrison. And the great gale which swept the area during August 1885, was remembered as much for wrecking the harvest of Goldings and Colegates as for pinning in the estuary forty-three large steamships and a dozen sailing vessels.

It was the Dockyard which had brought the Tizards to Gillingham, since H.M.S. *Triton*, commanded by Captain Thomas Henry Tizard, put in regularly at Chatham for stores or additional equipment required for the survey of British waters upon which she and her crew were engaged. The Captain traced his ancestry back to the Huguenot Tizzards, as they appear to have been known when they had settled in Dorset some centuries earlier. The name was well spread along the south coast, and legend speaks of a Captain Tizard who sailed into Plymouth Harbour with

two gold altar candle-sticks tied to his masthead*. Assimilation
into British life was thorough and successful, and it is only in the
early nineteenth century that the family records become distin-
guishable from the fabric of the times. They tell of Joseph Tizard,
ship-owner and coal merchant of Weymouth whose third son,
born in 1839, was educated at the Royal Hospital School, Green-
wich, entered the Royal Navy as a master's assistant in 1854, and
in the same year saw action in the Baltic on H.M.S. *Dragon*. He
served in the survey ship, H.M.S. *Rifleman* on the China Station, as
Senior Assistant Surveyor on H.M.S. *Newport*, led the procession of
British ships through the Suez Canal on its formal opening in
1869, and three years later became navigating officer to H.M.S.
Challenger for its four-year voyage round the world. This was the
Captain Tizard of H.M.S. *Triton* whose officers, hearing their
commander's good news in August 1885, drank the health of his
son in champagne.

His wife was Mary Elizabeth, daughter of William Henry
Churchward, the civil engineer who had helped build first the
Malta and then the Pembroke docks; a remote ancestor through
her mother's family, the Shordiches of Ickenham, had been Sir
Paul Rycaut, F.R.S., to whom she bore a likeness judging by his
portrait in the Royal Society's possession. She was a clever woman,
highly temperamental, constantly worried, deeply religious, believing with her husband, no doubt, in Herbert's injunction to
'do well and right and let the world sink.'

By 1885 events had concluded their task of moulding the
Tizards to the classic pattern. They had come as emigrants seeking
refuge. They had taken to the sea. And they were now more
English than the English. 'With a name like mine', said Sir
Henry in later life, 'you have to be.'

The young Tizard had two elder sisters, Aimée born in 1882,
and Ethel born in 1884. Two more girls followed within the next
few years, Dorothy in 1886 and Beata in 1888. Their brother was

* 'Fortunes of almost fabulous magnitude had been made by lucky privat-
eersmen during the last war; and was there not even then living in Weymouth
the heroic Captain Tizard, who had captured a Spanish Plate ship and sailed
into Plymouth Sound with his prize in tow, and a massive gold candlestick
glittering at each mast-head?' *The Log of the Privateersman*, Harry Collingwood,
pp. 15 and 16.

shortish, quiet, and unremarkable except for his shock of red
hair. His father was much at sea, his ship putting in to Chatham
only at long intervals, and one of the first persons to influence the
young boy was Canon Robins, the blind parson of Gillingham,
to whose church the family would walk across the fields every
Sunday evening. He had been baptized there with the third name
of Luke. He was brought up, as he later described it, as 'a proper
little Christian boy', and from the time that he began to read he
received an admonitory letter each birthday from his godmother,
Sister Esther of the Sisterhood of St Thomas Ye Martyr of Oxford,
reminding him that he was, as she stressed, 'enrolled in God's
great army'. The influence lasted long, so that he sloughed off his
religion but slowly, bit by bit, over the years. Yet before he reached
middle age it had been born in upon him that doubt, questioning,
the determination to follow facts wherever they might lead, was
the very rock on which science was founded, just as faith was the
theologian's. Thus he felt agnosticism to be part of the scientific
inheritance; he could never justify to himself the blind faith of the
atheist.

The abiding memories of Tizard's childhood were of the sur-
rounding fields and it was here, in the Kentish countryside, that
his father aroused his interest in science, explaining how the
height of trees could be measured by the use of elementary trigo-
nometry, throwing stones in ponds and explaining what it was
that caused the circular ripples. With his father, he visited the
dockyard and there was one notable occasion when it was 'a
beautiful day, and a lark was singing high in the sky'. The sailors
encouraged him to climb rope ladders, talking about distant ports
and the great seas whose deeper mysteries the Admiralty was now
beginning to probe.

In 1891 the Captain was promoted from the *Triton* to the post
of Assistant Hydrographer of the Admiralty, and elected a Fellow
of the Royal Society. The family moved to Surbiton, a name which
then stood not for the apotheosis of suburbia but for a pleasant
township among the trees, reaching back from the River Thames
and up through the orchards of Ditton towards the open country
of Chessington. The Tizards settled down in the comfortable quiet
of Berwick Villa. This stood on high ground, was separated only

by a single line of houses from the green country that stretched south to Old Malden Church, and to it there came during the summer the sound of threshing from a distant farm. It was a spacious, undistinguished building, with a long garden to which was eventually added the orchard of a neighbouring house.

Here Tizard observed his two pet tortoises and noted their predilection for fallen tulip petals. 'When they had eaten them all I observed one of them knocking down a fresh tulip and lying on the stalk, while its mate ate the flower', he later wrote. 'Then they changed places for the next tulip. It was intelligent, but it was not popular.' In the orchard there were pear trees, plum trees, and one big apple tree – 'a good tree to climb', he recollected. 'I remember spending happy summer afternoons in it reading *Vanity Fair* and occasionally stretching out my hand for another apple.'[1] Like so many memories of nineteenth-century childhood, Tizard's give the impression that much of life was a long summer afternoon interspersed with Sunday evening walks across the meadows to the church, broken by winters as cold as that when the Thames froze and an ox was roasted whole on the ice beside Kingston Bridge. It was a boyhood which rose slowly to a climax in which there bowed from an open carriage an elderly widow – Victoria, by the Grace of God, ruler of the United Kingdom of Great Britain and Ireland and the British Dominions beyond the Seas, Defender of the Faith, Empress of India. Tizard remembered the Golden Jubilee procession; he remembered the sights and sounds of traditional English customs, the pomp and ceremony which appealed to his imagination as strongly as humbug irritated him; and he remembered all his life the sound of the newsboys crying the death of the old Queen.

The early years were hard. The Captain, as Tizard wrote much later, 'was a truly religious man; he really thought that God would provide. What would have happened to us if he had died before he was 65 I do not know.' Henry dug a small allotment patch in the garden and was glad to make a profit of 4s. a year by selling vegetables to his mother – a sum 'about equal to the cash I received during a year from all other sources.' He made his own toys. He spent many of his holidays at home, although occasionally he went to Weymouth, and later Sandown, frequently cycling most of the way. He visited an uncle in the Prescelly Mountains who awakened an interest in fishing. And in 1898 his mother took him across the Channel to Bourbourg where he was left at a *pension* in the hope that he would improve his knowledge of French. 'F[ather] sent me 5s. as a birthday present', he noted. A few days later there followed a message saying that the Captain would be posting his son the money for the journey home, and in due course there arrived an Order for 16s. 'I had a happy but far from opulent childhood', he noted in his Personal Record for the Royal Society.

One thing helped to compensate for the frugality which in-fluenced most of his early life. His father might not have spent his years acquiring much money, an occupation for businessmen and similar individuals, but he had certainly secured a distinguished place in the Royal Navy. And his son, also, was destined for the same Navy where, given hard work, honesty, and a measure of good luck, he would at least live within the security of a Service which offered the prospect of honourable reward. Tizard's early education was thus undertaken with entry into the Royal Navy as the object of all hope and endeavour. He went first to a nursery school and then to Enfield House, kept by three maiden ladies only a few doors from Berwick Villa. Here he received the ground-ing in mathematics which was later to serve him so well – both in sensing the relationship between economics and the industrial application of science, and in evaluating, from among the jungle of defence ideas of the later 1930's, just those which were likely to repay time and thought. The man most responsible was a Mr Verey who taught against the handicap of a stutter. 'His methods of teaching would be frowned upon nowadays', Tizard has written. 'He used, for example, to group a handful of boys round him, sit on a low stool in the middle of the semi-circle, armed with a cricket stump, and fire questions in mental arithmetic at us. If a boy was too slow in answering, he got a rap on the shins with the cricket stump.' Tizard's interest in team games was casual, al-though he was a good gymnast and had both strong nerves and a steady hand. Thus it was he, slight of build, imperturbable, who was chosen to hold an apple on the palm of his hand while the gym instructor, an ex-sergeant-major, cut it in half with his sword. 'I

could just feel the steel on my hand before the two halves fell
apart', he remembered fifty years later.[2]

More than one boy had graduated from Enfield House to
H.M.S. *Britannia*, the two old battleships, linked by a gallery and
moored off Dartmouth, which still produced the country's naval
officers, and it was in the confident expectation of joining them
that Tizard watched the Golden Jubilee naval review at Portsmouth from his father's old ship. A small boat had wandered
against orders in and out the lines, outpacing each naval picket
that attempted interception. 'This', Tizard recalled, 'was the
Turbinia which Charles Parsons had built to demonstrate to an
unbelieving Admiralty that they had better sit up and take notice
of the new invention of turbine engines. He succeeded.'

Next summer the family spent their holidays at Weymouth.
Tizard, studying his papers in later life, noted that he had
written against the date 5 July: 'Father looking forward still to
my going in the Navy.' This remained the situation the following
year. As the summer of 1898 approached, he began his final preparations. There then descended the *deus ex machina* who was to
mark a turning-point in his life and fortunes. It descended in
the shape of a humble fly which entered his left eye. 'I closed it',
he recalled 'and discovered to my horror that I was blind in the
right eye.' He was not, in fact, completely blind, but he had a
blind patch. The specialists to whom he was taken claimed that
this would eventually clear. It did so, even though he was to
suffer from eye trouble for the rest of his life. And all thought of a
naval career now had to be abandoned.

This unexpected misfortune produced a traumatic result not
only on Captain Tizard but also on his son. For the father it was
difficult even to consider what career there could be for a boy
whom cruel fate had barred from the Royal Navy. For the son,
looking to a future that might be austere but was also assured, the
uncertainties of the world now loomed up menacingly and un-
expectedly. The shock left a scar which in after years was to show
in many ways. There were to be occasions when Tizard clung to
the financially safer post or appointment. There was to be a
minute detailing of personal expenditure in which he persisted –
not only as a young man, when it would merely have reflected

prudence, but as an established public figure when he would record the amount spent on a newspaper or the laundering of a collar. His financial principles were quixotic, and as the £3,000-a-year Rector of Imperial College in the 1930's he more than once refused money for Government services which included, in passing, the salvation of his country. More than once he refused, or returned, hard cash given for what he felt should be unpaid public work.

The circumstance which in barring Tizard from the Royal Navy helped to produce this attitude, presented his family with a problem that was resolved when he sat for a scholarship at Westminster. At the Challenge, as it is called, he failed to be elected into College; however, his mathematical training enabled him to win a Bishop Williams Exhibition, and on 28 September, 1899 he was admitted as boarder Up 'Rigaud's' under the House Mastership of the Rev. Watson Failes. From the first, Tizard's progress at Westminster was rapid, and he was not destined to remain long Up Rigaud's as a Town Boy. In January 1900 there was a Bye-election, and of the six boys then elected as Queen's Scholars, Tizard was placed fourth.

The world into which he now passed was small and academically aristocratic. Westminster's forty Queen's Scholars were divided into 'Elections' – Juniors, Second, Third, Fourth Elections, and Seniors – and each might speak only to those in his own Election and in those immediately above or below his own. They were regarded as forming the senior branch of the School. They were fully conscious of the fact. They 'kept themselves to themselves', and they no doubt discouraged Tizard from pursuing any friendship he had formed during his few months as a Town Boy Up Rigaud's. The habit of exclusiveness may have been built into his character, but it was here encouraged.[3]

For two years life was demanding. There was a long list of Westminster words and phrases which the Junior had to master during his first fortnight; there were innumerable small rules which had to be strictly kept; there was still much fagging, monitorial beatings were frequent, amenities few. To all this there was added the fact that Tizard was a potential scientist in a predominantly classical world. There is no evidence that he complained about this natural order of things. Instead, he turned to the job in hand. He won the Junior Cheyne Prize for arithmetic in 1900 – being placed equal to the captain of the school, who won the Senior Prize – and the Senior Prize in 1901. He had by now reached the Modern VIth and here he remained, probably owing to his youth, until the summer of 1903 when he gained his remove into the Modern VIIth.

From the beginning of the third year, life became progressively pleasanter, and to this period Tizard always looked back with pleasure. One reason, no doubt, was that Westminster had now begun the real making of him. He may have been a scientific goose among the classical swans, but he had always enjoyed a love of English literature, and his Westminster years underpinned and strengthened it. The school's position, butting up against the Abbey, opened his eyes to the splendours of architecture and the continuity of history. For many boys this would not have been needed, but for Tizard, already directed towards a career in which science was obviously to play at least some part, it provided a counter-weight. It kept him on an even keel and it helped to save him from the aesthetic and moral illiteracy into which the scientist can so easily slide.

> Westminster was a splendid school for boys of sensibility [he subse-quently wrote]. We had history all around us; history made and in the making. Westminster Abbey and the Houses of Parliament were at our doorsteps. The Abbey was our school chapel. I got to love it. Another boy (F. M. Maxwell) and I found that a door to the tri-phorium at the north-west corner of the abbey was slightly off its hinges, and we used to creep through to the stone steps when no-one was looking. We got to know the whole of the abbey; often have I spent a hot Saturday afternoon on the top of one of the old towers. To get to the tower we had to cross the rose window above Poets' Corner, but no verger ever spotted us or, if they did, they took no notice.[4]

He already knew the glories of the Abbey when, at the post-poned Coronation of Edward VII the King's Scholars, as they had now become, exercised their traditional privilege of being the first to acclaim the new sovereign at his Coronation. To him they addressed their 'Vivat Rex Edwardus. Vivat, Vivat, Vivat', as the monarch entered the Choir of the Abbey – the last relic of the former spontaneous shout of recognition by the people before the Sovereign is formally presented to the congregation by the Archbishop as their undoubted King. Tizard enjoyed this as throughout life he was to enjoy the splendour and colour of materially useless but spiritually uplifting ceremonies. This enjoyment typified however, only one half of his dichotomous nature which carefully separated the pomp from the pompous and which relished the human footnotes to great events. It was typical that more than half a century later he should remember how a verger had told him after the ceremony 'that the King was given a stiff whisky and soda in the Annexe after the service was over, and sank back rather exhausted in an armchair saying: "That was a damned good show" '.[5]

At Westminster he enjoyed the privilege of going into the Speaker's Gallery of the House of Commons with no credentials other than his scholar's gown.

> Members of Parliament, and the policemen and other custodians of the House were very kind to us boys [he recollected]. We felt, in a sense, part of the show; and it was certainly a valuable part of my education . . . I never heard anyone mention science; I feel sure that if any member had urged expenditure on scientific research he would soon have emptied the House.[6]

It already seemed likely that his preoccupation with science would be a lasting one, and in 1903 he was dissuaded by his housemaster from trying for a 'close' scholarship at Trinity College, Cambridge – on the grounds that they were not given to scientists. Instead, in Lent Term, he successfully sat for an open Demyship at Magdalen, Oxford. A year remained before he was due to go up, and since his father could not afford to send him to Germany, then the scientific Mecca of the Western world, he stayed at Westminster. He took special mathematics; he studied English literature; he spent a great deal of time reading what he liked in the library; and – the first indication of things to come – he 'became quite an expert on the works of Mahan.' Then in 1904, he went up to Magdalen for Michaelmas Term, to the Oxford of *Guy and Pauline*, approached by leafy roads, still dreaming away among its water-meadows, unscathed by the motor-car or by industry, a quiet place in which an unknown William Morris was still repairing bicycles. Its beauty was an unexpected revelation, and for the rest of his life he could never judge Oxford quite by those same critical standards which he used for all else. 'I remember the joy of coming over Magdalen Bridge when I was an undergraduate', he said forty years later. 'One never quite gets over that.'[7]

He had decided to read mathematics and was lucky in finding himself with a really good man, A. L. Pedder. In 1905 he gained a First in Mathematical Moderations, because, he later claimed, 'the examiners, by setting a very difficult paper, did not find out what a little I knew. It was lucky for me, and it taught me a lesson in life which was valuable.' Others rated his success more highly than he did himself, and Herbert Warren, then President of Magdalen, wrote to him on 17 July 1905 saying

> . . . I always had, as I think you know, a very good opinion of your abilities but I did not know that it was possible for you, in the short time you have had, to take the highest honours in a subject not exactly your own, and I think it does you the very greatest credit, for it means honest and intelligent work. You are too sensible, I am sure, to be unduly elated though your friends and yourself may feel a very just pride and you ought to be encouraged to aim at the highest and the best . . .[8]

Now, in the summer of 1905, he reverted to chemistry, for which he had been given his Demyship. The initial choice had been largely the result of association with his Westminster master, E. C. Sherwood, a good teacher of chemistry but one who had neglected physics. Thus Tizard was deflected from the great prospects of experiment and speculation which were already being opened up by the discovery of the electron – a fact which in later life he appears to have regretted.

The Professor of Chemistry at Oxford was still William Odling, then aged 76, lecturing in his frock coat and exercising little if any influence on those who listened to him. 'I went to his lectures for a time', Tizard wrote, 'more in order to improve my perspective of history than to learn any chemistry. I got the vague impression that he and Dalton had been boys together. Of course, this was too good to be true, but he could have known him.'[9]

Magdalen had no tutor in chemistry so Tizard was sent to Nevil Sidgwick, who was to become one of the outstanding influences in his life. 'An elderly looking man, almost bald, with a fringe of grey hair, rose and greeted me pleasantly', he wrote. 'It was not till long afterwards that I realized that he was then in his early thirties. He asked when I had last done any serious chemistry.' When Tizard replied, he was told that he should settle down to some serious reading in the Long Vacation.

> Observing perhaps, a lack of enthusiasm in my face [Tizard remembered], he turned to his shelves and picked out a new-looking book entitled *Chemical Statics and Dynamics* by Mellor. 'This is an important subject' he said, 'but the book is rather too mathematical for me. I wish you'd take it away and see how many mistakes you can find in it.' I believe that this was the first time that any senior man had indicated that I might know more than he did about something that was worth knowing, and the first time that anyone had suggested to me that there might be mistakes in a printed book of science. I took it away: an early discovery of a mistake in the first chapter aroused a detective spirit and led me to consult works of reference; and I returned in October with a list the length of which surprised my tutor as well as the author (who wrote a charming letter of acknowledgement), and I learnt a lot of chemistry in the process.[10]

For the next three years, Tizard's life was happy and unexciting. Most Magdalen men were comparatively rich, and few had as little as his own £230 a year – the £80 brought in by the demyship, £30 from a Triplet Exhibition from Westminster, and £120 from his father. Thus he lacked the means as well as the inclination for the more expensive activities of University life. He was in no sense a hearty. His recreations – after a brief experiment with hockey and football – were tennis and golf, walking and cycling. His friendships with his fellow-undergraduates were numerous but rarely close, although some of them lasted throughout his life, notably his friendship with Dalziel Llewellyn Hammick, cheerful and engaging, who lived on the same stair.

On one occasion he went to discuss theology with a Father Waggett. Although still open-minded, he was becoming uncertain of his position in God's great army, and he was already moving along that path which caused him gradually to relinquish the beliefs he had been taught as a child.

> The older I have grown [he subsequently wrote], the more I have been confirmed in my disbelief of most of what the clergy teach. I

cannot believe that Jesus Christ was the Son of God, nor that he was born of a virgin. I cannot believe in an individual life after death, much though I should like to. Most of the Bible, to me, is a series of legends handed down from generation to generation by word of mouth, and getting mutilated in the process, until they were at last preserved more or less permanently in writing. Most of the New Testament consists of reminiscences and sentiments by the followers of Jesus Christ. All the same I am thankful for my upbringing. I believe that all children should be taught to believe in God and to model their lives on the code of conduct contained in the Bible, which has not been noticeably improved upon for 2,000 years. The more intelligent of them will modify their views as time goes on. And I hold, in particular, that no true scientist can be an atheist. The more his knowledge grows the more apparent is the depth of his ignorance.[11]

Most of his practical work at Oxford was carried out at the Daubeny Laboratory, Magdalen, and in Balliol and Trinity, since the University laboratories, like the instruction given in them, were in a lamentable state. There was little incentive to research of the kind on which Tizard's mind would have preferred to exercise itself. And the spirit of Oxford at the time was exemplified by a remark of the Provost of Oriel, Dr C. L. Shadwell: 'Show me a researcher and I'll show you a fool.' Most of the dons, Tizard added, were 'content to live like gentlemen, passing to the younger generation the knowledge that had been amassed by others.'

He sat for his Finals in 1908 and was satisfied with his performance on the theoretical papers. Then, with a week's practical examination before him, he was gripped by high fever which sent his temperature up to 104 and threatened to remove him from the contest. He was rushed to a nursing home, responded to drastic treatment, and on the second day was accompanied to the examination by a nurse. The External Examiner took one look at him and suggested that he should return to bed. He did so. On the third day he succeeded in putting in three hours, and on the fourth managed to last the full six. When the results were announced he was not unnaturally exhilarated to see that he had been given a First. A senior man put the result in perspective by greeting him with the words: 'Congratulations. It's a good thing to get because it gives you a start, but of course it won't matter two hoots in three years time.'

There now arose the question of what his next move should be. He had resolved to be independent of his father's help, and seriously considered joining the Board of Education where a Frank Heath, the director of special studies and reports, was looking for a man to study the German educational system. The starting salary would be £300 a year. But after a short initial period, the post would be merely an office one, and Tizard decided not to apply. At heart he wanted to continue his education and to continue research, and he turned to Sidgwick for advice.

> We discussed the United States [he later said], but Sidgwick advised that there was no School of Chemistry in the United States good enough for me. It is not for me to say if he was right; that is what he told me. He said that Professor T. W. Richards of Harvard attracted a good many young men to his laboratory, but he was famous then for his accurate determination of atomic weights, a subject which had no appeal for me. I was very interested at that time in chemical thermodynamics and thought I would like to sit at the feet of the great genius Willard Gibbs for a time.[12]

But Gibbs had died a few years previously. The argument returned more than once to Germany, as must have seemed inevitable. Finally, it was arranged that he should study for a year under Nernst in Berlin.

It was to be a difficult year. Magdalen renewed the demyship, worth £80. There was £50 left from the money which his father had provided. And in September 1908 Tizard set out from Oxford for Fräulein von Lubztow's pension at Wilhelmstrasse, 49, an address carefully picked from Baedeker's *Berlin*, with the prospect of working for a year in the German capital on a total of £130.

His journey to Berlin was to carry him into the main stream of European scientific research. It was to consolidate all he had learned at Oxford. Yet it was more important for Tizard personally in two other ways. For in Berlin he saw for the first time the dedicated application which the Germans were giving to science, and glimpsed the speed with which it was altering their position in the world.

And in Nernst's laboratory he met Lindemann.

Tizard was formally admitted to the University of Berlin as a post-graduate student in 1908. He attended Nernst's general

c

course of physical chemistry mainly to improve his German, as well as the course on advanced chemical thermodynamics.

> I intended also to put my name down for Planck's lectures, but postponed doing so because of the cost [he afterwards wrote]. Later on I was told that the lecture room, which held 400, was already crowded. How different from Oxford, I thought, where a professor of mathematical physics could count himself fortunate if he kept an audience of half a dozen.[13]

Nernst put him first to the study of the condensation of acetylene to benzene.

> I fancy he thought that there might be something of commercial as well as of scientific interest in this [Tizard wrote in his Personal Record for the Royal Society]. But it was a hopeless task. I did finally get some traces of aromatics in the condensate, but the usual result was a dirty mess. Early in 1909 I started investigating the action of hydrogen on carbon bisulphide which Nernst thought would result in an equilibrium with methane and hydrogen bisulphide at high temperatures. But it came to nothing, and so at the end of the semester I had nothing publishable to show for my work. I decided not to risk the waste of another year. But I learnt a great deal of value in Nernst's laboratory.[14]

However, even for a graduate of Tizard's shallow purse, life in Berlin had much to offer. There was skating on the Wannsee, that delectable stretch of water which leads the open country towards the heart of Berlin. There were parades to watch. There were the illuminations – Tizard meticulously recording in his expense-book that he paid out seven marks on a carriage tour of them. And, for a man with eyes to see, there was the ever-present sight of a nation so busily at work that it commanded a combination of respect, awe, and anxiety.

There were also the rather frightening formal dinners with Nernst, to the first of which Tizard was invited on 6 December.

> My dear Mother and Father [he wrote the same evening], I have just come back from what I thought would be an awful ordeal, but it didn't turn out at all badly. To come to the point, the Professor asked me on Saturday to come to dinner with him today. I imagined myself in the middle of about 20 Germans, not understanding a word of what was going on, but luckily there were 2 Americans there both of whom spoke German worse than myself, so I didn't feel at all

awkward. I sat, too, on the Professor's left, and he was extremely
affable. The whole thing was awfully comic. I had an irresistible
desire in the middle of the meal to lean back in my chair and shriek
with laughter. The Professor had an extremely good appetite and
fairly shovelled away the food which was very good . . .

There were more of these dinners at Nernst's, held between five
and six in the evening, formal and uncompromising, with white tie
and tails *de rigeur*. At many, Tizard was accompanied by Lindemann.

Now that the dust of controversy is settling, it is possible to see in
deeper perspective the relationship between these two highly
developed personalities whom only the irony of history would have
dared to bring together, on the field of science, as Germany's power
waxed and waned through forty years. It is possible to claim that
the conflict between the two men has been exaggerated and its
importance raised to heights which it does not merit; and it is
certainly true that the documents which both men kept throw a
mass of illuminating, qualifying, mitigating light on both their
friendship and their enmity. Yet Tizard amply provided the
scientific judgement which Lindemann frequently lacked; while
the political manipulation of events from which Tizard shrank,
necessary though this might sometimes be, was to Lindemann but
part of the great game. Thus to minimize the failure of two such
men to combine their intellectual resources for the common good
is to do more than turn from the clash of right against right: it is
also to ignore the impact of the personal scientific argument on
the duration, and the casualties, of the Second World War.

Frederick Alexander Lindemann had been born some eight
months after Tizard, at Baden-Baden. His mother was American,
his father an Alsatian who had settled in Devon and become
naturalized. Even in the early days some differences showed between the two men. Thus Lindemann, influenced by German
tradition, found it difficult to look beyond Nernst's curtain of
authority; one did not, after all, question professors. Tizard found
himself able to look on Nernst as fallible, like the rest of men.
Lindemann was proud of the 'cold dedication to his own ideas and
principles, a dedication which ignored opposition, friendship,
loyalty and ill-health'. Tizard was ever ready to see the other side

of the question. Lindemann revealed, in power, some quality of the Medici, hugely cruel when necessary and yet, when he wanted, hugely human; contemptuous in a manner that roused the most bitter resentment and yet, in oblique ways that he usually sought to hide, finely understanding of the human predicament. Tizard was altogether more normal. The two men perhaps truly agreed only on immortality, hoping for the best, expecting the worst, and sharing decent honest doubt.* All this would have tended to give a special quality to their relationship even had fate not thrust them at one another's throats. Yet the situation was further compounded. For Tizard's difficult financial situation was contrasted with the Lindemann wealth, so that in Berlin one was confined to two rooms of the Luebtzow lodgings, while the other could dine at the Adlon. To complete the picture there was the figure of Charles Lindemann, also able scientist, also brave man, brother of one, friend of both, bonhomous and avuncular, a charmer who even in his later years could never quite understand how two adults could spare time to fight the private war which brother and friend fought for more than a decade.

In Berlin, Tizard and Lindemann became close but not intimate friends

> There was always something about him which prevented intimacy [Tizard wrote in the first draft of his autobiography in 1957]. He was one of the cleverest men I have ever known. He had been to school in Germany, talked German very well – as well as he talked English – and was fluent in French. He was a very good experimenter. He also played games very well. He wanted me to share rooms with him, but I refused. I think my chief reasons for doing so at the time were that he was much better off than I was, and also that we should be speaking English all the time, for he would take no trouble to teach me German. It was lucky that I refused because we had a minor row later on. I had discovered a gymnasium in Berlin which was run by an ex-lightweight champion boxer of England. So I used to go there for exercise. I persuaded Lindemann to join and box with me. But one of his great defects was that he hated anyone of his own age to

* While Tizard held that 'no true scientist can be an atheist'. Lindemann, quoted by Lord Birkenhead (*The Prof in Two Worlds*, page 169) once commented to Father D'Arcy: '. . . your position is impregnable, granted the major premise of the existence of God. And what are we poor scientists to know about that'?

excel him in anything. He was a clumsy and inexperienced boxer, and when he found that I, who was much shorter and lighter than he was, was much quicker with my hands and on my feet, he lost his temper completely, so much so that I refused to box with him again. I don't think he ever forgave me for that. Still, we remained close friends for over twenty-five years, but after 1936 he became a bitter enemy.

The two men studied together, saw much of one another and skated together during the first months of 1909. When Tizard returned to Britain late in the summer he travelled via Copenhagen, going thus far with Lindemann who was on his way to Sweden, and spending an entertaining evening with him in the Tivoli Gardens before taking boat to England. He landed on the day that Blériot crossed the Channel by plane.

Tizard returned to Oxford vaguely disappointed, uncertain of his next move, and spent some weeks working with Sidgwick again, this time on the colour and ionization of copper solutions. He now had to decide what course his career should take. He lived with his family, hoping to carry on research in London, until there came the unexpected offer of a temporary science mastership at Eton. Tizard disliked the life and left at half-term. Then, late in the year, he was offered the chance of working in the Davy Faraday Laboratory of the Royal Institution; and here he settled down to produce his first independent and successful scientific work.

The colour change of indicators, such as litmus, had been used for centuries for the titration of acids and bases, but it was only with the emergence of physical chemistry towards the end of the nineteenth century that their behaviour was gradually understood. Tizard saw the possibility of using the colorimetric technique he had developed with Sidgwick to study quantitatively these colour changes in different solutions with a view to clarifying their behaviour still further. At the same time this would help in the right choice of indicators for the titration of weak acids and bases whose equivalence is not reached, as with strong acids and bases, at the neutral point.

By the end of 1910 he had produced two papers on the subject for the Transactions of the Chemical Society. In the following year his report to the British Association on 'The Sensitiveness of

Indicators' was published at length in their Transactions – and helped to gain him election to the Association's General Committee. These papers at once established Tizard as an investigator. But it was not the results themselves so much as his methods of obtaining them that did most to create his reputation. Indicators were being studied in many laboratories, but in none of them were their problems being tackled with the clarity and elegance which Tizard showed. It was symptomatic of his future work that he here attacked a practical task directly, working from first principles. His experiments 'cleared the air', and helped to sort out other people's thoughts on a complex subject. The fact that salt hydrolysis, then a problem in the Final Honours School, is handled today with comparative ease at school is largely due to Tizard's clear exposition of the subject.

His work at the Royal Institution continued for one year, and during it he produced a new English edition of Nernst's *Theoretical Chemistry*. 'I have revised and partly re-written the old translation,' he said in a prefatory note, 'incorporated the new matter, and made a few additions to the text here and there, at the suggestion of Professor Nernst, in order to bring the book up to as late a date as possible.' It appeared in 1911 and in the same year Tizard's position was transformed.

In March, Oriel offered a Fellowship to be held by a Resident Tutor in Natural Science. Strictly speaking, the appointment was to a Fellowship and Lectureship, the term Tutor being applied only to 'Moral Tutors' who were restricted by Statute to four. The election took place at Easter, *The Oriel Record* commenting that the 'field is a large and brilliant one, and includes several distinguished names'. This was during the Provostship of the formidable Dr C. L. Shadwell, and Dr Marcus Tod, then a Fellow of Oriel, notes that Tizard, who was elected to the new Fellowship, was 'always on good terms with the Provost, partly because he was never afraid of him, partly because of their common loyalty and affection for Westminster'.

The election completely changed Tizard's financial circumstances. The income from the Fellowship was £170 a year. An appointment by Professor J. C. Townsend as demonstrator and lecturer in the Electrical Laboratory brought an additional £150.

There was £50 a year from the Rhodes Fund, and £6 a year for every pupil whom Tizard took – figures which brought his annual income to more than £500. He was still a bachelor. He had free rooms and he could eat a free dinner each night. 'This was riches', he wrote in his autobiography '. . . the only period of my life when I was completely free from domestic and financial anxiety.'

That year he spent part of the summer touring the Black Forest with a colleague, R. T. Lattey, and was so impressed with what he saw of the inhabitants that he noted, almost half a century later, that since this visit he had 'never been able to think of Germans as wholly bad'. The two men arrived back in England in time for the meeting of the British Association in Portsmouth where Tizard read his paper on indicators and introduced his friends to Lindemann.

He was now committed, and he very quickly became absorbed in what was still a closed University world, a world from which it might have seemed unlikely that he would ever move. Yet years afterwards, looking back, he felt that even had the Great War not broken out, he would have prised himself from the comfortable Oxford surroundings. To a friend he recalled how he had break-fasted well one morning and then spent a few hours lecturing. He had lunched well, watched the College teams exercising, and had strolled back to his rooms where his scout had prepared tea before a roaring fire. He looked forward to a pleasant few hours of casual reading, an excellent dinner in Hall, enlivened by good wine and better company. Then he realized that this would probably be his future for countless terms, and across his mind there passed the resolve to leave Oxford for work of a different kind.

Before he could begin to put this resolve into action, there came what he subsequently described as 'the greatest piece of good luck'. Well before the end of the nineteenth century there had been suggestions that the British Association should hold one of its annual meetings in Australia. The idea had been shelved for a variety of reasons, then revived in 1909, and after considerable discussion it was agreed that the Australian meeting should be held in 1914. Following the South African example nine years earlier, it was proposed that the Association should visit each of the States in turn – thus giving the visitors as comprehensive a view as possible of the great and undeveloped sub-Continent. The Australian Government decided, furthermore, to set aside £15,000 'to cover passages of not less than 150 official representatives, including selected Dominion and foreign scientists.' Thus it was hoped to attract a number of young men who might otherwise shy at the considerable expense of the tour.

Arrangements were virtually complete when, three days before the party was due to sail, one of the 155 members whose passages were being paid for by Australia, was forced to withdraw. 'A kind friend suggested me as a substitute', Tizard has written, 'and I packed and got on board as quickly as I could.' He had every reason to be grateful for the opportunity. It introduced him, as pleasantly as possible, to the second largest of the Dominions, those huge undeveloped and vigorous countries whose powers of expansion and enterprise were to fascinate him for the rest of his life. Furthermore, it brought him into personal contact, on friendly terms, with the leaders of what would today be called the scientific Establishment. They included Sir Thomas Holland, whom Tizard was to follow as Rector of Imperial College fifteen years later; Sir Oliver Lodge, Sir James Jeans, and Sir Joseph Petavel who was to be director of the National Physical Laboratory throughout Tizard's future spell at the Department of Scientific and Industrial Research. There was also, overshadowing them all, Ernest Rutherford, already deeply involved in the first moves of the nuclear revolution. To Tizard, as to so many others, Rutherford gave the friendship and encouragement which was always remembered with gratitude. It also seems likely that the friendship was to influence future events in an unexpected way. For although Rutherford had, by the early 1930's, a secret feeling about the potentialities of nuclear energy which he confided to Lord Hankey[15], his public profession of scepticism remained constant. To the end of his days he maintained in papers, and on the lecture platform, that no more could ever be gained from the nuclear stockpot than was put into it. Tizard's initial attitude was no doubt conditioned by Rutherford – an attitude which he made no effort to conceal, and one which was to compound his problems during the bitter internal struggles of the Second World War.

Tizard left London for Australia in the s.s. *Euripides* on 1 July

1914, and the memories that he retained of the five-week voyage were dominated by Rutherford. 'I partnered him at deck-tennis,' he said years later. 'He used to stand at the back of the court where he was worth a good many points to the side by keeping up a running commentary on the looks and behaviour of the opponents.' Tizard and he won the deck-tennis doubles – so that Tizard used to say that he had shared in at least one of Rutherford's triumphs. One evening the great man lectured on radium. 'He dwelt upon its extreme rarity and value, and on the danger of keeping it for any length of time near one's skin,' Tizard remembered, 'and he then said: "Now, in order that you shall all know what radium bromide looks like I will hand round this tube." The tube was passed rapidly round, handled gingerly, and returned to him safely.' Tizard noticed that there appeared to be rather much of this valuable substance, and later discovered from Rutherford what the tube really contained – a mixture of common salt and sand.[16]

When the *Euripides* had sailed from Cape Town on 22 July there had been no indication that war was near. The news of its outbreak, received by wireless, was posted up on 4 August, and the details confirmed when the party arrived in Adelaide three days later. It was agreed that the meeting and tour should continue, and during the next few weeks Tizard travelled with the party to Melbourne, Sydney, and Brisbane. Then, like the other younger members of the party, he sailed home to enlist.

The war had come upon him suddenly. Surprisingly, in view of his subsequent career, he did not 'remember taking the slightest interest in the application of science to defence before 1914.' After the Agadir crisis of 1911 there had been talk of war, yet it was still intermittent, and little of it filtered into the Colleges. The mood of the times was set by one Oxford paper which, after reporting weeks of sunshine, added: 'The summer term has therefore begun under the happiest conditions, and as it is so short and so sweet, and so crowded with good things, let those who have youth and health on their side make the most of it.' There was an Officers' Training Corps in the University but Tizard held aloof from it. Like many of his colleagues, he had been fascinated by Norman Angell's *The Great Illusion*, published in 1909, which argued that while war was not impossible on economic grounds, no government would be silly enough to embark on it. 'Wrong though he proved to be, I was sufficiently convinced to believe that no great nation would be foolish enough to go to war with another great nation', Tizard wrote. 'It must be remembered', he added as if in mitigation, 'that in Oxford, at any rate, it seemed as if peace, perfect peace, had descended on the land.'[17]

His interest in aircraft, such as it was, had a purely scientific background and he encouraged others to share this. Thus when Lord Carbery visited Oxford in May 1914 and looped the loop over Port Meadow with a brave passenger in the rear seat of his 80 h.p. Morane-Soulier, Tizard invited five of his pupils to tea, and together they watched the spectacle from his windows. Within little more than a year, all six were in the Royal Flying Corps. Of the six, only Tizard survived the war.

He was already in his twenty-ninth year, yet his life was in many ways still 'crowded with good things'. So crowded, as we have already noted, that he had already begun to contemplate the more turbulent waters of the non-academic world. Yet until the chance of the Australian voyage had dropped into his lap he had lived a life that had little remarkable about it. He had coasted along, without any spectacular ambitions, conscientious and comfortable, enjoying, like many other wise men, the modest pleasures of an age that was ending. Now the war was to sort him from the rest.

CHAPTER TWO

The Royal Flying Corps

Tizard was one of those who leapt to arms unbidden. He arrived back in Oxford from Australia early in October and within a few days was travelling to London with Henry Moseley, the experimental physicist for whom such a brilliant future was forecast. Both men were commissioned, but in London their ways parted. Moseley received a short training and met an early death a year later in Gallipoli. Tizard, soon a Second Lieutenant in the Royal Garrison Artillery, reported to Clarence Barracks, Portsmouth. Within the month he had passed the necessary examinations and been posted to train a platoon of local Territorials in the use of the anti-aircraft gun.

It was at first difficult for a man with his background to take at their face value the various rudimentary exercises in manslaughter on which he was now embarked. They were, moreover, given a ludicrous and almost farcical air by the rigid army discipline within which they were formulated, and the rather primitive equipment with which they were practised. For the anti-aircraft procedure Tizard had only contempt. 'One might possibly have hit a low-flying Zeppelin with it', he wrote of the solitary gun available, 'but the chance of hitting an aeroplane was negligible.' Even the simplest elements of ballistics appeared to be ignored during training, and to help remedy their omission he drafted a concise memorandum for unit headquarters. This so impressed a visiting General that the young officer was invited to submit a further treatise to the War Office. He did so, but was disillusioned when a Staff Officer arrived some weeks later to lecture the unit and proceeded to use Tizard's original memorandum and diagrams. The twist of the knife was provided when the officer failed even to alter the lettering on his diagrams. 'Thus ended my first attempt to bring scientific thought to bear on the problems of war', Tizard commented, 'for, from that time, I was not concerned at all with aircraft gunnery.'[1]

Such early experiences may well have bred in Tizard an attitude which looked with quizzical eye at authority, which gave him a fellow-feeling with the rebels of the world, and which in later life was to counter-balance, and at times throw into strong contrast, his natural reverence for the proprieties of life. In the Royal Garrison Artillery, during the first months of the war, they certainly encouraged him to experiment with new, and strictly unofficial methods of training. His exploits with a squad of Maxim gun recruits caused regimental concern, and some embarrassment when a visiting General insisted on inspecting the recruits' performance. The General, intrigued by such excellent results produced by such informal methods, insisted that young Lieutenant Tizard should explain. The result was a verdict – given, one feels, against the advice of many regular officers – to 'go on training them as you like, Mr Tizard.'

Two events were now to help change Tizard's life. The first was marriage. Five years previously, visiting his first mathematical tutor, A. L. Pedder, he had been introduced to Kathleen Wilson, the daughter of Arthur Prangley Wilson, mining engineer, a girl a few years his junior. The Wilsons were then staying in Oxford; the friendship grew; and when Kathleen visited Norway in the summer of 1913 in a party organized by her uncle, Duncan Wilson, both Tizard and Robert Bourdillon, one of his Oxford friends, were invited to join it.

This was not the first time that Tizard had been tempted into mountain country, since the previous year he had visited Switzerland with Bourdillon and the latter's father, a formidable mountaineer who had out-distanced both of the younger men on the shale slopes of the Dent de Bonnaveau. Now he and Bourdillon spent some days in the Jotenheim on their own, ending their expeditions only when Tizard twisted his ankle and had to be brought down to sea-level on a sled.

His friendship with the Wilsons continued. But in spite of comparative financial security at Oriel he continued to be worried about the prospects of supporting a wife. Only now, in 1915, did he decide to wait no longer, even though relative luxury had been exchanged for the small pay and uncertain future of a junior officer's life in time of war. He asked his Commanding Officer for a week's leave in mid-April 1915, and on 24 April was married to Kathleen Wilson by the Provost of Oriel in Holy Trinity, Brompton Road, Knightsbridge. Bourdillon was best man, coming from Upavon, Wiltshire, where with another Oxford colleague, G. M. B. Dobson, he was by this time working in a small experimental unit on bombs and bomb-sights.

Marriage was only the first of the events which were to change Tizard's life during the first half of 1915. Earlier in the year Bourdillon and Dobson had decided that scientific help was needed at Upavon. Bourdillon had written to Tizard asking whether he would come to Upavon if transfer to the Royal Flying Corps could be arranged. Tizard agreed, the formalities were completed, and early in July he arrived at Upavon, 'on probation for appointment as an assistant Equipment Officer in connection with experiments.'

The Central Flying School, Upavon, had been opened three years previously, a venture under the control of the War Office, staffed jointly by the Army and by the Royal Navy which provided the School's first Commandant, the redoubtable Captain Paine. Here, on some 2,400 acres that spread across training gallops, small fir copses, and the undulations of Salisbury Plain's northern fringe, the pilots of the First World War were taught both the rudiments of flight and the more specialized problems of handling the quaint structures of lathe and canvas with the aid of which, their enthusiasts claimed, it would at last be possible to bring a third dimension to the battlefield. There had been some discussion about the best site for the School, which was considered by many who served there to be remote and unnecessarily exposed to the worst winds that came.

> However [wrote C. G. Grey, that paladin of aeronautical criticism], all is for the best, in this best of all worlds, and one may confidently expect that those aviators who survive the gorges and ridges, the upward and downward *remous*, the Arctic frigidity and Saharic parchedness of the Upavon School will develop into aviators of unsurpassed hardiness, so that the War Office's little £40,000 deal in land may justify itself of its children after all.[2]

There were eight sheds which were used as hangars; an engine

house and a store, both lodged in a grove of firs; and various other
minor buildings, all situated on the green slopes that stretch down
towards the village of Upavon and the river which here starts to
carve its channel from the Vale of Pewsey, across the Plain and
southwards to the open sea.

At this period, aeronautical research in Britain was still being
conducted by three technically separate bodies, a state of affairs
explained as much by the casual national attitude to research as by
the newness of flight itself. The Royal Aircraft Establishment at
Farnborough could trace its ancestry back to its foundation in
1878 as the War Office's Balloon Equipment Store at Woolwich.
In 1905 it had been moved to the heathlands of the Surrey-Hamp-
shire border and transformed into H.M. Balloon Factory. Four
years later the organization split into two wings, and while one
became in succession the Farnborough Air Battalion, the Royal
Flying Corps, and the Royal Air Force, the other became the
Army Aircraft Factory, responsible for producing and testing
balloons, other dirigibles, and subsequently the first aircraft; and
the Royal Aircraft Establishment. 'Farnborough', as it was
quickly known, was only one of the three legs on which aeronautical advance depended – albeit the most 'official' one, since
it was directly responsible first to the War Office and later to the
Air Ministry. But there were also two other bodies, both set up by
Lord Haldane in 1909. One of these – in turn the Advisory
Committee on Aeronautics (1909–20), the Aeronautical Research
Committee (1920–45), and the Aeronautical Research Council
(1945–   ) – was concerned with the fundamental problems of
flight. But it was merely advisory, suggesting to the government
what lines of research might most profitably be followed. The other
body was the Aerodynamics Department of the National Physical
Laboratory, set up 'for continuous investigation – experimental
and otherwise – of questions which must from time to time be
solved in order to obtain adequate guidance in construction'.
Technically, the Department had the task of carrying out the
Advisory Committee's recommendations, even though it was part
of the N.P.L., an organization which in 1915 was still both under
the control of the Royal Society, and financed by Government
grant.

To this involved and rather British structure there was subsequently added the Experimental Flight of the Central Flying School, occupying the hangars on the southern side of the Upavon aerodrome and sharing them with the regular training flight. At the time of Tizard's formal attachment its scientific members consisted only of Bourdillon and G. M. B. Dobson. In theory, the Flight's main task was to test new types of aircraft as these arrived from the manufacturers; in practice, it stretched across a far wider swathe of experimental country, a fact due largely to the shortness of aviation history and the immensity of the prospects which were now opening out and inviting investigation.

The whole system of aeronautical research at this period – if system it can fairly be called – was therefore untidy and improbable, empirical and wasteful, achieving the considerable success which it did achieve only for great expenditure of effort and as the result of a few brilliant minds.

To this extent, Tizard's arrival at Upavon was a classic example of the right man coming to the right place at the right time. Aviation was by now recovering from a first astonished surprise at its own continuing existence. It had been accepted, not only as a fact of life but as one which might well play a useful part in the current war – although outside the small exuberant circle of enthusiasts this belief was still strongly contested. The character of these enthusiasts, the new men of half a century ago who could 'stretch out and touch the face of God', brought handicaps as well as advantages to the development of the art at this particular moment in its history. To leave the ground was still an adventure; to fly was still to pioneer; to survive was still very largely a matter of wisdom, chance and the skill and expertise of one's own two hands. It is therefore hardly surprising that the men with wings were at times driven onwards by uproarious high spirits rather than by any sober feeling for scientific investigation. Yet courage alone was not enough. If flying was to be drawn onwards from its existing stage of hit-and-miss black magic, of trial and error, of crossed fingers and the hope that one would survive to try again, something more was needed. This work waiting to be done required careful planning and cool appraisal so that men could begin to learn why aircraft behaved as they did. It needed exact measurement of things that had not before been measured exactly. It needed end-less questioning, constant self-criticism, and a mixture of humility and vision. Scientifically, this was to be provided by Tizard, who from the spring of 1915 began to discover how best to evaluate both the weapons of air warfare and the planes themselves. The system was not so very different from that in use only a few years ago.

Tizard moved to Upavon in the summer of 1915, bringing his wife to settle first in one and then in another of the nearby Wilt-shire villages. Their inhabitants, he realized with wry amusement were in their own humble way doing as well as they could out of the war by raising prices to whatever level the Service traffic would stand. Eventually, in Rushall Lodge, the Tizards found pleasant quarters at a reasonable rent, and here they lived for eighteen months.

The current work at Upavon was concerned with testing the Royal Flying Corps' first bomb-sight, and an incident that took place soon after Tizard's arrival emphasizes both the primitive state of current knowledge and the spirit of the C.F.S. Captain Paine had very little scientific knowledge but he had, as Tizard later stressed, the real experimental spirit. What was more, he encouraged new ideas.

> Some young officer argued one day in the mess [Tizard said many years afterwards], that as the resistance to motion got greater the further anything dropped under gravity (which is true), it followed that if you dropped an egg from a sufficient height, say 3,000 ft., it would not break when it hit the ground. This outrageous statement was received with hilarity by the young scientists present; but the Commandant was not convinced by their scepticism, and decided to make the experiment.

A pilot was duly deputed to collect a basket of eggs. He was then ordered to take a Maurice Farman up to 3,000 ft. and drop the eggs overboard one by one.

> We all waited patiently while the machine climbed laboriously to this dizzy height [Tizard related], but no-one saw anything drop. When the pilot came down he said he had dropped all the eggs; so a search was made for them. No trace of them was found, so the question at issue remained open.[3]

This slightly casual attitude appears to have governed some of the work on bomb-aiming, even after it had been tautened by the scientific improvements which Tizard soon injected into it. Much of the operational bombing so far attempted had been carried out by the simple method of holding the bomb over the side of the plane and letting go at what appeared to be the most suitable moment. This rudimentary procedure had then been improved by strapping the bombs beside, or beneath, the plane by means of a mechanism that would release them when the pilot – or in some cases, the bomber – pulled a lever or pressed a button. Such primitive systems were now about to be revolutionized by use of a simple bomb-sight; simple of course when judged by current standards but complex enough in 1915. Before such a sight could be calibrated accurately it was necessary to time the fall of bombs from specific heights, and to measure the lag – that is, the distance that they fell short of the place which they would have hit had they been dropped in a vacuum. The first attempts were made with a stop-watch and field-glasses. It was found, however, that the delay between the bomb leaving the plane's carrier and the perception of this by the observer was appreciably longer than the delay between the explosion when the bomb hit the ground and the observer's reaction.

Tizard suggested to Dobson that the job could be done photographically, and with his help designed a form of mobile camera obscura which was taken out to the bombing range, erected in the roof of a small hut, and duly levelled. From this, Tizard was able to take one photograph every second while the plane was making its bombing run; at the same time, a crude radio transmitter installed in the plane gave a signal, audible in the hut, as the bomb was released. He at first spent much effort in attempts to have this radio signal automatically recorded; finally, however, he discovered that if he pressed a switch when he heard the signal the time-lag was not more than a twentieth of a second. The practice was for the pilot on the bombing-run to steer for the hut and release his bomb before he reached too dangerous a point. 'When he seemed to wait too long', Bourdillon wrote, 'a certain feeling of tension developed in the observer (at least in my case) although we only used tail-fused 20 lb. bombs, so that nothing except a direct hit on

D

the hut would have hurt us.'⁴ Tizard, who had designed the method, was usually the officer in the hut. He would obtain the height of the plane by measuring the span of its wings on the photographs, its ground speed by measuring the distance it had moved on successive prints. 'From these measurements I made a rough calculation of where the bomb had fallen, and then went out and looked for it', he wrote later. Throughout the summer and early autumn of 1915, he carried out scores of such experiments, and his papers are full of their records, many of them accompanied by diagrams showing the path of the bomb-fall.

There were other experiments, on other targets, and the occasional miscalculation is suggested by a letter which arrived one day from a friend.

> Dear Tom [this ran], Thanks for the bomb which fell just W of the garden in the field. Sorry we weren't there at the time as we did not arrive until an hour or so later. The village were much entertained and what with your show and daylight saving had the time of their lives this last week-end. I hope you got back without trouble. Mrs. Jones, the milkman's wife said that 'it was as good as seeing Hamel loop the loop except that he didn't loop the loop'.

The trials were eventually finished, but before the bombsight went into production Tizard wanted a check made on the theoretical calculations. These were discussed at a morning conference during which he briefly noted the calculations on the back of an envelope and threw it across the table to I. O. Griffith, a colleague who had recently joined the Upavon team, commenting that it was just the job for him. Griffith produced the detailed answer nearly a week later, worked out on three pages of foolscap. 'A week to produce that', Tizard exclaimed. 'There's a war on – and anyway I did it on the back of an envelope.' 'Ah,' replied Griffith, 'but mine was much the prettier method.'

Well before the completion of the work on the bomb-sight Tizard had begun to suspect – rightly as it turned out – that the lag-errors he had been taking so much trouble to measure, were in fact of far less importance to bombing-accuracy than were simple flying errors. 'I then came to the conclusion', he wrote, 'that it would be very difficult for any scientific man to do really important relevant work unless he himself learnt to fly.'⁵

There was, however, yet another reason for his request to be taught – less easily definable, but possible more important. Tizard was thirty. This was only a few years older than most of the pilots who passed through the Central Flying School, but they were years which could easily form a deep gulf – so that it became something of a convention to think, if not to speak, in terms of young pilots and old scientists. In addition, Tizard was married – another factor which singled him out from most of the flying men with whom he lived and worked. These differences, which he perhaps sensed more than logically appreciated, would have to be lessened if he were fully to understand the problems that arose when men handled the apparatus that enabled them to fly. There was more than the need to share at least a little of their dangers: there was the need to understand how they thought when flying, how they reacted to the unexpected terrors and glories of the natural world. All this and much more would come, he realized, if experience as a pilot were allowed to bridge the gap between the scientists who clinically evaluated the performance of planes and equipment and the men who flew them in battle.

Tizard therefore proposed to Captain Paine that he should be taught to fly. Paine agreed, but said that he would have to get permission from the War Office. Here came the rub. The purpose of the Central Flying School was to train pilots for operational squadrons. Tizard was a scientific officer and would not, presumably, fly in an operational squadron. Thus, with formidable logic, it was argued by the War Office that no instructor should be diverted from his main task. Paine himself appears to have been unhappy about the decision. 'When I said "What nonsense" ' wrote Tizard, 'he again agreed and rang them (the War Office) up in my presence. After a conversation of some length he turned to me and said that they would agree on condition that I was only taught on days when weather was too bad for the budding pilots to go up.' Tizard replied 'Done'. His later reaction was just as typical when he commented of the whole comic procedure: 'This was good because one got used to difficulties right away.'[6]

He took his first lesson on 8 December 1915, going up for thirty-five minutes in a dual-control Maurice Farman with Lt. Charles Breese, R.N., then O.C. Workshops and a steady reliable

pilot. Thereafter he flew about twice a week, on the days when
conditions were too stormy or otherwise too bad for normal instruction. Most of his flights lasted about half an hour and when
he first flew solo on 5 January, he appears to have been in the air
for something less than three hours. Twelve days later, with a
solo flying time of less than two hours, he qualified for his certificate. Then began the longer and more arduous business of gaining
his wings. His diary for the following four months is full of brief
but illustrative comments, such as 'lost prop on landing', an accident by no means uncommon in those days. Later he flew from
Upavon to Oxford, losing his way between Wantage and Oxford
in thick haze. 'Landed at Eynsham,' he noted in his diary. 'Went
on to Oxford. Land v. flooded. Landed near Cowley. Cracked
propeller blade taxi-ing, when starting off again.' There was little
doubt that he was by now thoroughly enjoying his work. 'I loved
flying in my early days as a pilot', he wrote. 'I used to land machines all over the place. I found it exhilarating and of absorbing
interest.' His sight was a handicap, and from the start he had to
get special permission to wear glasses under his flying goggles,
into which he later had special lenses fitted. By mid-May he had
logged considerable flying time, and when he passed his final test
on 23 May, this totalled more than thirty-three hours, of which
some twenty-eight were solo.

It seems likely that the authorities still found themselves unable
to accept that a scientist should thus be taught to fly. The Certificate of those days records that the holder has completed a course,
and is so printed that this can be described as either 'short' or
'long'. In Tizard's case, both adjectives were struck out.

Shortly afterwards he flew to R.F.C. Headquarters in France.
His object was to discover how accurate Allied bombing really was,
a task which is unlikely to have endeared him to the Staff. It was
here, soon after his arrival, that he had his first meeting with
Trenchard, later one of his friends and strongest supporters.
Tizard had been seen among the gun lines, unaware of persistent
reports that Germans in Allied uniform were operating behind the
British front, and was shown into Trenchard's office and asked to
explain his business. He did so, adding that he had come with the
full authority of the War Office. Asked to show his credentials, he

explained that he had given them to Colonel Brooke-Popham on arrival. Trenchard thereupon picked up the telephone, asked to be put through to the War Office, explained the position, listened to their reply, and put down the receiver. 'They say they have never heard of you', he said, turning to Tizard. 'Well, sir', Tizard replied, 'isn't that just like the War Office.' Brooke-Popham's arrival shortly afterwards failed to unravel the situation. He remembered Tizard's arrival but could remember no letter. 'If he doesn't mind my saying so, sir', stated Tizard, 'I noticed that Colonel Brooke-Popham's table was very untidy. Could you send someone to look through his papers, sir?' Trenchard agreed. The letter from the War Office was discovered. It says much for Tizard's ability in handling members of the human species that no ill-will appears to have remained.[7]

The conclusion that he drew from his visit to France was that the chance of a bomber hitting the target aimed at was small. This, he realized, was only partly due to the difficulties of aiming. There were the linked difficulties of target-identification, which could perhaps be helped by the growing arts of aerial photography and navigation. There was the problem of flying in cloud, increasingly useful in view of the expanding enemy defences but involving riddles of navigation, meteorology, and flight itself. There was, over all, the problem of measuring, with greater accuracy, the performance of the new and more efficient aircraft which were now coming into service; and it was to these more general problems that Tizard applied himself during the summer of 1916.

He tested new radio equipment that arrived at Upavon. He tested new cameras, taking with one of them an experimental photograph of Stonehenge that he believed to be 'the first that showed unmistakably the outer ring of the ancient monument.' He helped to encourage use of the new aircraft compass devised by Keith Lucas at Farnborough, and he did all that was possible to discourage the attitude of officers such as the Flight Commander who told him, when he complained of a compass when about to set off for Oxford, that he 'would never make a pilot' if he had to rely on instruments. Above all, he concentrated on new and more precise methods of testing aircraft performance. This was not an easy task, since the whole process was under the control of a Service officer not a scientist. The actual method of testing was, in the words of Sir Vernon Brown, then one of the test pilots, 'somewhat crude, and consisted of measuring speeds near the ground over a course approximately one mile long, and a climb to 6,000 ft. with several stop-watches and a barograph, if such an instrument could be obtained.'

Throughout this period Tizard retained his friendship with Lindemann, who had joined Farnborough as a civilian scientist and who came to Upavon to be taught to fly – apparently in the early summer of 1916. When his training was complete he returned to Farnborough, but Tizard would frequently fly over from Upavon to see him, and it was here, in the famous Chudleigh Mess, that the two of them were discovered one afternoon, very pleased with themselves, having evolved their own version of three-dimensional chess. Two photographs of the two men taken at this period are of great interest. One shows Tizard leaning nonchalantly against a plane, puttees correct, uniform correct, a figure which might as well be that of an airman as of a scientist. The other shows Lindemann standing beside a plane in a dark suit, long Melton Mowbray coat and high stiff collar, the dress in which he invariably arrived at an airfield before changing into flying kit. Here perhaps is a clue to the fact that Tizard conformed, at least outwardly, because he believed that it was fitting to do so, even if for no other reason. Lindemann felt no such need.

To this period belong Lindemann's celebrated 'spins'. In the early days of flying it was considered fatal for an aircraft to drop downwards in a spin, since there appeared to be no known method of correcting the movement, and the plane then plunged into the ground, inevitably it seemed. After the war there grew up the legend that Lindemann had worked out a theoretical solution to the problem and had, while testing his theories in the air, become the first pilot to spin and live. The truth is that Lt. Wilfred Parke, R.N. had successfully extricated himself from a spin during the British Military Trials at Larkhill, Salisbury Plain on 25 August 1912. Other pilots had subsequently shown how they might pull themselves from a spin by some purely empirical method. However, it remained an exceedingly risky business, largely because no-one yet knew exactly why it was that certain movements of the controls did the trick. It was the mathematics of this problem that Lindemann helped to solve by personal experiment – his exact historical priority still being the subject of conflicting and unresolved evidence. Tizard summed up the position in a letter to Sir Harold Hartley only a few months before he died.

> The Germans first mastered the spin technique [he wrote]. Many pilots got into and out of spins deliberately before Lindemann did his experiments. I did myself, but did not take exact notes of the manoeuvre. Lindemann did, and his paper on the subject was quite first class. Lindemann's *courage* has been over-praised; I had flown for much less than 50 hours when I first span deliberately. But his *coolness* in taking accurate observations under difficult conditions was remarkable . . .[8]*

Throughout this central period of the war Tizard was concerned in the testing of weapons as well as of equipment, and this soon brought him into contact with that ebullient and colourful character, Sir Richard Threlfall, inventor of the first effective phosphorus bomb, research director of Albright & Wilson who made it, and a future chairman of the Government's Fuel Research and Chemical Research Boards. Tizard long remembered how Threlfall had been called to Upavon to meet the Chief of the Imperial General Staff at the first trials of a new anti-Zeppelin bomb. 'Not knowing what might be considered correct dress on such an occasion, he and his party appeared in top hats and frock coats' writes Threlfall's son in recalling Tizard's account of the visit. 'As they walked on to the aerodrome, where a stiff breeze was blowing, a Farman biplane, whose pilot was intrigued by the appearance of so curiously arrayed an assemblage, dived upon it to investigate. The party, uncertain whether this manoeuvre were intended or involuntary, speedily flattened themselves – and away rolled their combined top hats.'[9]

There is every indication that during his early days at Upavon Tizard was engrossed in his work and fascinated by the opportunities for combined adventure and scientific enquiry that it held out. But he was soon making a complaint that was to echo through

---

* The history of the spin was discussed exhaustively in articles by Norman Macmillan, and subsequent letters, *Aeronautics*, July and December 1960, February 1961, and March 1962.

much of his life – 'about the misuse of many of our scientific people' as he described it to Rutherford as early as November 1915. Moreover there was, quite apart from 'misuse', the Service attitude which relegated scientists to the lowly level of fitters and mechanics. This was not, necessarily, the fault of anyone at the Central Flying School, but it was to Major J. E. Tennant, O.C. of the Experimental Squadron, as the Flight had by this time become, that Bourdillon, Tizard and Griffith addressed a significant memorandum on May 8, 1916.

> Sir [they began], We have the honour to lay before you certain views on our duties, rank, and pay, in the Royal Flying Corps, and to request that should you concur in these views you will forward this letter to the proper authorities for consideration. Our reasons for taking this step are as follows. We feel that our present rank is inconsistent with the amount and nature of the work we are called upon to perform, and with our positions in civil life; also that this work, entailing as it does a high scientific training and a great deal of responsibility and initiative, cannot be efficiently carried out by officers of the lowest rank. Further, officers occupying scientific posts in other branches of the army are given ranks more consonant with their attainment: for example we know of officers of similar or inferior positions to ourselves in civil life being gazetted Captains immediately on joining the Army; further, officers of the R.A.M.C. are always promoted Captains after one years' service. At the same time, we have felt that representations of this kind are out of place in war time. We understand, however, that some or all of us may shortly be transferred to the new Experimental station under new Commanding Officers, and therefore we are taking this opportunity to ask that our status as scientific officers be reconsidered.

The memorandum outlined their records and then described their duties at the Central Flying School.

> These [it continued], may be divided into two classes: (a) the testing of bombs; testing and reporting on new inventions and suggestions for new inventions as directed by the War Office; and in addition a good deal of work connected with the testing of aeroplanes. The new inventions and apparatus tested from time to time have included bombs, darts, bombsights and carriers, compasses, wireless apparatus, signalling lamps, range-finders, gyroscopic stabilisers etc. These are mentioned to show the varied nature of the work we have been called upon to do. (b) the initiation and development of new experiments and inventions. The work already carried out includes the designing

1A: Members of the Alembic Club, Oxford, 1907, showing: (*back row l. to r.*) Unknown, Unknown, Henry Tizard, Thomas Merton, Tom Lindsay, N. K. Chaney, J. C. Thompson: (*seated, l. to r.*) Harold Hartley, W. H. Barrett, H. J. Moseley, M. P. Applebey, N. V. Sidgwick, R. T. Lattey, N. P. Campbell; (*front row, l. to r.*) Donald Somervell, Unknown, Unknown.

1B: An unidentified Magdalen group *c.* 1906. Henry Tizard on extreme left of third standing row.

2: Kathleen Wilson, later Lady Tizard, shortly before the First World War

3A: British Association group at Whyaller (then known as Hummocky Hill), S. Australia, August 9th, 1914, showing: (*front of railway car l. to r.*) Mr. M. Warren, Sir Thomas Holland, Professor Borus, Dr. Holt, Prof. Gunnar Anderson, Miss Gregory, Prof. H. Bassett, Dr. N. V. Sidgwick (almost hidden), Dr. Chattaway, Prof. Gregory, Prof. Boulton, H. J. Moseley, Mr. Lamplough, Dr. Dwerryhouse. In railway car (*l. to r.*) Prof. H. P. Dixon, Henry Tizard, Dr. Essington Lewis.

3B: Henry Tizard (*standing left*) and Sir Ernest Rutherford (*standing right*) on the ss *Euripides* during the British Association visit to Australia in 1914.

4A: Henry Tizard at work at Upavon, *c.* 1915

4B: Henry Tizard and fellow-officers in the early days of the First World War, probably at Portsmouth.

of C.F.S. bombsights and bombcarriers, the experimental determination of the lag of bombs, the development of the camera obscura as an aid to bomb-dropping, the development of signalling lamps and search-lights for use on aircraft; and still more recently the improvement of methods for testing aeroplanes, especially as concerns their behaviour at great heights, the development of night landing lamps and accessories, of phosphorus bombs, and experiments on directional stability.

We might also add that we were requested to draw up a scheme for the establishment of an Experimental Wing in the Royal Flying Corps, that this was done, and the scheme forwarded to the War Office by the Commandant, and that we understand that it proved of value.

There is no evidence that much notice was taken of this plea. Matters certainly changed for the better from the summer of 1916 onwards but it seems likely that most of this improvement was due to the growing influence of Bertram Hopkinson, one of the most remarkable characters drawn into aeronautical research by the war.

In 1914 Hopkinson, the eldest member of a distinguished family of scientists and engineers, had held the chair of Mechanism and Applied Mechanics at Cambridge. He joined the Royal Engineers and on orders of the Department of Military Aeronautics built a model factory on a scale of one-sixth linear and subsequently demolished it to discover the best proportion of bomb-case to weight of explosive, and the best material for the case. He was also consulted by Farnborough about the design of bomb-sights, and in July 1915 was appointed to the panel of Lord Fisher's Board of Inventions and Research. Four months later he took charge of both the design and supply of bombs, bomb gears, guns and ammunition for the Department of Military Aeronautics.

His chief legacy to the Royal Air Force [commented Tizard], was the doctrine that in order to bring science most effectively to bear on the problems of the Service, it was necessary to carry all experimental work, under scientific direction, right through the laboratory and workshops to the final stages of use in the air; and that as the work progressed the close collaboration of scientists and fighting men became more and more necessary.[10]

It appears that Hopkinson first visited Upavon in the autumn of

1915. He quickly saw that whatever might be the attitude of individual officers, the authorities begrudged every machine and every hour taken from training by experimental flying. His first step, therefore, was to move the Armament Experimental Flight of the Experimental Squadron from Upavon to a site at Orfordness on the bleak coast of Suffolk. Success was so quick and so considerable that it was decided that the Aircraft Testing Flight should also be moved. A site within reasonable distance of Orfordness had obvious advantages and in the autumn of 1916 Tizard visited Ipswich with Hopkinson in search of a suitable place. 'Next day', he wrote, 'we walked over Martlesham Heath, near Woodbridge. We decided it would make an admirable aerodrome once an avenue of trees across it had been removed.' The War Office was told, and within a few weeks the flat sandy stretches, covered with short heather, and faintly enlivened by the wind off the distant sea, were being cleared to provide an airfield that was to become famous for forty years of R.F.C. and R.A.F. history.

Later that year Tizard was appointed scientific officer in charge at the new airfield, a change from the continuing battle which had been part of his daily round at Upavon. 'Now all was to be different' he wrote. 'I was at last promoted Captain and was to be in scientific charge of a purely experimental station, under the direction of a man whom I admired and trusted. Life looked as good as it can be in a war.'

*   *   *

Tizard began work at Martlesham early in 1917, when the airfield was opened under Major (later Lt.-Col.) H. L. Cooper who was to remain one of his life-long friends.* His first task was to lay out an accurate course for speed-tests, a process which involved 'erecting camera obscura at each end, calibrating them, seeing that the necessary instruments were acquired, instructing the test pilots, and the assistants who were to reduce the records'. The word 'approximate' was eliminated from testing, and instruments were issued to aircraft from the airfield laboratory

---

* The Testing Squadron, as it now became, moved from the Central Flying School to Martlesham on 16 January 1917, but only on 16 October 1917 did the unit become the Aeroplane Experimental Station R.F.C.

after they had been accurately calibrated, an idea which was still considered by some pilots as both revolutionary and unnecessary.

Throughout the first weeks of the new year, Tizard was fully employed on the supervision of the test-course; on meetings at the War Office; and on such matters as consultations with the Admiralty on the problems of test-flying. A typical day is recorded thus in his diary:

> Wrote to Short & Mason about 20,000 ft. aneroid. To Director Met. Office about meteorological instruments for testing squadron. Speed hut set up. Table in vertical camera half cemented in. Hopkinson here during morning. Discussed carburettor tests with him. Titherington brought down Sperry gyro for controlling rudder. Arranged to fix it to 2c. Discussed fittings. Mayor brought down new carburettor for rotary engine from W.O. Distinctly dud-looking.

The work which Tizard organized and directed from these early days of 1917 onwards formed the solid base of the phrase 'Martlesham test' which for more than twenty years – at least until the outbreak of the Second World War – was the synonym for a performance test whose figures combined scientific accuracy with aeronautical utility. 'He taught me to disbelieve all aircraft performance claims until they had been confirmed by in-flight measurements made by properly equipped independent observers', says Oliver Stewart, then one of the Martlesham test pilots. 'Manufacturers were sometimes carried away by enthusiasm for their products and made claims for the speed, rate of climb, ceiling, range, duration, stability, manoeuvrability and other features of their aircraft which were not borne out by the methods of in-flight measurement insisted upon by Tizard'.[11] To carry out such flights he had between twenty and thirty pilots who came from operational squadrons in France for a five- or six-week posting to Martlesham. In comparative terms they had a rest, although the business of test-flying was more strenuous than many of them had expected. It was also more complicated, and for two reasons. The first was that Tizard saw how test-flying could provide information not only on aircraft performance but also on a variety of subjects ranging from comparable petrol-consumption of fuels under different conditions to meteorology and instrument-performance. The second was the rigid system of performance-testing itself.

The first of these is illustrated by the 'Notes on Organisation of Test-Flights' which he appears to have written about the middle of 1917 and which suggest that some of the pilots took a slightly less scientific view of the business. 'Flying officers seem a little apt to think, especially when they are young, that when a machine has gone through its regulation tests, there is nothing for them to do except a few minutes joy-ride per fine day', this went. 'This is bad for themselves, for the men, and for the whole squadron.' Tizard then made two suggestions. The first was that every plane should make one or two long flights of about one or two hours' duration, since these would help to reveal oil consumption, which might be very important under Service conditions. The second was

> that we should start a series of 'tests on tests' by which I mean experiments on how the performance of machines is really affected by different conditions . . . By putting a machine (say the newly doped 110 Clerget Bristol) through standard climb and speed tests at intervals, we might get valuable results as to the effects of age on performance. At present I do not believe any definite data exist on these points.
>
> Such tests would be valuable in many ways. They could be used to train pilots and observers. Further, when properly organised, we should be carrying out climb tests every available day. This in its turn would lead to the amassing of a large amount of valuable meteorological data, especially if combined with the firing of Very lights over the cameras at different heights to measure the velocity and direction of wind. Testing of instruments would be carried out at the same time, so that eventually we may hope to have instruments which can be absolutely relied upon for tests of new aeroplanes which have to be put through quickly.

These notes, and the methods by which they were implemented, show the position from which Tizard viewed the practical application of scientific investigation. More important, however, was the system of testing itself. The principles on which it was based had already been worked out at the Royal Aircraft Factory, Farnborough. There, however, they were applied almost exclusively to the process of design and to the fundamental problems associated with this. It was Tizard's achievement to appreciate that these same principles should be applied – as they were not then being applied – to the finished aircraft, and so to adapt them that the results were of use not to the experimental designer but to the operational pilot. The way in which this was done was described in his first aeronautical paper, 'Methods of Measuring Aircraft Performance' which he read before the Aeronautical Society of Great Britain as it then was on 7 March 1917. He began by pointing out that until recently tests of new aircraft had produced two main figures; their speed, and rate of climb at 10,000 ft. 'What does 10,000 mean?' he asked. 'Do you mean that your aneroid read 10,000 ft., or do you mean 10,000 ft. above the spot you started from, or 10,000 ft. above sea level?' These, he went on, were questions which the intelligent designer would ask, and he would also ask whether, even at the same height, the pressure was the same on two different occasions. 'It follows', Tizard continued, 'that it is essential when comparing the performances of machines to compare them as far as possible under the same conditions of atmospheric *density*, not as is loosely done at the same height above the earth, since the density of the atmosphere at the same height above the earth may vary considerably on different days, and on the same day at different places.' To cope with this fact the old casual methods for determining rate of climb had to be abandoned, and the pilot had to make at least five different sets of observations at frequent intervals – aneroid heights at every 1,000 ft., time elapsed since start of climb, temperature, air speed, and engine revolutions. Three or more tests would be made, and from the resulting figures it was possible to produce an average rate of climb which represented as closely as possible the performance on a 'standard day' – and from which errors due to temperature, up-and-down currents, and similar factors had been eliminated.

Similar care was taken with speed-tests, in which he preferred to use his system of two camera obscuras. When this was impossible and a low-level test-run had to be made, human errors were minimized by means of radio signals.

There are two observers, one at each end of the course; when the aeroplane passes the starting-point the observer sends a signal and starts his stop-watch simultaneously; the second observer starts his stop-watch directly he hears the signal, and in his turn sends a signal and stops his watch when the aeroplane passes the finishing point. By this double timing, errors due to the so-called 'reaction' of the observers are practically eliminated, for the observer at the end of the course tends to *start* his watch late, while the first observer *stops* his late. The mean of the two observations gives the real time.

Such precision no doubt had a slightly academic flavour to many operational pilots. That Tizard was able to carry them with him, to gain not only their co-operation but their respect, is a measure of the man. With one solitary exception he had not been in action as they had. He was not only married but had his family close at hand, having moved his wife and small son, John Peter Mills, born on April 1, 1916, to quarters in nearby Woodbridge, where a second son, Richard Henry, was born on 25 June, 1917. Henry Tizard himself might regard the officers and staff at Martlesham as 'a happy friendly crew'; he might, and did, take his part in the sometimes uproarious mess parties where windows, chairs, and most other things breakable were duly broken. But he retained, as he had at Oxford, a certain aloofness from the hearties. He was a family man in the company of essentially non-family men, and it would have been easy for him to be perpetually out of step. That he was not, that he gained the confidence of very different sorts of people, was due partly to a certain built-in integrity, partly to his obvious ability – and partly to the fact that he himself flew with an abiding disregard for danger.

> He was one of the few scientists who could let his knowledge play upon ordinary practical problems in a simple, honest manner so that the practical man really felt he was getting somewhere [says Oliver Stewart], I do not think I knew anyone in aviation I admired more – and I met the whole of the scientific tribe either at Orfordness or at Martlesham.

Tizard's early delight in flying was gradually qualified; partly, he later thought, because he had flown so much, without oxygen, at 15,000 ft. or more. The cumulative effect drew on his stock of good health and by the end of the war he felt that he 'never wanted to fly again'. While the war lasted, however, he flew whenever chance offered, taking the first Sopwith 'Dolphin' to France to be compared with the S.E.5's of the famous 56 Squadron, testing much new equipment himself, and frequently piloting Hopkinson between Martlesham and London. It was on one such flight that Hopkinson noted a large thunder cloud nearby.

We had been having an argument at lunch about the effect of thunderstorms on aeroplanes [Tizard said later]. Somebody had said that when flying near a thundercloud the wires of an aeroplane would glow with electrical discharges, and we had said that that was very unlikely. We started off from Martlesham in beautiful clear weather, with a few clouds about in the distance. Before we had gone halfway the clouds in the east had increased in number and size, and looked dark and threatening. I was looking backward at one which was fairly close and saw a flash of lightning pass between it and another cloud. I am sorry to say that I experienced no violent desire to investigate the matter further, and kept steadily on my course. But soon afterwards Hopkinson began looking round, and, as luck would have it, saw another lightning flash behind us. He pointed eagerly in its direction, and I registered suitable astonishment. Then he passed me back a note with 'Let us go and see if the wires glow.' So we turned and flew towards the thunder-cloud, and round its edges. Then we went inside for a short time. It was quite dark inside, and the cloud was full of hailstones, as I discovered by incautiously putting my head out from behind the shelter of the windscreen. We got out all right without observing any glow from the wires; but when we eventually landed we found that the hailstones had chipped the propeller, and frayed the fabric on the leading edges of the wings so much that the wings had to be re-covered. However, we did not know that while we were in the air, so we were quite happy.[12]

Even in that age of heroic exploits, one flight of Tizard's achieved legendary quality. On the morning of 7 July a formation of Gothas was reported to be making for London as he was checking over a Sopwith Camel. Although the plane was armed only with untested guns, he took it to a height of 16,000 ft. and began patrolling between Rochford and Sheerness. After a short wait he saw the enemy formation, twenty strong, heading for home – and, to his surprise, 1,000 ft. higher. He began to climb, and reached 17,000 ft. in time to attack the last machine with a short burst. After less than 100 rounds had been fired, both port and starboard guns jammed. Tizard tried to clear them but was unsuccessful. However, if he could no longer attack he could at least observe. 'So I flew a little higher and alongside the formation and followed it out to sea', he later wrote, 'taking notice of the speed and other particulars. The German crews were all looking up at me, wondering, I suppose, what I was doing. I then waved good bye to them, they waved back, and I went home to lunch.' It was an interesting enough incident. Later, when Tizard had become a national figure, a more dramatic gloss was put upon it. According to one report, he had followed the enemy planes, noted their performance, and then dropped the record by parachute, appending the postscript 'I now propose to engage.'[13]

He had his share of near-mishaps, and remembered grimly all his life the occasion when one of the engine-cylinders of a D.H.4 blew up when he was 'only about 50 ft. off the ground and heading for a lot of cottages.' He managed to turn round and land down wind, an action contrary to all the recognized rules. There were only two incidents, other than the brush with the Gothas, during which he was shot upon in anger.

> The first [he wrote in a letter to Charles Grey in 1935], was when a battalion of infantry opened fire on an imaginary aeroplane at night at Portsmouth in 1915. I was in charge of an anti-aircraft gun, and the spent bullets pattered all round me. My gun did not open fire. It would not have done any good if it had. The second occasion was when I was fired on by British anti-aircraft guns, when I was flying the first Sopwith Dolphin to France. In this case the danger was remote, literally.

At Martlesham, he was responsible not only for aircraft-testing but for a multitude of ancillary tasks and problems. He thus became concerned, before the end of 1917, with the need to provide some substitute for the aircraft fuel which was being sunk in increasing quantities by German submarines. This fuel was made from Pennsylvania oil, and as more and more shipments were lost the shortage became acute. Tizard therefore suggested that tests should be made, purely as an experiment, with a mixture of standard aircraft fuel and the benzol obtained from gas-works. To the surprise of all concerned, including himself, the results were not merely satisfactory but actually better than those obtained with the standard fuel alone. There was, however, one difficulty, since certain constituents of the gasworks benzol tended to freeze out of the mixture at low temperatures. This was overcome by using, instead of the benzol, certain constituents of the toluene already being imported from Burma. Most of this was going to the explosives industry, but enough could be spared to ease the fuel position over a dangerous hump. For Tizard the work was to have one important result, for it was later to lead him towards an investigation of fuel efficiency which served both him and the country well – and played its part in providing the fighters of 1940 with that extra speed needed to defeat the Luftwaffe in the Battle of Britain.

By the end of 1917, much of the work at Martlesham Heath had developed into routine testing – in itself a tribute to Tizard's organization. This had little attraction for him and for some weeks his mind ranged about for a fresh and challenging activity. For a while he interested himself in the problems of cloud-flying, already investigated by his old friend Bourdillon. With Tizard's encouragement, a flight at Orfordness was now trained in this difficult and dangerous activity. Lindemann played his part, and from the work grew the concept of a special squadron, trained both to fly and to bomb through clouds. Tizard gave much thought to joining such a unit; however, before the need for decision arose, Hopkinson arrived at Martlesham with important news.

The reorganization which was about to produce an independent Royal Air Force from the Royal Flying Corps would bring under Hopkinson's control the experimental work of Farnborough and the Naval Aircraft Experimental Stations at Grain. His work would be considerably increased. Would Tizard come to the Air Ministry as his deputy? he asked. 'I did not hesitate for a moment' Tizard wrote in his autobiography. 'I said there was nothing I should like better. So I moved to London at the end of the year, as Assistant Controller, Research and Experiments, with the rank of Major.'

First in Savoy Buildings and, after these had been hit during an air raid, in West Africa House, Kingsway, Tizard now saw, for the first time and at close-quarters, some of the chopper-and axe operations which appear inseparable from politics, both Service and civilian.* To Tizard's unsophisticated mind the welter of intrigue and cross-intrigue out of which the R.A.F. was born

---

* 'When a new ministry is founded, or an old one expanded, civil servants and men seconded from the Services, tend to grapple for control' wrote General Sir Frederick Sykes, who replaced Trenchard as Chief of Air Staff in November 1918. 'The Air Ministry was no exception to this rule . . .'

E

and which enabled it to survive appeared more suitable to a small
Ruritanian State than to a great Empire; for he had yet to learn
that matters are frequently arranged thus – and even when he did
so the fact never ceased to shock him. At headquarters he also
made his first, apparently prickly, contacts with the recently-
appointed Minister of Munitions, Mr. Winston Churchill. 'I do
not remember seeing him then,' he wrote subsequently, 'but some
of his snappy minutes came my way.'[14]

Both Tizard and Churchill were to devote a major part of their
lives to the defence of Britain; both had some qualities in common.
Yet the similarities between them were superficial though numerous – the physical bravery, the nimble mind, the facility for the
pungent phrase. The differences went deeper. One trained his
abilities to discern the natural world; the other concentrated on
control of the men who might be able to rule it for a few brief
years. The one believed in rigid intellectual discipline which
allowed no deviation from the standards of academic objectivity,
however important the ends; the other well knew that in the rough
political world equally rough and ready means sometimes gave
the only chance of survival. For Tizard, who after the German
holiday had 'never been able to think of Germans as wholly bad',
it was easy to ask – though perhaps as Devil's advocate – why
in 1934 defence should be concentrated against Germany to the
exclusion of France; to Churchill it must have seemed, in the
summer of 1940, that the logical assessment of the scientist when
invasion was in question was a luxury which events could not allow.

In 1918 Tizard watched the political battle from a distance.
Hopkinson made such interventions as were necessary, while his
deputy spent his time at the work for which he had a genius – that
of evaluating scientific improvements in terms of operational use,
encouraging both the scientists and the flying men to speak their
mind, to state their problems, and to work together as a team in
solving them. Then, in August 1918, Hopkinson flew into the ground
while piloting himself on a routine journey to London – an accident whose repercussions on the Air Force were to be considerable.
Writing of his death, Tizard said that 'in his position, and with
his knowledge and character, he would have had a great influence
on Government policy between the wars. I would go so far as to

say that the chance of the second world war breaking out would have been greatly lessened. Certainly we would have been better prepared for it.'[15] The claim may at first sound extravagant. But when tracing the unhappy record of scientific research for the Services between 1920 and 1939 it appears to be justified. It is ironic that in 1924 Tizard, who might have exercised an influence comparable to that of Hopkinson, refused the post that Hopkinson would almost certainly have occupied.

Throughout the remaining three months of war, Tizard carried on Hopkinson's work at the newly-created Air Ministry. He completed his spell there without, as he put it in his Haldane Lecture of 1955, 'any great respect for the manner in which the Civil Service dealt with highly technical matters'. One day a file about a new invention arrived on his desk. 'I have tried in vain to disinter it from its grave – it was probably cremated long ago – so it may be pure imagination on my part to say that it started with a minute written in green ink over the well-known initials "W.S.C." ', he said.

> It certainly was not marked 'Action today' because it had gone through the hands of many able administrators before it reached me. The invention was that of a mysterious liquid one drop of which added to a gallon of water would make a first-class aviation fuel; and the sum asked for the secret was very large. The able administrators had enlarged on the diminishing stocks of petrol, on the rate of consumption, the sinking of tankers, and so on — the general conclusion, implied if not expressed, being that if only half what the inventor claimed was true it would be well worth while paying the sum asked for the secret. I returned the file to its source with what I think may have been the shortest minute ever written to a Minister.

He was now, in effect, a departmental head, but he allowed himself to be tied down to office work as little as possible, passing over much of this to his deputy, Melvill Jones, an aeronautical research expert who had reached headquarters via the National Physical Laboratory, Farnborough, the Armament Experimental Station at Orfordness, and squadron service as an Observer in France. Tizard himself flew wherever he could, personally visiting airfields, experimental stations, and the factories where arms were made. And early in November 1918, he met a young meteorologist

at Farnborough, Robert Watson-Watt, whom he unsuccessfully
tried to tempt into a post as investigator of Germany's war-time
weather research.

On 11 November, Tizard was visiting the Oldbury factory of
Albright & Wilson, and from the laboratory workshops heard the
whine of the hooters announcing the Armistice. 'When I went to
the station the streets were full of cheering men, many of them
young, who had been earning high wages safely during the war',
he remembered. 'I could not share their enthusiasm; my relief
that the war was over was clouded by the memory of many young
friends who had fallen by the way. I returned to London sad,
rather than cheerful.'[16]

Shortly afterwards he fell ill with influenza, and recovered only
after some weeks. He returned to the Air Ministry, occupied himself as best he could for the remaining weeks of Service life, and
was demobilized – with the Air Force Cross as a decoration for
test-flying – in the spring of 1919.

> The war [he later wrote], did me a great deal of good. It pulled me
> out of the ruck at Oxford. It forced me to do things which I should
> never have done of my own accord in peacetime, but which I found
> in practice much easier than I imagined. It brought me into close
> and friendly contact with all sorts and conditions of men, and it made
> me realize that a purely scientific education *was* of value for men who
> had to deal with the practical affairs of life.[17]

Now the problem had to be faced. Would he continue to devote
himself to these 'practical affairs of life', or would he return to
what many men still hoped and imagined would be the satisfac-
tions of an unchanged Oxford?

CHAPTER THREE

Scientific and Industrial Research

Tizard returned to Oriel in the spring of 1919, transformed more than many men had been by the rough touch of war. Yet it seemed that he might now submerge himself, as completely as he had during the years before 1914, in a purely academic life. He settled his young wife and growing family in a comfortable house in North Oxford. He committed himself to giving a full course of lectures in physical chemistry, apparently with some doubts of his ability. And in March he applied for the Dr Lees Readership in Chemistry at Christ Church – but refused the appointment when it was offered to him three months later.

At Oriel he now revealed a new and unsuspected talent for finance, which he no doubt regarded as the application of mathematical knowledge to hard cash. His advice, which he pressed on his seniors with persuasive argument, was that the College should sell three large farm estates and re-invest the money so gained. The proposal was, in the words of the Oriel Record, 'of a very important and far-reaching character' since it involved the sale of the greater part of the College's landed property. The advice was eventually taken, but there were certain misgivings. Only after Tizard had left Oxford for his first spell as a Civil Servant did the truth of the matter become apparent – that his simple proposals had greatly increased the College income.

> Roughly we doubled our nett external income, and many of the investments were made in dated securities bought well under par [he was told nearly forty years later]. . . . There is no doubt that the sales were made in most cases at good prices, many of them greater than the valuations, and it will be noted that as late as the thirties, when most of the properties unsold at the first rush were got rid of, Wadley Manor was sold well *under* the 1920 valuation. The College therefore

is to be congratulated on cashing in on a period when tenant farmers had prospered during the war and were keen to improve their status to that of owner-farmers, and also on investing at least part of the money in 1921 when the yield on gilt-edged was over 5%; by 1922 it had fallen to $4\frac{1}{2}$, but by 1934 to about $3\frac{1}{2}$ and it did not reach over 5% again until 1957.[1]

Meanwhile, Tizard was feeling his way back into University life. As a lecturer he has been described at this period as 'nervous', and more than one of those who read under him feel that he was uncertain and unsure of himself when dealing with younger men. It is difficult, in view of his later record – 'he was, above all things, a young man's scientist' is a comment from many colleagues of the Second World War – adequately to account for this, but the explanation seems likely to have lain in two things. One was the set of slightly restless mannerisms which he revealed while lecturing, and which he never entirely lost. The other was the gulf which existed between those who had experienced the facts of war and those who had not, a gulf which could separate not merely men from different generations, but those whose ages varied by only a few years. Whatever the cause of Tizard's hesitancy, it seemed unlikely to affect his University career. On 14 February 1920 he was appointed University Reader in Thermodynamics for five years. In April he was re-elected a Fellow of Oriel for a further seven. And a few months later he examined in Final Schools when, he commented in his draft autobiography, 'I gave First Classes, *inter alia*, to C. N. Hinshelwood, E. J. Bowen and Sydney Barratt (not a bad lot!)'.*

He remembered his own experience a decade previously, and his feeling that there was too great an element of luck about hard questions.

One of the two papers I set in physical chemistry was so apparently easy, that I feel sure that a more cheerful group of candidates never sat in the Examination Schools [he recalled]. I am confident, too, that there never was an occasion when an examiner found it easier to distinguish between the relative merits of different candidates. The first-class man answered the questions briefly, accurately and to

---

* Later Sir Cyril Hinshelwood, President, Royal Society; Dr E. J. Bowen, F.R.S.; and Sir Sydney Barratt, Chairman Albright & Wilson Ltd.

the point; the second-class man wrote pages of irrelevant matter, to impress the examiner; and the third-class man made elementary mistakes.[2]

He had only recently made an intervention in Oxford affairs that was to have significant results during the next two decades. One of the matters which the University was forced to settle during these early months of the peace was the succession to Professor Clifton as Professor of Experimental Philosophy. Clifton had given up the Chair in 1915 after holding it for more than fifty years, and to even the most charitable observer one thing was clear: that considerable efforts were necessary if the Clarendon Laboratory was to be raised from the trough into which it had quietly been sinking for half a century. Then, early in 1919, it came to Tizard's ears that the Cambridge electors were trying to persuade the Oxford authorities to accept a Cambridge man for the Chair. Tizard remembered Lindemann.

Even at this period there were flurries of argument between them, as there might well be between any two strong-minded men. At times these revealed a deep ferocity. It has been claimed – but seems unlikely – that Lindemann could never forget that while Tizard had been a commissioned officer, he himself had remained a civilian, and that these facts irked something in his German ancestry. It has been claimed, with more plausibility, that Tizard's delight in giving authority an occasional sharp prod offended Lindemann's stern beliefs. And it seems likely that whatever the truth of these speculations, Lindemann continued to envy Tizard's ability to retain the common touch. The keenness of their arguments was not confined to matters of moment.

> I remember how on one occasion Tizard and I bumped into Lindemann [says Sir Vernon Brown]. At first they were quite friendly. But it was not long before they were engaged in a heated argument. It was soon being conducted along the 'of course that's all nonsense' lines, and both were soon red in the face. The argument was about the most economical way of packing oranges in a box – whether directly on top of one another or in layers slightly off-centre.[3]

Yet Tizard retained a profound respect for his friend's ability. He brought Lindemann one day into the laboratory of Balliol's Natural Science Tutor, Harold Hartley, and evidently regarded

him, as Hartley remembered more than forty years later, 'as the
saviour of science in Oxford'. And he now suggested to his Oxford
colleagues that Lindemann should be considered for the Clarendon
appointment. Some time previously, when Lindemann had first
discreetly noted that Clifton had already been in occupation of
the Chair for more than forty years, Tizard had considered that he
'might get it'. Now he did more, advising him and pulling such
strings as were within reach. 'Dear Lindy', he finally wrote early
in 1919, 'I found your application in Oxford, and have sent it off
today with the collected papers, in a registered parcel to the
Registrar. The application was quite all right.'[4] Both Rutherford
and Lord Rayleigh were among Lindemann's distinguished spon-
sors, and on April 23 he was elected to the Chair.

> He was disappointing in some ways [Tizard subsequently wrote]. He
> was a destructive critic rather than a brilliant investigator. Not that
> he did nothing original, but his contributions to the great advance of
> physics during the next twenty years were much fewer than I had
> expected from him. He showed then, as he did later, that though his
> intellectual powers were outstanding, his judgment was poor. But
> he deserves the greatest credit for raising the status of the Clarendon
> Laboratory from the low point which it had reached during the long
> reign of Professor Clifton.[5]

Helping Lindemann into the Clarendon saddle was one of the
last services which Tizard was to perform for Oxford for some
years. For while the attraction of the purely academic life had
remained constant, there were already signs of a hankering for
work which touched those 'practical problems' with which he had
been dealing throughout the war. Early in 1920, he travelled to
Manchester and spoke to the University on 'Experimental Work in
the Royal Air Force during and after the War'. A few months
later he became a member of the Aeronautical Research Committee; while from the summer of 1919 onwards he had been
devoting much time and energy to a project in which theory and
practice joined forces in equal strength.

    This project was a massive investigation into the ways in which
the chemical components of a fuel affected the performance of the
internal combustion engine. Tizard's part in it sprang directly
from his work at Martlesham Heath. Early in 1918, he had been

introduced by Hopkinson to the consulting engineer, Harry Ricardo, who explained that he would like Tizard's help in a programme of experiments to be started as soon as the war was over.

> I had long been convinced that the onset of detonation or knock was the most important factor in limiting the performance of the petrol engine [says Ricardo]. And I had satisfied myself, at last, that it arose from the spontaneous ignition of a small part of the working fluid due to compression by the advancing flame front, and that its tendency to do so depended upon the shape of the combustion chamber, the movement of the gases within it, and, above all, on the chemical components of the fuel.[6]

He had already carried out some preliminary work, and this had come to the notice of the Asiatic Petroleum Company which now proposed that he should direct a major programme of research at his Shoreham laboratory when the war finished. Ricardo remembered Tizard's work at Martlesham, and suggested that he should join the venture.

Tizard accepted the offer of 'what was then the large sum of £1,000 a year, which came in very useful at the time'. However, he made one typical stipulation. He would collaborate in the series of experiments, which were expected to spread over a period of one or two years, only on condition that the results of the investigation should be published. Academic research might, in this fallible world, have to be subsidized by business organizations; but the principle of open publication should still be insisted upon. The company chairman, Sir Robert Waley-Cohen, agreed, stipulating only that nothing should be published within eighteen months of his organization receiving the report of the experiments.

Throughout the last year of the war Tizard had therefore been in close and regular touch with Ricardo, and the two men had worked out what equipment would be needed, as well as the campaign to be pursued. Tizard had suggested building not only the variable-compression engine already proposed by Ricardo, but also another unit, always known as the 'Sphinx' because of its peculiar shape, in which the piston would make only one rapid stroke and then be locked at top dead-centre. He also proposed that in the preliminary theoretical work he should co-opt David

Pye, a busy man of great industry who had added a postscript to
the pioneer days of Welsh rock-climbing before the war and had
worked with Tizard as Experimental Officer at Martlesham
Heath.

It was agreed that as soon as the war ended, and we were released
from our various duties, Tizard and Pye would return to Oxford and
jointly prepare a very full thesis setting out all the physical characteristics of all the light hydrocarbon fuels and also other possible volatile
liquid fuels such as Alcohol, Acetone, Ether, Carbon Disulphide,
etc. [Ricardo has written]. I and my colleagues would supervise the
building of our new laboratory at Shoreham and the construction by
Messrs. Peter Brotherhood of both the variable-compression engine
and the 'Sphinx' together with the collection of such other test
equipment as we should need.[7]

By the summer of 1919 all was ready. Tizard and Pye had prepared an analysis of all the physical properties of the fuels to be
used, and now came to Shoreham to help in the practical experiments. Tizard spent most of the Long Vacation there, came down
at intervals throughout the following autumn and spring, and
returned for a long spell during the summer of 1920. His value
throughout this period lay in his ability to devise ingenious and
successful methods of solving the specific problems that continually
arose. He also had a flair for translating the theoretical problem
into one that could be solved on the test-bench, and he was able
himself to carry out a good deal of the actual experimental work.

As had been expected [writes Ricardo], we confirmed that the inci-
dence of detonation was the most important single factor limiting the
performance of the petrol engine, and, at Tizard's suggestion, we
expressed this in terms of Toluene Number, that is to say, the proportion of toluene (the least prone to detonate of any hydrocarbon
fuel we had tested) which had to be added to heptane (the worst) to
match the fuel under test, for we had established a straight-line
relationship in the blending of these two. Several years later the
Americans substituted iso-octane for toluene and today the expression 'octane number' is universal.'[8]

Tizard thoroughly enjoyed himself at Shoreham. He was,
moreover, already showing his instinctive ability to work with all
manner of men. 'To his subordinates', he once wrote of Lord
Balfour, 'he was courtesy itself, and was repaid by loyal affection-

ate service. Like all really great men he treated them as equals; need it be added that he knew how to get the best out of men?' Much the same might be said of Tizard himself. During the summer of 1919 he stayed with the Ricardos and more than forty years later they retain memories of 'the ideal guest', the man with an inexhaustible fund of good stories; the man who, like Lindemann, was adored by children. He played a good game of tennis, was interested in Ricardo's boating activities, and enjoyed fishing off the coast.

By the end of 1920, the bulk of the purely experimental work had been finished. What remained to be done was a long series of relatively routine tests, and in these Tizard had little interest. His part in the programme now came virtually to an end and he devoted himself to setting down the information which had been gathered. The result was a series of six papers, most of them prepared in collaboration with others, the most important being 'The character of various fuels for internal combustion engines', written with Pye and published first in the 'Automobile Engineer' and then in the Report of the Empire Fuels Committee.

*   *   *

Tizard was now thirty-five, a family man with a satisfactory record of work accomplished. A safe if undistinguished rut stretched clearly before him. The private consultancy which provided jam for the financial bread and butter could not, of course, be counted upon for ever; yet his University appointments, with their promise of progress up the rungs of the academic ladder, offered the mixture of security and satisfaction that would have been sufficient for many men. There might have seemed, on the face of it, little reason for moving; least of all for moving back into that dark, turbulent, suspect world of controversial public affairs.

This was the situation when Tizard received a letter from Sir Frank Heath, the man who had suggested some twelve years earlier that he might be interested in joining the Board of Education. Heath's letter has not survived, but it is clear from Tizard's reply that in it he made the tentative offer of a post in the Department of Scientific and Industrial Research, set up four years previously to encourage the most efficient use of the country's resources.

Heath, by now the Department's Secretary, was a man of fifty-six. He had come to command the country's machinery for Government-sponsored research by a curious path which had started from a professorship of English at Bedford College and had led through academic posts as lecturer and librarian to the Universities branch of the Board of Education, from which the D.S.I.R. had eventually sprung. He was a man of wide learning and ingenious mind who early in the war had been responsible for the shape of the British 'tin hat'. While British troops had only their Field Service caps, he was told, the Germans had steel helmets. Realizing that the job was that of deflecting a large number of small high-velocity fragments as efficiently as possible, Heath pointed out that the National Physical Laboratory would no doubt be able to work out the best shape. Then came the brain wave. The problem had, of course, been tackled long ago by the armourers. 'Japan was in the Middle Ages, so to speak, only yesterday', Heath said, 'and their armourers must have known all about the problem. Go at once to the Victoria and Albert Museum and borrow a Samurai helmet. I will get the names of steel manufacturers this afternoon.' Thus there came about the prototype of the British 'battle-bowler' which remained unchanged in shape for nearly half a century.

In a wider field, Heath's preoccupation with the ways in which science could aid the war effort was to have great and lasting effect. Early in 1915 he submitted to the Board of Education a memorandum suggesting how science could best be mobilized. This memorandum was considered by a small committee which in May 1915 decided to set up a permanent organization for the development of scientific and industrial research. Thus when the Royal Society and the Chemical Society later proposed that the Government should form a National Chemical and Advisory Committee, an organization with a larger field of activities was already being formed. This was the Department of Scientific and Industrial Research set up under Heath in 1916 on the lines of his earlier memorandum. Research Associations, in which the leading firms in separate industries worked on specific problems with the aid of Government funds, were started in 1917. In the same year the Fuel Research Board was set up, to be followed in

1918 by the Food Investigation Board, and by the end of the war the main lines of the organization had been laid.

Now, with the settling down into peace, there came — quite fortuitously, and produced by the desire for economy – an attempt to see how research for the Services might be co-ordinated. On consideration of the estimates for 1919–20, the Cabinet decided 'that means should be adopted so to organize all the scientific work which is of common interest to the fighting services of the Crown as to ensure the utmost economy of expense and personnel, and the due co-ordination of the technical work of the various naval, military and aeronautical establishments, so as to avoid overlapping either with each other or with the research organizations of the Civil departments of State.'⁹ The method to be adopted was the setting-up of three Co-ordinating Boards, dealing respectively with Physics, Chemistry, and Engineering. Together with the existing Radio Research Board, which already had an inter-Service flavour, these would, in the first and slightly ominous phrase of the D.S.I.R. annual report, 'ensure the utmost economy of expense and personnel' as well as suggest the lines of research they might most usefully follow.

The man who would run the new Boards from his position as Assistant Secretary, would have to be a scientist, but he would also need a sound working knowledge of the Services. It would, moreover, obviously be an advantage if this civilian, who would have day-to-day working contacts with Service officers, had during the past war shared at least a little of their own dangers and difficulties. There can have been a mere handful of such men in 1920. Tizard was one of them, and it was to Tizard that Heath now offered the post.

Tizard thought over the proposal for a number of days, and replied to Heath on 25 April. His long letter, of which only a draft appears to have survived, and Heath's reply, combine to give an illuminating picture of how this early attempt to co-ordinate scientific research for the Services was about to be tackled.

> It seems to me that the real attraction of the work, and the possibility of doing it well, depends so much on the detail organisation, that I hope you won't mind being bombarded with a number of

questions [Tizard wrote]. I understand from you that the policy is that *all* scientific investigations and research which the Admiralty, War Office and Air Ministry wish to be carried out, with the exception of those which are considered particularly secret, will be referred to one of the three Committees (Phyiscs, Chemistry and Engineering) responsible to, and to a great extent nominated by, the Research department. These committees will examine the proposals critically, will endeavour to co-ordinate the work of the three departments, and will supervise such work as *they* decide should be carried out. The necessary funds will be found by the Research department. I am not clear as to the relation of the proposed 'Assistant Secretary' to these committees.

(1) Is executive action to be in the hands of the Assistant Secretary or the Committees? If nominally in the latter, will it actually be in the former?

(2) Will scientific initiative on the part of the Assistant Secretary be encouraged, or is his work to be purely administrative?

(3) Will the three secretaries of the committees form part of the staff of the Assistant Secretary or will they be independent?

(4) What will be the size and contribution of the Committees, and are any members yet appointed? Will the Asst. Secretary be ex-officio a member of each committee?

(5) What will be the relation of such experimental establishments as the RAE Farnborough, Woolwich Arsenal experimental station, Admiralty Compass department, to the Committee, and to the Assistant Secretary? I think such relations will have to be fairly closely defined, as otherwise I see difficulties ahead. I suppose the administration of these establishments will remain as it is at present. I think I can best make the possible difficulties clear by taking an example.

(a) A large part of the *research* work at Farnborough is of direct or indirect importance to the three fighting departments, and indeed to industry in general. Will such research work continue to be 'controlled' by the Air Ministry without reference to the Research department. I ask this because the success of the scheme will largely depend on the fighting departments referring practically the *whole* of their proposed scientific investigations to the Co-ordinating Committees.

(b) Although the initiative for all such research may rest on *paper* with the Co-ordinating Committees, yet in practice too much may be concentrated (in the minds of) officials of the different departments. Money difficulties are not likely to stop this, as the cost of the research work at Farnborough, and I presume at similar departments of the fighting services, is really only a small fraction of the cost of the three Establishments. But perhaps it will be an important part of the work of the new Assistant Secretary to arrange, as tactfully as he can, that everything possible *is* referred to the co-ordinating committees! A point that arises here is what is going to be the connection between the new Aeronautical Research Committee and (a) the Research Department, (b) the Co-ordinating Committee. The same question applies to the new Admiralty Experimental station at Teddington, the 'cryogenic' laboratory at Cambridge etc., and to any other [unclear] which are now in existence or may be set up in future by the fighting departments.

Apart from these questions, my personal difficulties can be summed up very shortly. Is the post primarily scientific or administrative? I don't want to give up my purely scientific connections. Of course I quite realise, that if I came to the Research Department, I should not have time, at any rate at first, to go into scientific research myself, but as I visualise the post, I do think it would be important to have the confidence of the scientific, as well as the military, world. This would mean keeping up a more or less independent connection with e.g. the scientific societies to which I belong at present. Also it seems to me that the more direct contact I could have with the various experiments being carried out under the supervision of the Dept. & of the Co-ordinating Committees, the better. All this means a good deal of freedom of action, and that the work would be by no means confined to the 'office'. I believe this is the view you take, but would like to be certain of it. As to the other conditions, I should lose financially by coming to the Research department, and considerably so if at the lower grade of £1,000 and no bonus, apart from the fact that I suppose there are little prospects of increase in the future. Presumably there are certain compensations in the way of pension, but this depends on the number of years of service, does it not? So that if I came in now I should never be eligible for the full pension.

One thing I ought to have told you at once, which may affect your plans, is that if I *did* come, I should not be able to do so before October, except unofficially, as I have to give at least a quarter's notice to the engineering firm for which I am doing the research work I told you about.

He concluded by apologizing for the length of the letter and proposing a number of dates on which he could discuss the matter. Attached to his draft there is a separate sheet of paper on which he appears to have jotted down the tasks of the Assistant Secretary as he envisaged them.

The A.S. is to keep in personal touch as far as possible with the fighting departments, in order to ascertain their needs [this reads]. He is to take executive action on the decision of the Co-Ordinating Committees i.e. it will fall to the Assistant Secretary to arrange for

research to be carried out at Government experimental establishments, universities, private firms, etc.

Heath considered the points which Tizard had raised, and replied on 5 May* '. . . you begin with a general statement of what
you understand the policy to be so far as research for the fighting
services is concerned, and I think it accurately represents the
position, though I should like to add one or two guarding statements', he said.[10]

He added that the Assistant Secretary would be responsible for
seeing that the decisions of the D.S.I.R.'s Advisory Committee
were put into action. He would not be a member of each of the
Co-ordinating Boards but would be able to attend their meetings
as he wished and he would have access to all scientific stations
where work was continuing under their direct control. While the
work would be primarily administrative, 'scientific initiative'
would not be discouraged – although, as Heath was careful to
add, this would have to be personal rather than official 'just
because of the doubts which might arise in the minds of other
Departments if an officer in the powerful executive position of the
Assistant Secretary had also the means of initiating research on
behalf of this Department in his official capacity'. And it was
essential for the man in the new post to 'try to get and keep the
confidence of the scientific as well as the military world'.

It was an encouraging letter. Heath clearly knew that he had
picked the best man for the post and he was willing to interpret
the rules as might be fitting. There followed only a brief discussion
about terms. Tizard accepted the post and on 5 June was formally
notified of his appointment at a salary of £1,360, his work being
control 'of the group of Boards and Committees entrusted with
the co-ordination of research for the fighting Services.' Nearly
forty years later, looking back, he put down on paper his reasons
for taking this decisive step.

(a) I had already convinced myself that I would never be outstanding as a pure scientist [he wrote]. Younger men were coming on of
greater ability in that respect. (b) My war experience had taught me
the value, and interest, of the application of science. It was a neglected
field in England. (c) I had to look forward to the education of my

* The full text of Heath's letter is given in Appendix 1.

family; and though the salary offered by the D.S.I.R. was less than my total salary at Oxford, more than half the latter was dependent on consulting work which might not continue. In addition I could reasonably look forward to promotion in a few years time. (d) The Oxford climate did not suit me. I had perpetual colds and slight fevers in 1919–20.[11]

Thus within little more than a year he had done two things. He had used his influence to ease Lindemann into an appointment which to a physicist was one of the most important in Britain; and he himself had stepped out of the purely scientific arena into one where judgement of how science might be applied was the yardstick of success. It seems likely that he was wise in both moves, an interesting gloss on which is provided by Sir Cyril Hinshelwood, who has written:

> I do not think that he (Tizard) had that deep feeling for natural phenomena which Lindemann had, and I do not think he was very remarkable for his intuition. On the other hand, he had extremely good judgement, and a much better practical sense than Lindemann. You can hardly imagine Tizard suddenly wanting to do an experiment to see what would happen, and I do not think that he had the instincts of a discoverer. On the other hand, curiously enough, if he had heard other people speculating I am sure he would at once have said, 'Why don't you try it and see'. This little contrast seems to me to be very characteristic. Incidentally, it reflects a difference between Tizard and Lindemann, who would at once have given them the answer (quite possibly right) to the speculations, but would probably have told the other people at the same time why anything they proposed to do was foolish.[12]

Tizard resigned his Fellowship at Oriel at the end of June, and was about to take up his new work when influenza struck him down. He appeared to recover quickly at first, suffered a bad relapse, and was seriously ill before finally taking up his new appointment in September. He had already moved with his wife and two sons from Oxford to Wimbledon, where a third son David Andrew Thomas, was born in 1922. He found it difficult to settle, moved frequently, and only after some four years took a lease on 3 Camp View, a house on Wimbledon Common commanding a fine stretch of green country.

He started well up in the hierarchy of Government service, a fact underlined by his large and comfortable room at the D.S.I.R.

F

headquarters in Queen Anne's Gate. From it he could look out across the garden and a corner of the Park to the white buildings which a quarter of a century later housed his office in the Ministry of Defence, and into it there intruded little more than the occasional music of the bandsmen marching down Birdcage Walk. Until 1923, when his orderly mind and his instinctive ability as a committee chairman eased him up into the position of Principal Assistant Secretary, he was mainly concerned with the Coordinating Boards, and was, in fact described in 1922 by 'The Provosts and Fellows of Oriel College, Oxford', as 'Director of Research to the Forces', a title which had it been noticed would no doubt have produced pain in many be-medalled breasts.

The Co-ordinating Boards whose administration and direction was now Tizard's first charge did more than attempt to rationalize the scientific work of the Services. They dealt in addition with the *ad hoc* scientific puzzles and problems that beset the Service authorities, and they sometimes arranged to carry on their grant research which was largely but not exclusively of Service interest. Before the end of 1921, for instance, there were passed on to Tizard by the War Office reports that the Germans had been able to produce powerful electromagnetic waves capable of killing men and of detonating explosives – reports which Sir Richard Threlfall, with long experience of death-ray stories, described as 'these venerable proposals'. Sir William Bragg, Sir Ernest Rutherford, and Sir Henry Jackson, all decided that the proposals were unworthy of serious consideration. The Physics Co-ordinating Research Board was more cautious. Its chairman, Sir J. J. Thomson, felt that the chance of detonating explosives could not be completely ruled out and a number of experiments were made. All proved negative and Tizard eventually informed the War Office that the reports were of no military importance. The following year, at the suggestion of the Physics Co-ordinating Research Board, but unlinked with the reports from Germany, the Russian scientist Peter Kapitza was appointed to the Cavendish where, under Rutherford, he began his important work on intense electromagnetic fields. He was provided with an assistant, and Rutherford was given £500 towards the initial cost of apparatus.

One of the problems inherent in the Boards' mechanism was illustrated when Thomson visited the United States six months later and gave the General Electric Company a brief account of Kapitza's work, and of its possible applications. Tizard was worried, both by the disclosure of the information itself and by its possible effect. However, Lord Salisbury, Lord President of the Council, subsequently saw Thomson and tactfully satisfied himself that no harm had been done.[13]

The main work of the Boards – and of the Fabrics Co-ordinating Committee which was subsequently set up – was, however, the co-ordination of research projects of specific interest to one of the Services. Most of these were carried out in Service research stations, but much work was also done at the National Physical Laboratory, and a smaller amount at other D.S.I.R. research stations. In addition, the Chemical Research Laboratory, today the National Chemical Laboratory, was established under pressure from Tizard when it became clear that facilities were insufficient for handling the bulk of the Chemistry Board's work.

The possible use of selenium cells in detecting X-rays, problems of aircraft silencing and metal fatigue, the possibilities of new materials and new techniques were only a few of the matters investigated by the Research Boards. They also dealt with such esoteric efforts as the culture of artichokes, which were to provide the Royal Navy with industrial alcohol. Most of the work contributed new information on how the natural laws operated undeh specific circumstances; much of it provided information whicr throughout the years was slowly incorporated into Service equip‑ ment. Yet it seems likely that by far the most important work initiated by the Boards was a project which at the time appeared to have only limited practical application. In the Department's report for the year 1924–25 it was revealed that Professor Appleton of the Radio Research Board had 'suggested and carried out on behalf of the Board, with the co-operation of the British Broad‑ casting Company, a series of preliminary experiments with a view to the determination of the height of the Heaviside layer, by observations at Oxford, on the interference of the waves travelling by different paths emitted by the Bournemouth Broadcasting Station.' At the time it appeared that better radio reception was the most likely result of the experiments, which were to be continued. Yet from them there was developed, almost exactly a decade later, the 'magic eye' of radar, brought to practical use just, but only just, in time to bring victory in the Battle of Britain.

The Co-ordinating Boards accomplished as much as could be expected of them within their limits of economy and in the climate of the times; and it seems fair to claim that if they were not a success beneath Tizard's guiding hand, they would have been a success under no-one else's. However, he soon appears to have become sceptical of what they might accomplish, and one of his first reports on them, sent by Heath to Lord Balfour, Lord President, was accompanied by a note describing it as being 'very frank, too frank in its expression for any but your own eye, or perhaps that of any individual minister to whom you may think it wise to show it.' Early in 1927 a sub-committee of the Committee of Civil Research recommended that the Boards should be dissolved and their work handled in future by *ad hoc* committees. When the recommendation was implemented only the Radio Research Board remained.

Sir Harry Melville, writing three decades afterwards as a later Secretary of the D.S.I.R., comments that

> the reasons why this experiment in co-ordination was abandoned were complex, but a primary one was, no doubt, the difficulty of embracing within their scope the constantly widening field of applied research for purposes of defence. Each Board was confronted with a diffusive subject-matter and a growing number of active centres of work with which it ought to maintain a close contact. These and other factors made its task increasingly difficult. It is perhaps significant that in radio, where there was least diffusiveness, the Board went on.[14]

Quite as important, perhaps, was the fact that throughout the 1920's, expenditure on the Services was a political liability. Had this not been the case there would still have been little enthusiasm in either the Royal Navy or the Royal Air Force, and none at all in the Army, for giving more than the most cursory lip-service to to the suggestions of scientific men. And, even had the Services been aware that their life's-blood might, quite literally, depend one day on scientific ingenuity, they would still have remained cautious of pooling their research wholeheartedly in an age of continuing inter-Service rivalry.

However, so far as Tizard himself was concerned, his early experiences at the D.S.I.R. were to make him the man who knew better than most just how science could be applied to the Services. As Assistant Secretary he was the natural link between the laboratory and the Service user. He heard both sides of the question. He was, to an extent not given to most men, unswayed by personal ambition. And it was clear to all concerned that when his advice was asked for it would be given with an almost clinical objectivity. Thus from these early days his integrity earned him a trust that was to be of crucial importance.

*   *   *

Well before the demise of the Co-ordinating Boards, Tizard's facility for coping with the problems of co-operation between scientists and the Services had been recognized, and in 1924 it was suggested that he should become Director of Scientific Research in the Air Ministry, a post whose creation he himself had recommended. To see the offer in perspective it is necessary to realize why, in the organization of the Co-ordinating Boards, aeronautical questions had been the most intractable.

During the immediate post-war years, the problems of flight itself were relatively new and unexplored, while industrial expansion – for civil aviation if not for the Royal Air Force – was potentially great. The machinery for research which already existed had grown up largely as a series of inspired improvisations, while the bitter political battle on whose outcome the continued independence of the newly-fledged Service rested had added yet a further complication to an already complicated issue. As Assistant Controller of Research and Experiment in the Air Ministry for the few months following the death of Bertram Hopkinson, Tizard had already seen something of this developing problem. Hopkinson himself had suggested, shortly before his death, that aeronautical research might best be tackled by common action between the Air Ministry, the D.S.I.R., the Education Authorities, and the aircraft industry. This proposal was given more concrete shape by the Committee on Education and Research in Aeronautics set up in October 1918 under the chairmanship of Sir Richard Glazebrook, Director of the National Physical Laboratory, then still responsible for the Advisory Committee on Aeronautics. Tizard, soon to be demobilized, was a member of the Glazebrook committee, which in March 1919, reported to the Minister of War and Air, Mr. Churchill. Its main recommendation was that a Board of Aeronautics, run jointly by the D.S.I.R. and the Air Ministry, should be set up on a budget of £500,000 a year. This brought the expected recommendation from Air Marshal Sir John Salmond, then Commander of the R.A.F. in the Field, who maintained that the Air Council alone should be responsible for all research and experimental work undertaken for the development of aeronautics carried out with Government money. No action was taken on the Glazebrook Committee's recommendations, and the unsatisfactory system of divided control, with only haphazard liaison between researcher, designer and user, continued throughout the first years of the Co-ordinating Board's existence.

The first solution to the problem was provided by Tizard himself at the beginning of 1924, when he wrote to Air Marshal Sir Geoffrey Salmond, Air Member for Supply and Research. The existing functions of the Directorate of Supply and Research should be separated, and the latter expanded. A Director of Scientific Research should be appointed in the Air Ministry with duties roughly the same as those of Frank Smith, Director of Scientific Research at the Admiralty. In particular, the new Director should be responsible for the work of the Aeronautics Department of the National Physical Laboratory, and of other work carried out and paid for by the Air Ministry; for the work of the small Air Ministry Laboratory which had been set up in Imperial College under H. E. Wimperis; for the engine work by Ricardo at Shoreham; for all work on the research programmes of the Royal Aircraft Establishment; and for the miscellaneous smaller researches which were carried out at Air Force stations and Universities, and by a small number of minor firms. This was a tidy, clean solution which could in theory at least provide the necessary liaison between those who carried out fundamental research on the problems of flight, those whose task it was to translate theoretical results into planes that flew, and those who physically piloted the planes either in battle or, when fundamental research affected civil aviation, on the world's airways. This proposal had the support both of Salmond and of Rutherford, whose advice had been privately sought by the Secretary of State for Air. Much rested, however, on the calibre of the man who would fill the post, and on the position which he could gain for scientific advice at the level where plans and decisions were made. Salmond, Frank Heath and Sir Richard Glazebrook all felt that the one man qualified for the post was Tizard, and to Tizard it was offered during the first days of 1924.

He quickly drafted a reply to Salmond. It is not clear whether he sent it, or whether he decided, instead, to see Salmond personally. The points he made were of two kinds. First, he wished to know exactly how the new Directorate would be organized, what its powers would be, and how it would deal with various problems which he had already seen from his vantage-point while guiding the Co-ordinating Boards. Secondly, there were personal matters.

I came into the Civil Service for special work which demanded scientific qualifications [he wrote]. I am now paid at the same rate as that offered by the Air Ministry. My present position has this measure of security, that I can disappear only in two events, (a) the abolition of my post owing to ineffective work, (b) the abolition of the Department. But these prospects appears to be sufficiently remote not to be worth serious consideration. I also have prospects of promotion in the Civil Service, which, remote though they may be, still exist. I do not see any corresponding security or prospects in the post the Air Ministry is offering. Probably it is wise on the part of the Air Ministry not to offer a corresponding security; but then I am bound to take that into account. To put it bluntly, I see no personal advantage, but definite disadvantages, in my going to the Air Ministry under the conditions offered. The only inducement that is held out is that the work is of urgent national importance. Even on this point I am not at all sure that the work here will not be in the end of greater national importance, though it does not appear to be of such immediate importance. I may appear to be labouring these personal considerations, but it is not a bit of good my coming to the Air Ministry, either from your point of view, or from mine, unless I am going to put my back into the work. You express confidence that I could do the work, but I fear I have not the same confidence in myself! I think it will be very difficult work for anyone, and all the more so since the present policy of the Air Council was not put into effect directly after the war. I think it will be *impossible* for anyone to see it through without the fullest encouragement and support of the Air Council. Finally let me say that if the conditions are right, I think there is a great opportunity for someone, and personally I should enjoy the work. Many thanks again for your kind letter, and apologies for the length of this one.

On 11 February 1924, Salmond assured Tizard regarding the organization of the proposed Directorate.

As I assume you know [he wrote], the scheme we are adopting is based on your proposals, which have been followed in almost every particular. The D.S.I.R. will be directly under me and will control all the Air Ministry activities in regard to scientific research within the Ministry, at the R.A.E. and outside. I am not quite certain as to wireless and armament, but I have an open mind on the subject and wish to discuss this aspect of scientific research with the new Director. The functions of the other Director, who will be Air Commodore Halahan, will be confined to Technical Development only.[15]

Tizard remained undecided for five weeks, but on 19 March he personally discussed the matter with Salmond who two days later wrote to say that he was unable to secure better terms. More than one friend again urged acceptance – including Heath, his immediate superior, and Glazebrook, the chairman of the Aeronautical Research Committee as it had by this time become, who on 21 March wrote:

There is, I suppose, some risk, but it is a great opportunity. You will be welcomed by all who have the welfare of the Air Force at heart; you are trusted and believed in to a remarkable degree; you can secure a place in the regard of the Service like that which Smith has taken; you will have the support of an enthusiastic body of workers. Don't disappoint us all.[16]

It seems unlikely that he failed to give serious consideration to these exhortations. However, on March 27, he wrote to Salmond formally refusing.

The decision reached as to salary [he explained], means that the official view of the Treasury, accepted by the Air Ministry, is that the post of Director of Scientific Research in a Service Department carries no greater responsibilities than a principal assistant secretary-ship in the Civil Service, and is a less responsible position than that held by a Service Technical Director, e.g. the Director of Technical Development in your own Department.

At first it looked as though he might bring the Treasury to heel, for the post was left vacant even though H. E. Wimperis was appointed deputy-director of the new department which was now created. Wimperis, who had been an Experimental Officer, first in the Royal Naval Air Service and then in the R.A.F., was an old friend of Tizard from the days of the First World War. He was an able engineer, inventor of numerous devices of which the most famous was his eponymous bomb-sight, and it appears likely that by this time he had been recommended for the post of Director by Tizard. However, the post was left vacant, and throughout the summer and autumn of 1924 various kites were flown by the Air Ministry. A non-aeronautical scientist might be appointed; a professor might be brought in from one of the Universities; and in any case the Treasury might eventually veto the appointment on the grounds of cost. The only clue to the negotiations which took place during this period is given by a single passage written by Tizard in the draft of his autobiography more than thirty years later. 'Eventually', this records, 'the Treasury agreed to pay me £2,000 a year.' But the authorities refused to raise the salary of a scientist in what Tizard considered to be a comparable post. 'I refused on principle,' he says.

Tizard's action, which appears to have been taken in the autumn, was revealing and typical. It is frequently difficult for a man to do what he believes to be right. He may hold strong views about vivisection, education or the nuclear deterrent, but the burden of conformity tends to blunt the edge of his actions or, more conveniently, to provide an ample case for doing nothing at all. To Tizard all such compromises or silences were repugnant. At times, like all men, he would trim. But he did so rarely, and there can be little doubt that the fact circumscribed his efforts, as it did now, when he stuck not to his own guns but to those of a fellow-scientist.

However, this was not to be the final move. In the second week of December, Sir Samuel Hoare, the new Air Minister, himself met Tizard. Exactly what he proposed is not known, but Tizard subsequently wrote to him saying that 'you were kind enough to hold out possibilities of my coming to the Air Ministry under conditions which would have made me feel I could undertake wholeheartedly work which is absorbingly interesting as well as of great importance.' But he had held his hand too long, and was now striking while the iron was cooling off. On 16 December, he received a memorandum from Hoare in which the Air Minister said that he had discussed the whole matter with the Lord President of the Council, Lord Curzon.

> I had a long talk to him upon the subject this morning and I much regret to find that he is strongly opposed to your leaving the Department of Scientific and Industrial Research [he wrote]. Whilst I am as anxious as ever to obtain your services at the Air Ministry, I feel that I cannot press the transfer against the wishes of the Head of the Department concerned. I fear, therefore, that in the circumstances I must abandon the idea of your coming to the Air Ministry and devote my attention to finding some other candidate for the post.[17]

It was to be a hard task. Only six months later did he formally appoint Wimperis, thus recognizing the work which Wimperis had in fact been doing for some sixteen months.

This whole episode brings out, to a remarkable degree, many aspects of Tizard's character which were to be of importance both to himself and to Britain during the next two decades. His dogmatic integrity is well illustrated by the foundering of negotiations – when, it appears, they might otherwise have sailed forward – on the Treasury's refusal to give another equally competent scientist the pay which Tizard had wrung from the authorities for himself; so is his continuing worry about personal finances and his bad timing when it came to a matter of politics. Finally, there is his judgement of how science would be regarded by the members of the Air Council, and his implied suspicion that the scientist would be kept firmly in his place. At first, he gave them the benefit of the doubt, as was shown in his lecture on 'Commonsense and Aeronautics' read before the Royal Aeronautical Society in 1924. Speaking of the newly-created Directorate, he said:

> We look for the closest co-operation between the executive and the scientific branches; between, in short, the user and producer. The war showed us the value of that; but we seem to have been forgetting the lesson. Our little aeronautical world has tended to be divided into

so-called scientists (a small, slightly troublesome, and wholly incomprehensible sect) and practical men (who do the work). Placed on close but parallel lines, they only meet at infinity. Four years of experience on the Aeronautical Research Committee has taught me the danger of this; but we hope that the new organisation will avoid it.

Events showed, however, that this was to be a largely unfulfilled hope. Writing years later on the powers of the new Director, he put the matter briefly and damningly. 'He had no responsibility, for instance, for radio research; was only partly concerned with armament research and development; and had no scientific control over large-scale trials, under conditions simulating those of war, of weapons and tactics of offence'.

The results of Tizard's initial refusal were unfortunate for the country and for the Air Force. It might well have marked a point from which he would never look forward, and it was saved from this significance only by circumstances which still lay a decade ahead. Had Tizard become Director of Scientific Research during the nineteen-twenties there is little doubt that the Air Force would have been less inadequately equipped when war broke out; that the various scientific committees on which both air defence and air offence were to depend would have been able to force through their recommendations against lighter opposition; and that in the summer of 1940, when the heavens were falling, Tizard and those who stood for the cool scientific appraisal of the situation would have been able to appraise it not from the position of outside advisers with little official status, but from the higher ground. There is only one rider to this; for sixteen years, it would have been necessary for him to survive the political hazards of command.

*   *   *

What the Air Council lost the D.S.I.R. gained. For by 1924 it was already quite clear that Tizard's influence and work would spread far beyond the sphere of the Co-ordinating Boards. He had already become Principal Assistant Secretary, was helping Heath on matters only marginally connected with inter-Service co-operation, and was beginning to cut a figure not only among Civil Servants but among the leading scientists of the day. Rutherford, J. J. Thomson, Sir Richard Threlfall, Chairman of the Chemistry Co-ordinating Board and the first director of the Chemical Research Laboratory; and Sir William Hardy, the first Director of the Food Investigation Board; these were only a few of those among whom he now began to mix, not on equal terms but as a man who in the art of scientific administration was beginning to make his own mark.

In the summer of 1924, he attended the British Association's meeting in Canada, and in later years he enjoyed describing how a touch of fish-poisoning on the far side of the Atlantic had, as he liked to think, affected Britain's National Grid. The poisoning revived his old eye trouble, and he found that one effect was to reveal a flicker in the local lighting system. This operated on a 25-cycle frequency of generation and while it was no doubt efficient for most purposes, it obviously had disadvantages which had not so far presented themselves. These were taken up by Tizard back in England. For here the introduction of the grid was under discussion and it seemed likely that the 25-cycle frequency would be adopted. This would enable the Authorities to buy equipment from the United States while the new system could be co-ordinated with the small grid scheme already operating on the same frequency on the North-East Coast.

> I discussed the scheme with Lord Balfour who had succeeded Lord Curzon as Lord President in 1925 and told him of my experience [Tizard wrote in his autobiography]. He acted promptly and had an enquiry made in which the Medical Research Council took part. The result of the enquiry was that the Government insisted on the adoption of a 50-cycle frequency, much to the annoyance of certain electrical engineers. There can be no doubt that this decision was right, and I like to think it was all due to my eating fish on the way to Toronto.

In September 1925, while Heath made an eight-month tour advising the Australian and New Zealand Governments on the organization of scientific and industrial research, Tizard became Acting Secretary; from now onwards his influence became more explicit, his grasp on the reins of the Department continually stronger. This was as well. In many quarters there still existed suspicion of the possible impact of science on industry and an even deeper suspicion of Government influence on private enterprise. And while it would be wrong to imply that the venture would have foundered without encouragement from men such as Tizard, it would doubtless have had a far rougher passage. It would have been in worse condition when the stormy times of the 1930's arrived, and it would have been less able to help win the Second World War.

Tizard exercised his influence partly by force of character, partly through his broad scientific background. He had a temper, and forty years later men still remember hesitating before knocking on his door and entering the presence. Yet in spite of occasional impetuosity, he had an almost crippling facility for seeing both sides of a question, an honesty which insisted that both sides should be equally and fairly represented. Thus he often appeared, in the words of one contemporary, to have doubts. This wisdom frequently made his task more difficult.

In the craft of administration he had the knack of assimilating documents quickly and of nuzzling down to the hard core of a problem. Above all, he had outstanding ability as chairman of the innumerable committees through whose operations business was so largely conducted. In such he was a master tactician. At times he would disagree with apparent irritation or annoyance, but few would know that he had carefully calculated exactly when such an explosion would have the greatest effect. Another favourite practice was his method of dealing with items expected to provoke controversy. Before these were reached he would encourage small objections and comments. He would stimulate discussion about the wording of a paragraph, the phrasing of a remark, or even the punctuation of a sentence. Only when many of the committee were nearing exhaustion would the contentious item be reached. It usually had an easy passage.

He was a good committee-man; he made the right responses. Yet he never quite inured himself to Government procedure, and years later he quoted with relish the remark that the Americans had a new missile, 'called the Civil Servant because it didn't work and you couldn't fire it'. He enjoyed pulling authority's tail. Once,

when asked by a member of the Bridge Stress Committee whether
he would be watching the Oxford and Cambridge Rugger match,
he replied that he wouldn't, but added that it 'should be a good
opportunity for the Committee to observe the effect of repeated
impact stresses.' His assistant thereupon wrote a solemn minute
explaining that a team of thirty skilled investigators were to give
a public demonstration of the effect of repeated impact stresses on
a prolate spheroid. Could the expenses of the Committee be provided if they attended? Tizard could not resist sending this to the
Departmental pundit on Treasury regulations and asking if the
expenditure could be passed. The official failed to see the joke and,
Tizard noted with delight in his autobiography, 'replied with a
long dissertation about Treasury rules and concluded that there
was no necessity to get special permission; he could authorize the
expenditure'.

That he had an acute awareness of life beyond the Civil Service
was shown when Horatio Bottomley appeared in the office with
a hardy annual – the story that an inventor had offered him
a liquid, one drop of which would convert water into petrol.
Bottomley thought the idea was ridiculous; but would not the
authorities carry out an impartial test – charging him for this, of
course? The proposal appeared harmless, and was about to be
accepted when Tizard intervened. No-one else had appreciated
the implications – that the news: 'Government testing water-into-
petrol device' would be quickly headlined; that oil shares would
fall; and that Bottomley would no doubt make good financial use
of the fact.

Tizard brought to the D.S.I.R. a policy of seeing for himself
and an interest in staff relations which was in advance of current
practice. He enjoyed doing things rather than seeing things being
done. He liked to take part, and he managed to transmit the enthusiasm that he felt for practically every job in which he became
involved. This is clear from his account of how he rode on the
footplate with a very keen engine-driver during the work of the
Bridge Stress Committee. The test was carried out on a Sunday
when the lines were comparatively clear, and the engine was taken
across a bridge first at 50, then at 60, 70, and finally 80 miles an
hour.

Then the driver said: 'I think I can whack her up to 90, sir'. So we did another trial at 90 m.p.h. [Tizard recorded]. The driver seemed disappointed that the bridge hadn't broken, and suggested that we should try 100 m.p.h. But the Committee, to my relief, announced that they were satisfied with the results, and the driver took his locomotive back to the shed.[18]

In his relations with the staff, he would forgive almost anything except sloppiness or pomposity. He was conscious of class, but had his own idea of what the word meant. He would have rated a good dustman higher than a poor physicist, and in his personal dealings there was often a hint of Drake's injunction to 'let the gentlemen haul with the mariners, and the mariners with the gentlemen, for we be of one company.' He felt that the ladder of promotion should be available for all, but he believed it was there to be climbed.

He was constantly on the watch for human ability or human weakness, and he encouraged his staff to help themselves out of any troubles they themselves had created. Heath had decreed that proofs of official publications to be issued by the Department should be read by himself. In practice, this meant that most of the material was read by his Private Secretary who had the task of pointing out mistakes, solecisms, poor English, or anything else which might draw the fire of critics. The custom was continued under Tizard's rule, and on one occasion a graph in a research station's report was brought to his notice. The plotted results between which the curve was drawn appeared to be too random and scattered for any serious conclusions to be drawn, and it was suggested that, even if only as a protective measure, the graph should be taken out. Tizard disagreed: they must fight that one out for themselves.

He succeeded in getting his way in a high percentage of the controversial issues which arose. One of the few on which he laboured in vain was the management of the National Physical Laboratory, the Executive Committee of which was still appointed by the Royal Society although the Laboratory was financed by the Department. Tizard believed that the committee should be appointed by the Department and that the Royal Society should act in a purely advisory capacity. Sir Richard Glazebrook, the first director of the laboratory, strongly disagreed, and friendly guerilla warfare continued between them throughout much of Tizard's life in the Department.

> . . . Meeting of the NPL Organisation Committee in the afternoon [he noted in his diary for 22 June 1927, shortly before he took over as Secretary from Heath]. A large majority of the Committee were in favour of my plan that the Department should definitely take over all responsibility for management, leaving the Royal Society acting in an advisory capacity only. But Glazebrook objected; Rutherford, while agreeing, thought camouflage desirable, and Petavel sat on the fence. Eventually it was agreed that Heath should draw up a scheme with as little camouflage as possible and send it to Rutherford. I said that now Rutherford had heard the subject thoroughly thrashed out, I was willing to try and make work any scheme he put forward after further consideration. No further meetings of the Committee were thought necessary, so we broke up without making any final decisions. Vagueness is to continue.

Much the same scheme continues today but, as Tizard commented a few years before his death, 'No great harm is done; one can make almost any scheme work if there is a general desire to do so.'

Heath retired in 1927 and the Permanent Secretaryship was formally taken over by Tizard, a man who was, in the words of the *Manchester Guardian* when it announced the appointment, 'widely read, a clever and witty speaker, and with a fund of broad common sense that is considered unusual in one of his training'. The main belief which underlay his work was that a nation's industrial success in the twentieth century – and perhaps its industrial survival – can only be achieved by the planned utilization of scientific knowledge. He believed that much of the necessary research could best be achieved on a co-operative basis by firms in the same industry. He believed that the foundation of a nation's defence was industrial rather than military, that all strategic plans must be made within a framework not only of troops and arms but also of industrial power-resources, necessary food imports, and scientific economic planning. And he believed that the huge resources of the Empire could and should be better mobilized – a belief which had grown from his contemplation of the unexploited stretches of Australia and Canada in 1914 and 1924.

The extent to which he was successful in pressing these ideas is written into the record of the Department during the 1920's, a record of detail piled upon unspectacular detail – the extension of a laboratory; the founding of an outstation for specialized research; the successful piloting of a difficult measure through tricky Treasury shoals; and, on occasion, an almost imperceptible yet significant change in the balance of a particular policy. Such a change is provided by the attitude to the Research Associations, which had been started before the end of the war and were chiefly supported by grants from 'The Million Fund', the lump sum of £1,000,000 which had been voted by Parliament principally for this purpose. The general policy was to make the Research Associations self-supporting as quickly as possible. Tizard thought that there was much to be said against this, and by 1925 was pressing for the policy to be reviewed. The argument was continued the following year, with Tizard chiding a section of the scientific world which did ' not appreciate either the actual or the potential value of the Associations and tends to judge them by their capacity to produce striking industrial advances or public scientific discoveries'. The result was that the Research Associations were pulled, surviving, through a difficult period.

If his views about them were apt to vary – and his views about the extent of Government aid or intervention did vary – Tizard was constant in his belief that they should strike out beyond the bounds of pure research, get to know the problems of industry, and then apply themselves to those problems. It was typical that in his efforts to encourage this application he should arrange a three-day residential course at Oriel for the British Non-Ferrous Metals Research Association at which he brought laboratory workers and industrial managers face to face. At least a few problems were solved. And, as he later commented, 'I hold very strongly myself that in applied science it is far better to do one thing and get it applied, than to do two or three things and write papers about them.'

Tizard believed in the possibility of peace with continuing if unjustified optimism. But he saw, more clearly than most men, how science should be applied to war. And throughout his period at the D.S.I.R. the need to prepare the country lay constantly at

G

the back of his mind. This shows in his efforts to make Britain less
dependent on imports; in his constant support for Empire sources
of supply; and, above all, in his perpetual emphasis on the harsh
fact that Britain relied entirely on overseas supplies for oil, the
life-blood of modern battle. He always remembered the crisis of
1917 when supplies of aircraft fuel began to run dangerously low.
Surely, he argued, it was wise to investigate any means of turning
the country's large deposits of coal into the liquids so necessary
in modern war? It was therefore largely under pressure from
Tizard that the Advisory Council agreed in July 1925, to examine
the possibilities of the Bergius process, a method of producing oil
by the hydrogenation of coal. There seemed little likelihood that
this method would be economically viable, but the Council
'agreed that it was probably worthwhile to secure at the price
agreed all the knowledge which the Germans had obtained by
eight to ten years work at a cost of probably more than half a
million sterling', and a draft agreement was drawn up between
the British Bergius Syndicate, the International Bergius Company,
Dr Bergius himself, and the D.S.I.R. Tizard subsequently pointed
out to Balfour that 'the Advisory Council of the Department
holds very strongly the view that the Bergius process holds out no
hopes of being a commercial success. I thought that even if the
results of experiments were negative it would be wise to spend the
£30,000 for which we already had sanction. From the point of
view of National Defence it is important to investigate the whole
matter thoroughly.'[19] Balfour was also convinced – largely, it
appears, through Tizard's advocacy, and in the face of opposition
from the Advisory Council – and the formal agreement was signed
on 3 February 1926.

Within two years, experiments at the Fuel Research Station
had shown that the process was practicable, but that for Britain
it would be uneconomic. The experiments were therefore dis-
continued, but they were to have an interesting sequel. The
British Bergius Syndicate was taken over in 1927 by Imperial
Chemical Industries who subsequently concentrated at their
Billingham plant on various specialized applications of the processes involved. One of these, supported by the Air Ministry, was
the production of high-octane fuel. And it is therefore possible to

trace back to the 1926 agreement both the high-octane fuel from Billingham which helped Fighter Command to win the Battle of Britain, and the 'super-fuel' which gave British planes the short extra burst of speed needed to beat the 'buzz-bombs' of 1944. Tizard, as we shall see, had insisted for years before the outbreak of war, that new engines should be tested at the high pressures produced by such fuel – even though it was not then in existence.

He made his mark on the petrol industry in one other way while he was at the D.S.I.R.; for it was Tizard who, as the recently-appointed Secretary, put it to Lord Balfour that the fuel tax might be re-imposed.* His memorandum on the subject was passed to the Chancellor of the Exchequer, Mr Winston Churchill, who in March 1928 appointed a Committee to investigate the matter. Tizard, giving evidence before it, offered to bet that consumption of petrol would increase in spite of a tax, a proposition to which Churchill replied that there would have to be relief on something else – such as sugar. Tizard, asked what he meant by the comment that this would be appropriate, explained that it would be putting a tax on hydro-carbons and taking it off a carbohydrate. 'I could see Churchill storing this remark up in his mind', he later commented, 'and I have been under the impression that he used it in some public speech. But it is not in his Budget Speech of 24 April 1928.' However, the tax – 4d. a gallon – was brought in.

Tizard was now only 43. By a mixture of good judgement and good luck he had reached the top of his particular ladder in eight years. He was one of the most influential scientists in full-time Government employment, and to those who studied Civil Service form there must have seemed no limit to the heights which he might reach. All these prospects were to be snuffed out the following year.

Early in May 1929, he received a letter from the Imperial College of Science and Technology offering him the post of Rector at a salary of £3,000 a year, some £800 more than he was then receiving as Secretary of the D.S.I.R. The offer was tempting, since his family expenses were rising and the education of

---

* Taxes on various forms of oils and fuels go back to 1826, while a tax of 3d. a gallon was put on motor spirit in 1910, raised to 6d. in 1915, and abolished in 1921.

three sons now loomed as a steadily growing financial burden.
Yet he had been Secretary for less than two years. He liked the
work. He had ambitious plans for the future. He prepared, as was
his habit, to weigh the pros and the cons with deliberation and
care. And he then wrote to the College explaining that if he had
to make an immediate answer it would have to be 'no'; but that
if this were not the case he would be willing to consider the offer
very seriously – although, he warned, the eventual answer might
still be the same. Simultaneously, he wrote to Sir William
McCormick, Chairman of the D.S.I.R.'s Advisory Council, outlining the offer, describing his reply to Imperial College, and
implying that he would like to discuss the matter. His intention,
although he did not say as much, was to see if the Treasury would
raise his salary by £300. On that, he estimated, he could just
manage; and if he could just manage he would prefer the D.S.I.R.
to Imperial College.

So far so good. McCormick, however, appears to have taken the
view that Tizard's letter – of which neither original nor copy can
be traced – meant that he was willing to leave the D.S.I.R. if a
substitute could be found. Within the next few days, therefore,
McCormick sounded out Frank Smith, the Director of Scientific
Research at the Admiralty, apparently implying that Tizard was
in fact resigning. On 27 June, he wrote to Tizard saying: 'F. E.
Smith, I understand, will take the D.S.I.R. Secretaryship if it is
offered him', and adding, 'What we are going to do without you
at the Research Department, Heaven knows.'[20]

Tizard had no option. 'There was really nothing for me to do
then but to accept the offer from Imperial College', he wrote.
'McCormick's impulsiveness had pulled me over the edge.
Obviously the Treasury would have no inclination to raise my
salary once they knew that they could get a good man at the same
price.'

He had enjoyed himself at the D.S.I.R. 'It was a new venture of
Government and I think that I have always enjoyed myself most,
and perhaps been more useful, in the nursery stage of new developments', he commented in his Haldane Lecture. Yet more than one
friend wondered whether he had made a wise choice. 'You may
imagine the taking our friend Mac [McCormick] was in over it all,

and how he called on the Deity for assistance', Sir Richard Threlfall wrote to a friend some days later. 'Anyway this cuts me off from the D.S.I.R. even more than leaving the Council, but I hope Tizard is doing a wise thing for himself.'[21]

The news that he was leaving the Department just as he appeared to be getting into his stride was received, as the *Chemical Age* put it, 'with considerable interest not unmixed with a little surprise.' Reaction inside the Department was summed up by the Lord President in the new Socialist Administration, Lord Parmoor, who wrote to Tizard on 5 July, acknowledging his resignation, and sending him best wishes for the future. 'I find it hard to forgive you', he added ' – but as a Christian I must do my best.'

CHAPTER FOUR

Imperial College

One result of McCormick's speed in offering the Secretaryship of the D.S.I.R. to Frank Smith was that Imperial College gained a vigorous active administrator just when its need was greatest. The Government, however, lost a good servant, a man who, in the dangerous decade that now lay ahead, might have been of even greater use than he was. It is possible that had Tizard remained at the D.S.I.R. he would within a few years have been diverted to full-time study of how science could help the Services; that the nettle of defence problems would have been more surely and firmly grasped; and that the long pull between 1939 and 1945 would have been less arduous as a consequence. Instead, for half a decade he was to be partially immersed in the quieter waters of the academic world. During these same years, events conspired also to push Winston Churchill from the public stage. Thus both men watched from the touchlines as Hitler came to power; and thus between 1935 and 1939 it was mainly by quasi-official means that both were able to mould events. This had its compensations; and there is no doubt that Tizard, for one, relished the freedom which was an advantage of his position outside the Government hierarchy. Yet during the 1930's every touch of firmness on the helm was of importance; it might have been possible to provide that touch more readily from within than from outside the official machine.

Tizard went to South Kensington at a time when there was ample outlet for his organizing and administrative talents, his art as a chairman, and his flair for inspring young people with the adventure of scientific enquiry. He threw himself into the work with enthusiasm, and he had rarely been happier – except perhaps in the days at Martlesham when physical and intellectual adventure were uniquely combined.

He had a firm grasp of what the College would require in material needs if it were to expand as he hoped; and his ability as an administrator enabled him to pilot affairs through a difficult transitional passage into the position from which these needs could be attained. It is no more than true to say that without Tizard's delicate handling of matters in the 1930's, Imperial College would hardly have been able to reach the position it occupies today. Perhaps quite as important, there was the relationship which he established between students and authorities, a relationship commonplace today but then almost revolutionary. He managed to forge that personal link without which no head of a College can succeed. Yet he had an undeniable authority and 'desk tops ceased to be dropped quasi-accidentally when he was about', as one of his students has metaphorically remarked.

In addition, he persuaded both students and staff to think of themselves as belonging to Imperial College rather than to one of the three constituent organizations – the Royal College of Science, the Royal School of Mines and the City and Guilds College. This was a delicate operation and its success helped eventually to reveal Imperial College as one of the leading educational institutions of its kind not only in Britain but in the Commonwealth. The whole exercise, comments Dr Ellingham who as a colleague was an eye-witness to much of it, was like that of a Minister of Defence trying to persuade the three branches of the Armed Forces to refrain from fighting one another and to serve their common purpose. Tizard passed the first stage and went a long way towards achieving the second – not only by patience and tact but also by throwing his weight about when the time arrived for action on controversial issues.[1]

For the first year or so of his new appointment, he continued to live at Wimbledon, making the daily walk across the Common, and then going by train to South Kensington. Eventually, and largely at the wish of the Governing Body, he moved to London – first to Queen's Gate and then to a furnished service flat in St James's Court, Buckingham Gate, searching meanwhile for a week-end house in the country. This was eventually found by his wife on the shores of the Solent. At Hill Head, a few miles from

Fareham, 'Keston' stood in what was then lonely isolation, looking across the waters towards Cowes. It was a house more beautiful in situation than in architecture; nevertheless it was to provide Tizard with a second home to which he could retreat when the pressure of events in London daunted even his ability to take punishment. Disillusion came over the years, as Portsmouth and Southampton stretched out to eat up the open country between them and to turn Hill Head into a suburban marine parade.

At South Kensington he was, from the first, beset with problems involving the expenditure of large sums of money, and the future of the College for many years ahead. The most urgent of these problems concerned the Beit building, which had been launched by a substantial endowment from Sir Otto Beit, the financier and philanthropist. A five-storey building had been designed, and substantial work had been carried out by the end of September 1929, when Tizard took up his appointment. Now, however, it was becoming clear that the money available was sufficient for only three of the five storeys. The solution advocated was to roof over the third floor, and to leave completion of the building to the indefinite future. Less than three months remained before the decision had to be made.

At such an early stage in a new career, many men might have burked an issue so rich with possibilities of future trouble. Tizard, however, decided that to complete the five floors as a unit would be more economical in finance, space, and general utility. Within a few weeks of taking office, therefore, he decided to approach private donors for the required £33,500 – a figure perhaps comparable to £100,000 today. By December more than half of the sum had been promised, but the other half was still not forthcoming when the architects announced that a final decision had to be taken. Tizard insisted that the work should go on and succeeded in persuading the members of the Governing Body to take a chance over the deficit – most of which was eventually met by a special capital grant from the new University Court.

Tizard's concern over the proper completion of the Beit building was symptomatic of his belief that a satisfactory University education had to be based on adequate material foundations. He had no time for the theory that good work could be done in bad buildings and – not unlike Sir John Cockcroft today – was keenly aware of the effects which aesthetically pleasing surroundings could produce. 'I believe in the beauty of schools and colleges' he said a decade later when being admitted to an honorary degree at the University of Queensland. 'I have felt its effect; I have seen the effect on others. I hate ugly educational buildings of all kinds. I hate to see a technical school looking like a factory building in a crowded town. The technical school ought to be in just as beautiful surroundings as any other kind of school: perhaps more so than an art school for instance, which does not matter so much, as the students get their sense of beauty and dignity in other ways.' Writing in similar vein of his Imperial College days to his old friend A. P. Rowe, he later commented: 'I agree that if students are given nice things to use, they respect them. I don't think it wise to give them luxurious things. When I was at Imperial College we decided to make a garden on a waste piece of ground. A good many people said that the students would misuse it. I won the bet.'[2]

This emphasis on the physical background was exemplified by his plan for the re-development of the South Kensington site – perhaps the most important problem of organization which he set himself to solve. Bounded by Queen's Gate, Prince Consort Road, Exhibition Road, and Imperial Institute Road, often known as the 'Island Site', it was owned by the Royal Commission for the Exhibition of 1851 although largely leased to the Government, and used in the early 1930's for a hotch-potch of purposes. In Tizard's uncompromising phrase, it was 'the slum', and in his early days at South Kensington he began planning its future. It was typical that he not only sought professional advice but also asked a small group of lecturers – all under forty – to try their hand at drawing up their own unofficial plan. 'You should be interested in a future development which you may expect to live to see', he commented.

His first objection was to the Office of Works' heating station at the north-western part of the site. Its chimney was continually belching black smoke, and characteristically he did not merely complain. He had photographs taken of the chimney in full smoke, and then sent them with a humorous letter to the head of the Office of Works Engineering Section, a personal friend. Having achieved some results in this minor matter, he combined with Sir Evelyn Shaw, the Secretary of the Royal Commissioners for the Exhibition of 1851, to have a wooden model made of the entire Island Site. Would it not, he asked, be an admirable idea eventually to move all the museums to the south of Imperial Institute Road and to keep the island site exclusively for education?

Tizard thus staked the interest of the College in the site. This was just as well, since in 1937 the Ministry of Works – as it had by then become – revealed plans which would have ruled out any future use of the whole site by the College. On Tizard's recommendation this Government plan was reconsidered, his own was brought out of cold storage, and it was agreed that something based on the original 'Tizard solution' should be worked out in the future. This future, due to the war, was to be almost two decades away. But when the massive expansion of Imperial College was decided upon by the Government in 1953, the 'Island Site' was still available for development, and Tizard's original plans were still available for adaptation to the needs of the 1950's.

By this date another project which he had inaugurated was also about to mature. This had been started in 1935 when the Royal School of Needlework, occupying buildings adjoining the City and Guilds College, was in financial need. Tizard quickly came to an arrangement which involved their purchase within twenty-one years, during which period the Royal School was to use one half of the buildings and Imperial College the other. 'One result', comments Dr Ellingham, 'was that the Electrical Engineering Department of the City and Guilds College utilized the basement of the School – thereby confusing the public, who were apt to assume that an array of dynamos, electric motors, and other heavy equipment represented the machinery required for needlework in a technological age.'

Throughout the first five vital years of his Rectorship Tizard was hampered by the repercussions of the world slump which limited expenditure and trimmed plans for expansion. Consequently, most of his innovations were minor, although he was forever devising schemes for new College ventures. He established a series of lectures in Industrial Economics. He introduced German Exchange Studentships. He tided the Biological Field Station over an anxious period when, in 1933, it found itself in difficulties following the abolition of the Empire Marketing Board which had been its financial mainstay.

This consolidation of the College's material position which he directed with such sophisticated skill was merely one result of the new breeze which was soon invigorating the College. The central problem which Tizard felt he had to solve was neatly put when he asked in 1934 what should really be covered by a general scientific education. 'How' he demanded, 'is it possible, in a few years, to give a boy some insight into the beauties and wonders of the physical and biological sciences, some real conception of law and order in the universe, some true appreciation of the scientific method, without running the risk of leaving him with a mere smattering of uninspired knowledge?' It was an enlightened question, particularly for the 1930's, and his attitude to what would now be called the problem of the two cultures was clear and revealing. 'No scientific man wishes to see scientific education pushed to the neglect of literary studies', he continued. 'All of us recognize that a properly balanced diet for the mind is as important as for the body; what we do think is that science, well taught, can supply all that is best in the classical tradition: can "teach accuracy and exactness; can give a discipline in clear thinking; can teach boys to recognize differences in things which seem alike; can brace with its difficulties minds that are not afraid of difficulties; can inspire with its beauty minds not insensitive to beauty" – to quote the recent words of the Headmaster of Rugby in praise of Greek.'[3]

It was typical that he should not only cogitate over this problem but should put forward a solution. This he did in the spring of 1933 when a meeting of the Science Masters' Association was held at the College.

In the informal discussion the usual criticism was made that boys who took science scholarships very often could not write English [Tizard later wrote to Sir Gavin de Beer]. One of the masters present said that this was entirely the fault of the Universities because they had such a high factual standard for science scholarships that the

masters at school were forced to concentrate on the scientific parts
more than they would wish to do if they had more freedom. I said
that I was very sympathetic with this view and that we should consider whether we could not set an example.

The consideration was quick and effective. On 2 May 1933,
Tizard outlined to the Board of Studies a new Scholarship Scheme
designed to attract boys who had not specialized in science at
school, and whose education might have been mainly on the
classical side. The Board agreed to set up a committee and this
made practical proposals which were accepted by the Governing
Body in January 1934.

> We got the co-operation of Professors at (the) University (College)
> and King's College, and devised an examination which would allow
> a candidate to have a wide choice of papers, including Latin and
> Greek, English, Mathematics, Science, History, French and German
> etc. [Tizard continued to de Beer]. There were two compulsory
> papers, namely the English paper and the Mathematics. The latter
> was by no means up to scholarship standard.

The results of the scheme, which went on until the outbreak of
war in 1939, justified his optimism.

He had a broad liberal view of the task which education should
do. Thus he could talk with genuine fervour of the beauty and
mystery of science. And he could, with equal honesty, write to a
former student: 'I always say that a University education does
not fit a man at once for a practical job but if it is worth anything
it helps him to climb the ladder more quickly than other people
who have not been at a University.' However, whichever side one
was emphasizing, one thing was essential. 'Don't worry about the
Professors' he wrote many years later to A. P. Rowe, then Vice-
Chancellor of the University of Adelaide, 'it is really more important to have the respect of the students.'

One of his first tasks on becoming Rector was to investigate the
conditions under which these students worked and lived, and the
ordering of their various organizations. He unearthed a curiosity.
Their own social and athletics activities were less under student
control than was customary elsewhere. Yet the students themselves, for reasons that went back two decades, had almost complete control of College catering arrangements, the only Refectory

available being part of the Students Union. After a long round of discussions with the leading students Tizard introduced a complete overhaul of the rules and regulations controlling both matters. Only when they were effectively in operation, and the Refectory working smoothly under a joint-committee, did the authorities realize how well the possibilities of protest had been quietly dealt with before the new régime began.

Tizard's ability to get the best out of the students did not rest on any of the more likely reasons. He had never been a 'games man'. His heartiness rarely went beyond a round of golf or his favourite exhortation to friends and family: 'Who's for a good brisk walk?' His personal success rested, rather, on his integrity, on his delight in pulling the mat from beneath the feet of the pompous, the self-satisfied and the complaisant, and his puckish humour. At first sight he appeared slightly pedantic, rather precise, while at this date a pair of pince-nez added to the air of a thoughtful schoolmaster. Then, just when this impression was gaining ground, there would issue a phrase or a comment which brought young men closer to him – as when he described the members of one Henley crew, most of whom had failed in their examinations, as 'eight men with but a single thought – if that'.

Throughout the whole of his time at Imperial College he was frequently amused by the misunderstandings to which his title of 'Rector' sometimes gave rise. During the first few years of his appointment he received a succession of letters from which he got much pleasure – those addressed to Lord Tizard, Dr Tizard, the Rev. H. T. Tizard and even on one occasion, the Venerable H. T. Tizard. He was forbearing with the students' reaction when he banned them from using the Royal School of Mines' lift. Many had made their keys for this, but since the lift was in regular use and extremely slow, great delay was caused. The Rector let it be known that any student found in possession of a key would be severely dealt with. This was the time of the much-publicized case of the Rector of Stiffkey and Tizard found that he had at once been dubbed the 'Rector of Liftkey'. Another incident during the lift campaign that tickled his sense of humour occurred when he caught a student in the act of opening the lift-door. 'What the devil do you think you're doing?' he asked. The student, who did not know the new rector by sight, replied: 'Come to that, who the devil are you?'

In spite of his College and public commitments he somehow found time to attend most student functions – the dinners, boxing matches, plays and sporting events which are an essential part of College life. 'As soon as he arrived we noticed the difference', says one student of those days. 'It was just that we seemed to see him every where.' At the annual boat race for the Morphy Cup, rowed by the three constituent Colleges, he always followed in the umpire's launch and spoke at the dinner following the event – off-the-cuff and invariably to the delight of the audience. And it was typical that after he was created a K.C.B. in 1937 he should go straight from Buckingham Palace to a students' dinner – the organizers thus being able to say that theirs was the first function he had attended as a Knight.

His appearances were more than perfunctory.

As secretary of the Imperial College Boat Club [says one former student], I used to keep him informed about rowing and regattas. I well remember how on one occasion, at Walton regatta, I had not been feeling very fit, and was quite exhausted after the race. Sir Henry was watching, as he often did. On the following Monday morning I had a message to see the Rector. I went up to his room looking on to Prince Consort Road with no idea of what he wanted me for. He told me that he was at the regatta and thought that I was overdoing things and working too hard while spending so much time on rowing. I tried to assure him that there was nothing wrong, but to my great surprise he insisted that I go to see his own personal doctor in Sloane Street at no expense to myself.[4]

He kept a close watch on College athletics and maintained a keen interest in the other, more adventurous extra-curricular activities. When, in 1937, it seemed likely that the proposed College expedition to Jan Mayen Island would founder for lack of funds its organizer, Alexander King, personally sought Tizard's intervention, asking whether he would help to raise the necessary £3,000. 'Of course I will', was the reply. The expedition sailed on time. When four Imperial College members returned from the Finmark Expedition the following year, Tizard squeezed in an hour to watch a private showing of the expedition films.

He naturally showed a special interest in the Service side of student activities. Soon after his appointment he became a member of the University of London Military Education Committee, and when a subcommittee was formed in 1935 to supervise the foundation of a University Air Squadron, Tizard was its obvious chairman. The headquarters of the Squadron, set up in September 1935, was luckily enough in Imperial College, and this no doubt helped him to keep a benevolent eye on its activities. The squadron used Northolt aerodrome and here Tizard would often be flown by members in training; when they went to annual camp at an R.A.F. station he would invariably visit them – a practice which he continued to within a year or so of his death.

Tizard stabilized Imperial College when it needed stabilization, and set it on a sure course. In a way, he prepared it for the postwar world. And he helped to establish a new relationship between staff and students. Little of this would have been possible, however, had he not impressed his own personality on the staff and on the University authorities whose good-will the College sometimes needed. In this, he was usually but not always successful. He loathed pomposity, made no bones about it, had a pungent way of expressing himself, and would trim a man down to size with an ease that came from long observation and an appreciation of the English language. Thus one friend, already ripe in years, 'should have been gathered long ago'; while another, of notorious Civil Service timidity, 'came of a long line of maiden aunts'. At times he had a nervous fear that he might have gone too far, and after one dinner of the College Chemical Society earnestly enquired whether he had been quite in order. This was one of the more solid events when most of the staff brought their ladies, when a more-than-normal formality imbued proceedings, and when the correctness of the after-dinner speeches was apt to be equalled only by their length. On this occasion Tizard had got some way through his speech when he startled the company by saying casually that he was reminded of an unrepeatable story. There was a silence before he went on to say that in fact it was unrepeatable even though it had been told to him by – and he mentioned a nearby colleague of notably Presbyterian background. Many of those present knew how strongly Tizard objected to the telling of smutty stories on public occasions. The silence grew a little louder, and one guest commented later that there was a nasty feeling that for once Tizard had forgotten exactly what the occasion was. 'Of course I mean unrepeatable' he continued, 'in the sense that it was told with a Scottish accent – which I cannot imitate.'

There were, it has been said, 'undoubtedly a certain number of University Senators, College Governors and Professors and others who smarted under his lash and found it difficult to forgive him' – hardly surprising in the case of a man who could describe one rich and slightly pompous professor as a 'stuffed old peacock'. However, the animosity that Tizard was apt to rouse in certain breasts was more than off-set by the loyalty which he drew from the great majority of his colleagues and especially from the younger men. Two examples will illustrate why this was so.

> On the evening of the day I was appointed to the teaching staff of the Royal College of Science [one of his staff has said]. I was playing Bridge in the College Union with three other demonstrators. Tizard walked over and watched the play until the end of the rubber. Then he said 'Will you come and see me at 11 tomorrow morning'. I did not even know that he knew my name and as it was my first interview with him I was somewhat nervous. Tizard began: 'You keep curious company, at night anyway. Why does your partner fan his cards so that neither he nor anybody else can see the pips?' 'He is training his memory – having sorted the cards normally, he fans them in the opposite direction so that he must draw the cards from memory.' 'Well, I hope it works. I noted that it cost you the rubber and it's very hard on kibitzers. What time do you get up in the mornings?' 'Nine o'clock – but I don't have to be at College before 10.' 'That's all right, I approve. I find that people who get up early in the morning are conceited all the morning and stupid all the afternoon.'

That ended the interview.[5]

There was also the case of Bill Carpenter, the Chief Messenger and Head Porter, an ex-Army heavyweight champion who lived in Poplar and in his spare time took great interest in the local boys' boxing clubs. Tizard heard that Carpenter was organizing and refereeing boxing tournaments in the Poplar Public Baths and thus raising considerable sums for the local Hospital. Thereafter, he always bought two tickets and took a friend, usually from the College, to each tournament, sharing beer and sandwiches with Carpenter in the interval.

Tizard's success is well explained by G. C. Lowry, Secretary of the College for many years.

> Scientists, and particularly pure scientists [he says], tend to be tidy-minded; they like to have rules about everything; some mathematicians take it almost as a personal insult that their fellow human beings are so unwilling to conform. Tizard, being by training a chemist, was quick to detect flaws in organisations, and eager to put things right; but he was also practical enough to realise that human beings tend to react violently to changes laid down from above, unless the reasons for the desirability of these changes are patiently explained to them.

This belief in explanation, all down the line, was to be a vital factor in affairs far removed from Imperial College. For the College absorbed only a portion of his time and energy. He had multiple interests and activities, ranging from the Association of Special Libraries and Information Bureaux of which he was President in 1930, to the numerous scholastic and academic societies and associations dealing with education in general and scientific education in particular.

However, it was with the air, and the development of flight for use in peace or war, that his mind was so much occupied throughout these years.

*   *   *

Tizard had become a Fellow of the Aeronautical Society in 1917. Seven years afterwards he gave the Wilbur Wright lecture on 'Fuel Economy in Flight', and later in 1924 was elected Chairman of the Council. In a provocative inaugural address, 'Commonsense and Aeronautics', he staked a claim for the building up of a self-supporting civil aircraft industry independent of Service needs. Much would have to be changed, he stressed – the attitude not only of the public, but of those who should know better. The Insurance Companies still took an antiquated view, and he instanced his own case. 'I may do almost anything but fly', he commented. 'I may even commit suicide and the money is paid; the only thing I may not commit is aviation.'

In 1920 he had become an independent member of the Aeronautical Research Committee; subsequently he represented the

H

D.S.I.R., then reverted to his independent status in 1929. Four years later he became chairman, an appointment which he occupied for two five-year periods, during which he saw the substitution of the highly streamlined monoplane for the biplane as the standard fighter; the development of the mass-produced heavy bomber; and the birth of the jet-engine. Membership of the Committee consisted of four representatives of the Air Ministry; two from the aircraft industry and the same number from Imperial College; one each from the Royal Aeronautical Society and the D.S.I.R.; and five independent scientists. The brief of this assorted band was as follows: (1) to advise on scientific and technical problems relating to the construction and navigation of aircraft, (2) to undertake or supervise such research or experimental work as is proposed to the Committee by the Air Ministry and to initiate any research work which the Committee considers to be advisable; to carry out such work itself or to recommend by whom the work should be carried out; (3) to take over complete responsibility for the Air Inventions Committee and for the Accident Committee; (4) to promote education in aeronautics by cooperating with the Governors of Imperial College; (5) to assist the aeronautical industry of the country by scientific advice and research, and to co-operate with any Research Association that may be established; (6) to prepare for the approval of the Air Council a scheme of work and estimate of expenditure for the year, and to administer the funds placed at its disposal by the Air Council; and finally, (7) to make reports from time to time to the Air Council.

Tizard's influence on this body was unspectacular but pervasive, and from 1920 onwards he was involved with many of the sub-committees, boards, and panels which the Committee sprouted during the years between the wars. He knew everyone in the world of aeronautical research; he knew what investigations were going on, and where. If fresh work had to be started, he knew the best men for the job; whether or not they were available; and, in many cases, how they could best be approached. His position is indicated by the remark of Sir Roy Fedden who described him as 'refreshing and stimulating as compared with some of the heavy weather scientists of that period who looked down on more practical people who did things only with their hands'. Fedden, responsible for the design and development of all Bristol engines for more than two decades, saw much of Tizard in the latter's capacity as chairman of the Engine Sub-Committee. 'He was', he says, 'one of the most jolly senior people to take round the works, and I always looked forward to his coming. He was like a boy in his excitement and interest in looking at some novel or tricky machining operation or running rig.'[6]

It was on this Engine Sub-Committee that Tizard's insistence on one particular policy, and his support for one new 'invention' were to have crucial long-range results. The policy was that of demanding that all new Service engines should be tested on fuel of higher octane number than was then generally available. Against all protests, Tizard insisted that fuels of this higher quality would be produced if war came; it was essential, therefore, that engines should be able to operate at the higher pressures involved. This policy was followed; and when such fuels were available in 1940 from I.C.I.'s works at Billingham and from the United States, they were used with confidence in engines already tested to utilize them.

The 'invention' was the jet, and it is no overstatement to claim that without Tizard's support the jet project in Britain would almost certainly have been still-born through lack of funds. He had, as we have seen, played a vital part in increasing the efficiency of the piston-engine, and it would have been human enough if all his sympathies had been ranged on its side. This was not to be the case.

His first contact with what was to become the jet was in 1926 when as a member of the ARC Engine Sub-Committee he discussed a paper on the aerodynamic theory of turbine design written by Dr A. A. Griffith. The idea of using a gas turbine as an aircraft engine to drive a propeller had been investigated in 1920. However, results had been severely discouraging, due mainly to the difficulties of designing, with the materials available, a compressor that would be both light and efficient. Weight, size, and fuel consumption appeared to rule out any serious consideration of the new method. Then came Griffith's paper. Tizard felt that the possibilities which this offered should at least be investigated, and proposed that the theory should be examined at Farnborough. The examination indicated that further work was justified. An experimental rig was set up, and in 1930 Tizard became the chairman of a panel to consider the results. These results were inconclusive, and although Tizard himself felt that experiments should be pressed far enough to solve the scientific problems involved, he agreed with other members of the Panel that there should be no great financial outlay. Thus matters rested for five years.

Meanwhile, independently of any official body, Frank Whittle was working away at his plans for a turbo-jet – the 'real' jet-engine in which large quantities of air are drawn into the engine, compressed, heated, and ejected at high velocity. His company, Power Jets, was formed in March 1936, and in the same month Tizard met Whittle for the first time at a Cambridge University Air Squadron dinner. From the start, Tizard was interested. 'Whittle's suggestion was undoubtedly streets ahead of any other suggestion for the development of aircraft engines at the time', he wrote to Lord Halsbury sixteen years later. 'I knew it would cost a great deal of money; I knew that success was not certain; and yet I felt that it was of great national importance to spend the money.'

However, Tizard was cautious as well as interested, and it was October before he was finally convinced that the project warranted serious official support. Whittle was induced to send a full account of his work to the Aeronautical Research Committee, and this was discussed at the 105th meeting of the Engine Sub-Committee on 2 February 1937.

> I said that I thought insufficient time was being devoted to problems relating to possible future lines of development [Tizard noted later], and that the Sub-Committee would be of more use if it devoted itself to such problems as the provision of high powers and the possibility of internal combustion turbines and of jet propulsion. I added that in problems of this type it was necessary to envisage expenditure on a large scale if results were to be obtained in a short enough time to make them of competitive value.

The vital meeting came a month later, on 16 March.

> In summing up the discussion [Tizard noted], I said that when due allowance was made for natural optimism there was a very strong case for vigorous development of the device, which should result in a

very fast machine driven by a jet or combination of jet and airscrew. I added that the scheme appealed to me as being one calling for a concentration of effort and large-scale expenditure.

Then, largely as a result of Tizard's influence, the sub-committee recommended

> that the Air Ministry should explore the possibilities of encouraging the development of the Whittle jet propulsion scheme so as to ensure that everything possible was done to make the tests of the plant a reliable indication of its possibilities . . .

This was a minor triumph and it was achieved in the face of considerable opposition.

> 'I remember a very well-known engineer saying that he would stake his whole reputation on his opinion that the scheme would not work, and that it would be a waste of money to encourage it [Tizard wrote in describing the Whittle scheme twenty years later]. I said at the time that we would guard against the loss of the gentleman's reputation by omitting his opinion from the Minutes.[7]

However, the official mills grind slow, and only in June, says Whittle, were negotiations opened between Power Jets and the Air Ministry to find ways and means by which the Ministry could contribute to the cost of the work. In the middle of the month L. L. Whyte, managing director of Power Jets and the man who had succeeded in getting it financial backing, met Tizard and asked him to put on record his views on the project. Many men might have vacillated, for there was still considerable opposition to expenditure on what to many seemed a purely speculative scheme.

Tizard gave his own judgement in a letter to Whyte dated 22 June.

> You ask for my opinion about Whittle's scheme [this began]. I think there is nothing inherently unsound in his ideas. He may possibly be somewhat optimistic in some of his predictions, but even allowing for that, I think it highly probable that if he has the necessary financial support and encouragement, he will succeed in producing a new type of power plant for aircraft. I am particularly interested in this work because I think that if we are to provide the high powers which will be necessary for the aircraft of the future, we must develop some type of turbine. Further, the fact that such an engine would use heavy oil is of great importance from the point of view of defence and commerce.

I have a very high opinion of Flight Lieutenant Whittle. He has the ability and the energy and the enthusiasm for work of this nature. He has also an intimate knowledge of practical conditions – this combination of qualities is rare and deserves the utmost encouragement. I sincerely hope he will get the necessary finance because I think you will have to make up your mind that a large expenditure will be necessary before final success is reached. My general opinion of the importance of this work leads me to express the hope that the money will be raised privately so that the knowledge that it is going on will not be widespread.

P.S. Of course, I do not mean to imply that success is certain. All new schemes of this kind must be regarded as 'gambles' in the initial stages. I do think, however, that this is a better gamble than many I know of on which money has been spent.

This letter was in its own way quite as important as the formal blessing of the A.R.C. sub-committee three months earlier. It 'transformed the situation' Whyte says, 'for it meant that we had the support of the highest opinion outside the Government, and it enabled us to obtain modest financial support and technical help from engineering companies who were already engaged on secret work and could therefore be trusted'.[8] Tizard thus nursed the jet-project through its early years, although after the outbreak of war there were unhappy disagreements between Whittle and himself as to how the project was to be brought to success. That story, however, belongs to the 1940's.

Tizard's connexions with aeronautical research were not limited to his official work on the Committee. It was partly at his instigation that in 1935 the A.R.C. asked the Council of the Royal Aeronautical Society to co-operate in arranging an Aircraft Conference at Imperial College 'to discuss the present state of aeronautical research in this country in relation to the needs of the British aircraft industry'. The Conference was successfully held from July 10 to 12. There was a free interchange of views, the Press being excluded from the meetings after a good deal of heart-searching and a polemical correspondence with C. G. Grey who pointed out that he would be excluded from attending as editor of *The Aeroplane* but would no doubt be welcomed in various other capacities. Two references in the notes which Tizard wrote after the Conference are of interest.

From the point of view of the Aeronautical Research Committee certainly I think contact with the view of flying personnel could be greatly improved [he wrote]. In conversation with one or two officers at lunch I have learnt a number of things which are of great interest and importance from the scientific point of view that I have not heard before. I have been suggesting privately that it would be a good thing for the officers of the Air Force to be encouraged to send accounts to the Director of Scientific Research of any unusual observations they make. Then it would be quite easy for the Director of Research to pick out important matters and bring them to the attention of the Aeronautical Research Committee . . .

The position appears to me that all the chief technical people inside the industry are anxious to have free interchange of information between each other, but that they are stopped by their financial directors on the grounds that such interchange would be injurious to shareholders. It is clearly in the National interest to get free interchange. My own experience of some other industries is that in the long run it pays shareholders of private concerns equally.

Both these points hinted at the growing need for the aircraft industry to brace itself for shocks ahead. Tizard, better than most men, knew of the need. For by the summer of 1935 he had taken up the work for which he will be remembered. This work was throughout the late 1930's to absorb more and more of his time, so that when war broke out the Rector of Imperial College had been transformed into the scientist who stood between victory and defeat more certainly than any other.

*   *   *

The transformation began at the end of 1934, by which time Tizard's mark had been not merely made but also noticed. In 1926 he had been elected a Fellow of the Royal Society, being proposed by Sir Richard Threlfall and seconded by Sir J. J. Thomson. 'This honour came as a great surprise, for I had not thought that my scientific work would be held to justify it', he noted in his autobiography. 'It gave me renewed confidence.' The following year he was made a Companion of the Bath, and early in 1930 was elected a member of the Athenaeum under Rule II, which allows the Committee to select a small number of eminent men.

By 1934 he was therefore in a position to press his ideas along

many channels, of which Imperial College was only one and perhaps not one of the most important. A different and more delicate
machinery could be operated by dropping a suggestion at the Club,
by proposing that a new industrial idea might be investigated
through the A.R.C. in a certain way, by agreeing that it would be
splendid if he were to speak to a small group or address the meeting of a professional society. He spoke often, engagingly, and sometimes nervously. 'You have an unconscious hand-technique of, as
it were, fumbling in your two waistcoat pockets, alternatively,
while you speak, as if in search of a railway ticket or watch' a
friend wrote to him after he had delivered the Rutherford Memorial Lecture to the Chemical Society in March 1939. 'Once or
twice the fumbling produced a pencil (I think) which you then
held in both hands and observed fixedly as you spoke, then it was
returned to one or other pocket, and the fumbling recommenced!'
The address was so good, the writer added that he doubted
whether the audience was much distracted by the gestures but
'the gestures were certainly not appropriate'.[9] Tizard's addresses
were invariably good, especially where he could feel his listeners
responding and was able to extemporise accordingly. Thus he was
better when speaking to a visible audience than when broadcasting
for here his dry though immaculately-turned sentences, spoken in
a clear, clipped voice, had a flat quality that disappeared on
contact with the man himself.*

He preferred speaking to writing, and many of his best analyses
of national needs survive only as the partially corrected typescripts
to which he did not necessarily adhere. 'The fact is that I have
been too fastidious, and have never liked to publish anything
which was not to my own satisfaction at the time', he wrote
regretfully shortly before he died. 'As it is, some of the lectures I
have published are not altogether to my satisfaction now. But I
suppose the real reason for my incapacity to finish things has been my
laziness. The effort of writing anything well has always been a pain

---

* His broadcasts consisted of 'Bertram Hopkinson' (5 March 1937); 'Airships' (9 May 1937); Introduction to 'What More Do You Want from the
Scientists' (15 October 1937); 'I Knew a Man – Lord Rutherford' (16 December 1945); 'High Altitude Flying' (18 December 1946); 'Re-Opening of
Simon-Carves Research and Development Block' (3 December 1951).

to me.'[10] This, of course, was looking at the subject from only one side; from the other, Tizard appeared the antithesis of laziness, cramming into the day enough activity for two men. But he rarely had time to tidy and polish and burnish up his paragraphs. When he had, the results imply that he might have been not merely a great explainer of science to the layman, but also a more than adequate writer. Anyone who could describe Rutherford as Tizard described him in his broadcast talk 'I Knew a Man' as one of those geniuses 'who seem to have been told a good many secrets of nature by a good fairy at their birth'; a man with 'the summer lightning of inspiration' always playing about his head – any man who could do that knew how to use the tools of writing. This ability lay also behind his hatred of slang. He detested the word 'boffin' and the phrase 'back-room boy' not only because he thought them derogatory – 'scientists should be in the front room not the back' – but because he regarded them as inaccurate, slovenly, short-hand symbols which failed to do their job properly.

It was as an established administrator that Tizard by the end of 1934, stood four-square in the scientific and educational worlds. His future now seemed to be plotted out, surely and far ahead. Barring the misfortunes of life, or its unexpected windfalls, the path seemed clear if unexciting, worthy and useful, avoiding the precipices if failing to reach the heights. At Imperial College he had established in five years a dual reputation as administrator and counsellor, so that he was both admired for his ability to squeeze the most from the authorities, and envied for the high regard in which he was held by so many bright young men. Financially, he felt himself as hard-pressed as ever, a matter which worried him only because he wanted his children to be educated in a fitting manner, because he wished to provide for his wife in case of accident, because he felt it improper that these things should weigh so heavily on a busy man doing a worth-while job. He was anxious that his ideas should be adopted, but he was as happy if they were driven home by the next man as by himself. He wanted due regard for science; for himself he wanted only the rate for the job – and this, he considered, should be a high one. Of any hungering for public applause he was singularly free, and he no doubt agreed with Bacon that 'it is a strange desire to seek power and to lose liberty'.

Tizard's habits and spare-time occupations were unexceptional. He had no natural eccentricities and had not reached the height where it was expedient to cultivate them. He enjoyed snooker and he enjoyed bridge, although in this second pastime he suffered from a handicap that was almost grotesquely out of character. 'He was', says one of his oldest friends, 'one of the worst losers I have ever known.' It is difficult entirely to account for this. At times he no doubt regretted that chance had not dealt the cards better; at times he may have regretted lost opportunities. But he was unable to brush these aside as the fortune of what was, after all, merely a game. He lost at least some friends by his failing, and in later life he may have noticed how his invitations to make up a four were sometimes declined.

His one major relaxation was fly-fishing which from 1922 onwards gradually replaced golf, even though he still enjoyed an occasional round with Wimperis. In 1922 he had been recovering from a severe attack of influenza and was helped by two men, one an understanding doctor of the old school, the other Sir Richard Threlfall, who invited him to spend a long week-end on the Vyrnwy.

> Thank you very much [Tizard replied], but I can't fish and I can't walk a hundred yards without getting tired. Never mind [said Threlfall], come along all the same; you can sit on the bank if you like.
> So I went [Tizard wrote later]. We spent the night in his house at Edgbaston, and started off the next day in a commodious car, loaded to the brim with fishing gear and tackle, and with good things to eat and drink. We stayed about ten miles from the river, at a little Welsh hotel, which, although it had no fishing of its own, was the right kind of hotel for a fisherman, a hot dinner being always provided half an hour after it was quite dark, whatever the time of year . . . Next day I was initiated into the noble art. With an empty beer bottle under my arm, to force me to use my forearm and wrist only, I strove in vain to get the line out respectably straight to a respectable distance. I don't think that my two kind teachers had much fishing themselves that day; they spent most of their time disentangling my line, and tying on fresh flies. But they got some fish; it looked exasperatingly easy. As for me, the interest of it all made me forget

my woes, and I tumbled into bed that night dead tired, but pleasantly so, and slept the sleep of the just and healthy.[11]

The enthusiasm grew. A visit to the Vyrnwy or, later on, to any other good fishing river finally displaced golf as his chosen pastime. 'He had good hands (he had flown aeroplanes), was an observant naturalist and quickly became proficient' writes R. E. Threlfall. 'Unlike many of the others, he at once realised that every square yard of the river was not of equal fishing value, and he did not waste his time on the bad bits'.

Tizard fished on the occasional holiday in Norway. He liked the chalk streams of southern England to which he was taken by more than one of his wealthier acquaintances, and he was not averse to sea-fishing, where he appears to have been intrigued by the difficulties as much as by the chance of success. He did not shoot; as he once put it to Thomas Merton, later a member of the Tizard Committee. 'It would be more accurate to say that I cannot shoot with sufficient accuracy to indulge in it.'

He had a modest collection of first editions, could quote Johnson to illustrate a wide variety of human situations, and ranged with pleasure over the English classics. He admired Kipling, had by heart long passages of Dickens, and held Macaulay among his literary heroes. At the height of the war he decided to read once more as necessary relaxation, Gibbon's *Decline and Fall*. He delighted in P. G. Wodehouse. He enjoyed Stevenson, having a particular admiration for *The Wrong Box* in whose honour he once organized a 'Wrong Box Dinner' at the Athenaeum. 'We had heard that Ronald Knox had discovered an error in it', says R. E. Threlfall, 'and we both separately went through the whole book with a tooth-comb, as it were, to find it. He or I found one author's error and at least one printer's dating from an early edition.'

He kept a rough file of quotations that had caught his attention, and they show that his interests varied from Gibbon to Bagehot, from Huxley to Masefield. He had the humility of the first-class scientist, and marked among his jottings were the lines that were a favourite of Sir Frederick Gowland Hopkins and also of Tizard – 'I often wonder as I go/What makes the little daisies grow/And when I die, as die I must/And dust at length returns to dust/Some other fool will want to know/What makes the little daisies grow'.

Tizard's characteristics thus combined to produce a typical picture of the successful British professional classes in season. And yet. One wonders whether there did not sometimes wander across his mind those words about the man 'always a step ahead of me, cool-eyed, confident, lean. The person I should wish to be, and never yet have been.' There had been his refusal to take over the Directorate of Scientific Research at the Air Ministry, so that now, in the mid-30's the Directorate was almost free-wheeling, faintly disturbed by the clatter of events, no doubt, but little more. He had been tumbled by unfortunate circumstance from his position as Secretary of the D.S.I.R. where he would, as he admitted, have preferred to stay had the Government increased his salary.

Now, at the end of 1934, the position was to be miraculously changed. In spite of the quiet overtones of his life; in spite of the fact that he hated war and most of the things to do with it; in spite of his long lingering desire for a happy existence, committed to peaceful scientific administration, devoted to the steady virtues; in spite of it all, the Gods were to play the game differently. Now that he was in his fiftieth year, they tossed him a key part in the human story. They insisted that he should play a vital role in preventing the German conquest of the Western world.

CHAPTER FIVE

The Political Birth
of Radar

By the summer of 1934 the island of Britain was becoming comparable to a rich orchard guarded only half-heartedly from plunder – in this case plunder by the growing German Air Force. The reasons for this danger lay almost exclusively in the strength of the bomber force as an instrument of offence, a strength first appreciated by Trenchard during the final years of the First World War, and then gradually forgotten until it was drawn into the light again by Stanley Baldwin's ominous, currently-accurate, and despairing warning on 10 November 1932 that 'the bomber will always get through.'

The force of Baldwin's warning, so far as Britain was concerned, rested on a combination of geography and the growing speed of the bomber *vis-à-vis* the defending fighter. This combination, so unhappy for Britain, meant that the time available for interception and attack after raiders had crossed the coast was not only short but was rapidly diminishing. With no point in the country more than seventy miles from the sea, with most important targets considerably less, the margin of safety had by the 1930's reached vanishing point. If, therefore, the defence of Britain from crippling air attack by a determined aggressor were to be practicable – a proposition which many airmen would have found it difficult to uphold at this period – it became essential to intercept raiding planes as they crossed the coast; or, should this be impossible, at least to plot their course, locate them, and direct fighters towards them before they reached their targets. The first of these operations was the task of standing patrols – small flights of aircraft which guarded allotted stretches of the coastline. The second was carried out by a somewhat sketchy system of regional observers, later to be strengthened and organized into the Royal Observer Corps. In

1934 the first operation was rendered nugatory by the reluctance of the British public to pay for the necessary number of aircraft and pilots; the second, by reluctance to take the threat of war seriously. Both operations might be superseded and the whole problem of air defence transformed, were it possible to devise a ubiquitous, reliable, and accurate system which would give early warning of raiders and would then track their course across country – or which would destroy them in the air by some new and hitherto unsuspected means.

The extent of this problem was first brought home by the summer Air Exercises of 1934. These consisted mainly of night attacks on London – with Coventry being selected as the most important provincial target – and in the first raid the Air Ministry itself was successfully 'destroyed'. Of a subsequent attack the *Aeroplane* observer wrote: 'Our targets were the Air Ministry and the Houses of Parliament, and we picked them up without difficulty, and after the two runs over them, during which the recognition lamps were flashed, the job was finished and, according to the rules, neither the Air Ministry nor the Houses of Parliament should bother any of us any more.' Air Chief Marshal Sir Arthur Longmore, commanding one of the two defence zones, subsequently summed up the results by writing that the exercises 'had shown that successful interception by fighters of raiding bombers required more accurate information from the ground as to movements of hostile formations than was at the time available.'[1] In fact, only two out of five bombers were intercepted, while on the last night of the Exercises roughly half of them reached their target. Baldwin's miserable admission that the bomber would always get through had been vindicated. So far as air attack was concerned, Britain was defenceless. Her capital was, as Churchill described it, 'the greatest target in the world, a kind of tremendous fat cow, a valuable fat cow tied up to attract the beasts of prey.'

There were three separate reactions to this intolerable situation whose awkward corners jutted out from beneath the Air Ministry protestations that all was well. In the Royal Air Force, Senior officers, led by Air Marshal Sir Robert Brooke-Popham, the A.O.C.-in-C. Air Defence of Great Britain, were formed into a special sub-committee of the Committee of Imperial Defence;

their brief was to improve the air defence of London in view of the threat from Germany – listed as the 'ultimate potential enemy' by the Defence Requirements Committee only five months earlier.[2] In the Air Ministry itself, A. P. Rowe, assistant to H. E. Wimperis, began an informal survey of the problem by studying the fifty-three files on Air Defence which he found in the archives.

> It was clear [he later wrote], that the Air Staff had given conscientious thought and effort to the design of fighter aircraft, to methods of using them without early warning and to balloon defences. It was also clear however that little or no effort had been made to call on science to find a way out. I therefore wrote a memorandum summarizing the unhappy position and proposing that the Director of Scientific Research should tell the Secretary of State for Air of the dangers ahead. The memorandum said that unless science evolved some new method of aiding air defence, we were likely to lose the next war if it started within ten years.[3]

Outside the Air Ministry, the reaction was led by Churchill – desperately trying to rouse the country with his warnings of the wrath to come – and by Lindemann, on whom Churchill was now leaning heavily for scientific advice. And it was Lindemann, who knew a good deal more about the human race than his enemies usually admit, who staked the first public claim to attention by a letter to *The Times*, published on 8 August 1934, under the heading 'Science and Air Bombing'.

> Sir [this read], In the debate in the House of Commons on Monday on the proposed expansion of our Air Forces, it seemed to be taken for granted on all sides that there is, and can be, no defence against bombing aeroplanes and that we must rely entirely upon counter-attack and reprisals. That there is at present no means of preventing hostile bombers from depositing their loads of explosives, incendiary materials, gases, or bacteria upon their objectives I believe to be true; that no method can be devised to safeguard great centres of population from such a fate appears to me to be profoundly improbable.
>
> If no protective contrivance can be found and we are reduced to a policy of reprisals, the temptation to be 'quickest on the draw' will be tremendous. It seems not too much to say that bombing aeroplanes in the hands of gangster Governments might jeopardise the whole future of our Western civilisation.
>
> To adopt a defeatist attitude in the face of such a threat is inexcusable until it has definitely been shown that all the resources of

science and invention have been exhausted. The problem is far too important and too urgent to be left to the casual endeavours of individuals or departments. The whole weight and influence of the Government should be thrown into the scale to endeavour to find a solution. All decent men and all honourable Governments are equally concerned to obtain security against attacks from the air, and to achieve it no effort and no sacrifice is too great.

Thus three separate groups were making efforts to deal with the growing danger – the Air Force officers under Brooke-Popham; the Civil Servants in the Air Ministry, spurred on by Rowe and Wimperis; and certain politicians, led by Churchill and provided by Lindemann with scientific ammunition. All brought to bear on Lord Londonderry, the Secretary of State for Air, as much pressure as they were able to exert. Their lines crossed at numerous points, and there should be little surprise that even today the respective actions of the three parties are always debated with vigour and sometimes with venom. The chronology is therefore important.[4]

During the first half of October, Wimperis wrote to Professor A. V. Hill of University College, proposing that they should meet at the Athenaeum. Hill was a physiologist with a long record of pure research, but during the First World War he had also, as Director of the Anti-Aircraft Experimental Section, Munitions Invention Department, helped to devise the rudiments of what was later called Operational Research. He had a facility, as had Tizard, for perceiving what scientific principle might best be utilized by the Services. And he had a reputation for straight-speaking as great as Tizard's own. The matter on which Wimperis now wished to seek advice was that of the 'death-ray'. During the ten years he had spent as Director of Scientific Research in the Air Ministry, proposals for some such killer had regularly been put forward. The first had come in the summer of 1924 when he was only Acting Director, and he and F. E. Smith from the Admiralty had in turn each had demonstrated to them the contraptions of one so-called inventor, an inveterate death-ray monger. 'We want a better test and are willing to offer £1,000 for a successful hour's test', Wimperis noted in his diary. The offer became known to the public, and throughout the following months both Air Ministry and Admiralty officials spent a fair quota of time examining the various proposals which were made. All the claims were unsubstantiated, if not fraudulent, but in the circumstances of 1934 it was natural enough that Wimperis should seek to discover whether such a weapon could still be ruled entirely out of court.

He lunched with Hill at the Athenaeum on 15 October. 'I wanted a good talk with him on radiant energy as a means of A.A. defence', he wrote in his diary that night. 'I think I must put up a proposition to the Air Council.' This proposition came a month later, but before it was written Tizard appears to have been drawn into the affair. His first connexion with the situation is by no means clear. He was closely in touch with Wimperis, both as Chairman of the Aeronautical Research Committee and as a personal friend of many years standing. He was an old friend of Hill, of Brooke-Popham, and of Air Marshal Joubert de la Ferté, who had commanded Fighting Area during the Air Exercises, and who was among the officers lobbying most vigorously for some solution to the menacing defence problem. He was also in touch with Watson-Watt, by this time Superintendent of the Radio Research laboratory at Slough. However, there is no documentary evidence that Tizard was consulted during this period, although common-sense suggests that he must have been.

However, Air Marshal Joubert remembers a meeting which took place at the Uxbridge Headquarters of the Air Defence of Great Britain at which he, members of his staff, and also Tizard were present. 'One by one', he says, 'Tizard ruled out the death-ray and various possibilities of early warning – the existing acoustic methods and supersonic means. He concluded by saying as he left us, "that leaves only electrical methods – and I think we'll have something for you", or words to that effect'.[5] Joubert believes that this meeting took place towards the end of October or during the first half of November 1934, and in Tizard's diary there is for 31 October, the tantalizing entry: 'Joubert?' If the meeting did in fact occur as early as this, Tizard's remark could only indicate that he had been discussing possibilities either with Wimperis or with Hill. There is no indication, either in Tizard's papers or in Wimperis's diaries, that either was thinking of what was to become radar. Whatever the truth of the matter, it is clear that the next step was made by Wimperis, who on 12 November drafted the 'proposition' he had first considered after his meeting with Hill on 15 October.

This document was a lengthy note which he sent to Lord Londonderry, the Secretary of State for Air; Air Marshal Sir Hugh Dowding, Air Member for Research and Development; Air Marshal Sir Edward Ellington, Chief of Air Staff; and Sir Christopher Bullock, the Permanent Secretary. This note was to unstopper the bottle and let the genie of radar loose on the world; and it was the document which was to bring Tizard, for the first time, to the centre of the stage where he really belonged.

When one looks back on the stupendous technical advances of the last 50 years one cannot but wonder what equally striking advances can possibly lie ahead of us in the next equal period of years [Wimperis began]. Apart from television and the use of new ways of deriving our food from the soil, it is difficult to forecast what important discovery the future may have in store, but I feel confident that one of the coming things will be the transmission by radiation of large amounts of electrical energy along clearly directed channels. If this is correct the use of such transmissions for purposes of war is inevitable, and welcome in that it offers the prospect of defence methods at last overtaking those of attack.

2. The defence of a great city against hostile aircraft, carrying bombs or gas, has now become increasingly difficult on account of higher speed, higher ceilings, less noisy airscrews and engines, and the ability to fly with an automatic pilot in clouds and fog. We need, therefore, to intensify our research for defence measures and no avenue, however seemingly fantastic, must be left unexplored. The idea of a ray of energy to put the engine ignition out of regular action has often been proposed, but it suffers from the vital defects that it is easy to screen the ignition leads and plugs. The further idea of detonating bombs by such energy is probably impracticable because the actual bomb case may be expected to afford an efficient screen against such radiation (though the idea will not be lost sight of).

3. There remains to consider the effect of this radiation on the human body (and perhaps on metal fuselage and wings). I therefore sought the opportunity of a discussion on the physiological aspect of this matter with Professor A. V. Hill, F.R.S., the Professor of Biology at University College, London, and an able worker on Artillery problems during the War. The result of our talk will be found in enclosure 1A. Certain possibilities are there revealed – for the future if not for the present moment – and these I think need careful watching.

4. Scientific surveys of what is possible in this, and other, means of defence at present untried are best made in association with two or three scientific men specially collected for the purpose; their findings may sometimes prove visionary, but one cannot afford to ignore even the remotest chance of success: and at the worst a report that at the moment 'defence was hopeless' would enable the Government to realise the situation and know that retaliation was the sole remedy – if such it can be called. I would submit, therefore, that the formation of such a body be now considered.

5. I submit for consideration that of such a Committee an excellent Chairman might be found in Mr. Tizard, the present Chairman of our Aeronautical Research Committee and a former R.F.C. pilot. The other members should, I suggest, be the Professor A. V. Hill, F.R.S., already mentioned, and Professor Blackett, F.R.S., who was a Naval Officer before and during the War, and has since proved himself by his work at Cambridge as one of the best of the younger scientific leaders of the day. The terms of reference which should, I submit, be sufficiently wide to cover all possible developments, might be: 'To consider how far recent advances in scientific and technical knowledge can be used to strengthen the present methods of defence against hostile aircraft'. The Committee should be at liberty to consult other experts (for example in radio technology) when they deem this to be necessary.

6. There is much to say in favour of such a body acting not merely under the Air Ministry but as part of the machinery of the Committee of Imperial Defence, seeing that the Admiralty and War Office are each concerned in anti-aircraft work, and that the existing knowledge of that Committee and its Secretariat might save the new proposed Committee from working on schemes whose merits had been investigated already.

7. In either case, D.S.R., Air Ministry, would need to serve on the Committee and see that its findings were brought to the knowledge of the Air Council.

Three days after Wimperis signed this vital document, Lindemann met Tizard at the Royal Society. They had remained on good terms over the years. Tizard had helped Lindemann on to the Council of the D.S.I.R. in 1926 and had probably aided his appointment to the Aeronautical Research Committee. In 1930, when he had visited Germany with Colonel Cooper to watch the gliding at the Wasserkuppe, he had suddenly said on the way home: 'Let's go and visit Lindemann'. They had, wisely no doubt, kept to their own paths but it was natural that the two men should exchange views on the problem that now confronted all those with eyes to see.

Exactly what passed between Tizard and Lindemann on the 15th is not known, but in view of future events it is likely that Lindemann put forward his proposal that the whole question of air defence should be considered by an independent body acting under the Committee of Imperial Defence. He 'explained his proposals and Mr Tizard undertook to support them if possible', according to the note of the meeting in Lindemann's papers. Twelve days later Lindemann himself met the sub-committee of the C.I.D. which was considering the air defences of London and again urged that some similar organization should be set up to deal with the national problem. Up to this date, 27 November, he was still ignorant of what was happening in the Air Ministry; this unhappy position was, as we shall see, also that of the Prime Minister himself. By this time, however, Tizard had been told, unofficially and no doubt by Wimperis, of the latter's proposal to Londonderry, and before the end of the month he asked Hill, after a meeting of the Council of the Royal Society, whether he would serve on the proposed body .'I said "Certainly" ', Hill comments, 'provided that every item of information we might need was open to us. I knew too much, even then, of secrecy being used as a cover for incompetence.'

Londonderry had approved the idea in principle, and it seems likely that Wimperis discussed the details on 29 November when he met first Wing Commander John Hodsoll, Assistant Secretary to the Committee of Imperial Defence, and then Tizard, who was formally asked on 12 December whether he would chair a small committee for the scientific survey of air defence. Its terms of reference would be Wimperis's – 'to consider how far recent advances in scientific and technical knowledge can be used to strengthen the present methods of defence against hostile aircraft'. Professors Hill and Blackett would be the two other independent members, while Wimperis would represent the Air Ministry, and Rowe would act as secretary.

Tizard did not leap at the idea; he warmed to the work over the weeks rather than jumped at it immediately, and his first action on receiving the official letter was to write to Hill and Blackett to learn their views. To Hill he suggested that it would be better if they all responded in the same way, and added 'We should be in a stronger position if we were not paid anything like a salary or retaining fee'. The committee was to be purely an advisory one, without executive power of any sort, without staff and, as Tizard was soon to discover, without even a typist to deal with the correspondence, most of which was for many months handled by him from his own private flat. All three independent members accepted the Air Ministry invitation and the first meeting of the new committee – the Committee for the Scientific Survey of Air Defence – was planned for 28 January 1935.

Meanwhile, however, Wimperis was pursuing his own enquiries. During the first fortnight of the New Year he telephoned Watson-Watt at Slough.* Would Watson-Watt visit him at the Air Ministry he asked, and advise him 'on the practicability of proposals of the type colloquially called "death-ray", that is, proposals for producing structural damage or functional derangement in enemy aircraft or their crews'. Watson-Watt arrived on 18 January, and returned, keenly sceptical, to Slough, where he asked his assistant, A. F. Wilkins, to calculate how much power would have to be re-radiated from a radio transmitter to heat a certain amount of water to a certain temperature at a certain distance.

> I noticed [said Wilkins], that the amount of water was just about the amount of blood in a man's body, and that the temperature given was about fever temperature, so it seemed very likely that what was wanted was a 'death-ray'. The power required was, of course, fantastically large, and when I took the answer along, it was obvious that there was no chance of a death-ray being produced by those means. Watson-Watt was not at all surprised. 'Well', he said, 'I wonder what we can do to help them.'[6]

It was now, on this bleak January day, that the raw scientific speculations, theory, and work of the preceding few years at last began to firm up into more tangible shape – into the possibility of

* Wimperis was a member of the D.S.I.R.'s Radio Research Board and was well acquainted with Watson-Watt's work first with the Meteorological Office, then with the D.S.I.R., and finally as Superintendent of the National Physical Laboratory's Radio Department, the field work of which was carried out under Watson-Watt's direction at the Radio Research Station, Slough.

the new instrument of radar whose significance was to be so decisively exploited by Tizard and his colleagues.

By the beginning of 1935 a few scientists already knew that aircraft could under certain circumstances be detected by the reflections of radio waves. Marconi had speculated on the detection of ships some thirteen years previously when he had said, on accepting the Medal of Honor of the American Institute of Radio Engineers in 1922:

> In some of my tests I have noticed the effects of reflection and deflection of these (electric) waves by metallic objects miles away. It seems to me that it should be possible to design apparatus by means of which a ship could radiate or project a divergent beam of these rays in any desired direction, which rays, if coming across a metallic object such as another steamer or ship, would be reflected back to a receiver screened from the local transmitter on the sending ship and thereby immediately reveal the presence and bearing of ships, even though these ships be unprovided with any kind of radio.[7]

In 1924 Professor Appleton had shown that by 'marking' the waves of radio transmissions by a slight change of wave-lengths, the distance above the earth of the wave-reflecting ionosphere could be measured[8]; and five years later still he demonstrated in Northern Norway that by using short bursts of radio energy this distance could be presented visually on a cathode-ray oscilloscope.[9] At this point there breaks into the chronological record what was, apparently the world's first rudimentary radar proposal. This came from W. A. S. Butement and P. E. Pollard of the Signals Experimental Establishment at Woolwich and was devised by them for the location of ships. The proposal, recorded in January 1931, in the Inventions Book of the Royal Engineers Board, envisaged the location of ships from the shore, or from another ship, by the use of pulsed radio transmissions and the reception of the radio echo received back in the intervals between the transmission pulses. A high frequency beam with a wavelength of about 50 cms. and a rotatable aerial system with reflectors to provide a narrow beam were to be used. Butement and Pollard carried out a number of experiments and succeeded, even with the primitive equipment available, in recording the first planned radar echoes from terrestrial objects, although only at distances of 100 yards or so.

Their scheme was passed first to the War Office and then to the Admiralty. Neither was sufficiently interested to support the work[10] and the possibility of progress had therefore moved back to square one when Post Office radio engineers, experimenting with short-wave communication between Dollis Hill and Colney Heath in December 1931, reported a fluttering of signals whenever a plane passed nearby.[11] Then two workers of the Bell Telephone Laboratory in the United States, also working with ultra-short waves, pointed out that they had detected planes even when these were out of sight.[12]

Thus most of the work from which radar might have sprung had, until the first weeks of 1935, been carried out in a purely scientific context; the sole exception had been rather brusquely brushed away by two of the three Services – and not, such was the ordering of things, even mentioned to the third. Only now did Watson-Watt, operating between Wimperis and Wilkins, provide the essential link between scientific possibilities and the Air Ministry's operational needs.*

> To find out whether it was possible to turn what was known to practical use [says Wilkins], Watson-Watt asked me to find out what power would be required to produce a detectable signal from an aircraft at such and such a range. I then did two things. I assumed that the aircraft would have the re-radiating properties of a half-wave aerial, and I took it that the plane would measure about 25 metres horizontally and $3\frac{1}{2}$ metres vertically.[13]

Wilkins' computations implied that a plane might in fact be located by the use of radio waves, and Watson-Watt said so in the reply which he sent to Wimperis, as promised, in time for the first meeting of the new Air Ministry committee on 28 January.

This Tizard Committee, as it was soon called, involved scientists in defence in a radically new way. Previously, they had been asked to provide more efficient weapons of attack or defence, to add a percentage efficiency to something already in existence. Here the

---

* All the evidence suggests that Tizard had no inkling of these early moves towards radar. Thus in acknowledging a statement on the subject sent to him by Sir Edward Appleton in October 1944, and referring to the G.P.O. incident, he replied, 'There are one or two points in it that are new and of interest to me, namely the statement on page 3 that the engineers of the British Post Office detected in 1932 the presence of aircraft by reflected short radio waves'.

gap which they had to fill was of a different order. For however the question might be wrapped up and disguised, their brief was to discover whether Britain could be defended at all from air attack within the next few years. The character of their work therefore brought them, whether they liked it or not, into the political arena, where the rules were very different from those to which they were accustomed. It is therefore hardly surprising that when the committee in a changed form was finally dissolved in the summer of 1940 – due to 'political intrigue' as Tizard put it – it had for long been battling uphill.

The five men who met under Tizard's chairmanship in Room 724 of the Air Ministry from 11 a.m. until 1.45 on the morning of 28 January 1935, were to help transform Britain's defences between 1935 and the outbreak of war. In the early days, Wimperis and Rowe formed the main channel of communication with the Air Ministry. Blackett and Hill added both scientific weight and a knowledge of Service problems – the first had been through Dartmouth and Osborne and had served in the Royal Navy throughout the war; Hill had been an Army Captain while organizing his anti-aircraft research. Tizard directed and controlled. He was uniquely valuable since he always remembered how 'things that seemed easy for other people to do or use in the air, when one was sitting safely on the ground, assumed quite a different aspect when one was in the cramped and cold cockpit of an aeroplane, cumbered with heavy clothing – quite apart from the fact that other misguided people might be trying to shoot one down.' It was this facility for instinctively understanding the problems of the men in the air that slowly but surely altered the personal standing both of Tizard and of his committee as the years passed and war lurched nearer. Their standing, that is, at operational level; higher up, where ignorance sometimes reigned and the word 'science' was apt to be linked with the phrase 'new-fangled', matters were not so easy. Neither were they helped by the fact that while fighter defence was the responsibility of the Air Force, anti-aircraft defence, the unsatisfactory system of acoustic warning which alerted it, and research into acoustic devices, were for long under control of the War Office.

The Tizard Committee was eventually to become the custodian

of the country's safety, and Tizard himself the Air Ministry's unofficial scientific adviser, yet the position of both was weak. During its first difficult years the committee introduced the primitive radar system of early warning that revolutionized defence. It helped coax past the financial defences of the Treasury increasingly large programmes, so that what began with the request for an experimental £10,000 became the basis of a massive electronics industry; and – largely through the personal ability of Tizard alone – it enabled the Royal Air Force to win its own Thermopylae. Throughout the whole of its existence, however, it lacked executive power, so that when Tizard wished new devices to be tested, planes to be flown, staff to be utilized, or Air Force machinery set into motion, these matters had to be organized by persuasion, on the 'old-boy net', through the goodwill of individual Commanders – and sometimes in the face of determined opposition from those resolutely preparing for the last war. The Committee had no offices, and much of the confidential interviewing that the work demanded was carried out by Tizard privately at his flat in St James's Court. The 'secretariat' for some while consisted solely of Rowe who for much of the committee's life was also the secretary of numerous other bodies. In the early days even a typist was rarely available, although on occasion kindly Commanders would offer to get memoranda and reports handled. 'After a time' Tizard later wrote 'I found myself involved in considerable expenses owing to this work and I could not afford to carry it. In particular I had to employ a special part-time confidential secretary.'[14] Thus, throughout the later 1930's, did the Air Ministry struggle to mobilize science for its coming battle with the Luftwaffe.

At the first meeting of the Tizard Committee Wimperis gave Watson-Watt's reply to his query about the death-ray, and said that a further and more detailed memorandum would soon be available. There was discussion of a proposed balloon barrage, and it was agreed as a matter of policy that this should operate at a height of 5,000 ft. The next moves were made on a purely personal basis, and on 14 February, Tizard, Sir Christopher Bullock, and Wimperis lunched at the Athenaeum and discussed with Watson-Watt the paper on 'Detection and Location of Aircraft by Radio Methods' which he had now produced. On the following day – before the Tizard Committee had met again – Wimperis boldly proposed to Dowding that £10,000 should be spent on investigating the new method of detection. Dowding suggested preliminary tests at Slough.

> Mr. Tizard and I have sufficient confidence in Mr. Watson-Watt's work not to regard this as a necessary preliminary [Wimperis replied], but should you prefer such a check made I can arrange for a metal aeroplane to fly from Royal Aircraft Establishment, Farnborough, to Ditton Park (Slough) in about ten days, by which time Mr. Watt would have had time to modify the Ditton Park transmitter (rather a feeble one for this task) so as to make it better suited for this variation from its normal duties. There would be some loss in secrecy in carrying out this experiment since many more would be aware of what was going on.[15]

The various possibilities were discussed at the second meeting of the Tizard Committee on the 21st. And on the 26th the test was held south of Rugby – outside Daventry through whose short-wave transmissions Squadron-Leader R. S. Blucke, Flight Commander of the Wireless and Electrical Flight at Farnborough, piloted a Heyford bomber. On the ground Watson-Watt, accompanied by Wilkins and Rowe – the latter present both as the secretary of the Tizard Committee and as the official Air Ministry observer – watched the green blob on a cathode ray oscillograph rise and fall as the Heyford approached and departed through the transmissions. Wimperis was told by Dowding, delighted at the results, that he could have 'all the money I want, within reason.'[16]

Thus the Tizard Committee was given, within a few weeks of its first meeting, the raw material from which the weapon of radar was to be hewn. It was only the raw material, however, and the speed with which the first stages of the transformation were carried out was largely due to Tizard's persistent prodding. Wimperis's diary is full of notes recording meetings between 'HT' and the other members of the enthusiastic band who were quickly gathered to work on this new and exciting defence project. Tizard himself kept disconnected notes and jottings recording the swift progress of the next few weeks.

Within a few days of the Daventry flight it had been decided that experiments should be carried out from the long low strip of Orfordness to which Tizard had so often flown from nearby Martlesham Heath to watch the Air Armament work of the First World War. On 1 March, Wimperis and Watson-Watt visited the site and agreed that it was suitable, Wimperis noting in his diary that he was 'most hopeful of the new system going almost all the way to make air attack on this country a very doubtful success'. Tizard called the third meeting of his Committee for 4 March, and at this Watson-Watt demonstrated what he hoped could be achieved by the new method of radio reflection. By mid-May when the Committee met to consider the draft of its first interim report, the Orfordness station had been opened 'to extend iono-spheric investigations' and by the end of the month the first echoes were being received from the ionosphere.

There had been five more meetings of the Tizard Committee by this time, and it was decided to hold the next at Orfordness. On 15 June, therefore, Tizard met Wimperis at Liverpool Street Station, and travelled with him to meet Blackett, Hill, Rowe, and Watson-Watt. They lunched at the 'Jolly Sailors', Orford, and the whole party then took the ferry to 'the Island', the long peninsula on which the experimental station stood. There Watson-Watt showed them the radar trace of a Valentine flying off the coast in thundery weather. 'Got some lovely records up to 27 km.', Wimperis noted in his diary. The following day they were out on 'the Island' by 7 a.m. The tests were repeated. Even better results were recorded. Then they returned to the hotel where, after break-fast, the meeting of the Committee was held. After lunch, Tizard, Wimperis, and Watson-Watt strolled for the afternoon up the sandy banks of the River Alde, discussing the immense possibilities which now seemed to held out by what Rowe had already christened R.D.F. (for radio direction-finding) – on the grounds that since the system could as yet reveal only the existence of planes, but not their direction, the name would provide a good cover.

On 16 July all therefore appeared to be flowing smoothly for-ward. However, at the next meeting of the Committee, held on 25 July, an additional member was present in the person of Professor Lindemann.

       *   *   *

The bare facts of Professor Lindemann's movement on to the Tizard Committee, and its sequel, have for long been known, while some of the incidents have been described in Lord Birkenhead's biography.* However, only with the aid of both the Tizard and the Cherwell archives, and of Wimperis's diary, is it possible to piece together the details of this fascinating and cautionary episode: fascinating because it illustrates the mechanism of politics as much in use today as in the 1930's: cautionary because it indicates the problems of any scientist, or scientific group, which attempts to operate in a political vacuum when defence policies are involved.

Lindemann had followed up his letter to *The Times* of August 1934 by lobbying with Churchill's aid for a scientific investigation of air defence by a non-departmental committee.

> What I have in mind is a committee under the Chairmanship of a man of the type of the late Lord Justice Fletcher Moulton or the present Lord Weir with two or three service representatives and two or three scientists whose definite instructions would be to find some method of defence against air bombing other than counter-attack and reprisals [he wrote on 3 November 1934 to Mr. Baldwin, then Lord President of the Council].[17] It is essential [he later noted to T. J. O'Connor, K.C.] that work should be pressed on and that there should be a chairman of Cabinet rank who can go straight to the Prime Minister if he finds he is being held up by departmental slackness or ill-health.[18]

He was still unaware of what was happening in the Air Ministry, and in December he wrote to Londonderry again, renewing his suggestion for an independent, non-departmental committee. In reply he was informed that an Air Ministry Committee was already being set up under Mr Tizard; would it not be a good idea for him to get in touch with this? Lindemann, wary of the word 'departmental', invoked the aid of both Churchill and Austen Chamberlain. The latter in turn solicited the Prime Minister, Ramsay Macdonald, who replied agreeably on 10 January that 'it should not be a departmental committee', adding, 'it was something the C(ommittee of) I(mperial) D(efence) ought to take in hand', and exhibiting complete ignorance of what had by this

---

* *The Prof in Two Worlds*, the Earl of Birkenhead, 1961.

time been done by the Air Ministry. Only now, it appears, did he approach Londonderry, who five days later instructed Wimperis to draft a letter for Macdonald. With this to hand the confused Prime Minister was able to explain to both Chamberlain and Churchill that a departmental committee was already preparing for its first meeting. The result was hardly what Wimperis had hoped. For he was now informed by Londonderry that the Cabinet – presumably acting on Macdonald's advice – wanted Lindemann added to the Committee for the Scientific Survey of Air Defence.

At first it appeared that any such addition would be avoided. Lindemann stuck to his guns, and on Austen Chamberlain's advice delayed replying to the invitation which was made. 'As you will see, the constitution of the Air Ministry Committee is not very satisfactory and its terms of reference are altogether inadequate' he wrote to Churchill. 'Tizard of course is a good man but both he and Wimperis receive salaries from the Air Ministry' – in Tizard's case presumably a reference to his chairmanship of the Aeronautical Research Committee. On 12 February he took his protest personally to Londonderry, who agreed to write to the Prime Minister. And two days later the Prime Minister met Lindemann, Austen Chamberlain, and Churchill. The only note of this intriguing interview which appears on record lies in the Cherwell archives: 'The Prime Minister', it says, 'agreed that they had made out the case, and promised to get the Tizard Committee to present a report at an early date and then to wind it up and form the sort of Committee under the C.I.D. which had been demanded. On being pressed, he undertook that this should be done before the Air Estimates were introduced.'

This must have looked encouraging, and a few days later Lindemann followed up his tactical success by a speech that would have been anathema to Tizard who believed that science and politics should be kept, wherever possible, in separate water-tight compartments – a speech to the Conservative 1922 Committee vehemently calling for a complete reappraisal of the country's air defences. With a Socialist Prime Minister weakening, it was natural that Lindemann should appeal to the Conservatives' Praetorian Guard.

In my view [he said], the best procedure would be to set up, with the full authority of Parliament, and with the collaboration of the Committee of Imperial Defence, a small and powerful committee consisting of a few scientists and a few Service members and presided over by a man of Cabinet rank though not necessarily a member of the Cabinet. This body should have the right to claim and secure priority for its research in the various experimental establishments of the Defence ministries. It should be given means of supervising the work and assured of the full support of the Government. Its cost, which in any case would be insignificant compared with the sums habitually spent on defence, could if necessary be met by a supplementary estimate. Some such procedure seems to me infinitely preferable to any proposal for a departmental committee such as the one about which I have recently been approached.[19]

He still delayed accepting the invitation to join the Tizard Committee, a fact which was apparently noted with satisfaction in the Air Ministry.

For an influential friend of Tizard in the Ministry now wrote to him privately, thanking him for accepting the 'irritating political intervention', and explaining that there were difficulties in withdrawing the invitation to Lindemann. There would be no question of renewing it, or of stirring him up to reply. And it was thought improbable that he would be invited to join 'the main committee'.[20]

Comforting as such support no doubt was, the 'irritating political intervention' and 'the main committee' were references to what had been the first success of the Churchill-Lindemann lobby. For Macdonald, half-redeeming his promise of 14 February, had now agreed that a sub-committee of the Committee of Imperial Defence should be set up under Sir Philip Cunliffe-Lister – Secretary of State for the Colonies and soon to become Air Minister as Lord Swinton – to consider not merely the scientific but also the political and more general problems of air defence. In many ways this was an admirable move. Swinton was possibly the public servant *par excellence*, open-minded, experienced, knowledgeable, uncommitted except to duty – one of the few politicians whose pre-war courage did so much to win the Battle of Britain. Yet the new situation was deeply fraught with the possibilities of ill-will and confusion; for the Air Ministry's Tizard Committee was now made – whether additionally or alternatively no-one appears to have been quite certain – a sub-committee of this fresh C.I.D. organization. Thus Tizard's departmental committee had been overtaken and passed in authority by the Churchill-Lindemann late-starter, the body which was, in Macdonald's words in the House, to 'have the direction and control of the whole enquiry.'

Tizard himself was a member of both committees, but this increased rather than eliminated the chances for confusion. 'The terms of reference are unusual are they not', he wrote to Hankey, Secretary of the C.I.D., after being offered the seat on the new Committee. 'If they are to be interpreted literally, all initiative will be taken away not only from my Committee but also from such bodies as the Ordnance Committee. However, I assume from the last paragraph of your letter that they will not be interpreted too literally'. Hankey reassured him. However, the Gilbertian element was not entirely removed from the situation. As Dowding later pointed out to Tizard, a difficulty arose

> owing to the fact that political considerations brought about the existence of another Committee after the birth of your own.
>
> 2. You therefore have a dual function; firstly (in point of time) that of an Air Ministry Committee, and, secondly, a Sub-sub-Committee of the Committee of Imperial Defence.
>
> 3. Some of the problems which you are specifically asked to consider by the political Committee might, perhaps never have been referred to you by the Air Ministry, and *vice versa*.
>
> 4. It is clear, however, that the subject dealt with by the paper now in question [apparently pilotless planes] was specifically referred to you by the Political Committee and the answer should be addressed to them.
>
> 5. It would, nevertheless, be unfortunate if the Air Ministry Committee, through lack of knowledge of Air Ministry policy, should recommend to the Political Committee some course which would subsequently be opposed by the Air Ministry, and therefore I think it would be a wise move if the Air Ministry were given an opportunity of seeing and commenting on such papers before their transmission to the Political Committee . . .[21]

The first meeting of this 'Political Committee' – officially the Air Defence Research Sub-Committee of the Committee of Imperial Defence and soon known as the Swinton Committee — was

held in the House of Commons room on 11 April. Wimperis 'had
to speak for the Tizard Committee's findings' as he reported in his
diary, since Tizard was in bed with a poisoned hand; 'all har-
monious and intensely interesting.' Churchill and Lindemann had
at last achieved one of their objects in moving control of the whole
subject up to a non-departmental level. Neither man was slow at
exploiting success. They did not have long to wait for the opportunity.

On 7 June Ramsay Macdonald stepped down to take Baldwin's
place as Lord President, and Baldwin stepped up to become
Prime Minister. The previous day Wimperis had seen Macdonald
in his private room in the House of Commons. 'He was' he noted,
'v. frank about Lindemann and most realistic in his attitude.' On
the 7th he spent nearly half an hour with the new Prime Minister
and with him 'drafted the germ of the statement to be made on
Air Defence and in reply to Churchill.' The result of the Ministerial
Box-and-Cox switch was seen within the month. Swinton suggested
that Churchill should be brought on to his Committee, and
Churchill agreed, making 'it a condition that Professor Lindemann should at least be a member of the Technical Sub-Committee, because I depended upon his aid.'[22]

This technical Sub-Committee was, of course, the Tizard Committee, and Swinton immediately conferred with Tizard. He then
saw Lindemann and on 21 June wrote to Tizard informing him
of what had passed.

> I talked to him fully about the whole position [he said]. He was a
> little inclined to go into past history. I said I was really not concerned
> with that at all; indeed I had deliberately avoided doing so. I was
> merely concerned with the matter from the time the C.I.D. Com-
> mittee was established; that everybody concerned attached the utmost
> importance to the work; that there was the most cordial co-operation
> between everybody; that a vast amount of very valuable work was
> being done, and that I was sure he would come in the same spirit as
> everybody else concerned. I emphasised the vital importance of
> absolute secrecy, and the exceptional steps which we were taking to
> ensure it. I asked him to get into direct touch with you. He said would
> I approach you myself first. I said that of course I had already seen
> you and told you that I was asking him again to join the Committee
> of Scientists and that I had already been informed . . . that he
> (Lindemann) would accept.[23]

Thus the ground was now clear for personal tragedy. So far, Tizard and Lindemann had gone their parallel ways, alternately friendly and critical, acknowledging the situation with mutual common-sense. Now events had touched the helm of each so that they no longer steamed on similar tracks but had been swung out and turned to face one another on what could only, human weakness being what it is, be for each a direct collision course.

Animosity between Lindemann and the other members of the Tizard Committee developed from his first attendance. Yet it was not caused solely by his bellicosity or by the fact that he aroused their personal dislike; men can jog along satisfactorily with the most unexpected companions if only they have a few points of contact on the main issues. But it was exactly on these that Lindemann and the others were perpetually facing in opposite directions. There were in fact, two issues, one technical and the other political. The first is exemplified by the memorandum which Lindemann sent to Tizard early in July outlining his current thoughts on air defence. The ideas in this memorandum, Tizard wrote later, 'depend largely on two pre-conceived notions, both wrong. The first was "that the only hope of stopping aeroplanes by means of artillery consists of using a barrage . . .", from which he deduced that it would need 90,000 shells to bring down an aeroplane. The second is "that a machine, if it is to fly, must be comparatively light, and if it is light it must be fragile." Hence, "the line of development of which I have most hope, is to attach small mines of high explosive in suitable cases to parachutes." He "supposed" the weight of parachute and mine to be of the order of 100 grammes and the total weight of parachute and mine to be 200 grammes, but was sufficiently cautious to add that "the figure might require modification to the extent of a factor of 10."

'His second suggestion', Tizard continued, 'was to produce a cloud of substance in the path of an aeroplane to produce detonation in the engine. (Many interested amateurs make this impracticable suggestion from time to time.)

'As for the detection of aeroplanes, he alludes to the scattering of wireless beams by an impracticable method, which misses the whole point of R.D.F., and which has been tried without success in U.S.A. and Austria.'[24]

K

Today it is easy to see that most of the points in Lindemann's memorandum were unsound – although five years later Tizard was recommending that short aerial mines were one of the eight projects to which the Air Force should give priority. More revealing is the assumption on which they were based and which Lindemann had made in the footnote of a letter to Londonderry six months previously. 'I am not making a great point of day bombers as I take it the Air Force can deal with these' he wrote.[25] The Air Force could not as yet deal with these, and it was this underlying ignorance of Service requirements, as much as any technical inability, which lay at the root of much later disagreement.

However, even this was perhaps less important than the fundamental difference in outlook between Lindemann and the rest of the Committee members led by Tizard. Lindemann believed that only by taking whatever political action was expedient would it be possible to prick the authorities into action. Tizard believed that this was no part of their task; by making it so, he felt, they would merely be stepping into deep waters where they had no right to be. At base, therefore, the trouble lay not only in personalities, whose raspings might have been born with for a common cause, not only in technical differences, which could have been straightened out with good will, but in a fundamental difference of attitude. This was to be underlined, rather remarkably, in a letter written by Tizard himself almost exactly one year later. Meanwhile, he replied cautiously to Lindemann on 16 July.

My dear Lindemann [he wrote], I have been very busy with an Aircraft Conference* or would have written to you before. I have read your memorandum again, and can safely say that if you come on the Committee, you will find plenty of interest taken in your ideas, both by members of the Committee and by members of the various experimental stations.

There are really only two other observations worth making at this stage: (1) Obviously the Committee has had no right to demand secrecy from you in the past. But if you come on the Committee it means you will not in future be entitled to discuss things with anyone except with the previous knowledge and agreement of the Committee. We all work on that understanding. Also you come under the Official Secrets Act.

* See pp. 98–99.

(2) What disturbed me in our conversation the other day was your attitude that the people at the various Research Establishments were sure to be unhelpful, and slow to work out any ideas but their own. If you start with that attitude I am quite sure that it is going to be difficult to get full co-operation. At present we have no criticism to make of anyone in any of the Services whose help we have wanted. So my advice is, either come on the Committee wholeheartedly, without misgivings, or don't come on at all!

Please let me know if you accept this position, and I will then see that the papers are sent to you. The next meeting is to be held at 10.20 a.m. on Thursday July 25 at the Air Ministry. By the way, your opening paragraph reads as if you had frequently discussed matters with me. I don't remember having any conversation with you about them previous to our lunch the other day. Yours ever, H. T. Tizard.

By this time, however, the matter was out of Tizard's hands, and nine days later Lindemann attended the tenth meeting of the Committee. Fittingly enough, on the same day Churchill made his first appearance at the Swinton Committee. Here, after another offer of a death ray from a persistent inventor had been quietly turned down, it was decided that the radar experiments at Orfordness were sufficiently promising to justify executive action. There was some discussion about whether the new method was so sure to do its job that it was worth taking action. Most members of the committee had been convinced, but Churchill, after discussions with Lindemann, was still doubtful. While the others were talking he remembered the seventh verse of Neale's hymn, 'Art thou weary, art thou languid, Art thou sore distrest?', scribbled four lines on a postcard and handed it across the table to Wimperis. On it, Wimperis read the words: 'Seeking, Finding, Following, Keeping,/Is he sure to Bless?/Angels, Martyrs, Prophets, Virgins/ Answer, "M'Yes" '.[26]

CHAPTER SIX

The Great Debate

The family tree given below illustrates the relationship between the main defence committees which Tizard chaired, or with which he was closely connected between 1935 and 1940. Confusion can spring from the fact that the Tizard Committee, set up by the Air Ministry at the end of 1934, later became answerable also to the Swinton Committee of the Committee of Imperial Defence which was formed in the Spring of 1935. The Committee for the Scientific Survey of Air Offence was set up early in 1937.

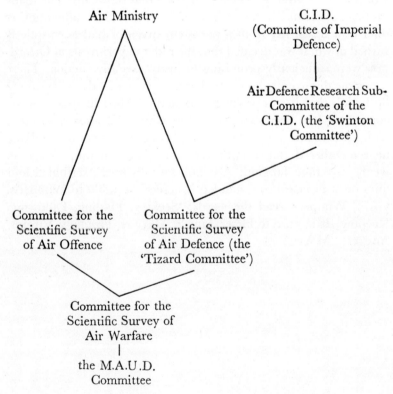

Air Ministry

C.I.D.
(Committee of Imperial Defence)

Air Defence Research Sub-Committee of the C.I.D. (the 'Swinton Committee')

Committee for the Scientific Survey of Air Offence

Committee for the Scientific Survey of Air Defence (the 'Tizard Committee')

Committee for the Scientific Survey of Air Warfare

the M.A.U.D. Committee

From the summer of 1935 onwards, Tizard described to the Swinton Committee, to politicians such as Churchill and Civil Servants such as Sir Warren Fisher, the scientific results which were being produced under the guidance of his own Committee for the Scientific Survey of Air Defence. In this he had to nurse through its difficult early stages the evolution of radar, and to sense just what particular line of development, if pushed hard, would be of greatest use if war came. With other members of the Committee, he had to filter the new ideas for defence, based on science or pseudo-science, which arrived in growing numbers as knowledge of what the Tizard Committee was doing seeped slowly down through the intricate channels of the Civil Service and the Royal Air Force. Further, he had to explain in persuasive terms not only to the R.A.F. but to the other Services, that they might soon have to alter their concept of the militarily possible.

'I remember well going home one day after a visit to the experimental station', he later said, 'and thinking that however important R.D.F., as it was then called, was to the Air Force, it must be just as important, if not more so, to the Navy. Full of this, I sought an early interview with a naval expert. I told him of the work, and drew upon my imagination a little. I was even bold enough to say that in a few years R.D.F. would make accurate blind firing possible from ship to ship. He listened to me patiently then he said: "May I ask if you have ever seen a warship?" I said "Yes, many times". "And have you observed the aerials?" "Yes" I answered. "Well" he said, "if you had observed them closely enough you would know that there was no room on them for any more." "Well" I answered, "my advice is that you take some of them off." '[1]

Even the Royal Air Force, by tradition the least conservative of Services, was at first not over-anxious to consider the implications of the new sense being given to the watchers on the ground. Reactions were mixed when the Tizard Committee first reported that if money was not stinted a practical system for detecting and locating aircraft fifty miles away could be developed within two years. 'Why', said one high officer 'if that is possible, the whole plan of Air Defence will be revolutionized!' 'Why not start revolutionizing it now', was Tizard's reply.

That a good deal of the necessary revolution did take place in time, before the outbreak of war, was due very largely to the Tizard Committee's practice of encouraging Service officers to give evidence, or to serve as co-opted members of the Committee. The atmosphere even at this early date, was already becoming very similar to that suggested by Mr Justice Du Parcq when, seven years later, he reported to the Prime Minister on various problems of wartime radio and radar production. 'In the actual working out of the problems on which research workers are engaged, there seems to be full and enthusiastic co-operation between Service representatives and the scientists. The former suggest in oral discussion what they would like done, and the latter suggest what might be done, and there is fruitful exchange of ideas across the table.'[2] This, in fact, was the direct legacy of the Tizard Committee.

It was within a somewhat half-time atmosphere of outside advice, with decisions on new defence enterprises being taken between the Athenaeum and Tizard's flat in St James's Court, that radar was encouraged into existence. The second half of 1935 saw the new science over its first hump. By mid-July the range of the Orfordness echoes had been extended to forty miles, and on 24 July there came an historic occasion on which a 'blip', estimated to indicate a plane some twenty miles away, was seen to alter. Then it was learned that the 'blip' had in fact revealed three Hawker Harts breaking formation. In August the first efforts were made to locate the height of planes, as distinct from their distance, and by the following month the Orfordness workers were finding aircraft fifteen miles away, and pinning them at 7,000 ft. with an error of little more than 1,000 ft. in height. All this had been achieved by Watson-Watt, seconded from Slough to Orfordness and working with a handful of scientists drawn off from other jobs. Now more effort was called for.

At the fifth meeting of the Swinton Committee, held on 16 September 1935, the efforts of Tizard and his Committee produced two results. It was agreed that the Orfordness work should be expanded and moved to larger quarters in Bawdsey Manor, a site a few miles away already reconnoitred by Rowe and Watson-Watt. And, more important, it was agreed that Treasury approval should be sought for the building of a chain of radar warning stations along the British coast, from Southampton to the Tyne – a decision made less than seven months after Blucke's metal Heyford had flown through the Daventry transmissions. Six days before Christmas, Treasury approval was given for building the first five stations – between Bawdsey and the South Foreland, and thus covering the approaches to London up the Thames Estuary. The confidence was to be justified; within three months Watson-Watt had solved the most important remaining single problem, that of inducing the radar echoes to reveal not merely distance and height but also bearing. By the middle of March 1936, it was therefore possible, always in theory and frequently in practice, to pinpoint the position of a plane in the sky even though it was still seventy-five miles from the coast. It now seemed that there was a good prospect of the country's air defences being strengthened in time to face daylight attack.

The Tizard Committee, which had brought about such a revolution almost alone, was not of course occupied only with radar and its potentialities. There was also Lindemann's persistent demand for investigation of aerial minefields which could be laid at night when even radar would not be able to bring fighter close enough to bomber to provide interception. This demand lay behind a curious letter in Tizard's papers reporting his demand for supplies of fishing lines, ink bottles and small parachutes. Lindemann had raised the question of aerial mines during his first attendance at the Tizard Committee and had continued to press the matter throughout the summer and early autumn of 1935, demanding that efforts should be made to discover exactly what happened when planes ran into wire from which mines were suspended. At first, since it was considered that the operation was too dangerous to be undertaken by a piloted plane, it was proposed that the experiment should be carried out by a radio-controlled Queen Bee aircraft. Then it was discovered that no Queen Bee would be available until late in 1936. Lindemann thereupon offered to pilot a plane himself in such an experiment, but was told that under the circumstances this would be considered offensive to the Royal Air Force. Finally, on 4 December 1935, it was decided that scaled-down experiments should be made, using fishing-lines instead of steel cables and small fragile vessels filled with ink which on being broken would reveal where they had hit the wings of the plane.

Much valuable time was also taken up with various claims put forward by scientists and inventors – serious and uninformed, crazy and crooked. Many of the schemes, worthy of Dr Strabismus himself, could be quickly dismissed. Others had already been found impracticable – although Tizard, in his purely unofficial and advisory capacity, frequently had difficulty in revealing why they had to be turned down. But there remained a minority of ideas about which there hung just the faintest trace of scientific plausibility, and these had to be investigated. Many of these propositions concerned a death-ray; and, since radar itself had sprung from a suggestion for this very thing, it was difficult to dismiss such claims too hurriedly. Thus the seventeenth meeting of the Tizard Committee cross-examined one gentleman on 24 March 1936. The claim in its original form had involved the killing of experimental animals on the Tempelhofer Airfield in Berlin. It was a very old tale that had always been disbelieved, Rowe noted in a memo which he circulated on behalf of Wimperis, to whom the story appears first to have come. However, 'the present story is quite different from anything we have had before, and lends some colour to the possibility that the claims are not absurd' he added. 'Whether [he] has anything is another matter.' He had nothing. 'I remember asking him what the animals had died of, to which he could not give a satisfactory reply. He had not expected to meet a physiologist on the Committee', says Hill. 'The consensus of opinion', Tizard noted later, 'was that his claims were fraudulent'.

Such probings occupied only a part of the Committee's time. For as its members listened to the evidence of Air Force officers concerned with the operational need of early warning, of anti-aircraft gunners faced with the problem of hitting planes flying at faster and ever faster speeds, and of experts who underlined the massive problems of dealing with individual raiders, their task was seen to involve matters of ominous complexity.

Basically there were two problems, each of which was itself subdivided. There was first the need for finding approaching

5: The Officers (*upper photograph*) and other ranks of the Aeroplane Experimental Station, R.F.C., Martlesham Heath, *c.* 1917. Henry Tizard is seen fifth from right in front row of upper photograph, sitting on the left of Bertram Hopkinson.

6: Bertram Hopkinson, *c.* 1917

7: The members of the Tizard Committee as formed under Henry Tizard in January, 1935, showing Dr. A. P. Rowe, secretary (*top left*); H. E. Wimperis (*top right*); Professor P. M. S. Blackett (*bottom left*); and Professor A. V. Hill (*bottom right*).

8: Professor F. A. Lindemann, later Lord Cherwell

raiders in time: this demanded a more accurate solution by night than would suffice by day. Secondly, there was the problem of destroying enemy planes once they had been found, and this again required different solutions by day and by night. These matters did not exist in separate water-tight compartments but were inter-related. It was possible to place varying degrees of urgency on each, and it was largely around this that friction between Linde-mann and the other members of the Committee grew and festered throughout the months.

So far as interception by day was concerned, radar at last began to offer a panacea. To this, Lindemann was always ready to stress two limitations. The method might not be operationally viable; and it might, in any case, be rendered ineffective by jam-ming or other methods. The other members of the Committee were, of course, aware of such potential limitations; but radar had grown up under their own loving eyes, and it was natural enough that they should tend to deal with such criticisms more leniently than did Lindemann.

Effective interception by night was still impossible, although considerable efforts to alter the situation were about to be made under the code-name 'Silhouette'. These involved lighting-up the clouds, against which the enemy bombers would, it was hoped, be seen in outline. 'Some pretty intensive work', in Tizard's words to Vannevar Bush, on 19 August 1941, was done on this, but the scheme was found to be impracticable, due to the vast amounts of power required and to other technical difficulties. There re-mained two other possibilities. One was the production of a radar set small enough and light enough to be fitted into a fighter plane and with which a pilot would therefore be able to feel his way towards a bomber until the enemy was visible. The other, develop-ment of a system to pick up the infra-red rays produced by an aircraft in flight, had been listed for consideration at the first meeting of the Tizard Committee. It had quickly been over-shadowed by the development of radar, and from the first Tizard himself believed that an airborne radar set offered the best solu-tion to the problem of night defence. Lindemann had proposed the use of infra-red for detection during the First World War and his interest had been revived, almost fortuitously, when he

learned that a young scientist in the Clarendon, R. V. Jones, was
making thermopiles for a U.S. inventor preparing to demonstrate
an infra-red detector to the R.A.F. Why not, he suggested, bring
Jones into the investigations?

> The Tizard Committee [Jones has written],[3] doubted whether infra-
> red techniques were worth developing, in view of the ease with which
> aircraft engines could be screened, but Lindemann (who had now
> joined the Committee) contended with reason that there must be
> much energy radiated from the hot exhaust gases, and he insisted that
> trials should be undertaken, although it was known that an investiga-
> tion by Dr. A. B. Wood in 1926 had yielded negative results . . . The
> trials, which began on 4 November 1935, bore out Wood's results:
> with the 500 h.p. piston engines and infra-red detectors then current,
> there was insufficient infra-red radiation from the exhaust gases, at
> least outside the atmospheric absorption bands, although there was
> considerable energy radiating from the hot surfaces of the engines.
> Despite this negative result, the Tizard Committee – rather surpris-
> ingly in the strained circumstances – asked me to continue the work
> on a full-time basis, with the object of developing an airborne infra-
> red detector.

However, detection provided only one half of the problem.
Planes, once found, had to be destroyed whether they were found
by day or by night. The day problem – now that the question of
interception appeared potentially capable of solution – was largely
that of providing the fighter with better armament. But it still
seemed unlikely that at night the fighter could be guided to within
the necessary range. The suggested alternatives were numerous,
and ranged from balloon-borne wire networks to short wire barrages, aerial mines and wire-carrying anti-aircraft parachute
shells.

Lindemann, apparently overlooking the remaining problems
of the day battle – or taking it for granted that they could be
solved – persistently pressed for more research on methods of
destroying the enemy at night. Tizard, convinced that perfection
of the radar chain must come before all, worked for the concentration on to this of all the manpower, money, and materials that
could be screwed from the authorities. Thus far, the differences
between Lindemann and his colleagues – other than the purely
personal ones – were those of emphasis. Now, as the summer of

1936 neared, a more important difference arose – that of the pressures which it was right and fitting for a scientific committee to bring to bear upon the authorities.

Before dealing with the great schism which this question was to produce, it is perhaps useful to quote a memorandum which Tizard prepared for Dowding at this point. For it adequately underlines the position reached, and it shows that his mind was already turning both to airborne radar and to what was to be a crucial aspect of the new scheme of defence – its operational integration with the officers and men of the Royal Air Force whose task it would be to utilize it in battle.

The work of the Committee [Tizard wrote on 27 March 1936], falls into two distinct parts. On the one hand we are dealing with the vital problem of how to find the enemy in the air under all conditions, and on the other with problems of what to do when the enemy is found.

2. The phrase 'finding the enemy' wants clear definition. By the methods we are at present exploring we hope to detect the enemy when within 100 miles of the coast, and when within say 50 miles to locate him to an accuracy of one mile in plan and ±500 feet in height. If this is achieved it is highly probable that defending aircraft can be directed from the ground to such a position that they will see and intercept the enemy on a high proportion of occasions in daylight. To provide additional help at night or in very cloudy weather we hope to develop some instrument which can be carried in defending aircraft, and which will give an indication of where the enemy aircraft is when they are within say five miles.

All this part of our work, though difficult is going on quite satisfactorily. I feel quite confident that the experimental work is in good hands, and that money is not likely to be wasted. We shall probably spend some money on ideas which lead to no practical results, but that is unavoidable. Further, the problem of location and detection is essentially a scientific problem, demanding the most up-to-date scientific knowledge and experience, and needing, at this stage, very little practical flying experience. It does not matter to the pilot *how* detection and location is effected, so long as it *is* effected; he need be no more concerned with the methods than he is concerned with the design of any other instrument he uses.

4. On the other hand I am not at all happy about the other side of the work. We have initiated, or are concerned with, much experimental work which has as its object the devising of methods of defence when the atmospheric conditions are such that fighter aircraft are unlikely to make sufficiently close contact with the enemy to ensure

effective attack. Such conditions may often occur by night above
clouds, when the enemy cannot be illuminated by searchlight; or
by day in very cloudy weather. These are tactical problems. Scientific
problems are involved, in which the help of a scientific committee
is useful, and perhaps essential; but they are far from being purely
scientific problems. Practical experience of flying, organisation and
command is essential if this side of our work is to be fruitful and not
wasteful. I feel that we want much more constructive criticism from
experienced officers of the R.A.F.

This, then, was the position in the early spring of 1936, a position from which a solution to the menace of the day bomber
appeared to be within reach, but one from which the threat of
the night bomber looked as dangerous as ever. This showed, of
course, that the right priority had been followed. Failure to win
the battle against the night bomber might prolong a war; failure
to win the Battle of Britain would probably have lost one.

The Tizard Committee's internal battle during the summer of
1936 was to be of importance not only because its outcome
affected the developing pattern of air defence but because it left
a legacy of bitterness which was to affect the coming war. The
entries are by no means all on one side of the ledger. And Tizard
insisted more than once that he did not wish the story to be told
until it was possible to consult Lindemann's papers as well as his
own. This was in keeping with his sense of fair play; for he knew
that although a black-and-white picture could easily be constructed, fairness to Lindemann demanded something more.

The first public references to the schism that developed during
the summer of 1936 were made more than twenty years afterwards
in 'Nature's' obituary by R. V. Jones of Lord Cherwell, as Lindemann had become, and then in Sir George Thomson's Royal
Society memoir. More details were given in Blackett's Tizard
Lecture to the Institute for Strategic Studies in 1960, and these
were subsequently added to and popularized to form part of
Sir Charles Snow's Godkin Lectures the following year. In 1962
Lord Birkenhead, using the Cherwell archives as well as memory
and reminiscence, presented Lindemann's view of events in his
biography, *The Prof in Two Worlds*. Great controversy grew up
round the Tizard-Lindemann disagreement as revealed to the
general public by Snow's lectures. Not all of this was due to the

partisanship shown in them; at least some of the reaction from scientists reflected the view that Snow had 'brought into the open something which we always hoped would have remained concealed'. This attitude is natural, if open to criticism. All closed sects, military, scientific, and religious, prefer to keep their own private skeletons locked away from public sight. In this case the attitude gives scant regard to the millions whose lives were affected – and in some cases lost – by the war-time repercussions of the argument.

The positions from which the argument was carried on, as well as an indication of the tactics to be used by Lindemann, is revealed by a letter written early in February to Lord Swinton:

> I have been giving the question of our air defence policy very careful consideration and think it only right that I should in the first place submit my conclusions to you [this went]. I would desire to make it perfectly clear that I am writing as a private individual and taxpayer, and not as a member of the Sub-Committee working under your Department. In so far as my submissions may come within the terms of reference of the Sub-Committee I hope to carry them with me, but they have expressed no definite opinion as yet and have no responsibility whatever for anything I may say.[4]

The letter, which went on to say – quite rightly – that there was no prospect of being able to deal effectively with the individual night bomber, was a clear example of personal lobbying, but one which Lindemann no doubt felt the circumstances warranted. He took care to forestall the most obvious accusation by informing Tizard, in a letter the following day, that he had written to Swinton in his private capacity; however, he does not appear to have enclosed a copy of the letter itself.

On the personal level, matters remained quiescent until the summer. Then, on 2 June, Churchill wrote a memorandum which was circulated to the members of the Swinton Committee in preparation for their next meeting. He stated that he had pressed at an early meeting of the Committee for work to be done on aerial mines; that 'nothing was done'; and, further, that 'all sorts of difficulties were raised.' Tizard's brief comment was that short wire barrages and aerial mines had been discussed in the Tizard Committee before Churchill raised the matter and before Lindemann had joined it. 'I said', he noted later, 'the fact was that, during the summer months, continuous experimental work was going on on lines laid down by the Committee.' Churchill's memorandum had clearly been prepared from Lindemann's brief and it consisted, as all concerned realized, of a frontal attack on Tizard's work. Shortly afterwards Wimperis noted in his diary that '. . . Winston's latest will, I think, take L. off the C.A.D. [sic] – H.T. says so, anyway'.

All now appeared to be set for a major discussion in the Swinton Committee on 15 June. Before this, however, another match had been struck in the already explosive atmosphere. On 12 June Lindemann took Watson-Watt to a private meeting with Churchill at which Watson-Watt said that 'he was dissatisfied with the policy which attempted to operate the normal ministry machinery at an abnormal speed, instead of setting up new machinery designed for a normal speed greatly exceeding that which existed'.[5] For it was true that Lindemann, while pressing for more work on aerial mines was at the same time anxious to speed up development of radar. Tizard felt much the same. But while neither was an Air Ministry employee, Tizard felt it improper to utilize political lobbying. Lindemann used any weapon to hand.

Three mornings after the Watson-Watt–Lindemann–Churchill meeting, the members of the Swinton Committee gathered. 'A vehement meeting', Wimperis noted in his diary, 'controversy between Churchill on the one side and Swinton and Tizard on the other. All about Lindemann and Watt. H.T. did exceedingly well . . . Long talk with Freeman who is much incensed by Watt's having talked to Churchill against the A.M. . . . H.T. to see me later as to seeing Hill and Blackett as soon as possible – & as to the future.' The significance of this ominous comment is explained by the letter that Hill wrote to Tizard the following day. 'I fully understand your unwillingness to continue as Chairman with L. a member of the Committee', he wrote. 'If L. succeeds in getting himself made Chairman of the Committee, then I resign forthwith.'

This note might suggest that although Tizard had done 'exceedingly well' he was in fact preparing to withdraw under heavy fire. Such was not the case.

Dear Lindemann [he wrote from St James's Court, on 17 June], No doubt you already know that as a result of your personal criticism to Winston Churchill he made a written attack on the Research Committee without taking the trouble to ascertain my views first. I was obliged to answer this categorically, whereupon he followed up in Committee with other wild criticisms presumably based on information from you. Needless to say I have no objection to your discussing with him the work of the Committee – on the contrary everyone concerned would welcome this if the object were to produce fresh ideas and constructive suggestions. But if the only result is to produce ill-founded criticisms then I am bound to say that however good your ultimate motives are, the only effect of your actions is to retard progress. I should really enjoy working with you if you were ready to work as a member of a team, but if you are playing another game I don't think it is possible for us to go on collaborating without continual friction. I have told Swinton this – so you ought to know.

I wish we could have settled such differences of opinion that exist in a friendly manner in our own Committee, but you have made things very difficult, if not impossible.

I am writing a general statement about the policy underlying the priority attached to different items of our work. I will let you have this next week. If agreed by members it will be circulated to the C.I.D. Committee.

Yours sincerely,
H. T. Tizard

On the following day Tizard wrote to Swinton, proposing that Professor Appleton should join the Tizard Committee, a suggestion which had already been made by Wimperis and one which would only be implemented, one can assume, if Lindemann's presence on the Committee had somehow been eliminated.

Meanwhile, however, Lindemann had conferred with Churchill and the two men now loosed a double-barrelled attack. To Swinton, Churchill sent a more-in-sorrow-than-in-anger epistle, regretting what he called Tizard's 'very offensive letter' to Lindemann and re-iterating his own constant theme that research on air defence should be pushed on even more quickly. To Tizard, Lindemann wrote a letter on the 25th.

I thank you for your letter of the 18th June [this went]. It is obviously impossible for me to attempt to discuss statements made at the meeting of the C.I.D. Committee in my absence, but I am sure anything deriving from me was strictly accurate. If you will send me a copy of the statement of which you complain and of your 'categorical' reply I shall be glad to deal with the matter.

The point upon which we seem to be in complete disagreement is the different urgency which we attach to our endeavours to find some method to deal with air attack. Your procedure would no doubt be excellent if we had ten or fifteen years time. I believe that the period available is to be measured in months.

Apart from Watson-Watt's work you will scarcely claim that any appreciable advance towards a solution of the problem has been made since the Committee has been in being. You appear to be perfectly satisfied with this rate of progress. I am not.

In view of the immense importance of the question, and holding the views I do as to its urgency, you will not be surprised that I have used every means at my disposal to accelerate progress and that I am determined to continue to do so. I am sorry if this offends you, but the matter is too vital to justify one in refraining from action in order to salve anybody's *amour propre*.*[6]

Yours sincerely,

F. A. Lindemann

Lindemann's position was underlined in a note which he wrote to Churchill. 'My feeling', this said, 'is that if they ask me to resign, as seems not unlikely in view of Tizard's letter, this will justify me in raising cain, and might do more to accelerate work than anything else.'[7]

His premonition was justified. For Tizard, after receiving Lindemann's letter of the 23rd had sent a copy of their exchanges to Swinton, commenting: 'It is difficult to see how we can usefully remain colleagues. I can hardly call a meeting of my Committee in the circumstances: I fancy that nothing useful would be done. However I have written him a further letter, a copy of which I also enclose. If he does not respond to it I feel that I must press you to remove him, in the interests of the work.' This, due to a concatenation of circumstances, was not to be necessary.

One phrase in this further letter, written by Tizard on 5 July, crystallizes the main point at issue between the two men. Tizard believed that it was 'not for us to decide' whether the Committee should be merely advisory or should seek executive powers. Lindemann believed that it should decide.

* Lindemann drafted his letter on the 23rd and it is this draft which is quoted in Lord Birkenhead's *The Prof in Two Worlds*. The letter which Lindemann actually sent on the 25th is slightly, but not importantly, different.

Dear Lindemann [this letter said], The general statement to which I referred in my letter of 17th June has been delayed because I asked Rowe to prepare a draft for me, and he has been so busy with more important matters that he found it difficult to get down to it. However, I hope that you will get it on Wednesday.

I got your letter of the 25th June in reply to mine. You need not worry about salving my amour propre. I haven't got any. My quarrel with you is not that my dignity has been affronted, but that your way of getting on with the job is the wrong one, and that far from 'accelerating progress' you are retarding it. Of course I know you want to get on with the job, but do try to realise that other people are just as anxious about this as you are, and are really putting in just as much work. Up to now I have never heard you put forward any criticisms of the progress of the Committee's work except in relation to the work on Aerial mines. I differ from your views on this matter, and so, I believe, do the other members. But we are all quite ready to be convinced if you put forward convincing arguments. On more than one occasion I have asked you to put your scheme on paper *in detail*, but you have not yet done so. If you want to have the work pressed with greater vigour, at the expense of other important work, you must surely start by convincing willing colleagues of the wisdom of doing this, instead of complaining to other people that they are slackers, which does no good because it is so obviously false. Remember, too, that we are advisory, not executive. You may feel that this is wrong; but I do not think we can possibly be executive. In any case it is not for us to decide.

If you persist in the attitude disclosed by your letter I do not think that we can remain members of the same Committee; but do give co-operation a further trial. I am much more interested in defeating the enemy than in defeating you! Yours sincerely, H. T. Tizard.[8]

Five days later Lindemann received from Rowe the long-awaited draft report.

Dear Rowe [he replied immediately], I have just received from you the 'draft report' by the Tizard Committee. I regret to say that I disagree with a very great deal of the draft.

What I disapprove of most, however, is the procedure which has been adopted. If a report was asked for, the proper course was to call a meeting of the Committee, discuss the general tenor of the report, get a draft made and then have another meeting of the Committee to discuss the draft and if possible approve it as amended. It is quite intolerable that a draft purporting to represent the views of the Committee should be produced without these views ever having been ascertained, that it should be circulated on Friday and that we should

L

be asked to send amendments, if any, so as to reach you by the Monday, so that the report can go straight on to the main Committee. Neither the general outline of the draft nor the details are to be discussed by the Committee as a whole nor are the members to be afforded an opportunity of hearing one another's views on the various topics. As I said, I protest vigorously against this procedure. Nearly four weeks have elapsed since, as I gather, this report was asked for and there would have been ample time to have as many meetings as we required to draw up a report in consonance with the views of the various members of the Committee.

It would be almost impossible to detail all my objections to the draft and in view of what I have said I hope it is not necessary and that we shall have a proper opportunity of discussing the position before any report goes forward. If this is not to be done, I must request that a brief report I shall draw up will be circulated together with the report whose draft has been sent to me and for which I cannot accept any responsibility.

I should be glad if you would communicate my views to the proper authorities and remain with kind regards, Yours sincerely, F. A. Lindemann.[9]

However impracticable Lindemann's proposals may have been, however importunate his methods of pressing them, it is difficult not to feel that but for one fact he would have had a case worth making. But the secretariat of the Tizard Committee had in fact planned a meeting for 15 July, nine days before the 'draft report' could be considered by the Swinton Committee.

On 11 July, Lindemann was to write two more letters. Their repercussions were, between them, to help shatter the existing Tizard Committee. One letter was to Rowe, noting that he had been asked for any 'material amendments' and saying that he would prefer to substitute his own draft, of which he enclosed a copy, 'as a basis of discussion'. The second letter was to the electors of Oxford, who were now informed that Lindemann would be standing as an independent supporter of the National Government in the impending election for one of the two University seats. He was in no doubt about the implications. 'I hope', he wrote to his brother a few days later, that 'the mere fact of my standing will stir up the Air Ministry even if I should fail to get returned.'

Events were thus simmering as the members of the Committee prepared for their twentieth meeting, to be held on 15 July. The evening before, Tizard called on Wimperis at his Chelsea home where they had 'a long talk over Air Defence matters so as to be ready for the morrow'.

Any hope that the critical meeting might pass off without major dissension was diminished by the morning's papers, which made it quite clear that one of the main planks in Lindemann's electoral platform was to be the state of the country's air defences. This development, as well as the Progress Report and Lindemann's suggestion that he might write for the Swinton Committee a minority note on it, were all discussed and in the words of a subsequent letter from Rowe, Tizard himself 'advised Professor Lindemann to write such a note if he wished'. Then the meeting broke up, if not in disorder at least in such a state that both Hill and Blackett were determined to resign.

Hill went immediately to the Athenaeum and there drafted a letter to Swinton.

> Dear Lord Swinton [it stated], I was present this morning at a meeting of the Committee for the Scientific Survey of Air Defence, at which a Report of the Committee was discussed. Prof. Lindemann raised various objections to the Report & finally his own relations with the Committee and with Mr Winston Churchill were considered. You know the whole story, but my view of it is as follows. Instead of being frank and open with his colleagues & the Chairman he went behind their backs & adopted methods of pushing his own opinions which – apart from anything else – would make further cooperation with him very difficult. It is clear, moreover, from paragraphs in this morning's Press, in reference to Prof. Lindemann's candidature for Oxford University, that he intends to use any available method of advertising the unique value of his opinions; & no doubt, to use his membership of the Committee, while criticising it behind its back, as a means to his own ends. The other members of the Committee are only anxious to work as quietly & efficiently as possible, & to avoid publicity of any kind, which can only be harmful in such work as we are undertaking.
>
> The very undesirable publicity of 1935 was directly due to Prof. L. & his friends. Under the circumstances I regret that, so long as Professor Lindemann remains a member of the Committee, it will be impossible for me to serve on it. I have nothing but admiration for the work of the Chairman: and in all other respects my relations with the Committee have been entirely happy. Various important applications are in view, & many preliminary difficulties in the way of

further progress have been got over. It is clear, however, after the unpleasantness which culminated in this morning's meeting, that the Committee cannot go on as it is, & I wish to place my resignation in your hands.

I write to you personally, so that you may know at once what the reasons are for a decision which, on every other ground, I regret. I have informed the Chairman that I am writing to you in this sense. Yours sincerely, A. V. Hill.[10]

The position was now fluid. Wimperis had gone home from the Air Ministry that evening uncertain if Lindemann would carry out his threat to write a Minority Note – and no doubt anxious as to what might soon be heard from the election platform. Tizard, acknowledging Hill's account of his resignation, appears to have been equally uncertain. 'We are in a strong position' he wrote, 'for we want to do a useful job of work, we don't want notoriety, we don't advertise, and we don't mind if the Government decide they would rather do without us.' This was unlikely –

I very much hope that you will continue that work, which is becoming more important, and I think more fruitful, all the time [Swinton wrote to Hill on the 16th].

Nevertheless, there did remain the possibility of the Government doing without them, and Tizard can hardly have been reassured when he heard from Rowe on the 21st of Lindemann's Minority Note. This was, he was informed,

much more restrained than the one he prepared for circulation to members of your Committee, and it seems as well to regard it possible that some of the members of the A.D.R. Sub-Committee will think he has made some kind of a case for parallel action upon location methods and on methods for destroying aircraft.[11]

In this critical situation, Hill and Blackett – who had also resigned – stood firm, seeing Swinton for an hour and a half on 22 July and leaving him in no doubt as to their positions. 'Poor man', Hill wrote to Tizard the following day, 'he *is* in rather a fix, but he had better get out of it now, rather than later. He understands that our refusal to continue to serve with L. is quite definite; and – as he says – he absolutely refuses to accept our resignations: so there we are . . .'[12]

The situation was resolved on the 24th when the Swinton Committee met for the tenth time. The chairman read the letters he had received from Hill and from Blackett who, according to a later note by Tizard, 'said that his views as to the best procedure of expediting the study of air defence differed so widely from those of Lindemann that he felt further work together would be too difficult to be fruitful'. Tizard put his case to the Committee – 'strong enough to make C. conciliatory: a great change from the aggression of the previous meeting', Wimperis wrote in his diary – and the general feeling was, in the words of Tizard's later comment, 'that there would be no course but to reconstitute the Committee of members who could work effectively together.' It was, Wimperis noted, 'a useful, peaceful meeting. Winston in a chastened mood'.

In addition to cutting through this knot of personalities which had brought the work of the Tizard Committee to a standstill, the Swinton Committee also took note of the Progress Report and of Lindemann's Minority Note on it. That the differences in these were rooted in the Committee's concentration on the day-raider, and in Lindemann's concern with the possibility of heavy night attack, is implied by the brief summaries of each which Tizard himself later made; so is the question mark which at this date still remained against the value of radar. The contents of the Committee's Report, Tizard describes as follows:

> The probability of interception of hostile aircraft by defending aircraft when visibility is bad was still small. The existing means of tracking and intercepting hostile aircraft had not been adequately tested. In the opinion of the Committee the efficacy of this means will remain unknown until the results of a number of exercises have been scientifically analysed.* The practicability of fitting aircraft with radio equipment enabling them to home on hostile aircraft was being investigated with considerable hope of success. The balloon barrage was considered to be the only defensive measure independent of location of enemy aircraft which could be available in the near future.

Lindemann's Note, Tizard commented, said that the Progress Report 'led to the completely novel conclusion, from which he

---

* These formed the 'Biggin Hill Experiment' described on pp. 149–156.

dissented very strongly, that work on aerial mines need not be of the highest priority'.*

The digestion of these delicate personal and difficult technical questions by the Swinton Committee continued during a quiescent six weeks. Not until 3 September did Swinton inform Lindemann that he had received the resignation of three of the non-Air Ministry members of the Committee, and therefore had no choice but to dissolve it. The third resignation came from Tizard himself, but this was a formality, since few people can have known better what was to follow. Six days later, Swinton informed him that he proposed to reconstitute the Tizard Committee in accordance with the decision of the Swinton Committee, which the Cabinet had now approved.

Lindemann, however, was not a man to give up easily. Acknowledging Swinton's news that the old committee was to be dissolved, but not yet knowing of its reconstitution, he concluded his letter by saying that

> in the circumstances I hope you will agree that I was justified in pressing for greater speed and drive. The whole of this work was being carried out in a half-hearted manner, and I can only trust that you will take this opportunity to reorganize it, and see that a new spirit is brought into play. As you know, I have never been enamoured of the lines on which it was being run, and I trust that the dissolution of the Committee portends that this extremely important work will now be pursued more effectively and with due energy.[13]

He knew that he was out – for the time being at least. But, like Churchill, he relished the battle.

Within a fortnight, on 8 October, the Tizard Committee, reconstituted on the lines that Tizard himself had suggested, with Blackett and Hill re-appointed, met once again. 'Lindemann not present, Appleton added to Committee', he later noted. 'Much better discussion.' He had nerved himself for the struggle, had

---

* Disagreement arose on the question of 'highest priority' rather than on the merits of aerial mines themselves. Almost exactly three years later, on 13 April 1939, the Tizard Committee did, in fact, agree that in certain circumstances such weapons appeared to have advantages; and recommended that early consideration should be given to their production and the provision of suitable minelaying aircraft. Two months later it repeated the recommendation.

fought the good fight and had won. Now he could go on, with increased confidence and vigour.

Thus was the matter arranged. It is quite clear from the documents that the priority to be assigned to methods of attack as distinct from location was only one of the issues which contributed to the break-up and reconstitution of the Tizard Committee, and to the lasting schism which it created, with all that that was to mean for the conduct of the coming war. Tizard, it is true, stood for a calculated, concentrated, attack on location, which for most practical purposes meant radar; Lindemann, in the words of Rowe's note to Tizard, 'for parallel action upon location methods and on methods of destroying aircraft'. Tizard urged concentration on the day-threat; Lindemann wanted, in effect, to deal with the night-attack simultaneously, a matter of priorities on which Tizard was obviously correct. Both assumed, it appears, that money, men, and materials could be spared to keep the country safe only by night or by day – a verdict which even on the Baldwin Government seems hard, though no doubt justified. Yet this issue of priority was overshadowed by two others. There was first the status of the Tizard Committee itself, which Lindemann felt to be too low and which he believed should be raised. Support for this view can be found in many quarters, and Professor Hill himself wrote to Tizard at the height of the argument on 16 June 1936, saying he was 'convinced that the Committee, through no fault of yours, has failed as yet to achieve what it ought to have achieved owing to our inability to get large-scale trials carried out, involving the extensive use of Service aircraft'.[14] The same theme runs through much of Tizard's own correspondence. Even more important was the difference between Lindemann's views of how this handicap should be overcome and the views of other members of the Committee. Tizard believed that it was 'not for us to decide' on the matter of pressing for executive power. Lindemann felt that the position was too serious for scientists to abide by the normal rules of conduct. In this he might well have gained support had it not been for his own personal failure in this particular exercise in human relationships, a failure which was so largely responsible for the foundering of the original Tizard Committee.

However, the purely personal issue cannot be dissociated from the future of radar, although for reasons more complex than have so far been suggested. Had Lindemann contrived to seize control of the Tizard Committee it seems certain that the purely technical development of radar would have been pressed on with as much speed and urgency as could be mustered. Watson-Watt, apart from anyone else, would have seen to that. But something would have been lacking. Without Tizard at the helm, the integration of the developing system into the operations of the Royal Air Force must have been left to others less experienced, less competent, less able to get scientists and Servicemen hammering out, round a table, the best practical answer to the current problem. It might even have been left to Lindemann who could charm birds out of trees when he wanted, but who also had an incomparable facility for doing the reverse. Had Lindemann been 'in' rather than 'out' during the crucial period between September 1936 and the autumn of 1938, it is likely that Bomber Command would have entered the war less ludicrously ill-equipped for the task in hand. But unless he had sprouted a hitherto concealed genius for marrying up the scientific and the operational, radar could hardly have been integrated into Fighter Command in time for the trial of 1940. Without that, the Battle of Britain would have been lost.

CHAPTER SEVEN

Biggin Hill

The year and a half which followed the reconstitution of the Committee for the Scientific Survey of Air Defence witnessed the greatest achievement of Tizard's life. This was the transformation of the purely scientific wizardry of radar into a complex early warning system which could be used by Controllers on the ground and by pilots in the air, under the pressures of wartime confusion, in battle. Others had pulled radar out of the scientific bag at the eleventh hour; a few had seen with Tizard that only this device offered a chance of salvation in the crisis that loomed ahead. Only he, due to the chances of history, could explain, to slightly sceptical air-crew, what this new weapon really was and how it could do so much to bring the armament of the few level with that of the many. He was not, in the conventional sense, a religious man; but during this period, as events marched on from the occupation of the Rhineland towards the humiliation of Munich, he may sometimes have felt, as Montgomery felt when he flew to command the Eighth Army in 1942, that here at last was the task to which all circumstance had driven him.

By the summer of 1936 he had become optimistic that the experimental radar equipment then operating at Bawdsey could give viewers on the ground a continuous stream of visual information; information which would reveal the bearing, distance, and height of aircraft approaching the coast and from which it would be possible to estimate their speed and direction of flight. This was immeasurably more useful both in accuracy and in range than even the best results provided by sound-location. Yet it was, so far as the defence of Britain was concerned, a solution to only half of the problem, and it was in the realization of this fact that Tizard now showed his genius. The main operational value of an adequate warning and tracking system could be the elimination of standing patrols, with the resulting conservation of men and planes. But this could only be exploited to the full if some completely new technique of interception were devised; and it would, Tizard knew, be unrealistic to hope that this could happen amid the confusions of war. A peacetime experiment was therefore necessary.

Biggin Hill, the station chosen for this, lay on one of the main air routes between the Continent and London. It had already been the site of interception experiments carried out for the Air Defence of Great Britain with the aid of radio-direction-finding equipment, and on 13 July 1936 Tizard outlined to a number of senior R.A.F. officers in the Air Ministry his proposals for what became known as 'the Biggin Hill Experiment'.

He began by explaining that men on the ground could now be given warning of approaching aircraft when these were up to seventy-five miles away. And he proposed a series of experiments to discover two things: the percentage of occasions on which fighter-interceptions would be expected by day if the position of the raiding aircraft could be known at regular intervals with increasing accuracy as it approached the coast; and how close to a bomber – whose position and track had been found from the ground – it was possible to direct a fighter by the use of radio instructions from the ground. To many senior officers the proposals were novel if not revolutionary; to others they seemed a waste of time. In spite of the somewhat casual reception of the idea, Tizard succeeded in convincing the authorities that the experiments should be carried out. It was agreed that they should start on 4 August 1936, and last for two months.[1]

A squadron of Gloster Gauntlets (No. 32) was to be used for interception, while three Hawker Hinds were to simulate the raiding bombers. Rowe meanwhile discovered in Dr B. G. Dickins, a young man then working on engineering problems at Farnborough, a suitable scientific officer to supervise the day-to-day working of the scheme. Early in August Dickins arrived at Biggin Hill, as did Squadron-Leader R. L. Ragg, an experienced navigator and a former experimental pilot also from Farnborough, now seconded for the experiment. Neither Dickins nor Ragg, neither Flight-Lieutenant W. P. G. Pretty, the Station Signals Officer, nor Wing Commander E. O. Grenfell, the Station Commander, knew the object of the experiment until Tizard arrived. He explained that it might be possible for a station on the ground to get a fifteen-minute warning of enemy planes approaching the coast, together with approximate details of their height, speed and course – and the information might be brought up-to-date at five-minute intervals. Given this information, how would they set about planning fighter interceptions?

To solve the problem, up to five trial interceptions were made each day. The Hawker Hinds would simulate the bombers while Squadron-Leader McDonald of No. 32 Squadron would then be ordered off by Grenfell on a course that would be changed by radio instructions at five minute intervals. Interceptions were made in all weathers and with varying success, but for the first fortnight the whole experiment was limited by the fact that Tizard was forbidden to reveal the existence of radar – and thus explain that in practice information would, it was hoped, be available not at five-minute intervals but in a continuous stream. Within a few weeks the team was getting nearly 100 per cent interceptions. These were all being obtained, however, with bombers that continued on their first reported course, a circumstance unlikely under operational conditions. The experiments were therefore changed, with the result that success was greatly reduced. The cause of the trouble was that when the bombers were routed on to a new course, the fighter's interception course had to be recalculated – and the time taken for this drastically reduced the chance of interception.

It was here that Tizard's peculiar mixture of scientific awareness and Service experience came into play. In this case it was a combination of simple geometry and the knowledge that fighters fly faster than bombers, and it produced the beguilingly simple 'principle of Equal Angles' which, as Tizard noted to David Pye some five years later, was 'still irreverently and flatteringly known in some squadrons as the "Tizzy Angle" '. Tizard pointed out that once the bombers' course had been changed it was only necessary to draw a line between the bombers and the fighters and to use this as the base-line of an isosceles triangle. The bombers' new line of flight formed the second side of the triangle and the fighters best interception course formed the third. This course might have to be altered when fresh information arrived, but the fighters would always reach their rendezvous before the bombers. Later in the experiments it was found by Grenfell that the 'Tizzy Angle' did not necessarily have to be computed and worked out on paper. A controller watching the plots of the bombers and fighters' courses, as these were marked on the map, was able to judge the angle by eye, the minor errors involved being more than counterbalanced by the increased speed with which instructions could be radioed to the fighter.*

Tizard maintained close contact with the experiments and he also flew as an observer in the 'bombers' on one or two occasions. There were two reasons for this. As a scientist he wished to check how accurately their actual position in the air matched up with their positions as plotted at Biggin Hill. Secondly, just as typically, and possibly of even more importance, he wished to show the air crews of No. 32 Squadron that while this radically new system of interception was being tested by a scientist, the scientist was himself a flying man. He knew the problems and dangers involved. He spoke their language. He could be trusted. Although he was in his fifties, the head of a College, a man from a world very different from that of most flying men, in spite of all this, they found him worth listening to. In fact, if war really came, they realized that there might even be something of value in this new and somewhat alarming system which appeared to strip a pilot of initiative and place him under the control of some elderly gentleman on the ground.

This question of control from the ground was, in these early days, perhaps as big a hurdle to be overcome as the basic problem of making non-scientists believe that a defence system could be based on invisible rays that travelled as fast as light. The fact that radio direction-finding systems could pin-point a plane's position more accurately than any system of dead reckoning was, perhaps

---

* The discovery that the 'Tizzy Angle' could be estimated was quite accidental. During one particular run a mistake was made in working out the answer and in desperation Grenfell judged it by eye. This resulted in a successful interception and Ragg and Dickins quickly realized that this was the way to decide upon the angle.

a little grudgingly in some cases, now being accepted. But the new system being evolved at Biggin Hill did something considerably more drastic since it meant that the fighter pilot, the ultimate personification of Yeats's airman with his 'lonely impulse of delight', was now to be ordered about the sky in a way totally new to him. Tizard, with his instinctive understanding of how flying men thought, and his ability in oiling the machinery of human relations, did more than any other man to make the new system acceptable.

However, six weeks after the start of the Biggin Hill experiment, his hopes for radar received a brusque shock. So brusque that in mid-September, two months after the break-up of the original Tizard Committee, he felt that he might, under some circumstances, have to 'dissuade the Air Ministry' from continuing work on the radar chain. This grave, and potentially disastrous, possibility was raised by the poor results at the start of an Air Exercise carried out in the third week of September.

> To say that I was disappointed on Thursday is to put it very mildly [Tizard wrote to Watson-Watt on 20 September]. As you put it yourself, you have to face the fact that very little progress in achievement has been made for a year. I am surprised that you encouraged – indeed proposed – the September exercises. Unless very different results are obtained soon I shall have to dissuade the Air Ministry from putting up other stations. The Secretary of State must have got a very bad impression. What particularly disturbs me is that there seems to have been a lack of good judgement on your part. You have had good results in the past, but there has been little effort to ensure that those results are repeatable, before going on to get better results. Although the transmitter was blamed for Thursday's fiasco it seemed to me that you had no evidence for this. Surely it is not difficult to get a sufficiently accurate measure of the energy emitted on the right wave-length on every occasion when the transmitter is operated? If so, I don't understand why this was not done long ago. Also why you should court failure by running your valves at full power when you can only get a mile or so extra range by doing so, is beyond my comprehension. I think that it is of the utmost importance that you should find the real reason for these irregular results as soon as possible.
>
> I am sorry to write like this, but it will not help you if I conceal my feelings. A great deal depends on your work.

However, there was a recovery later in the Exercise, and after it was over Tizard wrote to Watson-Watt saying Joubert had told him that 'if we could always guarantee results as good as on the last two days of the Exercise, he would have almost as much information as he needed, provided he could get height'.[2]

Tizard may well have over-emphasized his concern. But it must have come as a startling shock to discover that perhaps, after all, the technical development of radar could be pressed so far and no farther. This was particularly discouraging since the Biggin Hill experiments were by this time showing better results than the Air Ministry appears to have expected, and Tizard was able to report to the Swinton Committee in November that even when fighters were navigated by dead reckoning alone, interceptions could be made in 85 per cent of the trials.

It was agreed to continue the experiments, while Dowding, by now Commander-in-Chief, Fighter Command, arranged that all other sectors would start practising the new methods. These continued to evolve during the first months of 1937, and on Tizard's suggestion attempts were made to intercept not the Hawker Hinds but civilian airliners making for Croydon from the Continent. The innovation was useful, since first attempts showed up the peculiar difficulties of interception under certain specific conditions. The eventual success of the whole series of experiments was emphasized in a note by the Air Staff on 1 July 1937 which, according to Tizard, concluded 'that the trials have shown that RDF gives very important information which could not be obtained by any other means and which is essential to the successful operation of fighters'.

Meanwhile, the system of ground control was being radically overhauled. It was found that when the horizontal blackboard first used to plot courses was replaced by a vertical ground glass screen, the whole system could be streamlined. The positions of raiders and fighters could be plotted from behind this screen by the use of numbered and differently coloured suction pads, and the increased ease of operation allowed one controller to handle at least two and up to four, interceptions simultaneously.* At the

* The actual screen used in the Biggin Hill experiments was destroyed only during the Battle of Britain when a bomb knocked out the Operations Room. This was the only Sector in which the ground glass screen was adopted, Fighter Command preferring to use a single plotting table for each interception.

same time a code was evolved by which instructions could be passed to the fighters with the minimum delay – and such R.A.F. terms as 'scramble' (for take-off), 'vector' (for course to steer), 'angels' (for height) and 'pancake' (for land) were all introduced.

Thus there grew up, between the summer of 1936 and that of 1937 the basic technique of operational control without which the Battle of Britain would not have been won and could hardly have been fought. It is ironic that the Biggin Hill experiment which made this possible was – like so much of Tizard's work – started with only tepid official support. This fact was underlined when a further continuation of the experiments was proposed in March 1937. 'Although the initiation of these experiments came from Sir Henry Tizard, I have always felt that the experiments were more of an operational than a research or scientific character', the Air Member for Research and Development, Air Vice-Marshal Freeman wrote to the Deputy Chief of Air Staff on 9 March. 'I have rather felt that the experiments have been urged on at the instigation of scientists, when the initiation should, in fact, if there is any prospect of their success, come from the Air Staff'. The D.C.A.S. replied six days later, noting that, so far as the Air Staff was concerned, the experiments had never, in fact, been official. But they should be continued. And to stress that they now really were being carried out they would, from 24 March, come formally under the executive control of Fighter Command.[3] The work went on until November 1937, but before this it was running into the problem of alleged interference with training, and in August Fighter Command warned Biggin Hill that the scientific experiments were prejudicing the training of the unit stationed there. Tizard, hearing the news, suggested that the Station Commander should offer to test the unit against any other, at short notice. From this period onwards it became evident that a solution had been found to the problem of flying standing patrols for which there were neither enough pilots nor enough planes. After the lapse of a few dangerous years, the air defence of Britain had become once again more than a theoretical possibility.

It is interesting to note that of those who took part in the Biggin Hill experiment, Ragg, Pretty and Mcdonald all rose to the rank of Air Vice-Marshal while Dickins has occupied a long series of important posts in the scientific administration of defence. At first it is easy to believe that Tizard picked his men well; yet their choice was out of his hands; and it is perhaps more accurate to say, instead, that all, able men to start with, benefited from the douche of friendly but cold common-sense that he administered to most of those with whom he worked.

*   *   *

By the autumn of 1937, it thus appeared that with continued progress, good luck and sufficient time – that commodity to be so dearly bought with honour at Munich – there was a steadily growing possibility that the battle against the day bomber could be won. If this was not so, further argument would be unnecessary. If it was, there seemed little doubt that the enemy would turn to night attack. Against this, the possibilities of defence were still uncertain, disputed, and extremely costly. This question of hard cash, and the extent to which it continued to hamper the application of the Tizard Committee's research work, is revealed by a note from Neville Chamberlain, then Chancellor of the Exchequer, written to Swinton on 4 April 1937 on the balloon barrage, a method of defence which it had been agreed could provide protection for the larger cities. Chamberlain, alarmed at the cost of the London defences, wanted no further extension of the scheme to other areas without full consideration. He suggested that the money involved should be carefully scrutinised by the air defence experts, and that they should take into account the possibilities of reducing the cost without 'seriously' impairing the defensive qualities of the barrage.[4] It is easy to imagine that Tizard's reaction would have been to ask, without the trace of a smile, 'How seriously?'

The balloon barrage, however, was merely one scheme, and further research had now enabled Tizard to turn a less critical eye to at least some of Lindemann's proposals. 'Now that Farnborough have developed a practical breaking link we must consider seriously the possibility of dropping long lengths of wire, say 1,000 feet, with bombs at intervals and a parachute at one end, in front of advancing bombers', he wrote. 'The old idea of 100 feet lengths of bolasses was, I feel sure, quite unpractical, but if

1,000 feet lengths could be dropped I think the scheme gets much more practicable.'

As far as night attack was concerned, even interception was still – and was to remain for another four years – a nagging problem whose solution appeared to lie mainly in the hopes held out by either infra-red detection or by airborne radar. Jones's infra-red efforts in the Clarendon Laboratory appeared to give only inconclusive results. Even so, in April an airborne infra-red device detected another plane in flight at a range of 500 metres, and it still seemed that the disadvantages of the system might perhaps be less than problems of devising radar equipment small enough and light enough to be carried in a fighter.

In June, Tizard recommended that the experiments which Jones was conducting at Oxford 'should continue in the hope that they will have an application to air defence other than the detection of aircraft from the air' – apparently a reference to Tizard's scheme for the bombing of large ships by making use of the infra-red transmissions in the funnel and an automatic infra-red control on the bombs. The two men met in the autumn – after Tizard, at the thirty-fifth meeting of his Committee on 27 October had agreed to discuss with Jones the possibility of his leaving the Clarendon. 'I have been expecting to hear from you as a result of our talk the other day', he subsequently wrote. 'I want to know in particular what you think of the idea of moving your work to London. I do not think the work can go on for very long at Oxford and the alternatives are probably London, Bawdsey or Farnborough.' Jones replied that 'it would probably help in reaching a wise decision if you could possibly come and see our establishment at work. Lindemann would tactfully arrange to be out of the way. Alternatively, perhaps D.S.R. (Pye) might come, as Lindemann has no quarrel with him.'⁵ The visit was never made and Jones remained at Oxford until, roughly a year later, he was formally transferred to the Admiralty and, on Tizard's suggestion, was later made responsible for providing the Air Ministry with information on German scientific developments; a move which was fortuitously to bring about a crisis in Tizard's work.

Throughout 1937 it became increasingly clear that any hope of night interception must be based on airborne radar. There has

M

been bitter dispute about the genesis of many radar systems and
the story of this one is not immune from them, even though there
is no doubt about the seminal part played by Tizard himself. This
is not unnatural, since ideas may arise simultaneously in different
places; a scientific sugggestion may be transmuted by operational
need; a Service request may be altered by the scientists almost
out of recognition before it becomes effective; and since a backward glance to a period of great stress provides ample enough
chance for genuine mistake and misunderstanding.

The lion's share of the technical work in creating airborne radar
was carried out by E. G. Bowen, a young physicist who had been
one of the first recruits to Bawdsey. 'But it was Tizard', he says,
'who had the broad concept.' This had been developed during
the closing months of 1935 as Tizard realized that although the
technical problem of interception by day might be solved, the
night problem would still remain. This was at the same time being
mulled over by Watson-Watt, although in a scientific rather than
operational context, and the whole proposition was discussed at a
meeting of the Tizard Committee on 2 February 1936. 'Tizard
was in fact the one who in 1936 first suggested that an attempt be
made to make a radar set small enough to go into an aircraft',
writes Bowen. 'As usual, his reasoning was crystal clear, and a
beautiful example of how he always anticipated future events. He
argued as follows. The success of early warning radar meant that
the German daylight attack would be beaten back – as it certainly was in the Battle of Britain. They would then turn to night
bombing. Under these conditions, ground control could put the
fighters within three or four miles of the bomber, but the fighters
could not see them until they were within 500 or 1,000 feet.'

The first crude set was installed by Bowen's group in a Heyford,
with the aerials extending between the wheels. Later equipment
was fitted to an Anson, with the transmitting aerial poking through
the escape hatch while the receiving aerial remained inside the
aircraft. These planes operated from Martlesham Heath where
Tizard visited them as soon as the work produced results. 'I have
a vivid recollection of the occasion', says Bowen, 'of how we gave
him a convincing demonstration, then got ourselves lost over the
North Sea and finally felt our way back to Martlesham along the

East Coast in some atrocious weather.' About a year later Lindemann also was given a demonstration, and it is explanatory of
much that he should have left such a different impression on the
same observer. 'Although the demonstration went off extremely
well', writes Bowen, 'and we went out of our way to fly him to a
destination near London so that he could keep a dinner engagement, he seemed rather peeved about the whole thing, and generally gave the impression that it was a bit of a fraud.'[6]

From this need for the night fighter to find his quarry in the
immensity of space there grew the air-to-surface equipment which
was to play such a crucial part in winning the Battle of the
Atlantic. For in the autumn of 1937 – stimulated, apparently by
the promptings both of Joubert, by now A.O.C.-in-C. Coastal
Command, and of Tizard, the Bawdsey team installed special
equipment in an Anson. Early in September Tizard enquired
what had happened. The report he received was an exciting one.
On the evening of 3 September, the Home Fleet had been passed
through the Straits of Dover on its passage to Invergordon.
Unknown to its Commander, Anson K 6260 took off from
Martlesham Heath, flew through the Straits, and followed the
south coast. At 18.50 H.M.S. *Rodney* and H.M.S. *Courageous* were
picked up on the radar screen and intercepted ten miles south-
west of Beachy Head. 'Several flights were made broadside and
end-on to Rodney and Courageous at 1,500 ft', Tizard was informed, 'and echoes were observed.' The following day even
better results were obtained, the cathode tube in the Anson
showing distinctive blips not only from H.M.S. *Courageous*, but
also from escorting destroyers. This test also gave the hope not
only of significant detection of ships at sea, but that airborne
radar might provide information at distances less than those of the
height at which the search aircraft were flying – something which
had so far been barred by technical difficulties.

Yet there still seemed little prospect of a night fighter being
provided, in time, with a satisfactory 'smeller', as Churchill had
dubbed the prototype, – officially known as R.D.F. 2.

My thoughts are mainly occupied with the night problem now
[Tizard wrote to Dowding on 7 February 1939]. I believe that, given
machines, the training and the organisation, we may optimistically

regard the day problems in process of being solved in the sense that it will prove too expensive for an enemy to carry out constant day attacks of any magnitude. But the night problem is different and more serious, and we do want much more experiments.

Three weeks later he wrote to Rowe, by this time Superintendent of Bawdsey in place of Watson-Watt who had reached the Air Ministry as Director of Communications Development.

We must keep it in our heads all the time that the present chance of intercepting machines at night is very small. You might easily put up the chance several times even by a rudimentary R.D.F. 2.

This plea for more research into defence against the night bomber had been urged by Tizard from 1937 onwards. He also maintained interest in the chain of warning stations by this time being extended to cover the whole south and east coasts. And he was increasingly preoccupied with multiple minor problems arising from the Biggin Hill experiment. For its lessons were now being applied throughout Fighter Command and as this was done Tizard frequently found himself regarded not merely as an outside adviser but as official Scientific Adviser to the Air Ministry.

All this, it might well be thought, would have been enough for any man. However, it must be remembered that he was simultaneously carrying on with his rectorial duties at Imperial College. By a masterly sleight of hand he appears to have so organized his life that few colleagues realized the extent of his work elsewhere, and only in the Governing Body had these been discussed, almost certainly at Tizard's own suggestion. Here the Chairman, Lord Rayleigh, had referred on 20 November 1936 to his work for Government departments. For Tizard had realized that with radar over the first experimental hump, his defence work would surely increase; and he had told Rayleigh that he could not continue this without the full knowledge and consent of the Governing Body. On Rayleigh's suggestion a Committee composed of himself, Sir Herbert Read, Sir Herbert Wright, Lord Falmouth and Mr Prideaux, was therefore appointed to give such advice or direction as might be necessary. Four months later the Rector's Committee, as it was called, reported that its members had considered a confidential statement from Tizard and were satisfied that there was no serious danger of his valuable work interfering with College duties. Thus matters remained until early 1939, when it was arranged that a payment should be made by the Air Ministry to the College, thus enabling it to appoint the retired Professor J. C. Philip as Deputy Rector.

So far, so good. But by early 1937 Tizard was already directing yet another line of Service research. Until this date it had no doubt been natural that his thought and energy should be concentrated on solving the over-riding problem of air defence. Now, however, there came the first faint misgivings that all was not well with Britain's own offensive air arm, formed in July 1936 as Bomber Command. Here much was exceedingly ill. Since the end of the First World War there had been a decent public revulsion against the bombing of all except the most obvious military targets. There had been scepticism in both the Admiralty and the War Office of what could, in any case, be achieved by such an untried method of waging war as an all-out bomber offensive. Money, men, and materials – as well as the services of such men as Tizard – had all been short, and it was no doubt good judgement to concentrate them first on the all-important defence of the island base. Yet the result was that Bomber Command was to enter the war in September 1939 un-equipped with adequate methods for reaching their targets, or for destroying them if they were lucky enough to reach them. 'Nothing had been done by experiment to discover what the difficulties really were', Tizard later wrote of the position in the summer of 1939, 'and it took over two years of war and the loss of the most valuable lives and aircraft to discover this.'[7]

The idea for a Committee for the Scientific Survey of Air Offence, as it was to be called, came from Wimperis, who submitted a scheme to Swinton in the late autumn of 1936. On 17 November Swinton wrote to Tizard asking whether he would be prepared to chair the new committee, whose terms of reference would be: 'To consider how far recent advances in scientific and technical knowledge can be used to strengthen present methods of offence in the Royal Air Force.' A few days later he replied to Tizard's acceptance, writing: 'I am terribly grateful to you. I seem to put more and more on you, and you always come up smiling; but you have got the confidence of all the Services in a unique way.'[8]

Wimperis and his deputy David Pye; A. P. Rowe; and Professor Melvill Jones, who had been Tizard's deputy at the Air Ministry in 1918, all became members of the new committee, the scope of which was further defined by Wimperis in a letter to Tizard of 7 January 1937. 'As the Offence and the Defence Committees will have quite separate and different channels of reporting' – the first being direct to the Air Ministry and the second to the Committee of Imperial Defence – 'it will be necessary to preserve a boundary line between their fields of activity', Wimperis wrote. 'I suggest that detection and location and the putting up of barriers is work for the Defence Committee, whereas the Offence Committee would deal with any active means, such as gunnery or bombing, which R.A.F. machines might have occasion to use in this country or elsewhere.'[9]

Tizard's records provide many indications of his long uphill struggle to secure adequate attention for such problems of attack. 'We first met nearly a year ago, in November last', he wrote to Freeman on 7 October 1937. 'Since then we have had six other meetings and some interesting discussion covering a wide range of subjects, but time goes on, and it seems extremely difficult to get some experimental work carried out. . . . I know of course about all the difficulties of providing for everybody's urgent needs and I do not in the least want to appear to be dictating on matters of policy. All I want is to make it quite clear that the scientific people cannot really discharge the responsibility put upon them unless the Experimental Departments get the equipment they need.'

By the following year it was becoming clear that in spite of the revolution which the original Tizard Committee had achieved, the official machinery could not yet cope with scientific advice on offence. On 12 November 1938 Tizard met Freeman, Sholto Douglas, then Assistant Chief of Air Staff, Tedder, Director-General Research and Development, and David Pye. 'I said', he later recorded, 'that if the Offence Committee were not going to be fully informed, and if their advice was not going to be sought, it would be much better if the Committee ceased to exist. I knew nothing of what was going on on the Fighting Committee, and nothing of the problems of the Bomber Command. We had given advice about grouping of guns and it did not appear to be followed. We had not been told the reasons.'

It was probably inevitable that Tizard should hammer away in vain. His Offence Committee, like the original Tizard Committee, was purely advisory and had been called into being to cope with a problem less obvious and less pressing than the desperate defence problem of 1935. Executive power lay in the hands first of Wimperis and then of David Pye, who succeeded him late in 1937; both able men but neither of them a Tizard – who must more than once have looked back with mixed feelings towards 1924 and his decision to refuse what might have been a key post in the Air Ministry. It was probably inevitable. But the result was, as Tizard later wrote, that Britain started the war 'with the most inadequate bombs, with rudimentary ideas of accurate bombing under conditions of war, with little, if any experience of the problems of flying in a "black-out", which might have been acquired at many places in the Empire, and with a fixed idea that Bomber Command would have to rely on sextant navigation over Germany, because any form of radio navigation would be dangerous.'[10]

It was not possible to do everything. But between the summers of 1935 and 1936 radar had become a practical scientific possibility. Between the summer of 1936 and the end of 1937 its transformation from a scientific into an operational system was half accomplished. Twenty-one months still remained before the outbreak of war.

CHAPTER EIGHT

The Last Months
of Peace

Tizard paid his own personal price for his concentration on the problems of defence during these critical years before the war. He had always been a man to draw down a curtain between his public and his private life, and although a few of his scientific colleagues – Harry Ricardo, David Pye, Harry Wimperis, for instance – were frequent visitors to his home, there was not the mingling of work and leisure that makes for a completely happy existence. Now, from the autumn of 1936 onwards, work began to claim more of his time, his energy and his thoughts. His visits to Keston became less frequent, the daily diary even more full of small pencilled times which showed appointments at committees, conferences, receptions, or with one of those quiet effective men with whom one could, after dinner at the Athenaeum, settle down in the library to discover just what could really be done about the latest worrying problem.

Yet in spite of his preoccupation with defence, he still managed to find time for an astonishing amount of other 'business' activity. He spent a busy life as Rector of Imperial College. He found time to see through the press the massive *Science of Petroleum* of which he was co-editor. In March, 1939, he gave the Rutherford Memorial Lecture to the Chemical Society, an address which involved, quite apart from much else, considerable difficult research into Rutherford's early life. He was a Trustee of the British Museum, and a Development Commissioner. He played a part in the work of such bodies as the Association of University Teachers, where his interventions could be embarrassingly unpredictable. Thus at a Conference of the Association held in May 1939, to discuss University salaries, he disconcerted listeners by claiming that more public funds were spent on each University science student in

Britain than anywhere else in the world, and that 'If more money was to come from public sources a strong case would have to be made out'. Twenty years later the memory remained among some of those present that he had 'more or less torpedoed an important part' of the Conference.

Tizard was considered for high office more than once, and might well have gained it but for his growing defence responsibilities. In the summer of 1938 there were rumours that he might be picked to succeed Sir John Reith as Director-General of the B.B.C. His interest in the Corporation was educational rather than scientific and after the report of the Ullswater Committee in 1936 he had prophesied that the coming of broadcasting might be recognized in time to be as important as that of the printing press. This, he maintained, was one reason why the Minister concerned with policy should be 'a Minister of Cabinet rank with a seat in the House of Commons, rather than the Postmaster-General who is primarily concerned with the running of a vast commercial undertaking'. It is not clear how seriously Tizard's name was considered for the post of Director-General, but he felt it necessary to write to Ronald Norman, chairman of the B.B.C. 'We have been less than a month, so far, in searching for a Director-General', Norman wrote to him on 7 July 1938. 'We all understand, I am sure, your position. You are not a candidate and never have been. You are one of a series of persons of distinction whose name we have considered to see whether we would invite one or other of them to succeed Reith.'[1] It seems likely that a discreet word from the authorities suggested that Tizard would, in any case, be unable to accept such an invitation.

In 1938 he was one of the hundred British Association members invited to the Silver Jubilee meeting of the Indian Science Congress Association, held in Calcutta in January and presided over by Sir James Jeans. 'We landed at Bombay, and after a night there got into a special train and went to Hyderabad, Agra, Delhi, Dehra Dun, and Benares, and then to Calcutta', he wrote to an old friend, H. O. Weller. 'Most of the party went to Darjeeling for three days to have a look at the Himalayas which, as I pointed out was rather like going to Switzerland for the week-end to look at the Matterhorn.'

Tizard went, instead, to the Tata Iron and Steel Works at Jamshedpur where he gave the first Perin Memorial Lecture, speaking on Industrial Research, past and future. His conclusions, significant in view of the post he was to hold nine years later in post-war Britain, were that 'there are some branches of industrial research which can only be effectively controlled and organized by the State'. The establishment and improvement of standards of measurement was an example which no-one would question, he continued. 'But if we consider the progress of industry as a whole and forget for a moment the spectacular discoveries which may lead at long last to the establishment of new industries, we must surely realize that the chief results of industrial research are to be found in the improvement of known processes in detail . . . . I feel that most industrial research should be carried out in the closest possible contact with the day to day problems of industry.'

On his return to Delhi, he flew up to Peshawar in an R.A.F. plane sent for him by Air Vice-Marshal Joubert, now A.O.C. Royal Air Force, India. He spent two mornings flying over the North-West Frontier and two afternoons exploring the Kohat and Kyber Passes.

I remember [he wrote years later], saying . . . to Sir Philip . . . that I could not imagine why the Air Council, and he in particular, did not take the wonderful opportunity of practising navigation in Indian conditions, where the distances between the centres of population were large, and where at night no light could be seen. There must have been immense opportunities for full-scale experimental work of the first importance elsewhere in the world. The trouble of practising night-flying in England before the war was that the ground was dotted with lights.

Tizard returned to England in February 1938. His position during the next eighteen months was to become increasingly ambiguous. On one level he was receiving, mainly at his St James's Court flat, a growing number of defence suggestions, official and unofficial but all passed on to him by authorities who took it for granted that Tizard was the one man to deal with them. Sometimes even the most farcical could not be brushed aside without bother – for reasons indicated by a scientific colleague of

Tizard's who on one occasion said in exasperation: 'You show me a man with fool, knave, charlatan, written all over him, who wants to hang flat irons in the skies to bring down aircraft, and I will find you fifty M.P.s to back him'.

At a different level, Tizard was making proposals for the general reorganization of science and scientists in war – even though he remained an outside, independent adviser. 'I should like to make it clear', he wrote to one young inventor who had proposed a new bombing device, 'that I am not an official of the Air Ministry nor of the Government in any way. My connection is merely that of a scientific man who is asked to advise on scientific and technical matters from time to time.' It can be argued that this gave him an ability to criticize and a freedom to experiment he would otherwise have lacked; that he could accomlish more from outside the machine than he could from inside. Yet his own complaints regarding the Offence Committee were evidence of the limitations that were thus imposed. And his position was, as we shall see, to be peculiarly vulnerable when war broke out. Even so, the choice appears always to have been his own. For he preferred the ambiguous role, whatever its problems; he chose to work beyond the limelight. However, there was an important difference between Tizard and the men who normally wish to exercise influence in such ways. He lacked personal ambition, at least of the conventional sort; nature had in fact cast him as an *eminence blanc*.

Three months after Tizard's return from India, Lord Swinton was replaced by Sir Kingsley Wood – the First Lord of the Admiralty, Duff Cooper, noting at the time that the new minister 'clings to the idea of friendship with Germany and hates the thought of getting too tied up with the French'.[2] The unfortunate move, brought about by a curious mixture of panic and political pressure, was part of a drastic reorganization which had its sensible points. Thus within the Ministry, the post of Member for Research and Development was expanded and split into two, Air Marshal Sir Wilfrid Freeman becoming Air Member for Development and Production, and Air Vice-Marshal Tedder becoming Director-General for Research and Development, both with seats on the Air Council. In addition, Mr E. J. H. Lemon, Vice-President of the L.M.S., was brought on to the Air Council as Director-General of Production. These moves were of particular significance to Tizard, since the new organization under Freeman was to be, in all but name, the fore-runner of the war-time Ministry of Aircraft Production with which he was to have dealings for more than three years. More important, he was to lose support where he needed it most. 'The Committee', he wrote of the C.S.S.A.D. to Freeman two years later, 'suffered a serious loss when Swinton went. He was the only Air Minister that I have had to deal with who could understand the recommendations and take action on them. I have had no help from the others; indeed, obstruction rather than help.'

The effect of Swinton's departure, unfortunate though this was both for the country and for Tizard, was lessened – in both cases – by the attitude of the new Chief of Staff who had succeeded Ellington a few months earlier. This was Air Marshal Sir Cyril Newall. Newall had no scientific background whatever but he sensed that Tizard should be backed up without qualification; and that the knowledge gained from the Biggin Hill experiment was pushed along the Service channels so forcefully was due more to Newall than to any other man.

Both before and during this period of reorganization, there was more than one suggestion that the 'secret' of radar might have leaked out. 'I was amazed in the course of experiments', wrote one of Tizard's friends, 'to discover that aeroplanes a mile or so away produced definite effects on the sound received. It was not difficult to prove without doubt that these effects were due to waves reflected from the all-metal aeroplanes.' There was the cutting from an American journal which said that 'According to British reports the displacement of the "ghost" image has now been correlated with the distance of the plane away from the television receivers. A system has been worked out whereby television receivers on England's eastern coast could thus serve as "spotters" for approaching enemy aircraft in time of war.' The cutting was sent by Hill who commented 'They have got pretty close to it. I wonder what the Germans know.'*

* The Germans knew a great deal; not through discovery of British secrets but by original research. This gave them, by the outbreak of war in 1939, a radar system of greater accuracy but shorter range than the British. What they

There was also the recurrent tale that car engines of British motorists abroad had been mysteriously stopped by invisible rays. 'I have heard that story many times during the last four years', Tizard wrote to one correspondent, 'I can never hear it first hand. It is always secondhand, like ghost stories.' Among the amateur brain-waves that came his way there were some hardy annuals – notably the proposal that a cloud of chemicals should be laid in advance of approaching bombers. C. S. Forester, the novelist, sent an ingenious idea, passed on by Liddell Hart, for an anti-aircraft projectile which would place a star or cross of piano wire across the path of an approaching plane. There were numerous variations on the plan for laying aerial mines; a suggestion that a moving body might be made to follow the source of a selected sound; and more than one proposal for wire barrages. The trouble, as might be expected, lay with the schemes which could not be ruled out even though extensive experiment was needed to reveal their qualities. Such, for instance, was a plan for producing shock waves which would affect an aircraft in flight. Lengthy negotiations were necessary before tests could be held at the National Physical Laboratory on the prospects of thus producing 'destructive flutter in aeroplane wings' – tests whose results were unimpressive. Even more esoteric projects could not be ruled out, and in May 1939 Tizard and Blackett were almost induced to visit Holland and investigate the claim of a Dutchman that he could create a special sort of magnetic field in which people were sent to sleep. 'The more we think about it, the less we like it', Tizard finally wrote. 'We think that the chances that this invention is genuine are almost negligible. If the man is not genuine it is a bad thing for people like Blackett and myself to go to Holland to see it. It gives him too much of an advertisement in Holland, and he will probably use it, as an unscrupulous inventor would in England, to get money for his plans.' He had no doubt remembered Bottomley and the water that could be turned to petrol. Lord Sempill brought him a foreign professor who had an ingenious de-icing scheme. Tizard glossed over this but wrote to Pye

---

lacked was any method of operational use as efficient as that evolved during the Biggin Hill experiment.

that 'what really interests me about him is that in conversation he came out with a new idea for wire barrages which appears to me at present to be quite practical and very important. I have asked him to send me a statement suggesting how he could get on with experimental work and what financial arrangements might be made.'

Meanwhile, Tizard was visiting airfields throughout southern England, reporting on experiments with short wire barrages, aerial mines, balloon barrages, and various methods of illuminating the clouds from the ground. He had an observant eye for detail, noting to Newall how absurd it was that the public should be allowed on roads through Martlesham Heath airfield and adding: 'We are a comic nation. Of course there is something to be said for being so completely comic that the foreigner may not be able to persuade himself that there is anything of importance to be got from Martlesham.'

He was, moreover, occupied throughout the whole of the period with quiet instruction of his subordinates in the best way of passing on the vital information with which they were dealing. A laboratory specimen of his kindly technique is provided by one report on the Balloon Barrage the draft of which came to him for approval. Criticizing one paragraph he wrote

> We want to explain in this paragraph why the size of wire as well as the present parachute device has been adopted. We want also to say what is likely to happen if bigger and faster machines collided with the wire. In fact you have to try in a short space of time to convince a few people who will see the report that the best possible action has been taken for the present.
>
> The next thing to deal with is what happens if machines are (a) armoured, (b) armoured and fitted with cutters. Deal with the plain armouring first, thus leading to the present experiments on swinging round small bombs, stating the experimental effects. The wording on page 3 is really too loose. Then give the actual results of experiments on cutters, and of the time taken to operate. I do not want in this report a vague statement that ground experiments have suggested that a very simple form of cutter will be effective. What is wanted is the experimental facts. Then state what we deduce from these facts so far as (a) the present barrage is concerned, and (b) any barrage that depends on the swinging round or pulling up of weights . . .

He retained his bite and his bark. But he was, overall, methodical and kindly, explaining to all except the more obvious fools how things could be done better, more efficiently, with the minimum expenditure of that valuable commodity, time.

He was also easing along unofficial channels a scheme which was to be of immense use when war came. By early 1938 it was becoming clear that manning the expanding radar chain, and developing new radar applications, would on the outbreak of war demand the attention of large numbers of physicists. These would all have to be trained in the principles and techniques of a new 'science' of which they would know nothing, since the secret of radar development had been successfully kept. These physicists could be found only in the universities; but there existed no machinery for bringing them into the world of the scientist working on defence. As was common in such cases, Tizard created his own machinery.

It was obvious that the Cavendish Laboratory, Cambridge, only a short drive away from Bawdsey, would supply many of the physicists needed, and in the spring of 1938 Tizard conferred with the Laboratory's Professor Cockcroft – who apart from being a first-class physicist was also a practical electrical engineer with the invaluable benefit of Service experience during the First World War. 'We met at lunch in the Athenaeum', Cockcroft later wrote, 'and there he talked to me about new and secret devices we were building to help to shoot enemy planes out of the sky. These devices would be troublesome and would require a team of nurses. Would we – the Cavendish – undertake to come in and act as nursemaids, if and when war broke out?'[3] This was the first move in a scheme that expanded throughout the following months. By the autumn Sir Lawrence Bragg, the head of the Cavendish, was writing to Sir Frank Smith, Secretary of the D.S.I.R. saying: 'Already a small number of University men are admitted into the inner secret councils of the Defence Services. Could not this number be somewhat enlarged? It cannot be too large, but it might include the important leaders of research in many Universities.' Bragg sent a copy of the letter to Tizard who replied by saying:

> You say in your letter 'sometimes a problem can be put to outside people which is of such a general kind that no secret is given away by formulating it'. This is just what I am proposing to do if I come up to

Cambridge to have an informal talk with the senior people there. What I thought of doing was to state as clearly as I can what the main problems are, without necessarily disclosing all the ways in which they are being attacked. It can do no harm to get people thinking on the right lines.

Subsequently a number of the Laboratory's senior physicists paid the first of many visits to Bawdsey. Men at other universities were warned that they had been earmarked for important unspecified tasks if war broke out, and by the early summer of 1939 it had been agreed that a number of them should be fully informed of the secrets of radar. They were grouped in parties of nine or ten from the Cavendish, the Clarendon, and from the Universities of Birmingham, London, Manchester, and Bristol. They were sworn to secrecy, but they were neither officially nor unofficially enrolled under any particular ministerial banner. They were not paid, although it appears that most received out-of-pocket expenses. And it was finally agreed that they would spend a month during the Long Vacation at the various chain stations around the coast which had, since Good Friday 1939, been operating twenty-four hours a day. It was arranged that they should begin their work at these stations on the morning of Friday 1 September.

Tizard thus played a key part, between the spring of 1938 and the autumn of 1939, in easing the young, mainly University, scientists into the defence system – and therefore doing for radar on the ground what he had already, through the Biggin Hill experiment, done for it in the air. Yet he was worried about the broader problems of the Services' use of scientists in time of war. Would it not be possible, he asked Sir Kingsley Wood in the summer of 1938, to introduce some 'better means of co-operation between the scientific men in charge of research for the three Service Departments and outside scientists?'

One attempt had been made nearly two years previously. Rutherford had then proposed to Sir Thomas Inskip, the recently-appointed Minister for the Co-ordination of Defence, honest but uncomprehending, that 'a scientific secretariat should be formed to bring together the mass of research work of all kinds then in progress in Government Departments.' Inskip took advice, and some months later tentatively launched the idea at Lord Swinton, who was not impressed. 'I am frankly rather alarmed at the idea of creating a new general committee which is to breed more sub-committees, the secretaries of which are to be staffed by drawing on a limited cadre of technical officers who are already over-worked', Swinton replied. He was reinforced by a memorandum from Freeman, which suggested that Wimperis had been spending roughly 80 per cent of his working time on matters concerned with either the Tizard Committee or the Aeronautical Research Com-mittee. Therefore the idea of a super-committee, possibly under the direction of Charles Merz, the electrical engineer who had organized and become first director of the Admiralty department of experiment and research, was killed partly by this fear of more committees. Tizard's intervention behind the scenes may well have given it a *coup de grace*.

> Lord Rutherford told me about these proposals at the time, after he had seen you [he later wrote to Inskip]. I disagreed with them and told him so. It seemed to me that the kind of central committee he had in mind under the chairmanship of Mr. Merz was liable to grow into a somewhat clumsy administrative machine, and to do more harm than good, the harm being done by the unnecessary calls on the time of hard-worked executive officers in the Service Departments, and duplication of the work of other committees. I fancy that Lord Rutherford was shaken by my criticisms; at any rate, the proposal fell through and so far as I know he did not press it.

Now, in June 1938, Tizard put forward his own plan to Sir Kingsley Wood. There were a number of scientific men whose advice would be helpful but who were not being asked for it. 'My broad suggestion therefore', Tizard wrote, 'is that the Air Ministry should try through its present Committee to enlist the co-operation of independent scientific men by asking selected individuals to take a special interest in particular phases of the scientific work, and to pay regular and frequent (say monthly) visits to the experimental stations at which the work is being carried out'.

This, however, formed only the first half of Tizard's proposals. It had already become obvious, with radar, that what had been developed primarily as a new tool for the Royal Air Force had many applications in the other Services.

> It is worth considering [he therefore continued], whether it would

N

not be wise to have a small scientific committee under the Minister for the Co-ordination of Defence, or under the Committee of Imperial Defence, which would have as its main responsibility the initiation of entirely new researches to meet Service requirements, and the selection of outside individuals to advise on particular phases of Service research work and to co-operate closely with members of the Service Research Staff. I am in general opposed to the formation of new committees. They are apt sometimes to make such calls upon the time of individuals who have the executive responsibility in Government Departments that the net result of their labours may be bad rather than good. But as it is quite clear that one can only defend this country adequately, now and in the future, by making the utmost use of scientific knowledge in every direction, there is something to be said for a small central scientific committee which has a wider responsibility than the present Defence Committee of the Air Ministry. To make the work of such a committee fruitful it would, I suggest, be necessary that it should be supplied annually with ample funds to spend at its discretion on new ideas, the actual spending of the funds being arranged through the appropriate Director of Scientific Research.

He got quick agreement to part of his proposals, and on 22 June wrote to A. V. Hill saying that he had been given permission to select individuals to take special interest in particular lines of work. As for the more radical suggestion of a skeletal General Staff for science, this was baulked by the persisting belief that there were already enough committees, and that science was hardly important enough to justify yet another. This was in harmony with the atmosphere of casual calm which had in some Government departments survived even the impact of foreign affairs and the British re-armament programme. Tizard himself was not immune from it. After he had talked over the use of scientists with Inskip on 25 July – less than three months before Munich – he noted that 'Sir Thomas finally said he would discuss the proposal with the three Ministers of the Service Departments, and would speak to me again about it in the autumn. We agreed that there was no great hurry.'

It was not only on the use of scientists, and of science, in the Services that he was beginning to advise. His positions in the D.S.I.R., at Imperial College, and as Chairman of the Aeronautical Research Committee, had combined to give him a unique insight into what could be accomplished in the border country where science and industry meet. His contacts and his influence ranged across most of it. With Barnes Wallis of Vickers he discussed the best size for bombers; with Handley Page, the method by which the aeronautical industry could get the right type of University man. And in October 1938, he wrote to Tedder saying that: 'In Freeman's absence you ought to know that I have written to the Secretary of State to say that I think a strong case can be made out for design and manufacture by the Air Ministry in defiance of the existing policy which has been confirmed from time to time. What I have in mind is the creation of a Corps of Aircraft Constructors corresponding to the Corps of Naval Constructors in the Navy.' He suggested that a committee might look into the matter – 'in spite of the fact that what we all want to do is to stop the multiplication of committees'.

His influence could be traced far back in most matters connected with science and defence. Even when the serious question of grain storage arose, it now became apparent that it was Tizard who had kept research alive in 1933. The Empire Marketing Board had then been dissolved and its research laboratory in Imperial College threatened with closure. The Government took no steps to prevent this.

'The Governing Body of the College, however, was so convinced of the importance of the work that they made special efforts to secure temporary grants from various bodies, including the Carnegie Corporation and the Imperial Council of Agricultural Bureaux, and were eventually successful in 1935 in securing an additional annual grant from University funds for continuing the scientific investigations on a small scale', Tizard reported in a subsequent memorandum. A year later, with J. W. Munro, Professor of Zoology and Applied Entomology at Imperial College, he saw Sir Frank Smith, Secretary of D.S.I.R., and urged that research on the problem of stored food should be increased. They received a dusty answer, and the work of discovering how Britain's wartime wheat stocks should be stored, continued to be paid for from the general funds of Imperial College. Only now, Tizard wrote in 1937, was the project for a permanent laboratory organisation – eventually set up as the Pest Infestation Research Laboratory – being considered by the D.S.I.R. And he concluded his memo with a fearsome description of what was going on in some of the existing Government stores of grain, where 'weevils were present in millions and their activity could actually be heard at a distance of five yards', and where 200 weevils per pound of grain had been discovered. 'The research aspect is certainly being tackled at last, the Ministry of Agriculture and D.S.I.R. both being interested', Tizard wrote to Dr Graham Kerr on 8 November 1938. '. . . It is a little late in the day now, but not too late if the thing is done properly. I am still anxious lest the support given to research will be on too small a scale. However, we must wait and see. The next important step, as you say, is to see that results of research are properly applied. This is a perennial trouble in this country.' And, to the same correspondent, two days later. '. . . time goes on and meanwhile the weevil is very happy. This business has been very badly managed.'

The truth, of course, was that only now, in the backwash of Munich, were the many gaps in the country's defences at last being seriously studied. This was as well. Even in the Air Ministry the gaps were enormous, for Munich had come before the radar and communication chains were complete; when of the twenty-nine fighter squadrons reckoned mobilizable, only five had modern aircraft; when of the 450 balloons in the London Establishment only 142 could be deployed; and when only about one-third of the country's required number of anti-aircraft guns and searchlights were available – most guns being 'obsolete or obsolescent and some not in working order.'[4]

The pressing need to tackle defence problems on a new basis brought to Tizard the first hint of a change in the balance of power. For the imminence of war had high-lighted the value of men such as Churchill. And sensing the change of emphasis with the instinct of the political master, Churchill had written to Sir Kingsley Wood on 13 October. Surely, he suggested, the Swinton Committee might well be reinforced by the addition of Lindemann. Sir Kingsley, blessed with a higher authority to whom such proposals could be quickly passed, invoked the aid of Sir Thomas Inskip, Minister for the Co-ordination of Defence. And on 15 November Sir Thomas explained to Tizard how 'Mr Churchill thinks that Professor Lindemann would enable him to put before the Committee valuable ideas and generally to supply him with technical knowledge which he does not possess himself. He assured Sir Kingsley Wood that he was making the suggestion with full knowledge of all that had happened in the past and in the public interest. . . . Mr Churchill has his own methods, but he is sincerely anxious to help and he feels very strongly that Professor Lindemann has a contribution to make which we ought not to lose.'[5]

This, Tizard no doubt felt, was the old story repeated all over again. He agreed to discuss the matter with Inskip and wrote to him on the 17th.

I will bring along with me correspondence that I have had in the past with and about Professor Lindemann [he said]. It might be helpful for us to have this correspondence handy at the meeting. The following remarks may be of use to you in the meantime.

It appears to me that the question whether it is desirable to add any other scientist to the A.D.R. Committee depends very much on what view you take of the functions and usefulness of that Committee. I myself have never regarded it as a committee which is suitable for the discussion of the scientific problems of air defence. Any such problems initiated by any remarks of members have to be considered by a special scientific committee, e.g. the one of which I am chairman at the Air Ministry. The usefulness of the Committee seems to me to lie far more in the decision of what to do when such decision does not rest on purely scientific grounds as is so often the case. It is quite true that we have technical papers sent to us and that there is often some loose discussion on scientific problems, mainly initiated by Mr. Winston Churchill's interest in such matters. But in so far as the conversation has become of a scientific nature it has been rather a waste of time. I myself think there are no strong grounds for adding another scientific man to this particular Committee, but if you feel that its scientific representation needs to be strengthened do you think it is wise to accept one particular individual whom you know already does not carry the confidence of many other scientific men who are working on these problems? Would it not be better for you to consult, let us say, the President of the Royal Society as the obviously suitable man to give you entirely independent and unbiased advice about strengthening the Committee?

I must say I feel in a personal difficulty about the suggestion. I fully realise that Mr. Winston Churchill's main object in everything he does is to strengthen the defences of the Country, and therefore it seems wrong to oppose anything he suggests unless one has very strong reasons for doing so. But I also feel that the real motive behind Mr. Winston Churchill's suggestion is that he does not altogether trust the advice I give, and that he prefers Professor Lindemann's advice. I could quite easily foresee occasions when Professor Lindemann and I should not agree on the advice we gave you. We do not want that kind of disagreement in the Committee. Of course, whatever advice I give on the Committee is not simply my own personal view. It is advice which I know would be supported by my colleagues on the scientific committees of the Air Ministry and elsewhere. In fact, in course of time I have rather drifted into being a representative of scientific opinion on these matters. Now if you have two such representatives you are likely to get confused. It would be like appointing a Chief of Air Staff and then appointing another unofficial one to tell you when he goes wrong. From a human point of view this does not work.

Reason, however, was not to have its way. Tizard described the outcome of his meeting in a letter which he wrote to Hill on 24 November explaining that Churchill and his supporters were, as he put it,

pressing Lindemann's claims to be the brains on defence. It is rather clever [he continued], the way they have waited until Rutherford was well dead, so to speak, before pressing this again.* Inskip and Kingsley Wood want to give in. They were quite frank with me in saying that the reason they wanted to give in was that if they didn't, Winston Churchill would go off the Committee and 'make a stink', and they don't want a stink just now. After saying exactly what I thought of the proposals and making other suggestions which they did not like, I said that if Lindemann was coming on I was going off. Whereupon they both completely defeated me by saying that in that case they would not have him on, and they would let Churchill go off and stand the consequences. So I said I would like a couple of days to think it over.

I think I shall have to give in. To stand out in spite of that would be hardly in the best scientific tradition. But I want to suggest that if they put Lindemann on they should at the same time put on either you, Blackett, or Fowler,† even if it is only to indicate that they do really appreciate all the work you three have done . . .

It must have seemed that his victory in 1936 had been no victory at all. It confirmed his belief that politics was a dirty business.

* Rutherford had died on 19 October 1937.

† R. H. Fowler, Plummer professor Mathematical Physics, Trinity College, Cambridge, already co-opted to help with the work of Tizard's scientific committees and later (see p. 247) to play a part in co-ordinating wartime research between Britain and North America.

And when he wrote to Inskip, the crux of his letter was '. . . I simply have to surrender'. This was true – so long as he felt that it was necessary to act, as he properly called it, in the best scientific tradition. Had he manoeuvred, had he brought Churchill into the open in the most disadvantageous conditions, it is likely that Tizard would have won this particular confrontation; but in the uproar it might have been even more difficult for the country to make use of the twelve months gained by the surrender of Munich. As it was, he succeeded in getting Hill on to the Swinton Committee as counterweight to Lindemann. That was something. But he may well have reflected that shunning notoriety and advertisement; wanting only, as he had put it in his letter to Hill two years previously, 'to do a useful job of work', was apt to involve its own limitations.

There was, he must have reflected, always the chance that the opposition might over-reach itself as it had in 1936 – 'the trouble about Lindemann is that he is getting so infernally unscientific', he noted to Pye a few weeks later. 'He takes no trouble to examine even his own proposals properly, let alone anyone else's'. The end of this particular affair in fact came six months later. On 26 May 1939, Tizard met Sir Edward Bridges, Secretary to the Cabinet, and General Ismay and Wing Commander Elliot, Secretary and Assistant Secretary to the Committee of Imperial Defence respectively. The four men mulled over the work of the Swinton Committee. 'We all agreed', Tizard noted privately afterwards, 'that it had outlived its usefulness, and that as at present constituted was too large and unwieldy. Further, that there was no point in submitting to the Committee long technical reports, e.g. those on the U.P. The difficulty is that the object of the Committee is really political; in fact, to give Churchill a chance to air his views. So Bridges thought that there was no possibility of its being abolished, although he did think that it might be reconstituted with less members.' Events were to make this unnecessary. The next, twenty-first, meeting of the Committee was held on 11 July – 'more nonsense about aerial mines packed in rockets', noted Tizard. A few weeks later the war tipped all such organizations into the melting pot.

*　　　*　　　*

By the beginning of 1939, Tizard was worried about what he
rightly considered to be his anomalous position in the defence
structure. He had no doubt that Lindemann's star was rising. But
he also felt that he himself might be wasting his time, since he still
apparently believed, as he had in 1913, 'that no great nation
would be foolish enough to go to war with another great nation'.
Thus he wrote on 18 January to H. O. Weller, an old friend of
the D.S.I.R. days then living in Kenya: 'We are still in the midst
of rumours of war, but personally I think that Hitler has rather
too much sense to press things to the last issue, although no doubt
he will try to get as much as he can by keeping the world on edge.
However, we have to be prepared for everything, which is exasperating because it takes up so much of the time of people like
myself who would rather be doing more sensible things.'

This hope, obliquely implying that Chamberlain might indeed
have achieved the chance of peace in our time, was typical of
Tizard's habit of giving all men the benefit of the doubt. It illumi-
nates the gulf that existed between himself and the Churchill-
Lindemann combination. And it no doubt influenced the letter
which he now, in January 1939, wrote to the Air Minister in an
attempt to clear up his own unsatisfactory position.

> Dear Sir Kingsley Wood [this went], Sir John Reith told me last
> week that he was thinking of suggesting to you the formation of a
> standing committee to be responsible for the ordering and develop-
> ment of aircraft for civil air transport, and that he wanted to suggest
> that I should be the Chairman of such a Committee. I told him that
> I could not possibly take on any more work of that kind in present
> circumstances. I do, however, sympathise with his difficulties, and it
> might be useful if I had a word with you about them sometime.*
>
> I also want to see you soon about my work in connexion with
> national defence. It is now over four years since I was asked to
> become Chairman of the Air Ministry Defence Committee. Other
> responsibilities have been added since. I was very willing to do what

---

* A committee was appointed with Harold Brown as chairman and Sir
Charles Bruce-Gardner and Sir John Reith, head of the newly-formed British
Overseas Airways Corporation, as members. It reported within six weeks, says
Lord Reith, its chief recommendation being that a permanent technical board
should be appointed, with Tizard in the chair, to co-ordinate and control
technical research and development for aircraft. Little could be accomplished
before the outbreak of war.

I could in the emergency, but my work for the Imperial College has suffered, as well as my private interests. This cannot go on indefinitely, and I think that the time has come when I can ask you to accept my resignation with a clear conscience. It should not be difficult to make arrangements to keep me in close enough touch with the work to ensure that I could quickly become efficient in a full-time post in war, if required.

My view of the present position is that I could only help materially by spending even more of my time and energy on problems of national defence than I do at present; but that is out of the question. I have considered the possibility of resigning from the College, and devoting myself entirely to aeronautics and defence problems, but I do not see any suitable opportunity of doing this. So rather than do two important things superficially and indifferently, I must really settle down to do one well! I can explain this more fully when I see you.

This was not the first time that the best way of utilizing Sir Henry Tizard's abilities in either war or peace had been considered by those in power. As the Munich crisis had come to a head it was mentioned by Freeman, in general terms apparently and on 27 September 1938, Tizard had written to the Vice-Chancellor of the University of London saying: 'I am already committed to assist the Air Ministry full-time if they wish me to do so.' Whether or not they did is uncertain, and on 29 September, Newall, the Chief of Air Staff, wrote to Tizard asking 'for first option on your services on behalf of the Royal Air Force should we become involved in a war'. The two men met a few days later and on 7 October Newall wrote again: 'Thank you for your letter of the 5th, and thank you also most sincerely for your willingness to help us on the general lines discussed between us, should the necessity arise. You ask me how far I feel inclined to take you into my confidence during peace. My answer is, without any hesitation, one hundred per cent, as clearly, if we are asking you to help, we must let you know the problem from all angles . . .'[6]

Yet nothing had been finally decided – for the simple reason, it appears, that there was no niche which Tizard could occupy, and that no machinery existed for creating such a niche. Now, however, two efforts were made to ease a way round the difficulty. On the day that Sir Kingsley Wood received Tizard's letter, the Chief of Air Staff either saw, or telephoned Tizard, who wrote to

him on 31 January saying: 'You said yesterday that you would
like one remark made on record. I write now therefore to say that
I have already made arrangements at the Imperial College which
would free me to come to the Air Ministry for any full-time post
in war if required at very short notice.'

The post itself was nebulous, but Freeman quickly suggested
one possibility. 'It seems clear to me that we cannot afford to let
you go', he wrote to Tizard. '. . . What I would like to know is,
first, would you be prepared to take office under the C.I.D. provided such matters as salary, pension, etc. could be arranged. If
you agree to this could you possibly let me know some idea of the
position which you think you should hold under the Government?'

Here, at last, it seemed that Tizard might grasp the position
for which all his experience and judgement so ably fitted him.
And here, tantalizingly, no record remains of his reply to Freeman, or of such negotiations as may have taken place during the
following months. All that can be said with certainty is that an
arrangement was eventually made, starting at the end of March
1939 and provisionally due to last eighteen months, under which
Tizard would be able, in the words of the Air Minister, 'to devote
even more time to Government and particularly Air Ministry
work'.

However, the fact that both the Committee of Imperial Defence
and the Air Council by this time regarded Tizard as their unofficial scientific adviser is illustrated by one development during the
last summer of peace. This involved Tizard in the long series of
events which were to lead, through an off-shoot of the Tizard
Committee, to the decision that a nuclear weapon was a practicable proposition; to the assimilation of British nuclear research
by the United States; the birth of the Manhattan Project; and
the mushroom cloud over Hiroshima.

*   *   *

Late in December 1938, the German chemist Otto Hahn succeeded in splitting in two the nucleus of the uranium atom. The
facts which made such an achievement possible were worried out
a few weeks later by Lise Meitner, who had worked with Hahn
until the German anti-Semitic laws had caused her to flee from

Germany, and by her nephew Otto Frisch. The implications of their theory of nuclear fission, as the process was now christened, were startling. In the earlier 'splitting of the atom' which had been achieved naturally by Rutherford in 1919 and artificially by Cockcroft and Walton in 1932, more energy had to be poured into the nuclear stockpot than was produced by the splitting. Nuclear fission, however, indicated that this might no longer be necessary, that it might be possible to release vast amounts of energy which could be utilized either as peaceful power or in a nuclear weapon. Such exploitation of the natural order of things, for so long merely the speculation of writers, became even more feasible during the first months of 1939. For a French team working with uranium and heavy water in the Collège de France under Professor Joliot-Curie showed that the process of nuclear fission might, under certain conditions, be self-sustaining – an essential if the power released were to be utilized.

Throughout the spring and early summer discussion continued. Professor Tyndall, Director of the Wills Laboratory at Bristol University, wrote a note on an atomic weapon which was sent to Tizard through the Air Ministry machinery. Blackett offered to mention the 'uranium business' when he next met Cockcroft in Cambridge. In Imperial College Professor G. P. Thomson, son of Sir J. J. Thomson and a colleague of the Chudleigh Mess at Farnborough during the First World War, proposed that Tizard should obtain, through the Air Ministry, the supplies of uranium necessary for practical experiment.

And now, enquiringly, the Committee of Imperial Defence turned its gaze on the subject. It was decided that the whole question of using uranium as a nuclear explosive should be investigated in extreme secrecy. Tizard was given the task. At this date, the bulk of the world's uranium supplies came from the Belgian Congo. The uranium ore was used mainly in the ceramics industry and the metal, the refining of which was a costly and difficult process, had previously had no strategic importance. Tizard decided to tackle matters at their source.

As on so many other occasions, his long line of acquaintances and friendships stretched back to the right people. At the end of the First World War, when he had served for a short while in the newly-created Air Ministry, the Parliamentary Under-Secretary of State for the Royal Air Force – as the post was then described – had been Lord Stonehaven. Now, in May 1939, Stonehaven was the British director of the Union Minière which controlled the Congo uranium stocks. A meeting was arranged in the Company's London offices between Tizard, Stonehaven, Baron Cartier, the Belgian Ambassador in London, and Edgar Sengier, a Belgian Director of the organization. 'Sir Henry asked me to grant the British Government an option on each ton of ore which would be extracted from the Shinkolobwe radium-uranium mine,' says Sengier. Tizard's request was refused, but as he left the meeting he turned to Sengier. 'Be careful', he warned him, 'and never forget that you have in your hands something that may mean a catastrophe to your country and mine if this material were to fall into the hands of a possible enemy'.[7] It was this warning, together with another which Sengier received from workers in the College de France a few days later, which encouraged him to despatch to the United States two shiploads of ore from the Union's mines in Katanga – shiploads which were to help provide the raw material for the world's first nuclear weapon. 'It is sobering to realize', General Groves, who led the U.S. bomb-project, has since remarked, 'that but for a chance meeting between a Belgian and an Englishman a few months before the outbreak of the war, the Allies might not have been first with the atomic bomb'.[8] The comment underlines the significance of Tizard's work – even though the record shows that the meeting was not by chance and that, in the words of the Americans themselves, evidence gathered early in 1945 'proved definitely that Germany had no atom bomb and was not likely to have one in any reasonable time'.[9]

British eagerness to push ahead with enquiries was largely due to fear that the Germans might already be working on a similar weapon, a prospect which in July brought to Tizard an ingenious idea. 'If it is true that the Germans are really trying to make a uranium bomb they may be anxious as to its possibilities in other hands', wrote Professor Thomson. 'Would it be possible to do a bluff, and get them to believe we really had a new and very formidable weapon? If so it might make them hesitate risking a war till they were sure, and so tide us over the dangerous period of the

next few months. I imagine our secret service has means which
would allow them to plant false information where it would reach
high German authorities. If so, it would not be difficult to concoct
something with the help of our explosives department which would
sound fairly convincing and be difficult to disprove in a short
time.'[10]

Tizard replied that he himself had made similar suggestions to
the Powers-that-Be. Would Thomson 'try his hand?'

Shortly afterwards there appeared on his desk a "Draft of formal Report from Martlesham".

Sir [it began], (1) In accordance with instructions received, I
arranged to test 10 uranium bombs (experimental) each of ½ ton
weight and numbered 1–10 supplied by Professor G. P. Thomson.
(2) The bombs were buried to the depth of two feet in sandy soil, and
exploded by means of the electric fuses supplied with them. (3) Of
the bombs tested, numbers 1 and 3 failed to explode, number 4
exploded giving a small crater of 2 ft. in diameter. Number 5, 6, 7, 8
exploded with the results shown in the table.

Number	Diameter of crater produced
5	50 ft. ?
6	45 ft. ?
7	400 ft. ?
8	450 ft. ?

The explosions in the last two cases were extraordinarily severe and
damaged the buildings of the station two miles away from the test
Pits. They were fully equivalent in effect to 25 tons of TNT exploding
under similar conditions. The corresponding figure for numbers 5
and 6 would be about 2–3 tons. (4) Numbers 2, 9 and 10 were not
tested, the last two because it seemed probable that their effects
could be so great as to cause serious damage at . . . I have the honour
to be . . .

This was only half of the scheme, however. Together with the
'official' report, Tizard received from Thomson a longer and more
discursive account which might also be allowed to come under
German eyes. It included, as Thomson said, just enough detail to
make it plausible, but not enough to enable anyone to repeat the
experiments and disprove the claims.

Briefly [it ran], the tests have been an immense success and there can
be no doubt that we have now got a weapon which will revolutionise
air warfare. Even with the relatively enormous amount of 2% of

cadium as a 'depressant' the mixture is more effective than TNT in its general explosive reaction. With 1% it has about five times the power and with ·5% *over* 50 *times the power of TNT!* The authorities here would not allow me to test the samples with ·25% as they felt the explosion would cause an amount of damage in the neighbouring villages which would be difficult to keep secret. It is therefore of the first importance to complete the arrangements for the island, as we must get some idea of the delay required to give the aeroplanes a reasonable chance of getting clear. The present experiments bear out the view that, with only the small amount of cadmium required as trigger, the half ton should give an explosion about equal to the great explosion of Halifax, but in view of the fact that the gross energy available is roughly that of 5 *million* tons of TNT the effect may well be a good deal larger.

To come to details: the new trigger mechnism worked well and gave no trouble. We have at last got the right activator, but the proportions are critical. The same with 20% hydrogen content (by atoms), the tests I have mentioned were done with 10%, and the 5% gave nothing till the cadium content was reduced to ·25% and then not much more. The circumstances of the tests were impressive. We were 3/4 mile from the explosion pits but the noise was deafening, even through cotton-wool, and gave that sensation of physical shock one gets from a shell exploding too near. Earth, sandbags, etc. were blown up to a great height, and all the windows and several doors were broken at the station two miles from the pits. In view of the enormous increase in power (by reducing the cadmium) there can be little doubt that each half-ton bomb would destroy buildings over a radius of at least half a mile in an ordinary city.

The draughtsmen are working out the final details of the case and trigger mechanisms. Fortunately, it is a very simple job, and production should be rapid. We are publishing some unimportant scientific points in 'Nature' as it is known that I am working on uranium and this is the best camouflage.[11]

This was the trap which Tizard should, it was suggested, lay for the unwary Germans. It appears from the record that he did attempt to have news of the alleged experiments placed in Germany. The authorities, he noted later, were 'horrified at the thought'.

Meanwhile, and more significantly, Thomson added in his covering letter to Tizard, that 'the serious side of the work goes well, and I see no reason to change my view that it will work'.

For at Imperial College Thomson himself had already started

experiments with uranium oxide obtained through the Air Ministry in the hope of discovering whether a chain reaction could be produced. Subsequently, at the forty-eighth meeting of the Tizard Committee, held on 17 August, it was decided that David Pye should be asked to buy a further ton of uranium oxide so that Professor Moon, Thomson's collaborator at Imperial College, now appointed to Birmingham, could continue experiments there under Professor Oliphant. The experiments with this succeeded in clearing a few corners of the undergrowth that still covered the subject. But it seemed unlikely that a nuclear weapon would be feasible.

This view was by now gaining strength. Earlier in the year theoretical work – mainly by Niels Bohr in Denmark – had shown that only a small percentage of the atoms in natural uranium were highly susceptible to fission. The vision of a new weapon of unparallelled power, which had been opening up during the first months of the year, was now fading. Once again, chance seemed to pick Tizard and Lindemann for opposite sides; for now Churchill, acting on Lindemann's advice, was able to write to Sir Kingsley Wood warning him not to take seriously the dire prophecies of what the discovery of nuclear fission would mean. 'On the contrary', he wrote, 'it is essential to realize that there is no danger that this discovery, however great its scientific interest, and perhaps ultimately its practical importance, will lead to results capable of being put into operation on a large scale for several years'.[12]

*   *   *

The extent to which Tizard was by now being accepted as the one man who could advise with authority on the Service applications of science was shown by the attitude not only of the Committee of Imperial Defence which had handed him the nuclear investigation, but of those within the Air Ministry. Throughout the summer a subtle difference in the tone of his multitudinous notes and memoranda can be discerned. He wrote to the Air Minister advising that aeronautical research should be taken more seriously, noting that there were only two first-class University institutions for such research and making a comment that must have brought a mild shudder from Sir Kingsley – that 'possibly some influence, now brought to bear on those individuals who are deriving large profits from the production of military aircraft, may help to finance the University aeronautical departments on a more appropriate scale'. As usual, his sympathies were with Undershaft rather than with Major Barbara. He had previously noted to Pye that 'there are too many eggs in one basket at Farnborough, and if a war comes there may be too many of the enemy's eggs there too'. He now wrote to Freeman following up his earlier proposals. 'I am making a serious suggestion', he said, 'that this scientific research which is looked after by the Aeronautical Research Committee should be removed from Farnborough and developed at some other and better aerodrome and kept apart from *ad hoc* experiments. The aerodrome I have in mind is the Portsmouth Civil Airport. I also think there is a great deal to be said for separating this research from the executive control of the Air Ministry, and putting it under an executive Committee, thus following the American plan.' He went farther when he pointed out to Pye that as Director of Scientific Research he was responsible not only for research at Farnborough but also for scientific research in the development of aeronautics generally. 'I think that this responsibility is much too heavy for one man to bear, however big his staff, and somehow or other it will have to be gradually delegated', he commented. 'I believe that there is a great deal to be said now for the formation of an entirely independent and executive aeronautical research group, rather on the lines of the American system. It will, of course, have to be financed by the Government, but would not necessarily come under Air Ministry control.'

Much of all this might indicate that Tizard was already occupying the post for which circumstances had fashioned him – that of scientific adviser to the Air Minister, a man who in the carefully-built pyramid would presumably move at Air Council level. It was in this atmosphere that he wrote to Sir Kingsley in May: 'It might be wise to ask Mr Churchill to pay a visit to Bawdsey', he said. 'A visit there would give him a much better idea of the work that has been done and all that it means, than he gets from reading a few summarized reports at the A.D.R. Committee. If I took him there I might then be able to have a talk with him about other matters when he is in a receptive mood.'

Churchill agreed to come the following month, and on 20 June was, as he later described it, flown down to Martlesham Heath in 'a decrepit aircraft'. It seems that he thoroughly enjoyed himself. 'We showed him the detection, including anti-jamming, the method for communicating the observations to headquarters and elsewhere, the coastal defence set and the gun-laying set', Tizard noted later. 'We also showed him at Martlesham the air to air method. The demonstration went very well and he got a clear grasp of the method . . .'

The ways in which Churchill then exercised his influence are not clear but there can be little doubt of their efficacy. Shortly after his visit, at which the early airborne radar set was found to be successful at ranges of between 12,000 and 1,500 ft. the order came that thirty 'smeller' sets should be completed, and installed in aircraft, by 1 September 1939 – a crash order which, as it happened, helped to accentuate the inevitable teething troubles of the new sets.

Tizard's official position in the Air Ministry during the last few months of peace may have been non-existent but his influence was unquestioned. This was shown not only by his minutes on numerous Air Force subjects but, perhaps even more significantly, by his tour of Bomber Command stations in July. Air Chief Marshal Sir Edgar Ludlow-Hewitt, the C.-in-C., lunched with him on the 4th and it was arranged that he should visit selected stations as soon as possible. In a letter which Tizard wrote a few months later the initiation of this is quite clear – 'Last summer I thought it was time that the independent scientific committees devoted much more thought to your problems. That was why I paid special visits to stations in your Command.'

On 6 July, less than eight weeks before the outbreak of war, the C.-in-C. sent a note to all Group Commanders saying that Tizard 'was now able to turn his attention to the requirements of Bomber Command', and that the main object of discussions would be 'to enable Sir Henry to help us to solve our problems and to overcome our difficulties'. To help in the mechanics of the task, Tizard was allotted Ragg of the Biggin Hill experiment, now a

o

Wing-Commander and Command Navigation Officer, and together they set off on 24 July for Great Driffield, Waddington,
Mildenhall and Wattisham. At each airfield the routine was
roughly the same. The collected aircrews would be introduced
by Ragg, and Tizard would then ask them what their problems
were in finding their targets, in hitting them effectively, in flying
a complex piece of machinery under difficult and dangerous conditions. Few of the air crews had heard of Tizard until a day or so
before his visit; many heard of him then merely as a scientist and
as Rector of Imperial College. The slightly luke-warm air that
this sometimes created was altered by two things. The first was
Ragg's introduction of Tizard as a pilot who had won the A.F.C.
in the First World War. The second was Tizard's immediate
appreciation of the problems with which he was confronted and
the difficulties of their solution in the air. As at Biggin Hill two
years earlier, the pilots, navigators and wireless operator realized
that here was a man to whom they could talk on equal terms, to
whom it was not necessary to explain all those things which separated the ground-tied from the airborne.

Tizard's brief tour did something to highlight the appalling
position which confronted Bomber Command – due, it must be
felt, to the late stage at which, in the words of one very Senior
Commander, the Command had 'got the scientists round them'.
Tizard's recommendations suggested further aids to navigation,
improvement of gunnery, and further research on a gyroscopically-
controlled automatic sight for high altitude bombing. 'As for the
more distant future', he concluded, 'what the scientist can do
depends largely on policy, e.g. on the policy with regard to low-
flying attack, and whether attacks are going to be made singly or
in large formations'. Most frightening in the hind-sight of experience, was his opening sentence. 'Generally considered, with
proper training', this went, 'it would be possible to be pretty
certain of being within one's objective by a distance of ten to
fifteen miles, even if one could not see the ground . . .' This was
but six weeks before the outbreak of war; the Germans were
already making preparations to 'bomb on the beam', a method
which could, until countered, provide them with an accuracy of a
few hundred yards; and although something similar was discussed

at one of the stations which Tizard visited, it does not appear to have been taken seriously.[13]

Tizard returned to London during the last week of July. He relinquished the tenancy of the flat in St James's Court, arranging that for the immediate future he would divide his time between Oxford, where his scientific committees were to meet, and make-shift quarters in Imperial College. His eldest son, Peter, was by now qualifying in the Middlesex Hospital and was soon to join the Royal Army Medical Corps. Dick had just graduated from Oxford; while the youngest son, David, was still at school. All personal matters were arranged suitably, with a lack of fuss, so that when the transition to war had to be made it could be made with a minimum of upheaval. He checked on the readiness of the Maintenance Party which he had set up with George Lowry in Imperial College at the time of the Munich crisis. It had been planned by the University that most of the College departments should be evacuated to Edinburgh if war broke out – a plan for which Tizard had little enthusiasm and which he was able to cancel when bombs were dropped near the Forth Bridge in October 1939.

In the Air Ministry he was now provided with an office, and there is a legend that he arrived for the first time to find a carpenter screwing up a notice on the door which read: 'Air Marshal Sir Henry Tizard'. His alleged reaction would have been in character – an annoyed 'take that down immediately'. As assistants in his work as Scientific Adviser to the Chief of Air Staff he was to have a secretary and two assistants, Squadron-Leader Helmore and Squadron-Leader Haslam.

Helmore, a colourful pilot from the First World War, was industrial inventor, one of the pioneers of air refuelling, and a character well-known to the general public for his broadcast descriptions of such events as the Schneider Trophy Races and the R.A.F. Displays at Hendon. He was also a fisherman like Tizard and when at the end of August both managed to take a few days respite from work, they decided to spend it on the Wylye.

At breakfast on the morning of Friday 1 September, they turned on the wireless in the small inn at which they were staying and heard that Germany had invaded Poland. They decided that the corridors of Whitehall would be full of excited people and the roads full of cars leaving the Capital. There seemed little point in rushing back to London. They spent a quiet day on the Wylye and landed several good trout. Only then did they return to the inn, pay their bill, and drive back through Salisbury and up the road to London, around which the barrage balloons were already hanging in silver clusters.

CHAPTER NINE

Scientific Adviser

For Tizard, as for so many of those whose lives were closely wrapped to one of the Services, the change to war was more nominal than real. The event had for some weeks been regarded as inevitable, and all personal preparations had been made by the time that Big Ben chimed the nation out of peace on the Sunday morning of 3 September.

In the complex plan of dispersal and evacuation it had been arranged that the two technical committees would operate from Oxford, and it was in Chatham House, Balliol, that their members were now to meet – the 'Balliol Beagles' as Tedder called them, on the grounds that they were always letting loose fresh hares before they had caught the last lot. Tizard could look back with mixed pride and disappointment at the progress achieved since the day, almost five years before, when he had been asked to accept the chairmanship of the first of them. So far as air defence was concerned, the country was on the verge of readiness. Massive efforts were still being made to put the finishing touches to the chain of radar warning stations, and cover against low-flying raiders was still non-existent. Yet in spite of these defects, the whole prospect of defending Britain against air attack had been decisively transformed by the combination of radar and its operational utilization which Tizard had pioneered by the Biggin Hill Experiment. It is doubtful if in modern times any comparable transformation in a nation's defences had taken place within so short a period.

In other spheres, however, the Royal Air Force was still lamentably ill-equipped to fight the battles which lay ahead. Its greatest problems lay in its inability to carry the war effectively to the enemy, on land, on sea, or in the air. Here Tizard's Offence committee had made scant impression. The result was that little progress had been made towards finding how targets could be satisfactorily reached. The problems of precision bombing had barely been considered, those of area-bombing barely contemplated. The available bombs, it was found some years later, were only half as effective, weight for weight, as those used by the Germans. All this was perhaps inevitable, given the climate of the 1930's; and it is a fine point to decide whether responsibility lay more with the members of the Air Council or with those who were their political masters. The result, however, was that while the officers and men of Fighter Command could use skill and daring to fight with the weapons most suited to the task in hand, those in Bomber Command had the scales constantly weighted against them by lack of suitable planes, by lack of adequate navigational equipment, and by armament which did relatively little damage for the high cost in casualties.

The Air Marshals and other high officers with whom Tizard's life was to be so closely connected for the first of the war years were mainly those who respected his work for the Royal Air Force and who trusted his judgement. But there were exceptions. At the top of the Service pyramid there was Air Chief Marshal Sir Cyril Newall, Chief of Air Staff, already more than two-thirds through his three-year span of office. Kindly, conformist, hating intrigue with much the same upright honesty as Tizard, he was at times uncertain of the way in which he could best utilize the abilities of this man whom he admired but could not quite understand, and whom he summed up as 'one of the hairy scientists, not one of the smooth ones'. Below Newall there was Pierce, his deputy; Freeman, who as Air Member for Development and Production – and later as Chief Executive in the Ministry of Aircraft Production – was to have constant and detailed contact with Tizard and his work; Portal, possibly the clearest-headed of them all, the Air Member for Personnel who after being C.-in-C. Bomber Command was to take Newall's place; and Welsh, Air Member for Supply and Organization. Joubert an old friend of Tizard, one of the few senior R.A.F. officers who had early sensed the value of radar, an old Harrovian moving nimbly up the ladder of appointments, was now pulled back from India for promotion to Assistant Chief of Air Staff. At Fighter Command there was

Dowding, abrupt when not silent, possibly the greatest commander of them all, yet lacking the facility for public relations that
was to become more and more necessary; at Bomber and Coastal
Commands, were Ludlow-Hewitt and Bowhill respectively, both
fighting desperately to retain their position in the queue for planes
and men. Overall, there sat Sir Kingsley Wood, cautious and apt
to become confused, the Secretary of State for Air who had told
the Committee on Defence Programmes and Acceleration that
at the time of Munich the position 'had been positively tragic.
We had then had no real reserve, whether fighters or bombers.'[1]

Thus the situation which Tizard was to find in the Royal Air
Force and the Air Ministry was perhaps typical of much elsewhere.
On the Service side stood a group of men variously equipped for
the work ahead but at least anxious to have done with the uncertainty and, in general, understanding of the ways in which
scientists could help. On the political side the position was different, for here there still remained a reluctance to throw heart and
soul into the war, a constant looking backwards over the shoulder,
and a belief that while scientists might possibly be able to help in
certain minor aspects of the struggle, they lived on a different and
lower level from that of their betters.

Throughout the last months of peace Tizard had increasingly
been acting, and had largely been treated as, the Air Ministry's
Scientific Adviser, a post which did not exist. He was, in fact,
Scientific Adviser to Newall – not to the Air Minister or the Air
Ministry, it should be noted. This was formally acknowledged in
an Air Ministry note dated 2 September which said that 'on the
outbreak of hostilities, Sir Henry Tizard will assume an appointment under the direction of the C.A.S.' A few days earlier he had
been asked by David Pye to fill in an insurance form which was, it
was explained, for 'those scientists who, although not civil servants,
are carrying on work on behalf of the Air Ministry'. However, any
belief that Tizard had now been brought within the body of the
kirk was ill-founded. When it was suggested some months later
that he might give part of his time to other Ministries, the officer
whose official opinion was sought firmly pointed out that 'Sir
Henry is working for the Air Ministry on a voluntary basis, and
consequently he is a free agent as to whether or not he accepts

membership of Ministry of Supply Committees'. Tizard himself stressed that he had 'made it a rule to take no fees of any kind for work, either pre-or post-war' while he was Rector of Imperial College. And any suggestion that he might have executive authority was firmly scotched by a note from Air Marshal Sir Norman Bottomley, Senior Air Staff Officer at Bomber Command, to Bomber Groups a few weeks after the outbreak of war. 'It is to be understood', this pointed out, 'that Sir Henry Tizard is appointed in an advisory capacity and that research and development within the Service will be dealt with as hitherto through the usual channels. . . .' All this was reinforced by one fact: that Tizard's name was not even included in the Air Force List – a list that included the names of other civilians far down the scale.

His position as Scientific Adviser to the Chief of Air Staff was thus a curious one. His two scientific committees remained purely advisory, as did the single Committee for the Scientific Survey of Air Warfare into which they were merged in October 1939. Much experimental work continued to be carried out on its recommendation, but this work might be duplicated or by-passed by that of other agencies. And the happy relations which its members retained with almost all flying units, with research stations such as Bawdsey, now moved north to Scotland, and with individual commanders, rested almost entirely upon the goodwill and understanding built up over the preceding years by the three original independent members of the Committee for the Scientific Survey of Air Defence – Tizard, Blackett, and Hill.

This state of affairs, unsatisfactory as it was, had its compensations. Tizard was by nature an adviser, the man designed to lay all the scientific facts on the line, to provide the information which the executives could study before they took the plunge. This was his métier, and it seems certain that no-one in the Britain of 1939 was more expert in it. Thus his position, outside the machine rather than inside, suited him personally and allowed his talents to be used to the full without ruffling too many official feathers; it made his influence during the first nine months of war far greater than his position would suggest, but his danger at the end of that period quite acute.

From September 1939, his influence sprang mainly from two

things. One was the constant barrage of exhortation and advice with which he bombarded Newall. This was not always heeded, sometimes due to factors beyond Tizard's ken, sometimes due to the lack of satisfactory mechanism within the Air Ministry for 'tying-in' the work of the Directorate of Scientific Research and the work of a purely outside, unofficial adviser. 'Thinking back to the *beginning* of Henry Tizard's time at the Air Ministry my main impression is that we, and certainly I myself personally, did not fully appreciate or know how to make full use of a really practical *scientist*' Newall said many years later.[2] 'I realised this in some measure at the time, and I used often to dine alone with him hoping to learn how best to make use of his talents.' Secondly, there was the plain fact that no other man in the country had so much, or so varied a knowledge of how science could be applied to war. It was not that he was a star performer so much as a great conductor of the scientific orchestra. 'If he couldn't himself play the oboe he knew where to find the best oboist, fit him into his orchestra and, from the score in front of him, bring him in at the right moment', it has been said.

Between September 1939 and the summer of 1940, the bulk of Tizard's most important work therefore continued under the umbrella of the Air Ministry. But his experience was so wide, his contacts so numerous, that he was sought out by many men trying to hammer together a war machine from the miscellaneous collection of pieces available. Thus on 11 October he was visited by Dr Gough, Director of Scientific Research in the War Office. He came, Tizard recorded in his diary to consult him 'about the formation of a Scientific Advisory Committee for the Ministry of Supply.' The Ministry had been formed the previous year but, in the words of the official history, *Administration of War Production*, its research on weapons was still 'cut off from the general body of scientific work'. Tizard gave what advice he could – and two months later was asked whether he would serve on the Advisory Council on Scientific Research and Technical Development which was to be formed. Air Ministry work would prevent him from attending regularly he replied, but with that proviso he would be glad to join. 'I might', he added, 'be useful in helping co-ordination between the research work of the Ministry of Supply and of

the Air Ministry. . . . As for *honoraria,* I do not wish to get any
personal remuneration for my work in connection with National
Defence so long as I remain Rector of Imperial College.'

Hill and Cockcroft were among the other members of this
twenty-man Council which met under Lord Cadman for the first
time on 25 January 1940. Tizard attended meetings for a considerable time but his initial impressions were but slightly altered.
'Proceedings are too formal for my taste', he noted in his diary.
'Unless the scientific men concerned can get closely into touch with
practical problems, it may be that not too much good is done.'
His criticism was not only that the Council was too large and too
unwieldy, too formal in its operation, but that its whole approach
to war was wrong. 'There is an obvious tendency to embark on
unimportant work, without consideration of military applications,
and of previous work by other departments', he noted on 28
March 1940. 'Said I would write a note about this.' This attitude
formed part of a more general appreciation of Britain's position,
which he expressed in a memorandum to the Council in May 1940.
He had claimed early in the month that the resources controlled
by the Ministry were being dissipated. His view did not receive
immediate support and he promised to write a memorandum
which was presented at a meeting on 25 May. This, he said, could
be very short, 'because everything that has happened since the
[last] meeting has made it quite clear that scientific and technical
efforts can only hope to make a real contribution towards winning
the war by concentration on a very few objectives. There is practically no new scientific discovery or new technical development of
importance that is going to produce a big effort unless it makes a
considerable call on industrial resources and involves training of
personnel on a considerable scale,' he continued. 'I, myself, feel
quite confident that there are not half a dozen new things that we
can hope to introduce during the war which would have any
material effect on winning it. Can we not try to make up our
mind what these are? We can only make up our mind if we discuss
realities with experienced members of the Service Departments.
I should like to suggest that the Ministry of Supply should do what
has already been done at the Air Ministry, that is to say ask all its
experimental establishments or committees to decide, in conjunc-

tion with high officers of the Staff, what new developments really show promise of great importance, and to give reasons; and to form some kind of forecast of the scale of production and operation that would be necessary in order to produce an important military effect; and to try finally to produce a list of not more than ten items; then let the Advisory Council view the position again and decide what steps should be taken in order to get the most rapid progress on each of these matters.' Just such an orderly, logical, concentration of available forces was an objective for which he strove throughout the war, and towards its close the logic of events, if not Tizard's advocacy, was forcing just such a concentration on the Government.

Between September 1939 and June 1940, however, his influence was felt mainly on the planning, equipment, and operation of the Royal Air Force, and from his office in the Air Ministry there issued many hundreds of letters, memoranda, and minutes signed in his spidery initials above the letters, 'S.A. to the C.A.S.'. He served on numerous committees and sub-committees, so that one day he would be advising on Heinkel wireless equipment, magnetic detection of submarines and pocket wireless equipments, and on the next on the armouring of bombers, problems of low-level bombing, construction of relief maps and better inter-communication between flying crew.

He travelled extensively, and few days went by without his visiting an airfield, without his physically handling the equipment concerned, and without his talking to the men who used it. Wherever he went, there was two-way traffic – Tizard both drawing out facts by his questions and giving advice from his store of experience. His diary shows how extensive the travelling was during the first weeks of the war – to Exeter on 6 September, where he discussed gunnery problems at the Armament Experimental Unit with G. T. R. Hill; to Farnborough the following day, and to the Admiralty's H.M.S. *Vernon* at Portsmouth on the 8th. By the 9th he was back at the Air Ministry, and two days later was down at the Army's radar establishment at Christchurch with Watson-Watt. On the 13th he was visiting Balloon and Fighter Commands, and on the 15th investigating armament problems with Melvill Jones at Boscombe Down on Salisbury Plain. The following day he was back at Exeter and on the next up at Oxford. The pace was maintained, and during the following months his diaries are dotted with notes of the radio problems of Bomber Command; attendances at Fleet Air Arm Research Sub-committee meetings; meetings with Gough of the Ministry of Supply, with Hankey, and with experts who sought his advice on towed bombs, aerial mines, and plans for photographic reconnaissance.

When in London, he would retire at the end of the day, first to the Athenaeum and then to Imperial College. 'In view of his strenuous war-work which usually lasted from early dawn to midnight or later', comments G. C. Lowry, the College Secretary, 'one would have expected him to go to bed and get the maximum possible rest, once he did get back to the College. Not a bit of it; he used to rout the College Secretary out of bed, often after midnight, and sit for an hour or two, discussing current College problems, and producing answers to them with uncanny speed and accuracy.'[3]

He also kept close touch with the members of the Maintenance Party, which included volunteers from all grades of the College staff. Among them was Sammy Silvester, a labourer who was a very good snooker player and who frequently used the second-hand billiards table bought by the Governing Body to help volunteers pass the time. The Rector heard of Silvester and whenever he had a spare half-hour would challenge him to a game.

*   *   *

During the seven months of the 'phoney war' Tizard helped to tighten the radar chain in preparation for the test ahead; he helped airborne radar, from which so much was to come, over a difficult period during which it might have died; and he mothered into existence the Maud Committee, the first organization in the world to decide that a nuclear weapon could be made. Yet these, as we shall see, were only some of the matters across which his influence ranged with lasting effect.

Tizard's long connexion with radar, as well as his reputation for an almost inhuman impartiality, made him the ideal man to chair a committee set up at the end of October 1939 'to investigate the working of the R.D.F. Chain, both from the technical and operational points of view, and to make recommendations for its improvement.' This was necessary not only to rectify the inevitable strains of a delicate machine during its 'running-in' period but to prevent the recurrence of unfortunate incidents, of which there had already been two.

The first concerned a small aircraft which approached England only a few hundred yards outside the Shoreham bomber lane a few minutes after war had been declared. There was no doubt that the plane was Allied and at first no alarm had been sounded at Fighter Command Headquarters. But the plane had of course been plotted on radar. It was not equipped with the radar identification device only then coming into use and the rules had to be obeyed. The sirens sounded.

The second, and more embarrassing incident took place a few days later when King George VI was visiting Fighter Command Headquarters. As on 3 September, a plane approached the coast without giving identification signals. As on the earlier occasion, fighters were sent up to intercept. This time, however, a defect in the radar system showed the fighters as being not so many miles inland behind the stations, but the same number of miles out at sea. Thus as the King was having the system explained to him by Dowding a raid was shown as developing, and further fighters were sent up to deal with the situation. Confusion increased until finally there appeared to be a major attacking force in the air which no-one had seen and which had certainly dropped no bombs. Meanwhile, the monarch wanted to know what was happening. The investigation which ensued is still spoken of in subdued tones as 'the Battle of Barking Creek'. Such incidents were only the more obvious of the matters which could be investigated now that the all-out enemy attack had not been made. And in the light of the recommendations which Tizard's committee made in November, the whole system was tightened for the trial to come.

The successful defence of airborne radar through a long period of disappointment was an almost personal achievement of Tizard alone. It will be remembered that in June 1939 there had come an order to press ahead with development as fast as possible. The order was followed, and on the night that war broke out a Blenheim bomber was patrolling above the London area with a primitive airborne radar set manned by a civilian from Bawdsey. Five other sets were being installed, and the thirty ordered were completed by the end of the month. They suffered, however, not only from the speed of development but from the difficulties inherent in the move of Bowen's airborne radar group first from Bawdsey to Perth and then to St Athan in Glamorganshire. The result, Tizard subsequently wrote, was that 'when the first A.I.'s were rushed prematurely into service at the beginning of the war, they were a failure, and scientists were told that unless they could reduce the minimum range from 300 to 100 yards night interception would be impossible.' Tizard himself did all he could. 'He spent a considerable time talking to technicians at the bench, to scientists in the air, and to the pilots and crew,' says Bowen. 'He was always keenly aware of their problems and clearly indicated the need for adequate training of personnel, maintenance of equipment, etc. However, the business was plagued with a headquarters staff which was largely ignorant of the problems and requirements, and Tizard's clear view of the problem did not get across to the people concerned. This was largely the reason why the successful use of airborne radar was delayed until 1941 and 1942.'⁴ Tizard refused to be dispirited. He believed that the troubles could be eliminated and on writing to Tedder on 22 January 1940, commented '. . . in fact I regard the successful solution of the A.I. problem as *the* biggest problem of the war.'

At this date the confidence in airborne radar of the few aircrews who had tried to utilize it was marginal and Tizard suggested to Newall that a special committee be set up to co-ordinate all the efforts being made to solve the night interception problem. At the first meeting of the new Committee Tizard expressed his very strong views that the principles of airborne radar were perfectly sound, that current defects were due largely to the haste with which development had been pushed ahead, and that the pressing need was for scientific trials in the air before any more work was done. This testing fell to the Night Interception Unit, later called the Fighter Interception Unit, formed at Tangmere on 10 April under the command of Group-Captain Chamberlain. The results were as Tizard had expected. 'When the Service A.I.'s were properly tested in the air, under scientifically controlled conditions, it was found that the real trouble was that they squinted, and that an aircraft which was believed, by the indications on the instrument, to be straight ahead, was in fact on the beam. When that fault was remedied no more was heard of the vital necessity of reducing the minimum range he later wrote.'[5]

Tizard's influence on the development of airborne radar was thus direct and vital; his connexion with short-wave research, which did so much to make airborne radar effective, was different, indirect, but in the long run just as important. From the early days it had been appreciated that the operational usefulness of radar would increase as the wavelengths on which sufficient power could be obtained were themselves reduced – for the shorter the wavelength, the greater the information which could be obtained from its reflection. Watson-Watt, Cockcroft, Lindemann, C. S. Wright, of the Admiralty – who before September 1939 declared that the side which had power on the shortest wavelength would win the next war – were only some of those who cogitated on how power could be produced at short wavelengths. Tizard was another, and it was Tizard and Sir Frank Smith who at the eighteenth meeting of the Swinton Committee on 14 November 1938, had been asked to report on how university and other scientists might be enlisted to carry out short-wave research. An inter-Service Committee for the Co-Ordination of Valve Development, formally under the aegis of the Admiralty, later became responsible for actually commissioning the research, and finally gave to Mark Oliphant, Poynting Professor of Physics at Birmingham, the work which produced that war-winner, Randall and Boot's cavity magnetron.

Tizard was undoubtedly the main influence which induced us to abandon, temporarily, the work going on in Birmingham on nuclear energy, in order to devote ourselves to microwave radar [Oliphant has written]. Our experience at the 'chain' station, where we were introduced to the mysteries of R.D.F., and discussion with Cockcroft, Bowen and Rowe, convinced us of the advantages which might be expected to result from the development of generators and detectors of radio frequencies far higher than those then in use. It was Tizard who persuaded me that a contribution in the field could be of immediate value in the war with Germany, and I have no doubt that it was Tizard who persuaded Charles Wright to propose to me a practical way in which we could work on these problems under Admiralty auspices.'[6]

Tizard was to have no direct responsibility and 'directly, had nothing whatever to do with the work.' Even so, in the view of those most closely concerned he 'was undoubtedly the main influence.' With Tizard, as with few other people, one can understand how this could be the case.

The need for pressing on at all speed with research into both short-wave and airborne radar was underlined by the fact that little was known about what the Germans were doing. Here the British position was weak, and would have been still weaker had it not been for Tizard's pressure before war broke out. In April 1939 he had persuaded Pye to ask for attachment to the Air Ministry of a special officer to deal with scientific intelligence. The Tizard Committee agreed to forward the recommendation, and R. V. Jones was eventually named as the man required. He was by this time working at the Admiralty Research Laboratory and could not be transferred to the Air Ministry before September 1. The results of this failure to secure adequate pre-war information were far-reaching. They included failure to appreciate, until many months had passed, that the enemy had evolved a radar system which was different from our own but not inferior to it. Perhaps most significant of all, there was the failure to appreciate that the Germans were incapable of building a nuclear weapon. For it seems likely that had Britain been better informed of German research in September 1939, no atomic bomb would have been made by August 1945.

The gap in Britain's knowledge of enemy weapons was thrown into relief when, on 19 September, Hitler made an important speech in Danzig threatening Britain and France with the wrath to come. In this speech he used a phrase which was variously interpreted as 'a weapon with which we could not ourselves be attacked' and as 'a weapon against which there is no defence.' Even though this *waffe* or weapon might refer merely to the Luftwaffe, it was natural in the circumstances that Tizard should be consulted. He proposed that further enquiry should be made about bacterial warfare and that the Chemical Defence authorities should be asked whether any particular gas or bacteria could be easily distributed in glass bottles. 'I had heard', he recorded 'that Germany had imported quantities of glass bottle machinery, and that window glass was short.' In addition, he suggested that the possibility of the enemy using large numbers of pilotless planes – previously discounted – should now be reconsidered. More important in its long-term, but unexpected results, the Tizard Committee suggested that R. V. Jones, by this time a one-man department in charge of Scientific Intelligence in the Air Ministry should be give *carte blanche* to check through the Intelligence Reports of all three Services and make a considered assessment of what Hitler had really meant.

One result of Jones's report was a proposal that all such material should be made available to the three Services, a suggestion which Tizard strongly supported. 'We had a discussion about a Scientific Intelligence Centre at the meeting of the Joint Intelligence Committee', he wrote in his diary for 31 January 1940, 'but the Admiralty were of course against it. However, the Committee agreed in principle and left it to me to convene a meeting of the three D.S.R.'s and put forward a concrete scheme.' The result was indicated less than a month later when he commented on a meeting with Hankey and Sir Samuel Hoare – the latter to be appointed Air Minister in succession to Sir Kingsley Wood within a matter of weeks. 'I told them of my feeling that we must have a Central Scientific Intelligence Service,' he wrote. 'The Committee to discuss this went wrong in my absence owing to Admiralty opposition. Hankey said he was already dealing with a similar problem in connection with wireless, and they both agreed with me in principle.' But at the meeting, attended by the three Service Directors of Scientific Research and the three corresponding Directors of Intelligence, the Admiralty stood out against a joint organization. The existing system continued until, almost exactly seven years later, a special section of the Joint Intelligence Bureau to deal with the subject was set up in the newly-created Ministry of Defence.

During these first months of the war one interesting idea of Tizard's for gaining more knowledge of German work bore fruit. This was his proposal that useful information on German science and technology might be obtained from the numbers of distinguished scientists among the Jewish refugees by this time in Britain. There were obvious problems of taste, tact, and politics,

P

but these were overcome by the plan which Tizard put up in January. A Committee was formed of a number of well-known Jews; this suggested possible helpers, whose names had first to be approved by Tizard. The refugees would then be carefully interviewed. They would not, however, be given any indication that the interview was official. The members of the committee should rather, Tizard advised, 'take the attitude that it is a private venture on their part to ascertain how far help could be given to the Government.' R. V. Jones was appointed liaison officer and the scheme went ahead.

During this same month of January 1940, Tizard found himself singled out for a mission whose unorthodox character emphasized his unique role, both inside yet outside the Air Ministry machine. On 4 January he learned that Newall wished him to go to Italy immediately. The object of his visit was to make a provisional agreement with the Italians for the manufacture of a small weapon, the Manzolini bomb, of which he had heard but of which he knew little. An odd task it would seem, and Tizard, an old hand at such matters, took the precaution of asking for instructions in writing. All he received was an Air Staff note dealing with possible uses of the bomb. Did this mean, he persisted, that he was to assure himself, with the help of technical advice in Italy, that the Italian weapon filled the Air Staff requirements; and, if so, was he to make a provisional agreement? The answer was 'yes', and he was assured that if everything were satisfactory a representative from the Contracts Branch of the Air Ministry would then be sent out to conclude the agreement.

Tizard reached Rome on 8 January, and there discovered the explanation for the Air Ministry's sudden enthusiasm for Italian weapons. The Embassy staff explained that money was no object; officials would, in fact, welcome a £4,000,000 order being placed for the bombs, since at present they saw no method of implementing the Government's guarantee that £20,000,000 would be spent in Italy during the year. Tizard became slightly cautious, attended a demonstration, made the necessary enquiries, paid a friendly visit to an Italian Aeronautical Research Institute, and arrived back in London on the 13th. His caution had been justified. The Air Staff, he now found, felt that there was no longer any need for the bomb – although, Newall subsequently assured him, a final decision would not be taken until its members had considered his report.

Meanwhile, Tizard passed on to Sir Kingsley Wood a proposition which had been made to him by the British Ambassador in Rome – that even if the Air Staff decided that they did not need the bombs, these could surely be bought and handed over to the Finns. 'If used against the Russians', Tizard commented, 'they might have more effect than if used against the Germans. This seems to me a suggestion worthy of your consideration as it may have political as well as material advantages.'

The fact that Tizard could be allowed *carte blanche* to spend up to £4,000,000 in Italy can give a false indication of the attention being given to him and to the work of his Committee for the Scientific Study of Air Warfare. He was worried about this, and his worry was highlighted one evening when, dining with the Chief of Air Staff, he was told that an inventor from Canada would be arriving within the next few days to discuss a new weapon. 'I asked him', Tizard noted in his diary, 'why he had a scientific adviser. Here is a man coming over at considerable expense without any kind of indication as to whether his ideas are of any value; probably a waste of money.' Newall, who appears throughout to have made every effort to utilize Tizard's ability as well as possible, asked him to elaborate.

The result was an eight-page memorandum which Tizard drew up the following day and which indicates that even by this time a sorry state of affairs was developing within the Air Ministry. He listed his complaints, technically, in detail and, judging by the evidence, very justifiably.

> Very little is ever referred to the Committee [he concluded], and the direct advice of the Committee on other matters is seldom ever asked for, and quite important variations in programmes which affect priority of work are made without the Committee being informed. For instance, there was a recent conference at Exeter, settling the priority of the work which affected the Committee's recommendations, and the Committee had no knowledge of it. All this gives me the impression, which I hope is wrong, that D.G.R.D.'s branch, particularly the armament branch, regard the Committee as, perhaps, a necessary nuisance, not a body which must be taken fully into

their confidence and used to the utmost extent. If this impression cannot be removed the Committee's work will suffer, and I believe the progress of the technical equipment of the Air Force will also suffer.

It was a complaint to which he returned a fortnight later.

I saw the S. of S. in the morning [he recorded], and told him that I did not think the position of the Scientific Committee and myself was anything like so influential in war as it had been in peace. The reason was that one was now working in a void. Everybody seemed to be too busy to discuss the general problems in the way they had been discussed and very often there was insufficient authority behind decisions. For instance, the Air Council had reached a decision about the Italian bomb without hearing my views at first hand, although I was in the building.

It might be thought that Tizard's frustration during these early months of the war was linked with Churchill's appointment as First Lord of the Admiralty and the installation there, as his own private statistical adviser, of Professor Lindemann. Such indications of this as there are, must be viewed with caution. So far as Lindemann was concerned there had been a slight and temporary lowering, in the temperature of his relations with Tizard. This had been brought about by his brother, Charles Lindemann, who on Tizard's suggestion had come to the Air Ministry soon after the outbreak of war and there discussed the need to worry more technical information from the French. The demand had been for a man with good scientific knowledge, able to move with ease at the higher Service and political levels, and with a feeling for the French. Charles Lindemann, a student of Nernst before the First World War – in which he had had a distinguished record – Vice-President and technical adviser to the British Military Claims Commission from 1919 to 1924, a cosmopolitan who was yet the most English of Englishmen, was ideal for the task. He was appointed within a few weeks, arrived in Paris shortly afterwards, and for the following nine months continued to provide the Air Ministry, via Tizard, with a continuous and detailed flow of information on how science and scientists were aiding the French armed forces.

Before leaving London he had arranged that he, Tizard, and Professor Lindemann should find themselves dining together one night in the Athenaeum. 'At that time', he says, 'I had no idea how serious their quarrel was . . . It is evident that he and my brother avoided discussing their troubles with me.' He did what he could. And he even succeeded in persuading them to shake hands – a gesture which on F. A. Lindemann's part recalls, as his biographer aptly remarks, 'the glacial handclasp between Giraud and de Gaulle.'

With Churchill, Tizard's relations were at this time more complex and less unfriendly than might have been expected. Rancour on both sides had sunk beneath the need to win the war, and such differences as existed arose mainly from the conflicting views as to how this might best be done. 'I have been so pressed in these early days that I have not had a moment for a talk with you, but I want to thank you for the help you are giving in bringing the Navy abreast of events in our secret sphere', Churchill wrote early in September. 'Please come to me at any time if I can reciprocate.' A few weeks later the two men lunched at Admiralty House and then attended a meeting at which both discussed, together with Lindemann, Ben Lockspeiser and others, the development of various new weapons. 'Winston Churchill told me', Tizard noted in his diary, 'that I was to be given all information I wanted at any Admiralty Establishment.'

Contacts with the First Lord were frequent and their general tone is indicated by Tizard's diary entries for 31 January and 1 February. 'A meeting at 10 pm at the Admiralty, the First Lord in the Chair . . . and the S. of S. also present' runs the first. 'The meeting was held to discuss the new rocket protection of ships. Crow explained his design. As usual much too much optimism was displayed. We went on to discuss the protection of merchant ships and I suggested the PAC scheme. He promised to discuss it further at the Admiralty the next day.' The following day they adopted the PAC scheme, upon which Tizard noted 'This will mean, unfortunately, that the Admiralty will get in the way of Air priorities. Other naval schemes were discussed. All of them seemed to me to be either quite useless or of very little value. However, they were going ahead with most of them.'

The question of priorities was crucial and persistent and under 1 April, Tizard noted of a meeting with Churchill: 'Sometime after this meeting (the next day I think) I had dinner with Winston Churchill and had a friendly talk with him afterwards. I told him that Admiralty requirements were likely to interfere with production of Air Ministry requirements, and it was difficult enough as it is to get anything produced quickly.' Tizard, pulling hard for the Air Ministry, naturally came up against Churchill, pulling hard for the Admiralty; but his opinion of how the matter might be solved is revealingly shown in a letter which he wrote to Churchill on 9 May. 'The best way to settle all these priorities on which there may be some differences of opinion, and to get the right kind of authority and drive behind the work', this went, 'is to have a special committee with yourself in the Chair, if possible another member of the War Cabinet, and high officers of the Service Departments.'

This need to get priorities right was for Tizard one of the central problems of the war and formed the heart of the private memorandum on 'Co-ordination of scientific and technical effort' which he sent to Hankey during the first weeks in April. In this he pointed out that when the Committee of Imperial Defence had become the Secretariat of the War Cabinet on the outbreak of war, many of its committees had automatically ceased to function. 'This involved', he noted, 'the disappearance of a centre of co-ordination where technical problems of great importance to the war could be discussed with Ministers and high officers of the Service Departments.'

> Technical progress is essential in the war [he continued]. The morale of the fighting man is soon broken if his technical equipment is markedly inferior to that of the enemy. But the scientific and industrial resources of the country are strictly limited, and it is essential to use them in such a way as to produce a decisive result as soon as possible, and to avoid dissipation of effort on things that do not matter much, or do not matter at all. If we try to do everything, we may do nothing in time. What is done must depend on higher strategy and tactics; but it is also true to say that high strategy may depend on what *can* be done. . . .
>
> Let me now attempt to be constructive by suggesting a course of action which will not add to the present complexity of organisation. Let the highest officers of the staffs of each Department, whose duty it is to guide and direct technical developments, meet to decide in

common on a short list of new requirements or inventions which, in their opinion, may have a big or decisive effect on the war. Let them be asked to give full reasons for their views, which should be placed before the Cabinet after submission to the Chiefs of Staff Committee. When the list has the final highest approval, let the Cabinet call for regular progress reports and, when necessary, arrange for inter-departmental control. Such action cannot do any harm; indeed it must do good by forcing attention on the things that really matter most. But the list must be kept small; say twenty items at the most.

As an appendix, Tizard added a list of the following 'important new requirements' for the Air Force:—(1) R.D.F. detection of, and homing on, enemy aircraft under 'blind' conditions. (2) Production of transmitters and receivers of very short radio waves (50 cms. and under). (3) Equipment to give quick and 'automatic' recognition of friendly aircraft, from the ground, from ships, and from other aircraft. (4) Improved means of radio navigation. (5) Jet propulsion aircraft. (6) Predictor sights for aircraft guns. (7) Stabilized bombsights, and (8) Short aerial mines.

Within the Air Ministry, Tizard had some success, and it was agreed that work should be pushed ahead on what was virtually this list, with one man in charge of each item. On the larger matter, results were different. A copy of Tizard's memorandum to Hankey was sent to the Prime Minister but before it could be considered the controversial issue of mining the Norwegian leads rose to its climax. On 9 April came the German invasion of Denmark and Norway, and in the ensuing weeks long-term problems were cast aside for more urgent matters.

*　　　*　　　*

As the war burst into activity Tizard was setting in train the long series of events which was to lead men over the frontier into the nuclear age. History has as many watersheds as the most complex mountain chain: yet it is difficult not to feel that one of the most important was crossed when Sir Henry decided in the spring of 1940 that the feasibility of producing a nuclear weapon should be investigated.

Almost a year previously, it will be remembered, Tizard had tried to stake a British claim on the output of the Katanga uranium mines. His action had been taken, however, largely as an

insurance against remote contingencies. He believed, as did the
bulk of his colleagues, that the construction of a uranium-bomb, as
it was long known, would not be possible, let alone practicable;
the results of George Thomson's experiments at Imperial College
had reinforced his views. That Tizard's attitude well fitted the
climate of the times is shown by an incident which took place at a
technical committee he attended early in the war. Lindemann
should have represented the Admiralty but decided to send one of
his able young assistants, James Tuck. 'Tizard is sure to try and
pump you as to what I am up to here', he told Tuck when briefing
him. 'We must have a plausible story to keep him off the scent' –
apparently a reference to Lindemann's latest scheme for the use
of aerial mines. 'You don't know what such a man can do. He can
stir up all sorts of inquiries into its feasibility and frighten the
R.A.F. enough to prevent their trying it. No, you say that our big
line is a uranium bomb. This is just the sort of thing that Tizard
would expect me to be thinking about. You know enough about it
to make a plausible story.' The curious thing, says Tuck, is that
Tizard did button-hole him after the meeting to ask: 'What's
Lindemann up to these days?' 'I duly whispered the astonishing
secret', Tuck says. 'He duly snorted and said: " 'Ha! Just what
I would expect! It will never be used in this war, if it works at
all!' "[7]

Tizard did not think it likely that the physics of the matter would
allow nuclear energy to be used; furthermore, he believed that if
for some unappreciated reason such a thing could be done, then
the men, materials and money required would be far better expended on other work. On the first of these points he erred in good
company. On the second, it can be claimed that he was right, since
even with the massive use of American industrial resources, and
the extension of the war far beyond the duration thought likely in
early 1940, 'the bomb' still came too late to affect the war with
Germany – the only war being waged in the spring of 1940.

By September 1939, two factors had combined to damp down
belief in the possibility of a nuclear weapon. One was the basic
uncertainty as to whether an explosive release of energy could be
obtained from the rare uranium 235; the second was the large
amount of the metal which it was felt would be essential for any

such weapon. Fresh information on both aspects of the problem had come to Tizard by the following March. The first move had been made by Professor Chadwick, the discoverer of the neutron, who had left the Cavendish for Liverpool University in 1935 and had shortly afterwards begun to supervise the construction of Britain's first cyclotron. On 5 December 1939, Chadwick wrote to Appleton, recently appointed Secretary of the D.S.I.R., reporting on work which had been carried out in his laboratory since the outbreak of war on the two different kinds of uranium fission. 'The conclusions I have reached are these', he said. 'It seems likely that both types of fission – the one due to thermal neutrons, the second to fast neutrons – could be developed to an explosive process under appropriate conditions.' Estimates of the amount of uranium necessary varied considerably – from about one ton to between 30 and 40 tons.

> The amount of energy which might be released [Chadwick continued], is of the order of the energy of the well-known Siberian meteor. The difficulty is really lack of data. Very few experiments have been made which throw any light on the actual mechanism of the fission processes; they have been mainly concerned with the radioactive products of the fission – interesting and important but apt to degenerate into a kind of botany. I think it would be desirable to get some information on the mechanism and if I can get enough uranium oxide I will do so. I have here a Polish research man (Professor Rotblat) who has some experience in this work and who is very able and very quick.'[8]

Appleton passed on Chadwick's request to Tizard, proposing that Thomson's uranium oxide might be handed over to Liverpool. Tizard referred the matter to Pye, and Chadwick in due course received part of the ore which had been delivered to Imperial College some six months earlier.

This had barely been arranged when Tizard received a second request, this time from Professor Oliphant at Birmingham. Oliphant himself was by this time deeply engaged on the problems of short-wave radar research, but he had been supplied with uranium oxide by the Air Ministry in 1939 for the use of research workers on his staff. Now, on 16 January 1940, he explained that further experiments were contemplated. Could he, therefore, have another five cwts? Tizard thought that it might be possible. But who would be using it? 'I am told that you have refugees in your Laboratory', he wrote, 'and it just occurs to me that perhaps it is a little hard on the English physicists who are interested in the same problem but who are now deeply engaged on war work, if the refugees get a good start on them by being in the fortunate position of being able to devote their time to pure science. However, I suppose that one should not grumble at this provided that the scientific work goes on.' Oliphant replied that the work would be done by Dr Otto Frisch – who roughly a year previously had, with his aunt Lise Meitner, provided the theory of nuclear fission. Frisch had been visiting Britain when war broke out and would be remaining for its duration. The matter was vital. And, Oliphant added, 'in my opinion it is much more important that work of this nature should be done than that any question should be raised about whose effort is employed to get the answer.'[9] The uranium oxide went to Birmingham.

Frisch was working with Professor Rudolf Peierls, a young Berliner of thirty-two, recently naturalized, who had come to Birmingham from the Cavendish two years previously. Together, during February and early March, they carried out the work, and made the calculations, from which could be extrapolated the possibility of a nuclear weapon. They wrote a two-part memorandum on the subject and addressed it, on Oliphant's advice, to Tizard. And it was this memorandum, with a covering letter from Oliphant, which arrived on Tizard's desk on 19 March.

One half, 'On the construction of a "super-bomb" based on a nuclear chain reaction in uranium', was a highly technical document. The other, headed 'Memorandum on the properties of a radioactive "super-bomb" ', was less technical but in some ways even more remarkable.* It contained not only the rough theoretical blue-print for the atomic bomb but also hinted in simple terms at those questions of strategy and morality which have since been exercising some of the nimblest minds in the world.

---

* The copy of this half of the Frisch-Peierls memorandum in the Tizard Papers appears to be the only one in existence. No copy exists in the official archives, nor have the authors retained one, a fact which accounts for the absence of any reference to it in the official history of Britain's Atomic Energy Project, '*Britain and Atomic Energy*, 1939–1945', Margaret Gowing.

The attached detailed report concerns the possibility of constructing a 'super-bomb' which utilises the energy stored in atomic nuclei as a source of energy [the memorandum began]. The energy liberated in the explosion of such a super-bomb is about the same as that produced by the explosion of 1,000 tons of dynamite. This energy is liberated in a small volume, in which it will, for an instant, produce a temperature comparable to that in the interior of the sun. The blast from such an explosion would destroy life in a wide area. The size of this area is difficult to estimate, but it will probably cover the centre of a big city.

In addition, some part of the energy set free by the bomb goes to produce radioacitve substances, and these will emit very powerful and dangerous radiations. The effect of these radiations is greatest immediately after the explosion, but it decays only gradually and even for days after the explosion any person entering the affected area will be killed.

Some of this radioactivity will be carried along with the wind and will spread the contamination; several miles downwind this may kill people.

In order to produce such a bomb it is necessary to treat a few cwt. of uranium by a process which will separate from the uranium its light isotope (U_{235}) of which it contains about 0·7%. Methods for the separation of isotopes have recently been developed. They are slow and they have not until now been applied to uranium, whose chemical properties give rise to technical difficulties. But these difficulties are by no means insuperable. We have not sufficient experience with large-scale chemical plant to give a reliable estimate of the cost, but it is certainly not prohibitive.

It is a property of these super-bombs that there exists a 'critical size' of about one pound. A quantity of the separated uranium isotope that exceeds the critical amount is explosive; yet a quantity less than the critical amount is absolutely safe. The bomb would therefore be manufactured in two (or more) parts, each being less than the critical size, and in transport all danger of a premature explosion would be avoided if these parts were kept at a distance of a few inches from each other. The bomb would be provided with a mechanism that brings the two parts together when the bomb is intended to go off. Once the parts are joined to form a block which exceeds the critical amount, the effect of the penetrating radiation always present in the atmosphere will initiate the explosion within a second or so.

The mechanism which brings the parts of the bomb together must be arranged to work fairly rapidly because of the possibility of the bomb exploding when the critical conditions have just only been reached. In this case the explosion will be far less powerful. It is never possible to exclude this altogether, but one can easily ensure that only, say, one bomb out of 100 will fail in this way, and since in any case the explosion is strong enough to destroy the bomb itself, this point is not serious.

We do not feel competent to discuss the strategic value of such a bomb, but the following conclusions seem certain:

1. As a weapon, the super-bomb would be practically irresistible. There is no material or structure that could be expected to resist the force of the explosion. If one thinks of using the bomb for breaking through a line of fortifications, it should be kept in mind that the radioactive radiations will prevent anyone from approaching the affected territory for several days; they will equally prevent defenders from reoccupying the affected positions. The advantage would lie with the side which can determine most accurately just when it is safe to re-enter the area; this is likely to be the aggressor, who know the location of the bomb in advance.

2. Owing to the spreading of radioactive substances with the wind, the bomb could probably not be used without killing large numbers of civilians, and this may make it unsuitable as a weapon for use by this country. (Use as a depth charge near a naval base suggests itself, but even there it is likely that it would cause great loss of civilian life by flooding and by the radioactive radiations.)

3. We have no information that the same idea has also occurred to other scientists but since all the theoretical data bearing on this problem are published, it is quite conceivable that Germany is, in fact, developing this weapon. Whether this is the case is difficult to find out, since the plant for the separation of isotopes need not be of such a size as to attract attention. Information that could be helpful in this respect would be data about the exploitation of the uranium mines under German control (mainly in Czechoslovakia) and about any recent German purchases of uranium abroad. It is likely that the plant would be controlled by Dr. K. Clusius (Professor of Physical Chemistry in Munich University), the inventor of the best method for separating isotopes, and therefore information as to his where-abouts and status might also give an important clue.

At the same time it is quite possible that nobody in Germany has yet realised that the separation of the uranium isotopes would make the construction of a superbomb possible. Hence it is of extreme importance to keep this report secret since any rumour about the connection between uranium separation and a super-bomb may set a German scientist thinking along the right lines.

4. If one works on the assumption that Germany is, or will be, in the possession of this weapon, it must be realised that no shelters are available that would be effective and could be used on a large scale. The most effective reply would be a counter-threat with a similar bomb. Therefore it seems to us important to start production as soon

and as rapidly as possible, even if it is not intended to use the bomb as a means of attack. Since the separation of the necessary amount of uranium is, in the most favourable circumstances, a matter of several months, it would obviously be too late to start production when such a bomb is known to be in the hands of Germany, and the matter seems, therefore, very urgent.

5. As a measure of precaution, it is important to have detection squads available in order to deal with the radioactive effects of such a bomb. Their task would be to approach the danger zone with measuring instruments, to determine the extent and probable duration of the danger and to prevent people from entering the danger zone. This is vital since the radiations kill instantly only in very strong doses whereas weaker doses produce delayed effects and hence near the edges of the danger zone people would have no warning until it were too late.

For their own protection, the detection squads would enter the danger zone in motor-cars or aeroplanes which are armoured with lead plates, which absorb most of the dangerous radiation. The cabin would have to be hermetically sealed and oxygen carried in cylinders because of the danger from contaminated air.

The detection staff would have to know exactly the greatest dose of radiation to which a human being can be exposed safely for a short time. This safety limit is not at present known with sufficient accuracy and further biological research for this purpose is urgently required.

As regards the reliability of the conclusions outlined above, it may be said that they are not based on direct experiments, since nobody has ever yet built a super-bomb, but they are mostly based on facts which, by recent research in nuclear physics, have been very safely established. The only uncertainty concerns the critical size for the bomb. We are fairly confident that the critical size is roughly a pound or so, but for this estimate we have to rely on certain theoretical ideas which have not been positively confirmed. If the critical size were appreciably larger than we believe it to be, the technical difficulties in the way of constructing the bomb would be enhanced. The point can be definitely settled as soon as a small amount of uranium has been separated, and we think that in view of the importance of the matter immediate steps should be taken to reach at least this stage; meanwhile it is also possible to carry out certain experiments which, while they cannot settle the question with absolute finality, could, if their result were positive, give strong support to our conclusions.'[10]

With this remarkable document, and its companion, there came to Tizard a covering letter from Oliphant.

I have considered these suggestions in some detail and have had considerable discussion with the authors [this said], with the result that I am convinced that the whole thing must be taken rather seriously, if only to make sure that the other side are not occupied in the production of such a bomb at the present time. In fact, I view the matter so seriously that I feel that immediate steps should be taken to consult with the necessary authorities concerning the possibilities of palliative measures if such a bomb should be used. . . . I shall be very grateful if you will bring this matter to the attention of those who should be informed, though I think there are two reasons why considerable secrecy should be observed. Firstly, if we should tackle the manufacture of such a bomb ourselves a great deal of the effect it might produce would be lost if knowledge of its manufacture should be available beforehand. Secondly, if the enemy are preparing such a bomb, which is not unlikely, we should endeavour to obtain information to this effect through our Secret Service without revealing that we ourselves are aware of the possibility. I hope you will not think this purely a hare-brained scheme. It may well turn out to be impracticable, but in any case it is put forward with sincerity by Frisch and Peierls, and with considerable belief by myself.[11]

The great step forward implied in the memoranda by Frisch and Peierls lay in the fact that they estimated the critical mass of the necessary uranium to consist not of tons, not of hundredweights, but of roughly a pound. To Tizard, concerned not with theoretical but with practical armaments, the position was now suddenly different. A uranium-bomb might still be the most remote of possibilities, but it could not be definitely ruled out. 'What I should like', he replied to Oliphant, 'would be to have quite a small committee to sit soon to advise what ought to be done, who should do it, and where it should be done, and I suggest that you, Thomson, and say Blackett, would form a sufficient nucleus for such a committee, and if you like to bring someone else in please make a suggestion.'

Shortly afterwards at a meeting of the C.S.S.A.W. in Oxford, Thomson was officially given the task of forming a small subcommittee whose brief it was 'to examine the whole problem, to coordinate work in progress and to report, as soon as possible, whether the possibilities of producing atomic bombs during this war, and their military effect, were sufficient to justify the necessary diversion of effort for the purpose'. The members of the

Thomson Committee, as it was to be called met for the first time in the rooms of the Royal Society. And here its members – initially Blackett, Chadwick, Oliphant, Cockcroft, Moon, and Thomson – heard not only the first definite plans for investigating the possibilities of a nuclear weapon, but also an extraordinary story from a French visitor. This was Lt. Jacques Allier, a French business man who a few weeks earlier had succeeded in spiriting from Norway the world's total existing stocks of heavy water, in flying them to Scotland, and in bringing them down the length of Britain to the French Embassy and then transferring them to the Collège de France in Paris, in whose vaults they now lay hidden.*

Allier had crossed the Channel with a letter of introduction to Dr Gough from M. Paul Montel, director of the Franco-British mission in the French Ministère de l'Armament, and he had come on a mission with a three-fold aim. He wished to draw the attention of the British to the work on nuclear fission done by the Joliot Curie team in the Collège de France. He wished to stress French fears that the Germans were working on similar lines. And he wished to prepare the way for an inter-change of nuclear information between the British and French Governments, and for permanent scientific collaboration between the two countries aimed at jointly developing nuclear research. Having addressed the members of the Thomson Committee, Allier was taken by Cockcroft to meet Tizard and Pye at the Air Ministry and to them he gave a list of German scientists capable of carrying out nuclear research. Would it not, he urged, be worth discovering whether such scientists were still working in their peace-time universities?[12] Tizard agreed, although his doubts were shown in the note which he sent the following day to Wing Commander Elliot at the Offices of the War Cabinet.

> M. Allier seems very excited about the possible outcome of uranium research, but I still remain a sceptic and think that probability of anything of real military significance is very low [this said]. On the other hand it is of interest to hear that Germany has been trying to buy a considerable quantity of heavy water in Norway. I think you ought to make enquiries from the Belgian company whether Germany has also been trying to get uranium. You will remember that the

* The details are given in *The Birth of the Bomb*, pp. 68–73.

head of the Belgian company promised to inform us whether there were any unusual demands from Germany. I have received no such information and I suppose you have not, otherwise you would have passed it on. It would be a good thing to find out the facts now.

If Germany is trying to buy heavy water and not trying to buy uranium, I cannot think why they want the heavy water. It may be, however, that they are terrified at intelligence of our own work in England and think they had better corner the heavy water so that we should not have it. This is always quite a possibility.'

Subsequently the idea was put forward that Britain might buy the stock of uranium then held in Belgium but Tizard proposed the more economical method of merely having it moved. 'We might share the cost of transport, and storage in this country, which would be very much cheaper than buying it', he added. 'Then we should feel we had an insurance against the occurrence of an unlikely event.' And on the 15th, he wrote to Charles Lindemann in Paris, saying that he had already seen the French visitors and adding: 'We have taken all necessary action, but for your own information I may say that the French are unnecessarily excited.'

This attitude was at the time just as widely-held in the United States as it was in Britain, and Tizard's scepticism was reinforced when in the middle of May A. C. G. Egerton, joint secretary of the Royal Society, passed on to him a note received from A. V. Hill by this time attached to the British Embassy in Washington as a special Air Attaché.*

It is not inconceivable that practical engineering applications and war uses may emerge in the end [he wrote of nuclear energy]. But I am assured by American colleagues that there is no sign of them at present and that it would be a sheer waste of time for people busy with urgent matters in England to turn to uranium as a war investigation. If anything likely to be of war value emerges they will certainly give us a hint of it in good time. A large number of American physicists are working on or interested in the subject; they have excellent facilities and equipment: they are extremely well disposed towards us: and they feel that it is much better that they should be pressing on with this than that our people should be wasting their time on what is scientifically very interesting, but for present practical needs probably a wild goose chase.[13]

* See pp. 250.

It was typical of Tizard, and of almost unparallelled significance for the future, that in spite of his personal scepticism, in spite of the scepticism of others, he should continue to give support, even though qualified support, to Thomson's committee. He believed that it was best not to argue but – so long as not too much energy was diverted from things that offered better prospects – to discover what the position really was. Thus from early May 1940 onwards – while the Ministry of Supply began to investigate the possible effects of a uranium bomb dropped on a large British city – the work of Thomson's committee began to branch out in Birmingham, Liverpool, Oxford, Cambridge, and a number of other universities. Over it Tizard exercised merely a watching brief and it is here only necessary to tell, more accurately than has been possible before, how it came to be known as the Maud Committee.*

Shortly after the invasion of Denmark by the Germans, Professor O. W. Richardson, Hon. Foreign Secretary of the Physical Society, received a message from Lise Meitner in Sweden. 'Met Niels and Margherita recently', this went. 'Both well but unhappy about events. Please inform Cockcroft and Maud Ray, Kent.' It was clear from this that Niels Bohr and his wife wished to tell their old friend John Cockcroft that they had not been injured during the German occupation. The 'Maud Ray, Kent' appeared inexplicable, and the message was passed to Cockcroft, who at first thought that the words might apply to some sort of ray. The matter was then referred to the military intelligence experts, one of whom soon provided an ingenious explanation: it only needed the substitution of 'I' for 'Y', he pointed out, to make the three words an anagram of 'Radium taken'. Other experts had other views, and one physicist thought that the words might be an anagram of 'Make Ur Day Nt.' – with an implied 'and' between the last two words, an explanation which, as Fowler wrote to Tizard on 28 May, 'is all very wild but just sufficiently reasonable to make one worry'. However, it was decided at a meeting of Thomson's committee early in June that henceforth it should be known by

---

* Various parts of the story have been given in print, including some by the present author in *The Birth of the Bomb*. The full details have become available only through the help of the Tizard Papers.

Q

the initials M.A.U.D. The riddle of the telegram was solved only three years later when Bohr arrived in Britain after a dangerous journey from Denmark. Had his message, he asked, reached his old governess, Maud Ray living in Kent – at an address which had been dropped in cable-transmission to Britain.

By the time that the Maud Committee was christened the Germans were already cutting their way through France, and the Chamberlain Government had fallen, protesting to the last, with a mixture of indignation and wounded feelings, that this was not at all the sort of war for which it had prepared. That the repercussions would affect Tizard was obvious. He, and those who thought like him, had often enough stressed that a major reorganization was necessary to prepare the country for survival and victory. What they had not perhaps realized clearly enough was that they themselves might be overturned rather than thrust upwards by the swift rush of events.

Tizard himself was affected by five factors – four personal and one historical. First was the increased power which Churchill's new ascendancy would give to Lindemann. He had, after all, been among the first to appreciate the German menace; had always believed that he, better than most scientists, could help to defeat it. Tiresome as it might be to those who disagreed, it was natural enough that he should try to further this with whatever power he could command. Secondly, there was the fact that Newall, the Chief of Air Staff whose personal Scientific Adviser Tizard was, had disagreed with the former First Lord of the Admiralty on the Norwegian operations; more unfortunate, perhaps, was the fact that Newall had been proved right and Churchill wrong. Thirdly, there was the installation of Beaverbrook as the head of the Ministry of Aircraft Production – basically Freeman's organization for Research, Development, and Production, now formally separated from the Air Ministry and given independent status. Thus the operational aspects of Tizard's work henceforth involved a Chief of Air Staff with whom the new Prime Minister had disagreed and its technical ones the agreement of a Minister whom Tizard at first considered to be merely a 'newspaper baron', a species for which he had little sympathy. Fourthly, Sir Archibald Sinclair, the Secretary of State for Air who now replaced Hoare, was a man whose links with Churchill went back to the days of the First World War when the new Prime Minister had been Colonel of the 6th Royal Scots Fusiliers and Sinclair had been his second-in-command.

These human factors on which events were to turn were important. So, also, was the fact that when the new Government came into office radar had yet to be proved in battle. All that Tizard had stood for during the previous five years had still to be put to the test. Ithuriel's Hour, when 'the sum of all our past, Act, habit, thought and passion, shall be cast in one addition', was now near. It was near both for radar and for Sir Henry Tizard.

CHAPTER TEN

Resignation

The translation of Churchill to No. 10 Downing Street, and the increase in Lindemann's power which accompanied the move, added weight to the forces now coalescing against Tizard. Yet this did not make his eclipse inevitable. His disagreements with the new Prime Minister appeared to be more concerned with policy and less with personality than had been the case a few years previously. His reputation in the Royal Air Force was unique; his position in the scientific establishment both secure and unerodable. He might well, but for the unhappy coincidence of affairs, have struggled on against the tide until the tide itself turned. However, this was not to be. The crisis came in mid-June, less than six weeks after the new Government had been thrust into the saddle. Its course was brief, and its result a crushing one for Tizard. It seems possible, however, that the affair might have gone differently had not Tizard's position *vis-à-vis* the Air Ministry – as distinct from the Air Force – already become somewhat uncertain.

Early in April, it will be remembered, he had achieved adoption of his eight-point priority plan. However, this was followed, little more than a month later, by the thaumaturgic reorganization which converted virtually half of the Air Ministry into the new Ministry of Aircraft Production. Much of the vitality thus injected into affairs had just that quality of urgency and concentration which Tizard had always demanded. Yet he had suffered under the older order for too long to be dissociated from it. And, increasingly, he found himself by-passed – a matter made simpler no doubt by the fact that he was responsible not to the new Minister but to the Chief of Air Staff. On 23 May he wrote a revealing letter to Hankey.

> I think I ought to let you know that if you want me to help you in any way I should be quite free to do it [this said]. The fact is that my own

work at the Air Ministry, far from increasing, has been decreasing considerably. You know that I have never had any executive authority, and the war now depends much more on getting things done and getting policy settled than on advising what things might be done in nine months time. . . . I do not really feel that I am being properly used, and it is better for me either to be properly used or to give up pretending that I am much use to the Air Ministry where they do not really seem to want me. Please understand that I have no grievance whatsoever, but I am not anxious to go on in a pretence position with people like yourself, and perhaps the Prime Minister also, being under the impression that I have more power and influence than, in fact, I have.'

There are two points about this letter which should be stressed. The first is that Tizard realized that opposition now came as much from within the Air Ministry as from the Prime Minister. The second is that he 'had no grievance whatsoever', an indication of that Olympian attitude which he could take to affairs: an attitude which was to handicap him considerably during the next few dangerous weeks, yet was to be largely responsible for his extraordinary influence during the following years.

He continued to advise one and all, and as the Germans brushed aside opposition on their way to the Channel coast, he remained in close touch with both Hankey and Newall. His comments contained the persistent warning that the airfields were far too vulnerable to attack by paratroops, and his records include notes of a memorandum on defence sent to Ismay and apparently used by the latter as 'a very useful brief' at a full-dress meeting of the Cabinet on 23 May. He had more than one ingenious idea. 'Has it been decided to resort to chemical warfare if there is an attempted landing in this country', he asked Hankey on 28 May. If so, he suggested, electric light bulbs filled with mustard gas might be strewn on the beaches, a proposition which the experts at Porton considered to be quite feasible. To Newall he wrote three days later with an idea for countering the alleged German practice of using despatch riders dressed in Allied uniforms. 'Has anyone', he asked, 'ever thought of using trustworthy Indian soldiers as despatch riders for the important order? A German cannot disguise himself as an Indian.'

Meanwhile, the crisis in his own affairs was approaching. The immediate cause was a new system of radio navigation used by German bombers. Its outcome, with all that this was to mean for the war, might have been different had Tizard for once approached a technical problem with less than his normal caution; or had he, once the facts became plain, begun adroitly to manipulate man and events in his own favour. He was not, however, the man either to forsake the scientific approach or to indulge in personal manoeuvrings. What for many would have been merely the techniques of survival, were inevitably summed up by Tizard in the one damning word 'intrigue'.

Even by the summer of 1940 relatively little attention had been paid in Britain to the possibilities of radio navigation. There were several reasons for this – the overwhelming need to concentrate all scientific effort on the defence of Britain itself, a sphere in which long-range navigation was of minor importance; strong views on the limitations believed to be inherent in radio-navigation over distances of more than a few miles; and the comfortable view that if astro-navigation had been good enough for the pioneers it was good enough for the pilots of 1940. These and other factors combined to produce scepticism when, early in 1940, it was first mooted that the Germans might be experimenting with a system of radio-beams which would enable them to pinpoint targets with considerable accuracy, at night, and under the worst weather conditions.

In Britain the nearest approach to beam-navigation was the blind approach system in which an aircraft was led down on to its home runway by means of a radio beam transmitted from the airfield. This was picked up by the navigator who in the simplest form of the device, heard a set of dots if he was on one side of the beam and a set of dashes if he was on the other. 'On the beam', he heard a continuous sound. Various technical problems involved were overcome one by one during the late 1930's but two things appeared to limit the use of the method for long-range navigation. One was the spread of the beam, thought to be inevitable; the other was the strength of the signals themselves, a strength which most experts believed would be too small to allow their use over Britain when transmitted from as far away as Germany. This theory – a complacent one when viewed by hindsight but reasonable enough at the time – was held by both Lindemann and Tizard until mid-May, and it is from this period that the crisis of Tizard's position began to develop, a crisis which is perhaps best explained and examined by a simple chronological account of events.[1]

On the outbreak of war, R. V. Jones was, as we have seen, charged with the task of investigating the scientific background of German weapons. Early in 1940 the technical feasibility of the enemy being able to concentrate a radio-navigation beam was mentioned to him by a colleague, and from then onwards this was constantly in his mind. During the spring a German bomber, shot down over Britain but not destroyed, was found to contain documents which mentioned that a 'knickebein beacon' was operating from dawn to dusk. With the nearest translation of 'knickebein' being 'googly' in cricketing parlance, it seemed likely that these beacons might be very different from the radio-beacons already being used by the Germans for homing purposes. Then a second crashed German bomber was found to contain a document bearing the 'knickebein' phrase, and on 23 May Jones wrote a paper claiming that after all a German plane might be able to 'bomb on the beam'.

Thus matters remained during the first days of June. On the 4th, Tizard visited Lindemann at 10 Downing Street, where he already appeared to be working on an open brief from Churchill to investigate anything of scientific importance. 'Apparently he has been told by the P.M. to "drive ahead" with anything new that may be of use this summer, and there is enough overlapping of responsibility to hinder almost anything useful being done', Tizard noted in his diary. The situation became clearer when on 7 June Watson-Watt, Director of Communications Development – a phrase which was used to conceal the existence of radar – suggested that he attend an informal meeting at which Sinclair would be present. Tizard, not officially invited, found that the object of the meeting was discussion of the priority list which he himself had arranged with Tedder some weeks earlier. Moreover, although Tizard was the Scientific Adviser to the Chief of Air Staff, Sinclair had at his elbow his own scientific adviser – Professor Lindemann.

During this first week of June, as it became clear that the Secretary of State for Air and the Chief of Air Staff were relying on different, if not opposed, scientific advisers, there came growing confirmation of some German beam system. This reached a peak when, on the 12th, Group Captain Blandy, a Deputy Director of Intelligence, handed Jones a slip of paper on which were the words 'Knickebein Cleves established fifty-three, twenty-four north, one degree west', and asked: 'Does this mean anything to you?' To Jones it appeared as conclusive evidence that a radio beam had been set up at Cleves – a few miles beyond the Dutch frontier and the nearest point in Germany to the British coastline. Later in the day, he was sent for by Lindemann who wished to discuss the possible existence of German radar. Lindemann then asked if there was any other news. Jones told him about the beams; and, after a good deal of technical argument he finally convinced Lindemann that such a system represented not merely a threat but a dangerous one. This view was reinforced a few days later when a bomber, shot down over Britain during a prowling night reconnaissance, was found to contain equipment which could be used not only for blind landing but for the reception of certain other radio signals on a specific wavelength.

Lindemann now prepared a note for the Prime Minister.

> There seems some reason to suppose that the Germans have some type of radio device with which they hope to find their targets [this said]. Whether this is some form of RDF and they have IFF [Identification: Friend or Foe] beacons planted by spies to guide them, or whether it is some other invention, it is vital to investigate and especially to seek to discover what the wavelength is. If we knew this, we could devise means to mislead them; if they use it to shadow our ships there are various possible answers; if they rely on I.F.F. beacons to find targets, we could lead them astray; if they use a sharp beam this can be made ineffective. With your approval I will take this up with the Air Ministry and try to stimulate action.

At the bottom of the letter, Churchill initialled a note for Sinclair: 'This seems most intriguing and I hope you will have it thoroughly examined.[2]

Sinclair acted without delay and on 14 June, as the Germans were about to enter Paris, appointed Air Marshal Joubert to take charge of the investigation. The following day, a Saturday,

9: The officers who with Henry Tizard were so largely responsible for the success of the Biggin Hill Experiment (ranks given as in 1936): Wing Commander E. O. Grenfell (*top left*); Squadron Leader A. McDonald (*top right*); Squadron Leader R. L. Ragg (*lower left*); Flight Lieutenant W. P. G. Pretty (*lower right*); and Dr. B. G. Dickins (*bottom*).

10: "A" Flight No. 32 (Fighter) Squadron, Royal Air Force, Biggin Hill, November, 1936

11: The Air Council, June 1940. Showing, at head of table (*l. to r.*), Captain H. H. Balfour, Parliamentary Under-Secretary of State for Air; the Rt. Hon. Sir Archibald Sinclair, Secretary of State for Air; Air Chief Marshal Sir Cyril Newall, Chief of Air Staff. On the extreme right is Sir Arthur Street, Permanent Under-Secretary of State for Air.

12A: Sir Henry Tizard and General Sir Bernard Montgomery, Oxford, March, 1944

12B: Sir Henry Tizard (*back centre*) and Brigadier Charles Lindemann (*back right*) at Indianapolis, September 4th, 1940, during the visit to the United States of the Tizard Mission

Joubert, Jones, Lindemann, and a number of other officers met in Joubert's room at the Air Ministry. Tizard does not appear to have been invited – possibly because he held no official position, possibly because his unofficial one sprang from the Chief of Air Staff rather than from the Secretary of State for Air. The meeting considered the latest evidence of a German beam-system; this had been building-up, with material from various secret sources, during the previous few days, and it now seemed likely that it would be technically possible to find such beams if they existed and take counter-action either by jamming or by other subtle means. It was agreed, therefore, that a meeting of the Night Interception Committee should be called for the following, Sunday, afternoon.

Tizard, who was of course a member of this Committee, was informed of this Sunday meeting by Joubert, on the telephone since he had travelled up to Oxford the previous evening. He appears to have regarded it as rather a routine affair, saw little special reason for his presence, and decided to remain in Oxford.

He arrived back in London on the Monday morning, amid the repercussions already following the downfall of the French Government, Marshal Pétain's order to the French forces to lay down their arms, and the negotiations with Hitler which were even then starting. He was soon informed of what had happened at the Air Ministry meeting the previous afternoon. 'It was a curious affair because at the beginning there was no regular member of the Night Interception Committee present except Nutting and myself', said a note from Dowding. 'Joubert was in the chair and Watson-Watt arrived after half an hour. The meeting was called to discuss some rather nebulous evidence about German long-distance navigation by Lorenz beam. Various plans were made to find out what the Germans were doing, and these may or may not be effective.'[3] And, although he did not add this, Watson-Watt had been put in charge of the technical work.

More information on the Sunday meeting soon came to Tizard not by letter but from Jones, Air Commodore Nutting, Director of Signals, and Group Captain A. F. Lang who arrived in his office on the Monday morning to inform him of events. He should, they urged, prepare a note for Newall on what they all considered

a serious and developing threat. They then agreed with the text
of the note which Tizard now drew up.

'I have just been informed of the discussion at the meeting
specially called yesterday (Air Marshal Joubert in the Chair) to
consider the evidence that German aircraft were using a Beam
System to locate themselves over this country, and to recommend
action to defeat this system', it began. The method, he agreed,
was no doubt technically possible and with it an enemy might
arrive over a selected spot in this country within a certain area.
'What is not known is the extreme range within which this system
can be operated – it is probably not more than 200 miles but the
extreme range would vary with the height, increasing with
altitude.'

Tizard put forward various counter-measures which might be
brought in if the threat of the beams were confirmed. Jamming
was one; another was the fitting of British bombers with apparatus
to enable them to follow the enemy back to his airfields. But both
his caution, and the way in which he had been ignored, are
apparent towards the end of his note.

> I may be wrong [he wrote], but there seemed to me to be unnecessary
> excitement about this latest alleged German system for dealing with
> the country. One cannot possibly get accurate bombing on a selected
> target in this way. It would, of course, be perfectly simple to use this
> system to bomb a place like London under completely blind con-
> ditions, but if we on our part had the task of bombing Berlin under
> blind conditions we could do it without this system. I feel that the use
> of the system is far more dangerous if it is looked at from the point
> of view of being able to concentrate large numbers of aircraft round
> a particular district in bad weather conditions by day. That is what
> we must be prepared for and it is on that occasion and that only that
> I should jam.

He went on to suggest that plans might be drawn up to
discover what equipment would be needed for a similar British
system and what sort of accuracy might be expected. 'Who
is really responsible for looking after this and deciding policy
under you? I have been trying to find out but have not been
successful. Someone should have the definite responsibility. At
the moment the responsibility for action and for advice seems to
be widespread.'

He took the note himself to the Chief of Air Staff's office, the note which his honesty, his ability to see both sides of any question, had prevented him from writing with anything more than caution. He lunched with Trenchard, whom he reported as being 'very gloomy. Had a row with Winston'; and took the afternoon train to Grantham.

While Tizard was sitting in the train and while Newall was still, one must assume, studying the latest account of what was really going on, the first action to counter the beams was already being taken in London. For on the afternoon of the 17th Watson-Watt convened a meeting at the Air Ministry at which steps were taken to equip aircraft for finding the beams, and to provide certain radar stations with the apparatus needed for the same task.

Tizard's attitude is made clear not only by his memorandum to Newall but also by his diary entry for the 17th and his reply to Dowding's note. The first reported that 'meeting yesterday nothing to do with Night Interception – general excitement unnecessary and engendered by Lindemann about beam system of navigation possibly used by enemy.' The second said that he was 'disturbed about the way certain people seem to panic suddenly about matters which, though important, do not give cause for panic. The result of these sudden committee meetings is that people go off at half-cock and no-one seems to have clear-cut responsibility . . .' The 'possibly' was of course scientifically justified by the knowledge then available, but the intensity of Tizard's implied scepticism is difficult to justify. As early as February he had been informed that the Germans apparently had 'an apparatus which is said to be termed the X-Geraet and to enable aircraft to be located by a new electric or radio-electric process'; and a fortnight later he had written, after hearing of recent Intelligence reports, that 'the Germans obviously have something in the way of RDF and have ideas of using it for bombing at night.' Weighing all this, it is difficult not to assume that for once he was unduly affected by the man on the other side of the argument. 'Tizard', says Sir Frederick Brundrett, who from the Admiralty played an important part in the war-time development of radar, 'was never prepared to accept any opinon emanating from Cherwell as an honest one, and I frequently found it necessary to prevent the circulation of some particularly acid comments which were quite unjustified by the facts of the actual case under discussion.'⁴ It is not quite certain that this fatal weakness was now the main cause of Tizard's scepticism but there seems little doubt that it influenced the tone of his note to Newall – and his attitude in the personal crisis which was now rising to its climax.

On the day that Tizard had written to Newall, Lindemann sent a second memo to the Prime Minister. 'In view of the extreme urgency of investigating radio methods likely to be used against us by the enemy, in the air or elsewhere,' this ran, 'it would seem desirable to have a ruling that such investigations take precedence, not only as regards materials, but especially the use of men, over any research whose results are not likely to affect production in the next three months.' At the foot, written and initialled in red by Churchill, was added the comment: 'Let this be done without fail'.⁵

The following day, the 18th, a small unit was formally set up to 'investigate signals of a suspected frequency both from a specially fitted van and from an Anson aircraft'. By the 19th, special ground observers had been selected, brought to the Air Ministry and briefed for their tasks – the speed of the whole operation stemming from Churchill's over-riding order that Lindemann could requisition research staff as required.

Tizard had been by-passed, but at this stage it would not have been too difficult for him to recoup. He had been sceptical of the beams rather than dogmatically opposed to their existence. Now that they were being taken seriously it would have been easy to show an anxiety he did not feel, to support whatever measures were taken, claim as much credit as possible if they proved justified and, if the reverse, to use their failure as a weapon in the personal battle. Tizard, however, was not that sort of man. Others might act thus. For him even the most necessary ends did not justify such means. You did not chip away at scientific integrity and you did not play politics. You resigned, however politically unwise this might be. This he now proposed to do.

On 19 June he travelled up to Oxford and from Balliol wrote two letters. After commenting on a technical matter to Pye, he continued 'On the other hand Lindemann is advising the Secretary of State directly about this and about 11 other matters concerning our short list of high priority items. I feel therefore that until the Air Ministry can make up their mind on whom they want to rely for advice it will only make the present confusion worse if I come in at this stage.'

He also wrote to Sinclair.

As you must be very busy, I think I should put down on paper what I want to say when I see you [he began]. There is considerable confusion not only in the allocation of responsibility for giving scientific advice on new developments, but also in responsibility for taking action. For some years, before the war, as well as since the war, I have had the chief responsibility for giving the Air Ministry independent advice, and have been Chairman of a strong committee appointed for the purpose. We have worked throughout in close personal touch with the Air Staff and I have made it my business to study the operational needs and difficulties of the Commands.

For some months past I have found that my advice has been seldom sought by the Ministry on important matters and, if given unsought has either not been taken or been taken too late. This has been specially noticeable recently. As an individual, I do not complain – the personal feelings of individuals are of no account in war. But I do think that it simply causes confusion to keep me in my present position, and then for you to rely on others as your principal advisers.

I attended your meeting on June 7th almost accidentally. I had no invitation from you but was told by Mr. Watson-Watt that you were going to have an 'informal meeting on gadgets' and that it would be a good thing for me to come along if I could. I saw Sandford* who told me that he did not think that it was important that I should attend. However, I put off another engagement and came. I was, therefore, very surprised to find a formal meeting on a high plane, with Professor Lindemann installed as your principal scientific adviser, discussing a priority list which I was primarily responsible in drawing up.

All the decisions taken at that Conference affect decisions taken by other responsible bodies. It is, if I may say so, of great importance that you, as Secretary of State, should be taking a close personal interest in the few new developments that may have a decisive effect on the war, but it is surely wrong to come to definite decisions at such meetings without either making full use of machinery and people already

* Sir Folliott Herbert Sandford, Principal Private Secretary to the Secretary of State.

existing to advise you about such decisions, or alternatively, abolishing
the existing machinery and people and replacing them by something
better. There is great confusion now because responsibility for advice
and action is not clear cut, and directions and suggestions for action
come from many sources, not properly co-ordinated.

Too many cooks spoil the broth. This is as true in the field of
scientific research and technical development as in any other field.
I feel, therefore, that I should now resign my position and thus rid
you of one of the spoiling cooks. I do so with great regret because I
think that in the past I have been of some help. But I am only adding
to the confusion, and not helping on the war, by hanging on now in
difficult circumstances: and I had better do nothing until you or any
other Minister feel that there is a position of clear cut responsibility
that I can usefully fill.'

To Sinclair, still grappling with his new responsibilities at the
Air Ministry, largely dependent on his permanent staff and the
goodwill of the Prime Minister, Tizard's letter came as a shock.
Now, perhaps for the first time, the new Secretary of State for
Air realized his involvement in this particular battle. At 7 p.m. the
following day, the 20th, he was available for Tizard at the House
of Commons. 'He had got my letter but had nothing to propose,'
Tizard recorded in his diary that evening. 'I promised to consider
the position further before deciding.' He was unimpressed by
Sinclair who, he wrote in a letter to Hill a few days later, 'ladled
soft soap over me – much to my annoyance'. But there was still
time for second thoughts. They might have altered the position
had it not been for the events of the following days.

Churchill, who had decided that the question of the beams
warranted his personal intervention, now called a meeting at No.
10 Downing Street for 9.30 on the morning of Friday 21 June. 'If
I had not written to, and seen, the S. of S. previously, I do not
think that I should have been asked to this meeting', Tizard subsequently wrote to Hill. It seems likely that he was right.

On the morning of the 21st Churchill, Lindemann, and Beaver-
brook seated themselves on one side of the long table in the
Cabinet room – while some fifty miles from Paris the desolated
French officers were being taken to an historic railway carriage
in the Forest of Compiegne to hear Hitler's draconian terms.
Facing the Prime Minister's party in No. 10 were Sinclair,

Newall, Tizard, Watson-Watt, Portal of Bomber Command, and Dowding of Fighter Command. The matter to be discussed was considered to be so vital and so secret that no Secretary was present. No minutes were taken. Arriving half an hour after the meeting had begun, and informed of it only a few minutes previously, came R. V. Jones. Lindemann waved him over to his side. But Jones was an Air Ministry employee; he resolved the situation by sitting at the short end of the table. There was a good deal of controversial argument about the practicability of the beams, and about their importance should they exist. Lindemann stressed the importance of the threat. Tizard asked whether we would adopt this system if we were in the Germans' position, and answered himself by saying that we would not. Jones, queried by Churchill on a technical point, briefly outlined the events which had led him to suspect the existence of the beams. It was then decided that investigations of this purely Air Force matter should be intensified, that preparations should be increased for dealing with the beams if they did indeed exist. But it was to Lindemann – not to Sinclair, not to Newall and not to Tizard – that the results were to be reported; and it was Lindemann who was to give a weekly report to the Prime Minister on the progress in what came to be known as the battle of the beams.

Churchill's view of the matter, and the way in which he felt it should be tackled are illuminated by this passage in his history of events:

Being master, and not having to argue too much, once I was convinced about the principles of this queer and deadly game I gave all the necessary orders that very day in June for the existence of the beam to be assumed, and for all counter-measures to receive absolute priority. The slightest reluctance or deviation in carrying out this policy was to be reported to me. With so much going on I did not trouble the Cabinet, or even the Chiefs of Staff. If I had encountered any serious obstruction I should of course have appealed and told a long story to these friendly tribunals. This however was not necessary, as in this limited and at that time almost occult circle obedience was forthcoming with alacrity, and on the fringes all obstructions could be swept away.[6]

If there remained any doubt that in this context Tizard was regarded as one of the obstructions, it was removed later in the day. After lunch another meeting was called to discuss the priority list. This time it was held in the Air Ministry and Sinclair, not Churchill, was in the chair. But, as in the morning, it was Lindemann who sat on the chairman's right hand. 'Most of the discussion was futile, and decisions were made contradictory to other decisions', Tizard subsequently wrote to Hill – phrases suggesting that his antipathy to Lindemann, and the way in which he was being treated, were at last beginning to sway his better judgement.

For the beams did exist. They were found that night by a specially-equipped Anson search aircraft which flew from Wyton in Huntingdonshire northwards across the Midlands in whose blacked-out factories men and women were making good the grievous losses of Dunkirk. 'We took off about dusk', says the pilot, Flight-Lieutenant H. E. Bufton, as he then was. 'It was a fine bright summer's evening. By the time we got up to four or five thousand feet, not very high, we found good clear signals – dots – on 31.5 megacycles. We turned north and after about ten minutes' flying crossed a very sharp beam into the dash sector.'[7] The beams led, clean and unmistakable, towards the heart of Derby where lay the Rolls-Royce aero engine factory, one of the most important targets in Britain.

The counter-measures, introduced just in time during the coming weeks, were to limit severely the value of the German technique. This was never used successfully for the night bombing of Fighter Command's airfields, an operation suggested by early investigations and one which might have had the most fearsome consequences. It was used, however, for many months in various forms. Coventry was bombed on an improved system and so was London on nights such as that of 29 December when the beams, still not consistently jammed, crossed above the tower of London University. It was bad enough.

From the meeting in the Air Ministry on the afternoon of the 21st, Tizard went to the Athenaeum and there wrote the draft of his formal resignation.

Dear Secretary of State [this read], Many thanks for your kind remarks yesterday. I feel convinced, however, especially after the meetings today, that I am right in resigning my present ill-defined responsibilities. If you are to have an independent scientific adviser it is

very important that he should enjoy your confidence, and also that of
the Prime Minister, and the Air Staff. I cannot pretend to fill that
bill, and it is harmful, not helpful, to progress to go on as at present.

My resignation as adviser must also include resignation of the
Chairmanship of the Scientific Advisory Committee. You will be
able to get another Chairman if you wish; but in my opinion the committee had better be abolished as in existing circumstances it cannot
be of much use.

I want to make it clear that my resignation does not mean that I
refuse to do anything for you. If you, or any member of the Air Staff,
want my advice on any specific question in future you have only to
ask, and I will do what I can. But it does mean that I shall not do
things and give advice, on my own initiative, as I have been trying to
do hitherto. As things now stand, that only leads to muddle and
confusion. Yours sincerely, HTT.

Tizard showed the draft of his letter to Newall. The reactions
of the Chief of Air Staff, and the atmosphere in the Athenaeum
on that warm summer's evening were described in Tizard's subsequent letter to Hill.

Newall . . . agreed that I could not do otherwise and asked me to
suggest some other way in which the Air Ministry might use me with
authority [he wrote]. I told him that I was going to make no suggestion now, and advised him not to do anything in a hurry, but to wait
for two or three weeks. The fact is that Winston is trying not only to
be Prime Minister and Commander-in-Chief, but also, through his
pets, to control in detail all the scientific work of the Department. Only
this morning, Stradling* told me of the same kind of interference with
A.R.P. work. If this goes on we are bound to lose the war. Something
must be done about it, but the question of timing is important.
Everything is in a muddle now.

He travelled up to Oxford on the Friday night, and the next
morning drove to Exeter. 'Picked up two sailors at Stonehenge
and gave them a lift to Exeter', he noted in his diary. 'They were
"guarding Salisbury Plain" as their ship was in dock. They said
they wanted to get to sea again as the Navy was grand. They had
been at Narvik and Dunkirk and were very fit and cheerful though
they had had no pay for three weeks.' At Exeter he met his son
Dick, temporarily serving there with the Air Defence Department

* Sir Reginald Stradling, Chief Adviser, Research and Experiments,
Ministry of Home Security.

R

of the Royal Aircraft Establishment and they spent Sunday fishing the Exe. On Monday he drove to Worth Matravers, on the Dorset coast, to which the Bawdsey research station had now been moved from Scotland, and then on to Cockcroft's Army radar establishment at Christchurch. He reached Oxford late that night and the following day was involved in discussions on the latest smoke and dazzle experiments. In the evening he wrote to Hill. And the following day he drafted a personal note to all members of the Committee for the Scientific Survey of Air Warfare, a note which really marked the opening of operations on the other side of the Rubicon.

> For some time past I have been very unhappy about the progress of work initiated by the Committee, and have felt that my position as Scientific Adviser to the Chief of Air Staff carries with it implied responsibilities which I am not able to discharge properly [this said]. With the change of Government matters have become worse in this respect; not better. There are too many advisers and too much conflicting advice; responsibilities are not clear cut, and in consequence action is slow. In the circumstances I have felt that for me to retain my present position is harmful, and not helpful to progress. I have therefore resigned my post as Scientific Adviser, and as Chairman of the Committee. I have also told the Secretary of State that I do not think that the Committee can continue to be of much help unless there is a change in the organisation. We have worked very happily together for a long while, and I am quite confident that an unprejudiced review of our work would show that we have made very few mistakes and that our judgment has been good. But this is not a time to dig up the past, and we shall all be able to do useful work in other ways. I shall take no further action until I have learnt your views.

Simultaneously he sent a similar note to Fighter, Bomber, and Coastal Commands. 'There are so many inside and outside advisers now available at the Air Ministry, so much contradictory advice given on important technical matters, and in consequence so much uncertainty and slowness of action', this started, 'that I have felt for some time that I am not effectively helping in the war by retaining my present rather vague responsibilities.' He went on to say that he was still willing to help the Commands personally in any way, but his letter must have produced a sinking feeling in many who read it.

The events of June 1940, marked a watershed in Tizard's career, just as they did in the story of Britain's survival. It was not merely that from this time onwards, in the words of a Senior R.A.F. officer closely involved, Churchill failed to trust Tizard's judgement. That would have been easy enough to bear; all men, even Churchills, make mistakes. Yet Tizard, self-critical man that he was, must himself have looked a little glumly at the future. For there was a treble irony about this incident which was to mean so much to him. One of his rare misjudgements had been made just when events cast their most flattering light on Lindemann's dogmatic, opinionated, and almost bull-dog qualities. The central figure had been R. V. Jones, whom Tizard himself had forced on a semi-reluctant Air Ministry and without whose persistence the danger might have burst upon Britain unawares. And without the discovery of that danger at the last minute of the last hour Tizard's own genius in enabling Britain to win the day battle of the air might possibly have come to nought – blown apart by accurate night attacks on the targets he had helped to safeguard by day.

Yet it soon became clear that this error of judgement, however grievous circumstances might make it, weighed little when placed in the balance against Tizard's long record of achievement. Thus the news that he had been forced out brought despondency to the Air Force and alarm to the scientific establishment. 'It seems to me intolerable that you should find your position usurped by Lindemann without any reference to you', wrote Freeman. 'The whole position is preposterous as are indeed many other things at the present time.' Dowding felt 'very resentful' of the treatment which Tizard had received. 'I feel', he wrote some weeks later, 'that we all owe a debt of gratitude to you for the commonsense and logical attitude which you have adopted to scientific problems – in fact I always say of you that no-one would suspect you of being a scientist (and I mean that in a most flattering sense). The present witch doctor is firmly established for the time being but witch doctors lead a precarious existence . . .' Bowhill, deploring the news, wrote that 'stations in Coastal Command are open to you whenever you want to visit them in order to study any question'. Trenchard at first refused to believe it. The scientists, less hampered by Service reservations, were even more outspoken. To Appleton, the resignation was 'a major tragedy', while Egerton wrote that it was 'quite terrifying to realize, when the country is in such danger, that things like that can be happening owing to personal intrigue.' Charles Darwin, head of the National Physical Laboratory, writing from Bushy House, expressed to Tizard his 'profound disgust' at the way he had been treated. 'It really does seem to me that we do not deserve to win when this sort of thing can come about by the agency of a pack of small-minded men', he added. Others, writing in similar vein, declared that their concern was 'shared by the whole of the scientific community'.[8]

This almost universal reaction was given force by the combination of two feelings. There was disgust at the shabby personal treatment meted out to a man who had created an air defence out of nothing. And there was distrust not so much of Lindemann himself – it being generally accepted that war makes curious alliances essential – not of his scientific ability, but of his ability to use science in the context of Service requirements. In fairness two other factors should be mentioned. To Churchill and those who supported him – as well as to many others – the 'miracle' of radar and the value of the machinery which Tizard had helped to create, was still a question-mark in the future; only from mid-July onwards was its unique value in full-scale operations put to the test. Secondly, only a few of those even at the highest levels, inside the Royal Air Force or out, knew the background of the controversy over the beams. Even in writing to Hill on 25 June of the vital meeting on the morning of the 21st, Tizard felt able to disclose only that it had been called 'to discuss an Air Force problem'.

It is easy for the conflict between Tizard and Lindemann to obscure the central fact that the issue was not merely personal; it was the manner in which the whole scientific direction of the war was to be conducted. This was brought out in the situation that now developed and which seemed likely, for a few critical weeks, to break into the open; that it did not do so – with all the repercussions which would have followed – was due largely to the fact that invasion appeared imminent and that all effort had to be concentrated against that one looming threat.

On 26 June Hill sent to Sinclair his resignation from the CSSAW. 'In the difficulties and confusion now confronting the Government', he commented, 'it would do no good to pursue the matter further at present; later on, however, it may be necessary, on some suitable occasion, to bring the matter up in the House.* I know that practically the whole of the Scientific Community would be of the same opinion about it.' Sinclair, worried no doubt that the controversy might be laid open for public inspection and appraisal, suggested that Hill might meet him; and he hoped that he would do so before the subject was raised publicly 'whether in the House of Commons or elsewhere'. However, the ripples were already spreading outwards. Trenchard was reported as being wholeheartedly on Tizard's side, and it was suggested that if Hill raised the issue in the Commons, Trenchard might do the same in the Lords.

Hill now agreed to see Sinclair, warning him meanwhile that here was something much more serious than a personal disagreement between Tizard on one side and Churchill and Lindemann on the other. 'In the ordeal which the country may soon have to face – and in preparing for it now – it will be disastrous if the best advice is not available and if action is not taken quickly on it', he wrote. 'It cannot be, unless the present unhappy situation is drastically altered. This is not a matter only of Tizard, but of the effective use of our scientific and technical assets and resources in waging war – and not squandering them in wild goose chases.'[9]

Sinclair met Hill a few days later and suggested that a small number of scientists might meet the Prime Minister privately to discuss the situation. Hill rejected the proposal, writing in his draft reply that 'they feel sure that nothing would be achieved that way. If such action is to be taken it must be by someone who will not be charged with having his own axe to grind. In the meantime trouble is blowing up with the Council for Sc. Res. and Tech. Dev. in the Ministry of Supply, who feel that a certain weapon has been pushed and is now being manufactured on a large scale, contrary to expert opinion which regards the decision as dangerous. There was also an idea which was even more questionable than this 'certain weapon', the aerial mine. 'Some of us', Hill

---

* Professor Hill had by this time become an Independent Conservative M.P. for Cambridge University.

continued, 'are very concerned about the possibility that an attempt may be made shortly to fire enemy crops. *Technically* this is pretty certain to fail, *morally* it will give the enemy a strong hand for propaganda, and an excuse for stealing the crops and stores of our friends in occupied territory, *economically* it would be better to concentrate all our bombing capacity on his coal-oil plants.'[10]

This subject was governed both by technical difficulties which were not overcome until late in the war, and by the feeling that while it was permissible to destroy wheat in the granaries or, at a later stage, in the bakeries, it was immoral to attack it while it was still growing. A small number of incendiary pellets, consisting of a sandwich of phosphorus between two layers of cellulose which was harmless when wet but which burst into flames when dry, were in fact dropped; their use was abandoned, partly because of the number picked up by children, partly because they failed to produce sufficient destruction.*

However, the problem of crop-firing was not, perhaps, as ethically clean-cut as some imagined, and Tizard himself had been investigating a method which, had it been used as a reprisal for similar German action, would have produced even greater protests. Earlier in the year he had enquired about particulars of arsenic for crop-destruction, and had asked experts to obtain more precise information of the potentialities. On 9 February 1940, he wrote a preliminary draft about the subject, and noted that 'the whole scheme does not look very promising either from our point of view or the enemy's'. However, at the beginning of the following month he met two well-known scientists both of whom, he appreciated, could give further advice on such work, and on 4 March he wrote to the Chief of Air Staff saying: 'I have been examining past work and recent suggestions on the possibility of destroying or injuring growing crops by dropping suitable substances from the air.' He went on to say that any such scheme had earlier been ruled out as impractical, but that latest

---

* An American suggestion was that such pellets could be dropped in grease-proof rags. They would then be retrieved by rats and mice who would drag them to basement crannies where they would be even more damaging than when used for crop-destruction.

reports suggested that only one-tenth of the amounts previously thought necessary might in fact be effective. He moved, therefore, that a small committee should be set up to make a serious scientific examination of the data. Two months later he examined various equipment which had been prepared, and noted: 'I saw spraying apparatus. New form, involving dropping the container, which sprays on descending, looks much better than the old form.'

All such work was merely tentative, however. One reason why it was never carried into operation is indicated by two letters from Air Vice-Marshal MacNeece Foster, A.O.C. No. 6 Group. The first was to Portal, C.-in-C. Bomber Command.

> My dear C. in C. [he wrote on 9 July], with reference to the comments of Tizard and Lindemann which I mentioned yesterday, there is one other point of some importance you may consider has a bearing on National Security.
>
> A good deal in the future depends on supplies from America. There are strong forces headed by Ford and Lindbergh which are against giving up these supplies.
>
> If they can say that we are deliberately destroying 'the kindly fruits of the earth' as a means of starving a Continent, they may make it very difficult for our friends who wish to help us.
>
> Some small knowledge of American politics and propaganda makes me feel that this is a point worth while taking into account, unless the blow we mean to strike is likely to be decisive; a question on which there appears to be some doubt.[11]

Later in the month, MacNeece Foster wrote to Tizard, saying 'I hope and believe that we may have had together something to do in saving the country from a possibly disastrous venture – morally, politically, and militarily.'

Meanwhile, the struggle to alter the existing system by which Lindemann appeared to have sole access to the Prime Minister's ear was continuing. In the van was Hill who drew up a secret memorandum which was approved by a number of scientists including Tizard himself. Its damning facts and figures were provided by a member of Pye's staff in the Directorate of Scientific Research.

The tone of this memorandum. 'On the making of technical decisions by H. M. Government', was set by the opening sentence which stated that 'a number of scientific men now connected with

work for the Services are gravely concerned at the manner in
which technical decisions are frequently taken by the War Cabinet without, or against, proper technical advice'. The memorandum cited the case of the incendiary pellets for crop-burning. It
cited the case of £1,000,000 to 'be spent in producing long aerial
mines, which would probably be useless even if the aircraft for
laying them were available, which they are not.' There then came
the nub of the matter, on which the opposition rested its case.

> The time is too grave to allow personal considerations to hinder one
> from making a frank statement, though I make it with regret [the
> document continued]. It is unfortunate that Professor Lindemann,
> whose advice appears to be taken by the Cabinet in such matters, is
> completely out of touch with his scientific colleagues. He does not
> consult with them, he refuses to co-operate or to discuss matters with
> them, and it is the considered opinion, based on long experience, of a
> number of the most responsible and experienced among them that
> his judgment is too often unsound. They feel indeed that his methods
> and his influence are dangerous. He has no special knowledge of
> many of the matters in which he takes a hand. He is gifted in explan-
> ation to the non-technical person; the expert, however, realises that
> his judgment is often gravely at fault. Most serious of all is the fact
> that he is unable to take criticism or to discuss matters frankly and
> easily with those who are intellectually and technically at least his
> equals.
>
> I realise that Professor Lindemann's presence may be indispen-
> sable to the Prime Minister, and the prestige and influence of the
> Prime Minister are now so important to the nation that some com-
> promise may be necessary. It is impossible, however, for the present
> situation to continue as it is. I possess detailed evidence in various
> instances of the waste of time, money and effort which his advice has
> caused, and of the improper methods by which he has worked. A
> large number of my scientific colleagues, inside and outside the
> Government service, will confirm these statements and they cannot
> be seriously disputed. I realise that the whole trouble is not due to
> one person, but that a system has grown up of taking sudden tech-
> nical decisions of high importance without, or against, technical
> advice. These decisions, as in the ill-considered case of the pellets
> designed to destroy enemy crops, may involve questions of high
> policy. They may involve grave loss of human life and of national
> supplies, as in the failure to provide protection for merchant ships.
> They may lead to ill-advised adventures which slow down the pro-
> duction of tried weapons. Unless the system is altered and a better
> one evolved the situation will become highly dangerous.[12]

Two appendices were attached. One consisted of 'notes on suggestions made by Professor Lindemann'. These included fourteen different proposals ranging from aerial mines and the use of butane gas for ground attack to that for crop-firing pellets. Beside each were the comments, damning but indisputable, which came – although this was not revealed – from David Pye's Directorate of Scientific Research.

The second appendix to Hill's memorandum consisted of notes by Tizard on Lindemann's proposals for Air Defence made in the Tizard Committee. 'Speaking generally', Tizard concluded, 'I cannot think of any original idea of Lindemann's which has been of any practical value. I agree, broadly, with his views on bomb sights, but they are not original. The trouble is that the man with the wrong ideas has had, to support him, all the drive and enthusiasm of Mr Winston Churchill, whereas my Committee has not had corresponding support. The result has been waste of effort and dislocation of work. There has been on the other hand a complete lack of executive drive behind the recommendation of my Committee, with the result that we are now short of weapons and methods that would have been available had we been in the fortunate position of advising Mr Churchill. I have documentary evidence for this statement and am preparing it.'

Hill's memorandum was only the most important shot in a campaign which was now being waged almost openly in the scientific world. 'RHF, I gather, has resigned from the Cttee and I gather Blacket is going to (or has)', Hill wrote to Tizard on 3 July. 'W. L. Bragg is writing to Herbert Morrison about it. Other groups of people are concerned. Altogether there are the makings of a first class row if something isn't done quietly about it soon . . .'[13]

While the repercussions of his resignation were rumbling round the scientific world, Tizard himself was continuing philosophically with his customary work of giving advice to all who asked him for it.

At the same time he was clearing up his papers. But he had not, after all, completely given up his advisory work. On 27 June Freeman had written to Sir Arthur Street, then Permanent Under-Secretary and Secretary of the Air Council, pleading that whatever

else happened, Tizard should not be allowed to resign from his
work on the Aeronautical Research Committee. Street drafted
the necessary letter but Sinclair refused to sign; the work of the
A.R.C., he pointed out, now came under the jurisdiction of Lord
Beaverbrook. Freeman explained the situation to Tizard who said
that since he would not, as he had imagined, be reporting to Sinclair, he was prepared to carry on. Similarly, Joubert wrote on
14 July hoping that Tizard would continue to attend meetings of
the Air Ministry's Night Interception Committee – although in
what capacity is not clear.

When it came to his position *vis-à-vis* the Chief of Air Staff,
Tizard went on unchanged, and in mid-July was stressing to
Newall that it was 'of the utmost importance that even at this late
stage we should concentrate on the large-scale production of
bombing machines in Canada with all that this entails. The engines would be bought in the United States and therefore the
machines would have to be designed for American-built engines.
The training would have to be done in Canada, and this should
include a development of radio navigation, which is behind-hand
here, but which, as a problem, could be well tackled in Canada.'
Shorts, he suggested, would be the best people to undertake the
engine work, and their men, he proposed, should be sent across
the Atlantic. 'I feel that if I were an autocrat and could do what
I like', he added, 'I should export as many skilled workmen as
possible, with the ultimate object that whatever happened in
England, I should have a factory over there which no enemy
could touch, producing weapons of great defensive value.'

In many ways he continued as before. An unreal touch is added
by a note sent to him by Air Vice-Marshal Saundby on 26 July,
saying that even by that time there had 'been no official or even
unofficial notification' of his resignation. Tizard himself, however,
appears to have been in no doubt about the position. He cleared
up his papers in Oxford and in London, and returned all official
documents. There were, however, his own private papers. 'The
question that arises', he wrote to Freeman on 2 July, 'is what
should happen to my records. Actually I have already begun
taking notes on certain important matters so as to have a precis
handy, with the idea of then burning the record. Another idea

has, however, occurred to me. Professor R. H. Fowler is leaving for Canada in the middle of the month as liaison officer to help the Canadian National Research Council to get going on experimental work which will be of value to us as well as to them. Would it not be a good thing for Fowler to take some of my more important records with him? This would have two advantages. (a) He would have first hand information which he could use in Canada, and (b) the records would be in a very safe place which might be rather a useful insurance.' Freeman agreed the following day and left it to Tizard to select what Fowler should take. This he did, going through the material with Fowler and handing him 'all Committee minutes, my pre-war notes, and other papers to take to Canada.'

On 26 July he wrote in his diary: 'Final cleaning up of papers and removal of some . . .' He was still chairman of the decreasingly important Aeronautical Research Committee and still a member of the Ministry of Supply's ponderous Advisory Council, but neither post now counted for much by comparison with the past. Yet the very qualities which had prevented him from fighting for his own position in the political melee now inhibited him from bringing his case into the open. It looked as though his influence on the war might be ending as the real struggle was starting. This, however, was far from the case.

CHAPTER ELEVEN

The Mission to the United States

There is some evidence that by the early summer of 1940 Tizard was tiring; at least a few of those who now saw him after a lapse of years were shocked by what they saw. He had, after all, been in the eye of the storm for five long years and the strain was telling. Throughout July, however, as the value of the radar chain became more explicit, and as he himself sat impatiently without a full-time job, neither in the war nor out of it, he rallied back with a vigour that surprised his many friends and shook those enemies who had written him off for the rest of hostilities. Within weeks he was leading the mission to the United States which he had been advocating almost since the outbreak of war.

The Tizard Mission of September 1940 – formally the British Technical and Scientific Mission to the United States – marked a watershed in Anglo-U.S. relatoinships. It handed over to the Americans the most closely-guarded of all British scientific secrets. And in the field of short-wave radar alone, as Cockcroft later wrote, 'our disclosures had increased the power available to U.S. technicians by a factor of 1,000'. The effects of the Mission were, moreover, to stretch far into the future. During the war, inter-change of information went on at an increasing pace along a number of channels, notably those at the office of the National Defense Research Committee in London and the British Common-wealth Scientific Office in Washington; while after the war such free interchange of information as continued rested largely on the basis of goodwill which the Mission had created and fostered. Yet it must be remembered that the British group which took British equipment and British ideas across the Atlantic as the Battle of Britain was rising to its climax, did not offer information on a reciprocal basis. Its whole concept as developed by Tizard was something very different from a market-place exchange of secrets, and the brief which he himself wrote gave his objects as head of the Mission in all-embracing terms.

It has become accpted that the Tizard Mission was the brain-child of the Churchill Government. This was not so. The seeds from which it grew were planted shortly after the outbreak of war in 1939. Interchange of information was discussed in December of the same year; it was discussed throughout the spring of 1940; and it was finally approved by the new Government only some three months after its accession to power, and only then with some reluctance and misgiving. Grounds for such reluctance were not lacking. Within the Admiralty there was a fear – unjustified as it later proved to be – that information given to the Americans would quickly be secured by German agents. There was a feeling in parts of the Air Ministry that while the Americans might help in the solution of British production problems, this was not certain and might not even be necessary; while those who were chary of presenting valuable wartime secrets to a neutral country were reinforced by the unhappy history of the Norden bomb-sight. President Roosevelt had been asked by Mr Chamberlain for details of this most valuable instrument shortly before the outbreak of war, but had given a non-committal answer. Mr Churchill, at the Admiralty, had taken up the request three months afterwards but even the offer of the latest British developments of Asdic in December 1939 had failed to produce results. Two years later, long after the success of the Tizard Mission, the Americans remained adamant on this point. 'A few days before Pearl Harbour', writes H. Duncan Hall, 'the American Navy was still considering the question of the release of the Norden sight and "still unwilling to do so for military reasons" '.[1] This was a rare case of American obfuscation, and it was, as we shall see, at least partly influenced by an unfortunate delay in Britain which sorely hampered Tizard's efforts. Yet its earlier stages must be borne in mind when considering the slow development of the Mission.

The first suggestion that scientific liaison should be established with the Americans was made by Tizard in November 1939, when he proposed to Newall that A. V. Hill, then one of the joint Secretaries of the Royal Society, should be sent to Washington as a scientific adviser to work with the Air Attaché, Air Vice-Marshal

Pirie.[2] Hill agreed. 'Brooding over our conversation re America, I think it is very important indeed that something of the kind should be done', he wrote to Tizard on 20 November. 'It seems rather likely that scientific liaison will be established with Canada, and the American proposal should – apart from anything else – make that much more effective . . .'[3] Tizard talked privately at this period of 'bringing American scientists into the war before their Government' but was thinking merely of liaison, without any hint that information should be exchanged. This later question came before the Cabinet in December, however, and the Admiralty, no doubt with the Norden case in mind were, in the words of the official historian 'reluctant to agree except on a basis of strict reciprocity – an Asdic for a bomber sight – as to which for some time there were difficulties on both sides.'

These difficulties spread to the proposed Washington appointment, and after a further talk with Hill at the turn of the year Tizard wrote to Newall again on 5 January. 'He (Hill) suggested that if there is trouble over a definite appointment and if the thing cannot be settled soon, it might be wise to send him over specially for three months, then let him come back and report, and on the basis of his report decide whether to replace him by anyone else. I think there is a good deal to be said for this. The scientific contacts that are important to make should be made quickly; all this delay is most disappointing . . .' Eventually, in February, Hill left for Washington, a supernumerary Air Attaché technically on loan from the Royal Society. The Air Ministry paid only his expenses.

Hill's contacts with American scientists were extensive and cordial. He quickly realized that they were already experimenting with radar, even though their work was taking a course unhurried by any spur of national danger; yet their potential facilities, both for research and production, were immense. In April he therefore recommended to Lord Lothian, the British Ambassador in Washington, that an exchange of detailed information and experience on radar should be made with the United States. Lothian cabled the suggestion to Britain on 24 April, together with his approval of the proposal. Pirie cabled his support, and the matter was discussed again on 26 April. The situation was slightly obscured by a statement from the Foreign Secretary, Lord Halifax.

The previous day, he said, the U.S. Ambassador, Mr Joseph Kennedy, had told him that the U.S. Government had already given the British all bar two of the secrets of their naval and military devices, one of these two exceptions concerning the Norden bomb-sight. Nevertheless, it was agreed that the matter might be pursued, and on the following day a meeting to discuss interchange was held in the Air Ministry and attended by Appleton; Watson-Watt; Charles Wright, Director of Scientific Research at the Admiralty; and a number of others concerned with radar. 'Dr Appleton suggests', Watson-Watt wrote to Tizard of the meeting, 'and I agree, that if recommendations are accepted, I ought to visit the U.S. to negotiate. I should have plenary powers.'[4]

It was from this meeting that the idea of the Mission crystallized, a hard proposal being made in a minute which Tizard now wrote to Newall.

I am definitely in favour of a frank interchange of all technical information with the American Navy and Army Departments [this went]. There is, of course, a risk of information going sooner or later to the enemy, but I think that we should gain more than we should lose by taking this risk. What we want most to do now is to get scientific results applied in practice, to supply the Air Force with suitable equipment as soon as possible. It must help materially to enlist the help and powerful resources of the American radio manufacturing industry; and we cannot get their help adequately without disclosing our technical information. R.D.F. is perhaps the best bargaining counter we have; if we use it properly we may well get in return the whole-hearted co-operation of the American authorities in other ways. On the other hand I do not think that Hill is the best man to convey the information and do the bargaining. He is not a radio expert, and Americans are such good salesmen that he may well run the risk of attaching too much importance to some of their claims. If you decide in favour of a frank interchange of information, I suggest that a special mission should be sent as soon as possible, and that Mr. Watson-Watt should go with the mission, which should be headed by an Air Force officer of high rank.

Tizard was by now seized of the idea and stoutly defended it at another meeting held in the Air Ministry a few days later. He found considerable opposition. Watson-Watt 'maintained that the Americans could not teach us anything, and that we should get much the worst of the bargain . . . that there was nothing in the

production argument, and that by the end of the year our facilities for production would be greater than theirs. I said that if so
it would be the first time in history that this had happened.' The
Admiralty, in the person of Admiral Somerville, believed 'that
anything told to the American Navy went straight to Germany',
an objection for which Tizard could subsequently find no ground
at all. This, judging by Tizard's notes, remained the main stumb-
ing-block throughout the next few days – despite his question:
'Are we to assume that our Intelligence Service is quite incapable
of extracting information from America and that the German
Intelligence Service find it easy?'

Thus matters rested during the first days of May until, on the
10th, the whole problem was transformed by the German offensive
in the West. 'It looks', Churchill's P.S. at the Admiralty wrote,
'like being a shorter war than we might have thought earlier.'
Then, on 18 May, the whole problem of exchanging secret information with the Americans was discussed by the Service chiefs.
Sir Dudley Pound supported the idea, saying he understood that
the Americans were working on the use of very short waves and
that their knowledge might be helpful. Newall said that he was
inclined to agree. So did Ironside, speaking for the Army and
giving what appeared to be sufficient reason: the Army, he explained, had no particularly secret equipment. The Chief of the
Air Staff was therefore invited to examine the proposal to pool
secret technical information with the United States of America,
and to report his conclusions. Hankey, Minister without Portfolio, and a man whose opinion weighed heavily if not decisively
in such matters, supported the exchange of radar information
two days later, and on the same day, the 20th, A. V. Alexander,
the new First Lord of the Admiralty, suggested to Churchill that
he should make a definite proposal to Roosevelt. 'I consider it
important', he added, 'if the offer is made, there should be no
appearance on our part of attempting to bargain, and I would be
prepared to release securities without restraint, including Asdics,
RDF, and measures for countering magnetic mines.' Churchill's
reply, commenting that he did not think that the wholesale offer
of military secrets would count for much at the moment, accurately
reflected the attitude of leaders hard-pressed by calamity.[5]

Meanwhile, on the far side of the Atlantic, the dour course of events in Europe had stimulated, among American scientists, the wish to aid the Allies. This fact is made clear in a personal letter which Hill wrote to Tizard on 20 May. He had, he said, done all he could in Washington, and he would now do more good by 'coming back and stirring up there', as he put it.

My main thesis [he continued], is that *we could get much more help in the U.S. and Canada if we were not so damnably sticky and unimaginative.** There is an intense eagerness to help which we do not exploit: (a) because we are such bloody asses, or (b) because we are so sure we can win without anybody's help. Illustrations. A. We could get hundreds of experienced pilots if we didn't demand allegiance to K.G. VI, and at the present critical moment the Americans would wink at their people going. B. All offers to exchange information with them would, I am sure, be welcomed, & would open up very great research & development & production facilities. (4) The general ideas about RDF are now coming to be commonly spoken of, so we need not imagine that anything except the details is secret. This morning 2 letters from 'inventors' came in offering us what was essentially AI, and also GL3 for directing and rangefinding for AA guns. Yesterday Aydelotte,† discussing Anglo-American cooperation with me, asked openly why we didn't share information on microwaves for AA gunnery: and Bush also yesterday asked me why we didn't use the resources of firms here for manufacturing such stuff. (5) It might be worth while having somebody permanently here to relieve the attachés of the burden of dealing with inventors and inventions – 99% of which are useless. Pirie's time is considerably wasted with inventors. Death rays (a flood now because of the stories of the Liege forts) are unusually numerous. Wearing carbon next to the skin is the latest device for avoiding them. (6) I hope to goodness something will be done to help the Canadians to use their resources more fully for research and development. Egerton & I tried last September but 8 months have been wasted. The same damnable lack of imagination. (7) I made an American rather sore and ashamed yesterday by saying that they get just as hot about *our* examining mails at Bermuda as about the *Germans* invading Holland and Belgium.

Well, best wishes to you: I wish I was coming back sooner, but I have engagements till 15 June: it is damnable being here now – though one's American friends are just as restless as one is oneself.[6]

* Doubly underlined in original.

† Frank Aydelotte, Director of Advanced Study at Princeton and American Secretary to the Rhodes Trustees.

s

Hill had, in fact, roughed out the framework within which he felt that exchange of information should take place. It is described in a memorandum which he had already passed to Brigadier Lindemann, who had moved from Paris to Washington on the fall of France and whose combination of knowledge and charm was already providing him with a useful if unofficial niche from which he could survey and at times influence Anglo-U.S. relationships.

> In present circumstances (18th June 1940) I suggest that the proposal might most suitably be put to the President of the United States as follows [Hill wrote].
>
> (a) That the British Government is extremely grateful for the generous help which is now being given or promised from the United States. (b) That the Government realises that it is in our own interest and in the interest of civilisation that the rearmament of the United States should be as rapid and effective as possible. (c) That the Government, therefore, will be glad, without condition, to give to the Government of the United States any scientific and technical information in connexion with the war, and any service experience relating to it, which they desire. (d) That the British Government would hope, in return, that restrictions on information or purchases now existing in the United States for reasons of secrecy, may be modified.
>
> The essential point of this is that we should offer any information desired, *without condition*, since we realise that America is fundamentally engaged in the same struggle for civilization as we are. The exchange would follow naturally.'[7]

In a memorandum written on his arrival in England, Hill was even more outspoken: 'Our impudent assumption of superiority, and a failure to appreciate the easy terms on which closer American collaboration could be secured, may help to lose us the war,' this went. 'An American said recently to Mr. Casey, the Australian Minister in Washington. "Why do the English always hold their friends at arm's length?" There is a very strong desire to help us, but of course the same fetish of secrecy exists in the Service departments in the U.S.A. as in Great Britain; it can be avoided in only one way, namely by a frank offer to exchange information and experience; without such an offer the resources of the U.S. will remain imperfectly accessible to us.'[8]

Hill's formal proposals, with their emphasis on an open exchange rather than on a one-for-one barter, had sprung from mutual agreement between Tizard and himself and were the principles on which Tizard finally insisted. They were submitted to Churchill via Professor Lindemann, whose Private Secretary replied on 21 June, saying that 'the question raised in your memorandum was discussed with the Prime Minister yesterday. The Prime Minister decided that a decision should be postponed for a short period, and that the question as a whole should be treated as part of the larger issue.'[9]

On 25 June, Sinclair wrote to the Prime Minister referring to Alexander's letter of 20 May and pressing him to agree. Three days later Lothian telegraphed to say that he believed Roosevelt would be willing to authorize an exchange of information, and urged the making of an immediate offer. The reply went on 6 July, when the Ambassador was told that it had been agreed to initiate a general exchange of secret information and that the British did not wish to make it a subject of bargaining. However, the idea of unrestricted exchange was by no means universal, and Churchill had concurred only on condition that 'specific secrets and items of exchange' were reported beforehand. 'I hope too much of the bargaining spirit and consequent delays will not spoil it', Hill commented in a letter to Tizard on 3 July.

Discussions on the Mission continued throughout the first three weeks of July. The most important was held in Joubert's room at the Air Ministry on 9 July. Hill was present. So was Watson-Watt. It was proposed that the leader of the Mission should be a senior R.A.F. officer, accompanied by representatives from the Admiralty, the War Office, and the Ministry of Supply, as well as by Watson-Watt.

> The terms of reference [it was suggested], should be, through the medium of the British Ambassador, Washington, to negotiate with the U.S. Army and Naval Authorities and men of science, and industrial firms, on the free exchange of information about matters to be put forward by the Admiralty, War office and Air Ministry, and to arrange for manufacture in the U.S.A. of the required equipment. To establish relations with the Canadian authorities with the object of commencing research and manufacture of required equipment in that country. In exchange for facilities afforded to us by the Americans, to provide full information on certain subjects which the Departments consider may be released to the American authorities.

I would hope [continued this note from Joubert], that the Mission
would be able to start for the U.S.A. on or about July 17th. I suggest
that the stay in America should be not less than three weeks.'[10]

Meanwhile, however, the Cabinet was still awaiting news from
Lord Lothian that the President was, in fact, as willing as was
hoped to accept such a Mission. He replied on the 22nd, adding
that the President would be glad if it came as soon as possible.

Three days later the Government authorized the Mission and
agreed that it should be led by Tizard. This latter idea had not
come entirely out of the blue. When the proposal that the Mission
should be led by an R.A.F. officer had been quietly dropped,
Joubert had at first put forward the name of Lord Chatfield and
then proposed that Sir Henry Tizard be asked to attend to 'the
civilian side of the Mission'. Tedder was more forthright. 'It is
clear', he wrote on 16 July, 'that by far the best leader would be
Sir Henry Tizard, who combines the wide scientific knowledge
needed with the knowledge of current operational requirements,
and who has also an international standing as scientist.'[11]

Tizard was, of course, the only man who had the required
combination of qualities and it is not surprising that Churchill,
accepting that the exchange would best be initiated by a Mission
headed by a personality of outstanding eminence in the scientific
world, should have proposed Tizard's name. However, it was
stipulated that precise lists showing the information it was proposed to impart, and the information it was hoped to receive,
should be prepared and submitted to the Prime Minister for his
approval.

Such was the state of affairs that Tizard himself only heard of
the proposal some five days later when Sinclair informed him of
the fact and added that he had probably heard the news already
from the Minister of Aircraft Production. That afternoon Tizard
visited the Ministry only to find that Beaverbrook had been called
to an urgent meeting. Instead, he saw Sir Archibald Rowlands,
the Permanent Secretary.

I asked him [Tizard wrote in his diary], what kind of authority I
should have, & was given a provisional list of 'secrets' I should impart, and of information I was to ask for. I said I certainly would not
go unless I was given a free hand & that I did not want to go in any

case unless the mission was really important for the war. It looked to me at first sight as rather a neat method of getting a troublesome person out of the way for a time! Rowlands said it was regarded as really important. I asked who, in that case, would represent the Service Departments. He rang up the Air Ministry & was told that a Flight Lieutenant had been selected! The War Office said they did not think it worth while to send anyone! I said that this was absurd. Rowlands agreed. Finally I said that I would think it over, but that I certainly would not go unless Service Depts. thought it important enough to send officers of high rank. Subsequently saw Joubert at the Club, & explained my attitude.

At this point the fate of the Mission still appears to have been hanging in the balance. However, the battle for control of the air-fields in southern England, the battle on which the German decision for or against invasion would rest, was now rising to its climax. In thousands of villages men waited daily for the ringing of the church-bells which would signal 'Cromwell', the news that invaders were, after nearly 1,000 years, once more approaching English soil. And in London even the most stout-hearted members of the Government must have wondered, in spite of their words, what the outcome would be. Tizard himself wondered. Such matters weighed in the balance. For the country might temporarily succumb, so that the battle would have to be continued from North America; if so it would be as well if the forces there could benefit from the knowledge that Britain had so painfully acquired during the preceding years.

With little settled, Tizard continued his preparations. On 1 August, he went to the Admiralty and the War Office to discuss the naval and military members of his Mission. He asked Tedder to select him a good Air Force Officer. He met A. V. Hill at the Royal Society where he wrote a note stating his views, later getting it typed at the M.A.P. so that, whatever happened, his opinions would be on record. Then, as requested he called on Churchill.

> Had to wait some time as the Archbishop was with him, which, as the private secretary explained, had quite thrown out the time table [he recorded in his diary]. The P.M. quite emphatic that the mission was important and that he particularly wanted me to lead it. I asked if he would give me a free hand, and would rely on my discretion. He said 'of course' – and would I write down exactly what I

wanted. So I said I would go, and went into the lobby and wrote out a paper which I left with his secretary.

This was Tizard's own brief, a virtually all-embracing one which said: 'To tell them what they want to know, to give them all the asisstance I can on behalf of the British Government to enable the armed forces of the U.S.A. to reach the highest level of technical efficiency.'

Every reservation now appeared to have been lifted. Tizard threw all his energies into the business of preparing for the Mission; making final decisions about its members; discussing, largely with Cockcroft whom he had commandeered as his deputy, what exactly should be taken; and, as a side-issue, settling his own personal affairs. There were some minor, irritating, developments and, as always, he seemed to be dogged by the more absurd and niggling of Civil Service rules and regulations. Thus on 2 August he was informed that the Treasury would not be able to pay his out-of-pocket expenses since they 'only pay them in exceptional cases to outside people travelling for short periods in this country on official business.' A few days later he was warned by Rowlands that it would probably be impossible to get him a seat on the Clipper service to the United States and he would have to travel by flying boat. They have, Rowlands added, 'been stripped of some of their passenger accommodation, and I do not think that they are very comfortable'. But efforts would be made for a Clipper seat 'if the P.M. gives the "All Clear" for you to leave'. For there had, even at this stage, been another hint of delay, and Tizard noted in his diary for 6 August that Rowlands 'told me that the P.M. had agreed to everything I suggested, but that it was not now considered urgent to send the Mission! Our politicians are quite impossible.' Later that day Tizard wrote again to Churchill urging that if the Mission were really to go there should be no delay in sending it. On the 9th the Prime Minister minuted that he was anxious that they should start as soon as possible and under the most favourable auspices. The check of 1 August was only temporary, he added.

Finally, the last doubts were cleared away, and on 10 August, Tizard took the chair at a meeting in the M.A.P. to discuss plans with members of the Mission. A. E. Woodward Nutt, who had taken Rowe's place as secretary of the Tizard Committee when Rowe had replaced Watson-Watt at Bawdsey in 1938, was to serve as secretary. Cockcroft and Bowen were the radar experts, while there were other Air Ministry and Admiralty officials. By an act of genius, however, Tizard insisted that the Mission be accompanied not so much by Serving Officers as by Serving Officers who had recently been in action, and who had operational experience of radar or similar aids. Thus from the Royal Navy, there came Captain H. W. Faulkner; from the Army, Lt.-Col. F. C. Wallace who had fought his way out of Dunkirk; and from the Air Force, Group Captain Pearce who had recently won the D.F.C. during operations over Norway. These were the men to whom Tizard explained on 10 August that the object of the Mission was largely to create goodwill. In general, he proposed to pass on full information about matters which had already reached a fairly advanced stage of development, but only very general indications of the lines on which we were working of subjects still in the early stages. The Admiralty were not anxious that details of the enemy's latest magnetic mines should be disclosed, while so far as jet engines were concerned only general matters would be discussed. In virtually all other spheres, interchange would be complete – on gun turrets, on rocket-defence of ships, multiple pompoms, chemical warfare, and explosives, as well as on radar.

Films of British equipment in action were to be taken, as well as actual equipment, notably a specimen of the magnetron, and micropup and millimicropup valves developed in the G.E.C. laboratories. The latter were provided with – an augury of things to come – the company's hope that the Mission would safeguard the company's interests when it came to revealing the valves' industrial secrets to the Americans.

Within a few days Tizard and Woodward Nutt had completed the special arrangements. Most members of the Mission were to sail from Liverpool. In the same ship would go the 'samples', and special arrangements had to be made for their containers – labelled not British Technical and Scientific Mission but 'Tizard Mission' – to be taken under armed guard to the docks. Prize specimen was the 'black box', an ordinary japanned metal trunk specially bought from the Army & Navy Stores, and containing among other things the famous cavity magnetron. All had to be immune from the usual Censorship and Customs clearance; and special arrangements had to be made so that if the ship were in danger of falling into enemy hands, the whole of this secret equipment could be sunk without trace.

On the morning of 14 August Tizard drove to Waterloo, breakfasted there rather bleakly, and then left for Poole with Woodward Nutt, discussing with him in the train the various matters whose ends still needed tying together.

They arrived at Poole about noon and lunched with the other passengers who were to travel in the flying boat 'Clare' – Captain Balfour, the Parliamentary Under-Secretary at the Air Ministry; Wavell Wakefield, his private secretary; and Group Captain Pearce. Then they were taken out by launch to the 'Clare', together with the crew of four whose Captain was making his first crossing of the Atlantic. They took off a few minutes after two, gained height, and were joined by the fighters which were to accompany them as far as Ireland. 'The escort was comforting as there had been heavy German raids the day before and a raider had actually been brought down in Poole Harbour', Tizard noted in his diary. They crossed the British coast above Barnstaple, flew uneventfully north-west and three hours later circled above Foynes before dropping down to the harbour.

'A magnificent tea which we all ate copiously', Tizard noted of his meal at the small hotel. 'Lucky I did because we had no dinner on board the Clare and I had not been warned. Then back to the Clare after a stroll, and got off again, fully loaded, at 7.30 pm.' Now perhaps for the first time, Tizard saw the point of Rowlands' warning about the flying boats that might not 'be very comfortable.'

The 'Clare' had been fitted up in only the most rudimentary way for the passengers, who looked down from improvised chairs as they crossed the coast of Ireland a few minutes before 8 p.m. Then they headed out to sea in the face of a strong headwind, flying at less than 1,000 feet above the white horses beneath them. At first they read and talked. After coffee and sandwiches, they tried to play bridge, but by this time it was dark and the single naked bulb gave little light. 'Settled down in our chairs to sleep, but my sleep was only fitful, as it was cold', Tizard noted in his diary. 'I had a chair by a draught. Ran into some bad weather at night judging by the bumps. In the morning, cloud and mist.' At first light they flew out of the bad weather, picked up a tail-wind, and continued droning westwards, flying monotonously, uneventfully, interminably it seemed, above a bank of low cloud that lay only a few hundred feet above the water. They breakfasted on Bovril, biscuits and fruit and a few hours later – having passed close to Tizard Harbour – circled above Botwood where they landed at 12.14.*

This was but the first leg of the journey completed. The four passengers now flew on to Montreal where Tizard was met by Dr Otto Maass of the National Research Council of Canada and driven to Ottawa. 'Had a bath, then a late dinner and to bed at midnight', he noted. 'Rather gloomy about news of heavy air raids on England.'

It had been Tizard's idea that he should 'clear the lines' with the Canadian authorities before starting the main work of his Mission with the Americans, and one of the first men he met was Dr C. J. Mackenzie, President of the National Research Council of Canada. 'I think few people in England at that time realised what this meant to us' writes Mackenzie, ' – most missions were going directly to Washington, which was at peace, and neglecting completely the potential of Canada which was a partner in the war.'

Tizard spent a week in Canada before going on to the United States, and more than twenty years later the impression that he created has remained.

> His arrival was like a breath of fresh air to those of us who were struggling with war research [says Mackenzie]. He quickly grasped all our difficulties, never flattered or patronised us, neither did he underestimate our potential because at the moment due to lack of contacts with the war we were not doing much effective work either in our laboratories or in our engineering firms.
>
> Tizard and I immediately became intimate friends, as we seemed

---

* Tizard Harbour was named after Sir Henry's father who had passed there on his naval survey work during the nineteenth century – a fact which Tizard later pointed out with considerable pleasure to his colleagues in North America.

to talk the same language and reacted to most situations alike. I could take Tizard into an officers' mess where at that time the senior officers knew very little about modern weapons, and Tizard would talk their language in connection with the fields in which they were competent. We moved through different groups – senior political figures, senior military staffs, university people and scientists, and everywhere we went Tizard was at home, and created a most favourable impression. He understood the practical problems of the Services and industry, and respected their outlook, but he also had a feeling for the young research worker filled with enthusiasm and bright ideas but with very little practical background.[12]

Within twelve hours of his arrival in Ottawa, Tizard was busy arranging for a personal demonstration of a new allegedly bullet-proof material which the Canadians were considering. He discussed with Mackenzie how the Canadians might start full-scale aeronautical work and the development of new radio navigation methods, and spoke of the need for a special experimental squadron to be set up in Ottawa to help the work of the National Research Council. He was soon advising Darwin at the N.P.L. in England that he should send members of his aerodynamic staff to Canada; despatching details of new materials to Pye; and writing to Freeman 'reminding him of my letter about sending Shorts design staff here, and asking him if it was too late.' For a week Tizard seems to have become three men – the diplomat dining with the Governor-General, the Earl of Athlone; the scientist discussing the likelihood of a pituitary extract increasing the performance of flying crew; and the airman lunching with pilots in their mess, going over the problems they faced and the ways in which science could help solve them.

He met Mackenzie King, the Canadian Prime Minister, who was visiting President Roosevelt the following day and who promised to discuss the Mission. By 21 August the lines had been cleared in Canada, and the next day Tizard travelled to Washington, where he was subsequently joined by Dr Mackenzie, representing the Canadian Government. That evening there at last caught up with him the formal permission by which Imperial College allowed him to leave Great Britain. 'So far as the consent of the Governing Body is concerned', wrote Lord Rayleigh, the Chairman, 'I think I can give it – at any rate I will take the blame if any.'

Tizard now turned to the main business of the Mission, which was to be divided into two parts. First, there was a fortnight during which he began discussions, sensed the position, and prepared for the arrival of the Mission and its secret equipment. After that, the British and Americans slowly but definitely began to learn each other's strengths and weaknesses in the vital subject on which their continued existence depended.

On his arrival in Washington Tizard met Lord Lothian, was welcomed by Charles Lindemann, and established his headquarters in the Shoreham Hotel. His first impressions tended to confirm his earlier doubts. 'No administrative arrangements made for my Mission', he complained in his diary. 'No office, no typists, etc. Felt rather annoyed. A good many people do not know what I am here for!' He found, moreover, that there was already a plethora of groups dealing with various aspects of Anglo-U.S. co-operation, ranging from the British Purchasing Mission in New York to two officers in Washington who were dealing directly with the U.S. Army for the supply of 25-pounders and of tanks. Tizard now prepared to find his way through the maze, and from the first had every help from the Americans in making the difficult journey. The day after his arrival he met Franklin Knox, Secretary of the Navy, who seemed cordial. Knox arranged for a meeting in the Navy Department and at this Tizard explained the object of the Mission to senior officers, and agreed with them on the various methods by which interchange of information would take place.

On the 26th, he saw Roosevelt, being taken to the White House by Lothian.

We went in back entrance to avoid the films [he wrote in his diary]. The President very nice, a most attractive personality. He said he was going to get his draft bill for conscription through Congress, but it would probably lose him the election in November. However that 'didn't matter'. He talked generalities, except that he explained that the withholding of the Norden bombsight was largely political and that if he could get any evidence that the Germans had it, or something like it, he would release it to us. I said we should like to feel that there were large numbers available for supply to us when he decided on release and that we should like to have dimensions, etc. so that we should be prepared for it. I said that we were more interested in production than in design; the principles of design of an accurate bombsight were well understood. I told him that we were bringing films to illustrate methods of detection, etc. He said that he would like to see them at the end of next week.

While Tizard was carrying out the preliminary work in Washington, the other members of the Mission were crossing the Atlantic in *The Duchess of Richmond*. She had left Liverpool on 31 August and also carried as passengers the crews who were to take delivery of the first over-age destroyers being handed to Britain in return for U.S. bases in Newfoundland, Bermuda, and the West Indies. They sailed in to Halifax Harbour on 6 September, and two days later Tizard met them in Washington. From now onwards the proceedings fell into a regular pattern. Offices were acquired in the Shoreham, and here the Mission held a meeting at 9 a.m. each morning. Cockcroft assumed responsibility for much of the discussion on radar; Bowen specialized on airborne equipment and on navigational aids. Faulkner, Wallace, and Pearce naturally dealt with the U.S. Navy, Army, and Army Air Force respectively, while Tizard handled the higher-level interviews with the Services, and with Dr Vannevar Bush, the Chairman of the National Defense Research Committee. All visited U.S. research stations and the Service units where equipment was being developed.

The stumbling blocks to free discussion, such as they were, came neither from the scientists nor from the Services. Their cause lay rather in the U.S. machinery of Government and in the complicated commercial and business factors which were involved in the interchange of patented information, a feature of Anglo-U.S. relations that was to rumble intermittently down the war years. The first problem came to the surface on 28 August when Tizard dined at the Cosmos Club. 'Bush told me after dinner that he did not yet feel free to discuss with me the work of his Special Defence Committee' Tizard noted in his diary. 'He would welcome such discussions but he thought that they ought to be initiated first by the Navy or War Departments. Following such initiation he would take his own steps to bring the discussions about.' The reason, which Tizard did not know and which Bush was presumably too tactful to mention, was that the National Defense Research

Committee had not been authorized to disclose anything to the British. Permission came from the Army only on 12 September and from the Navy, in more limited form, four days later.

The position is engagingly described in a letter from Bush. 'We conferred frequently', he says of his relations with Tizard during these weeks.

> But we were rather careful not to be seen together too much for fear that some of the people in Washington would conclude that there was some sort of conspiracy under way. Both Tizard and I were in somewhat of a quandary, for each of us would have liked to have told our own group that the other had made very significant advances which would be valuable, but we could not do that as we were both of us under severe limitations. I think you can well imagine the skill with which Tizard handled the affair, making contact with dozens of people and giving the impression, without saying anything definite whatever, that Britain had made an extraordinary advance, as indeed it had.[13]

More difficult were the problems that arose when Tizard met officials of the Navy Department, also on 28 August, and discovered that they were unwilling to discuss details of anti-aircraft work. He decided not to press the issue at the moment, but held his fire until he was next in the Navy Department. Here the matter was unravelled. 'It appears', he wrote in his diary. 'that an English firm . . . had sued the U.S. Government for infringement of patents. They had been refused access to the latest U.S. predictors for ship work and had been unable to prove their case. They had then shifted their attack on to Ford and were suing him. It was felt by Admiral Furlong that if we had full information about the predictor, it might afterwards be said that we handed some of this information to [the firm] to enable them to fight their case.' This, like subsequent and similar problems, was handed over to the legal pontiffs, either of the Embassy or of the British Purchasing Commission.

These were isolated cases, apparently as embarrassing to the U.S. authorities as to Tizard and the members of his Mission. Almost without exception he found that the Service chiefs with whom he dealt were anxious to co-operate, willing to reveal everything they had to show. There was sound judgement, as well as allied goodwill, about this. For it was soon clear that in the dominating field of radar the Americans were far behind the British. They knew the principles and they had begun to construct equipment for Service use. But they had had no Tizard to marry up scientific possibilities with Service needs; they had not been pricked by the threat of massive air attack into developing equipment beyond its early stages; and the experimental lash-up rather than the operational receiver and transmitter was what Tizard and his colleagues examined during their visits to airfields and research stations. Much of the position had become clear to Tizard during his first meeting with General Mauborgne, head of the Army Signals Division. 'We meant to have only a few minutes talk, but he got interested and went on until lunch time', Tizard noted. 'He told me that they had succeeded in locating aircraft at considerable distances, up to 100 miles in favourable circumstances, but on the other hand it was clear that they had not succeeded in doing what we were doing, and in particular they had no equipment for use in aircraft. When I told Mauborgne roughly what we were able to do he became extremely interested and promised full interchange of information.' Some days later, at Wright Field, Tizard was taken round the Laboratories and attended a long session in the Conference Room. 'The only thing of immediate practical interest to us was the portable vertical beacon, quite a small thing', he noted. 'The radio navigation was fully explained, and it seemed to be very good, provided it was not meant for use in war, in which case it seemed to me that the whole case would break down. As for the RDF, it was nearly non-existent. It was explained that the Western Electric Company had been employed on air to ground detection, but judging from the results shown to us they had not achieved any practical success.'

Tizard was impressed with the American work on radar aids for directing searchlights and for gun-laying, and at Indianapolis, where the Civil Aeronautics Administration had their experimental radio station he was much taken with their blind landing system which he himself tried in the air. 'It looks extremely simple in the hands of a good pilot, but I did not find it quite so simple, when I tried it myself', he wrote, 'mainly because I had had no practice in blind flying and played strictly fair. It is, however, quite evidently a perfectly practicable system.'

By the third week in September, Tizard and his Mission had revealed more than the secrets of radar which had by that time turned the scales in the air battle being fought above southern Britain. They had given details of the important predictor for the Bofors devised by Colonel Kerrison of the Admiralty Research Laboratories. Many of Britain's new anti-submarine devices had been revealed, as well as the proximity fuse. There were also more fundamental matters. 'The Tizard Mission brought in its "black box" some information about an explosive called RDX, which had been known since 1899 but had proved too sensitive and too expensive to win favour', says Baxter.* 'They had developed at Woolwich a method of manufacture and means to desensitize the product by mixing it with beeswax.'[14] There was only one minor trouble, and this was delay in the arrival of the Air to Surface Vessel equipment, and at first Bowen had to be content with describing verbally to the Navy Department what the equipment was and how it worked.

The climax of the Mission came during the week-end of 27–29 September. On Friday the 27th Tizard, back in Washington after a brief visit to Ottawa, met Bush and his colleagues. Together with other members of the British party they began to work out how the United States, Canada, and Britain could best exchange information in the future. These discussions went on after Tizard's return to Britain, and arrangements for continuing the work of the Mission were finally determined by a memorandum which Cockcroft sent to the Ambassador before he left the United States for Britain in December and which proposed the establishment of the British Commonwealth Scientific Office in Washington.

Tizard spent the 28th at the British Embassy, discussing with the authorities how the work of the various British Missions could be co-ordinated. Here he was also able to help Lothian deal with a would-be inventor whom the Ambassador had not wished to turn away before seeking scientific advice. 'Went to Embassy to see an inventor, Mr . . . . and his backer, Mr . . . . ,' Tizard noted in his diary. 'These two had been taken in to see Lothian and

---

* James Phinney Baxter, author of *Scientists Against Time*, the history of the U.S. Office of Scientific Research and Development.

McCormick-Goodheart.* I was asked to be affable, give them tea, and find out what it was all about. Result: Mr.[. . . . . . .] is mad, and his backer probably fraudulent. [The first] offered to blow up any French port in the English Channel on Wednesday next with his new machine. He would stay in the air for six months and communicate with me by high frequency. During that time he would blow up any other place designated by the British Government. Condition, that he should be paid 100 million dollars when the job was done. I said "agreed".' It would be nice to believe the persistent story that Tizard wrote the offer on Embassy paper and that unease was caused among officials by lack of Treasury sanction. Tizard's diary, however, states that he warned both Ambassador and others against making any offer in writing.

Cockcroft and Bowen were, meanwhile, taking part in discussions from which the Massachusetts Institute of Technology's famous Radiation Laboratory was to emerge. The spur for this was Randall and Boot's magnetron, 'the most valuable cargo ever brought to our shores' and 'the single most important item in reverse lease-lend' as Baxter has called it. Cockcroft had already produced the magnetron at a meeting of officers from the U.S. Naval Research Laboratory in the Wardman Park Hotel. 'I still remember the rather doubtful opening with the U.S. officers suspicious as to whether we were putting all our cards on the table', Cockcroft has written. 'The disclosure was the key point, and from then on we had no difficulties. We found the Navy Laboratory has been experimenting with klystron 10 watt transmitters and were intensely interested. . . . Our disclosures had therefore increased the power available to U.S. technicians by a factor of 1,000.'[15]

Now, on 28–29 September, there came an unofficial week-end party at the Tuxedo Park home of Alfred Loomis, Chairman of the N.D.R.C. Committee on Microwaves. Here a number of American scientists were using the relatively primitive klystron to detect training planes. The magnetron, explained once again by Cockcroft and Bowen, 'opened up new vistas' as Cockcroft put it. Then, as the potentialities of the new valve were discussed, there came the proposal for a new microwave laboratory. Cockcroft later stated that the idea was Loomis's. Baxter generously says that 'the

* Leander McCormick-Goodheart, Hon. Counsellor at the British Embassy.

members of the Tizard Mission urged N.D.R.C. to specialize in the microwave field and to establish a large laboratory for the purpose, staffed by scientists and engineers from both the universities and industry similar to the three created by the British'. The meeting had started in the evening and went on into the small hours. 'Running conferences continued till October 13', states an official account of the first five years of the Radiation Laboratory, 'and by that time practically everybody was agreed that what the program needed was a central laboratory built on the British lines: staffed by academic physicists, committed to fundamental research but committed even more than that to doing anything and everything needed to make microwaves work.'[16]

The first task of any such group, it was agreed, should be the development of a centimetric airborne radar set – the one piece of equipment which was more likely than any other to transform defence against the night bomber. Almost exactly three weeks later the Microwave Committee agreed to undertake the project, and unanimously voted to set up what later became the Radiation Laboratory – in which Bowen was to remain for many months as the British representative.

Meanwhile, Tizard was clearing up his papers, having final meetings, and preparing to hand over charge of the Mission to Cockcroft – to whom he paid five dollars, lost in a bet, made on hearing bad news from England, that the country would have been invaded by this time. On 5 October he flew out of Washington by Clipper for England via the Azores, but in spite of the secrecy of the Mission was caught by the photographers at the airport before the plane left.

The flight home was smoother than the journey out in the 'Clare', but on this occasion there was a different worry. 'A dagoish looking person shows an unholy desire to sit near me, and especially near my F.O. bag', Tizard noted in his diary. 'However, I finally hid it in my bunk, after persuading the steward to see that no-one had the upper berth.'

When Tizard arrived back in London at the end of the first week in October, the Battle of Britain had been won. The radar chain had held. The country had survived the threat of invasion. Yet all this is clearer today than it was during the heroic autumn of 1940

T

as the night blitz was rising to its height. He again took up quarters in Imperial College and here his first action was typical. He called for details of any damage caused to the College by air raids, and was told that there had been an unexploded bomb in the boiler house. But damage had been considerably lighter than it might have been, even though some of the water pipes had been fractured; for two of the men on duty had insisted on dealing with the emergency straight away, doing a lengthy repair job only a few yards above the unexploded bomb. Tizard immediately sought out the men and thanked them personally. One thing that he never missed was an opportunity of showing appreciation for, as he put it, 'a good chap'.

By the time of Tizard's return to London the Foreign Office had received a brief report on the Mission from Lothian, emphasizing that it had created a most favourable atmosphere of close collaboration between the United States, Canada, and Britain in the development of vitally important war equipment. Now he began to prepare a full report for Churchill on the results of his work. While this was being done he gave two accounts of what had been achieved. The first was on 14 October, when he reported to a meeting presided over by Freeman and attended by A. V. Hill and representatives from the Ministries of Aircraft Production and Supply, and from the Admiralty. So far as the U.S. Navy Department was concerned, he said, there appeared to have been frank disclosure, with the exception of the Norden bomb sight. 'I consider that there would have been full disclosure if the ASV apparatus had arrived in accordance with the arrangements made prior to the departure of the Mission', he later added.

Despatch of this equipment from Farnborough had been delayed by the desire to make doubly sure that it was working correctly. Tizard now emphasized the importance of hurry and the apparatus arrived in Washington on 1 November. Bowen had already arranged for an aircraft to be available, and on 2 December made a long flight over the Atlantic during which the set – first installation of airborne radar in any U.S. aircraft – was successfully demonstrated. 'Unlike ground and ship-board radar in which America had made a start, this was one type of radar in which the U.K. had it all over the U.S.A.' comments Bowen. 'This installation of a British airborne equipment in a U.S. aircraft transformed the situation for them. Next to the magnetron itself, it was one of the most important pieces of equipment handed over by the Tizard Mission.'[17]

Tizard's second account of affairs came on 4 November when he reported to the Defence Services Panel of the newly-formed Scientific Advisory Committee of the Cabinet.* Here he made four recommendations, all of which were subsequently carried out. Radar experts should be sent to Canada to aid production there. Samples of all new equipment should be sent to both the United States and Canada. Canada should be asked to test all new equipment under operational conditions, and to develop equipment and methods in the light of experiments in the air, keeping in close touch with radar workers in Britain and the United States. And British technical experts in the United States should arrange for the testing in Canada of any new device which might be of use to the British forces. As a result, co-operation between Britain and North America was to be increased considerably during the coming months, and from now onwards Tizard was to receive almost regular proposals and reports from both Washington and Ottawa outlining the extension of Anglo-U.S. or Anglo-Canadian collaboration. He had, as we shall see, some difficulty in dealing with them, for his position was now to become even more anomalous than before.

Early the following spring Dr James Conant, the newly-appointed Chairman of the National Defense Research Committee, led a mission to Britain which was the direct outcome of Tizard's work the previous autumn and the fore-runner of the firm Anglo-U.S. collaboration of the ensuing four years. 'He told me' Tizard noted in his diary on 9 March 1941, some five months after he had returned from the United States, 'that he had had lunch with the P.M. and told him how valuable my Mission to the U.S.A. had been. I was glad to hear this, as the P.M., who sent me there, had not found time to see me since my return, and had not even acknowledged a preliminary report that I sent him; nor had I been brought into any of the discussions on co-operation with America that had taken place since I came back.'

* Set up the previous month. See pp. 273–274.

CHAPTER TWELVE

Unofficial Adviser

The Britain to which Tizard returned in October 1940 was a nation very different from the one he had left two months previously. In those hot August days which now seemed a world away, disaster had seemed nearer with every edition of the papers. Few men, or women for that matter, looked much beyond the rim of the next day. The spirit of desperate resolution which Churchill had done so much to arouse had steeled the nation to the deeds of the immediate present, but there had been time neither to consider the deficiencies of the past nor to plan the battles of the future. Now all was different. The Battle of Britain had been won. Invasion had been at least postponed and perhaps even abandoned. While Tizard had been in Canada and the United States, the country had been able to take a deep breath – and had begun to feel, by instinct rather than by reason, that if the night blitz could only be ridden out, there might be a future after all. With the Germans in control of Europe, with Russia still locked in a pact of apparently indissoluble amity with the Reich, and with America still neutral, one could not yet speak of the organization of victory. But one had survived. In 1942, or '43 or '44, all might be possible.

First, however, there would have to be that ordered reorganization of the country's resources which Tizard, among others, had so long advocated. Industrially and scientifically, the haphazard improvization of the previous seven years was now thrown into relief by the prospect of the long haul ahead. There were exceptions, of which the Air Ministry's bomber programme was perhaps the best example. But in many fields, ranging from manpower to raw materials, from the supply of radar mechanics to the allocation of shipping space, it was becoming clear that the Continental defeats of the summer had merely compounded the penalties of a long era of casual mismanagement. From now onwards all had to be mobilized, marshalled, and directed in a way, and on a scale, totally different from that envisaged at the beginning of the year. For the first time, perhaps, it was realized that total war would have to be total.

However, it was not only the need for a new and massive industrial mobilization that had grown with the events of the previous few months. The need to make the best use of the country's scientific potential was equally urgent, and it existed at separate levels. 'It is by devising new weapons, and above all, by scientific leadership, that we shall best cope with the enemy's superior strength', Churchill had minuted in September.

> If, for instance, the series of inventions now being developed to find and hit enemy aircraft, both from the air and from the ground, irrespective of visibility, realise what is hoped from them, not only the strategic but the munitions situation would be profoundly altered – we must therefore regard the whole sphere of R.D.F., with its many refinements and measureless possibilities, as ranking in priority with the Air Force, of which it is in fact an essential part. The multiplication of the high-class scientific personnel, as well as the training of those who will handle the new weapons and research work connected with them, should be the very spearpoint of our thought and effort.[1]

These were fine words. What was needed to carry them into effect, however, was some scientific body which could, by giving constant advice at the highest level, ensure that effort was coordinated rather than duplicated; that research and development projects had a measure of scientific scrutiny before they were allowed to swallow up men and materials; and, above all else, ensure that at both Cabinet and Chiefs of Staff level, the interdependence of science and strategy could be at least duly considered before decisions were taken. The problems involved in such a requirement were considerable and they were still only partially solved when the war ended.

By October 1940, however, a half-measure which was to do duty for the duration was already being brought in. It consisted of a body whose influence rested on the standing of the Royal Society and its members rather than on the work which it was allowed to handle. Two previous efforts had already been made by Sir William (Henry) Bragg, President of the Royal Society, to ensure that the nation's scientific knowledge should be available at the highest level – one a few weeks before the outbreak of war, the second a few days after it. On both occasions he had written to Lord Chatfield, Minister for the Co-Ordination of Defence, proposing first that a small group of Fellows of the Royal Society might advise the Committee of Imperial Defence; then, more ambitiously, that the two Secretaries of the Royal Society, Professor A. V. Hill and Professor A. C. G. Egerton, 'should be attached in some appropriate way to the establishment of the War Cabinet, which would then have at its disposal a direct connection with the scientific community'. Neither suggestion was accepted.[2]

In September 1940, the Royal Society tried once again, this time proposing that a committee representing the scientific societies should be set up under a Cabinet Minister. The Government acquiesced and in October 1940, Neville Chamberlain performed his last official act as Lord President of the Council by signing the papers which brought into being the Scientific Advisory Committee of the Cabinet. Its first Chairman was Lord Hankey; its members, the Royal Society's two secretaries, and the secretaries of the D.S.I.R., and the Medical and Agricultural Research Councils. Its terms of reference, considerably more limited than those proposed the previous year, were threefold; 'To advise the Government on any scientific problems referred to it; to advise Government departments, when required, on the selection of individuals for particular lines of scientific enquiry or for membership of committees on which scientists are required; and to bring to the notice of the Government promising new scientific or technical developments which may be of importance to the war effort.'

This was adequate, as far as it went. But the new organization was tolerated by the Prime Minister only on the understanding that 'we are to have additional support from outside rather than an incursion into our interior',[3] and it was at times either ignored or short-circuited by the one-man recommendations of Professor Lindemann. It was further limited by the Prime Minister's awkward belief that most scientists were necessarily different from other men, revealed in his comment to Oliver Lyttelton, Minister of Production – 'it does require people of the *métier* to compose some of the quarrels amongst the scientists. A won't talk to B because B has invented something A thinks he ought to have invented, and so on.'[4]

The Scientific Advisory Committee studied a wide range of *ad hoc* problems varying from the need to secure the country's food supplies to reports that the enemy was building a Channel Tunnel. It was in a good position to collect expert evidence, and it controlled a number of specialist Panels and Sub-Committees such as the Defence Services Panel which considered the results of the Tizard Mission. But Tizard himself was never under any illusion that it was likely to play an important part in guiding the country's scientific effort. It was 'really very ineffective', he stated years later in a letter to Professor J. R. M. Butler, then Chief Historian for the Military Histories of the War. 'I fancy that the Prime Minister did not like at all the suggestion of the setting up of the Committee under a Cabinet Minister, but he thought it politically wise to do it', he explained in another letter to Professor Butler. 'I think the Committee did some useful but not out-standing work, and that . . . it was not particularly concerned with the needs of the fighting Services.'

Tizard's own position – described in one Government minute as Technical Adviser to Lord Hankey – was to become the paradoxi-cal one of unofficial adviser to many of the advisers. As a friend and close colleague of those forming the Scientific Advisory Com-mittee, his influence, as so often, was pervasive, but difficult to define. To understand the extraordinary circumstances in which it was exercised, it is necessary to recall Tizard's situation when he returned from the United States. He was still Chairman of the Aeronautical Research Committee, but this was a body whose influence, concentrated on longer-term projects as it inevitably was, had tended to decline on the outbreak of war. His Mission had technically finished with his report to the Ministry of Aircraft Production and, as we shall see, he lacked official authority even to deal with the multitude of enquiries that came to him from across the Atlantic, directly as a result of his work. His Scientific Com-mittees had dissolved, leaving not a wrack behind. Moreover, and even more unfortunate for Tizard, the immense value of radar in turning the tide during the Battle of Britain had yet to be properly understood. Churchill, and others, of course knew what it had physically accomplished; but only a little was yet known of what had been happening on the other side of the hill; and few if any would have given the verdict which the historians were eventually to give. Yet 'among the material factors which contributed to Fighter Command's success, by far the most important was a system of early warning and control unparalleled outside Britain. . . . had lack of an early-warning and control system forced Dowding to rely on standing patrols, most of his squadrons would have been worn to a standstill long before Goering launched his main assault.'⁵ In later years Dowding's successor, Air Marshal Sir Sholto Douglas, as he then was, commented that 'the word radar should be written on Tizard's tomb.' 'Battle of Britain' would be just as fitting.

In the autumn of 1940 all this was of little help. Newall, his term of office as Chief of Air Staff ending, was about to leave Britain as Governor-General and Commander-in-Chief, New Zealand; his successor, Air Marshall Sir Charles Portal, saw no need to enquire for Tizard's services. Dowding, his great battle won, was about to be succeeded and sent to the United States for special duty with the Ministry of Aircraft Production. 'Like all men', as his biographer noted, 'he had made mistakes, though fewer, perhaps, than most of his contemporaries. But he had been so often right in his frequent conflicts with the Air Ministry that the few occasions when he was wrong were not likely to be forgotten.'⁶ Circumstance had combined with the new brooms to sweep very clean, and Tizard now found himself without a post, without an office, and with an entrée to Air Ministry and Royal Air Force stations and commanders that, however ubiquitous, sprang merely from his chairmanship of the Aeronautical Research Committee if it sprang from anything other than official goodwill.

Yet throughout the height of the war, from the beginning of 1941 until the summer of 1943, Tizard's influence was to be remarkable. For many crucial months he was head of the Chiefs of Staff sub-committee which controlled and directed the growth of radar. He hammered through, against considerable opposition, both the development of the jet engine and, on another level, the use of Barnes Wallis's bouncing bombs for the 'dam-busters' raid.

He was picked as leader of a Scientific Mission to Russia which, had it not been abandoned at the last moment, might have had repercussions as great as those of the Mission to the United States.

Most of this sprang from the opportunity provided by Lord Beaverbrook in the autumn of 1940. The fact that the first Minister of Aircraft Production's recollection of Lindemann was 'of an uneasy and far from popular figure without any settled office or portfolio, whose entry into other Ministers' offices was seldom solicited and whose departure was invariably welcomed',[7] may have played its part in this. Two guides through the scientific maze were no doubt better than one, particularly if they were likely to act as check and counter-check. More important, it had become necessary for Beaverbrook to have a qualified adviser of the highest scientific rank, one whose impartiality was above suspicion, who had no personal, Ministerial, or Service axe to grind, and who could be relied upon to give an honest as well as an informed judgement however damning it might be. He needed a scientist of unqualified integrity and the opportunity to acquire Tizard came in November 1940, when Freeman – airman, not scientist – left his post as Air Member for Production and Development in the Ministry of Aircraft Production to become Vice-Chief of the Air Staff under Portal.

A good deal of apocryphal nonsense is talked about the relations between Tizard and Beaverbrook, and a good deal of it is refuted by Tizard's own papers. The two men presented, it is true, a pair different enough to raise comment. Compared with Beaverbrook's love of operating the political machine there was Tizard's evident belief that politics is, in Roseberry's words, 'an evil-smelling bog'. Compared with the elfin delight in power there was contempt for it. The difference in outlook was basic, and during one encounter Beaverbrook expressed amazement that a man of Tizard's ability should eschew all interest in making money. Yet it is in fact quite clear that personal contact qualified Tizard's opinion of Beaverbrook. There were many things that he failed to understand about the man, and some which he continued to dislike. But he had no doubt that he was a war-winner; wrote in 1941, when the political gulf between the Air Ministry and the Ministry of Aircraft Production appeared well-nigh unbridgeable, that he saw no reason

why he 'should not work happily with' him; and a few years later
went out of his way to praise Beaverbrook's 'ability to get things
done.'

Early in November Tizard submitted to Beaverbrook a memorandum on the transfer of experimental work to Canada; work
which he feared – unduly as it turned out – might be critically
disrupted by German air raids. Beaverbrook was not convinced.
But he appears to have suggested that Tizard might take over, on
an unofficial, temporary, and advisory basis, the work which Air
Marshal Freeman had been carrying out in the M.A.P. on research, development, and production. Tizard replied on 4 November, saying: 'I have seen Freeman today and will do the best I can
till the end of the month . . .' He was, in fact, taking up work
which he would carry on, to a lesser or greater extent, with varying
authority, and under various titles, for more than two and a half
years. At first, he was hardly happy about it. 'I fancy I may have
misled you yesterday by giving you too much of an impression that
I could spend my whole time here', he wrote. 'Actually I am still
on this night defence work for the Air Ministry and still busy over
matters arising from the American Mission which affect other
Departments. I have some College business to attend to also. I
shall do what I can to fit everything in. I thought I ought to make
this clear as if you attach great importance to the presence of a
temporary deputy at Headquarters it would be better to get someone else.' He stressed what he felt was the temporary nature of the
work when, on 11 November he wrote telling Portal that he was
'occupying Freeman's chair until the end of the month in order to
give the Minister my views about the state of Research and
Development for the R.A.F., and advice about future organisation.' So far as the R.A.F. was concerned, this was an ideal situation – Portal being, according to Freeman, horrified at any idea
of Tizard's leaving the Ministry 'for he feels that in your independent position there you are able to watch our interests in a general
way probably better than anyone else.'

The position was thus in strong contrast to that of the early
summer. Then Tizard had held his ambiguous semi-official position
as Newall's Scientific Adviser, and if he appears not to have been,
at any time, 'on the Air Ministry's books', the Government had at

least reimbursed Imperial College. Yet events had cold-shouldered him away from the Air Council when he would have preferred to remain in close contact. Now, with payment for his services having stopped in October, he was, with the exception of his post on the Aeronautical Research Committee, merely the Rector of Imperial College. And now he was being begged to stay.

Tizard thrust himself into the work of unofficial adviser with immense energy. His notes, diaries, and extensive memoranda show that within a few days he was minuting Beaverbrook on Blind Landing aids, on a proposed reorganization of radio research, and on what should be done about the Whittle Scheme. Within a few weeks he had picked William Farren as the new head of R.A.E. – in itself a tribute to his judgement – and his work could soon be described as part-time, or advisory, only by the greatest stretching of words – even though it was still unofficial. On 10 December he visited the Martin-Baker Aircraft Company at Higher Denham and then drove on to Boscombe Down. The following day he arrived at the R.A.F. station at Middle Wallop and continued on to Cheltenham. On the 12th he had a long series of interviews with officials of the Gloster Aircraft Company at Hucclecote and continued northwards to Blackpool where, on the 13th he visited the Vickers-Armstrong works. At Barrow he spent the night with Sir Charles Craven, Beaverbrook's Industrial Adviser, and the chairman of the Air Supply Board, as the former Air Council Committee on Supply was now called. Next day he had the comparatively restful experience of driving on to Glasgow where, on the 16th, he visited the Marine Aircraft Experimental Establishment at Helensburgh.

All this was purely unofficial.

I hope [he said in the draft of a letter to Beaverbrook a fortnight later], that my position at M.A.P. will be settled very soon. It is very difficult for me to go on in the present vague way. As I told you, I should welcome the opportunity of being responsible for Research and Development provided I enjoyed your confidence as well as that of the Royal Air Force.

I do want to make the point that responsibility for research and development cannot effectively be discharged from an office chair. I think it is essential to keep in close personal touch with the user, i.e. the Royal Air Force, and with the place where research and development is done. Also it is very important now to concentrate on things that matter. There is a constant tendency to embark on new work simply on the proposals of outside enthusiasts backed by influential people. I do hope that if you give me the responsibility you will feel able to rely on my judgement about new proposals, and that nothing new will be started about which I have not been consulted.

I assume that the post would carry with it membership of the Air Council as heretofore.

You have had nearly two months opportunity of seeing the worst of me! If you now feel you have sufficient confidence in me, do say so, and let us regard the thing as settled. If you are still uncertain, however, I would rather go off and do something else. Do please decide soon! Remember that I am still trying to do my normal peacetime work in addition to my (temporary!) war work!

On the last day of 1940, Beaverbrook received from Tizard a memorandum on aircraft production accompanied by a brief note which said: 'The following programme is agreed with the Air Staff. Do you approve?' From now onwards his presence was taken for granted, and he became installed in a first-floor office in Thames House, a large close-carpeted room with veneered walls in the discreet but more opulent I.C.I. manner. Opening off it there lay a smaller room where there worked his scientific assistant and his secretary, both of whom were kept almost as occupied by the stream of visitors as by the constant flow of work. Sir Henry would arrive punctually at 9.30 in the car which was allocated to him from the Ministry pool, a big yellow Rolls-Royce for the first few months and subsequently a Packard. The first of the visitors would often arrive before he had finished dealing with his post – officials from within the M.A.P., senior officers from the Air Ministry, operational Commanders with whom he had previously discussed specific problems, scientists from other Government organizations, or – in later months – friends from America who felt that Tizard, above all other men, would know the best way of unravelling their own particular problem. 'It was', one of Tizard's scientific assistants commented, 'rather like a bus-stop.'

His work covered the vast, and steadily growing range of M.A.P. acitivities. On more than one occasion he aroused opposition as much by his superior knowledge as by his attitude. This could be brutally direct. 'He didn't suffer fools gladly and there were a lot of fools around at that time', says Lord Tedder. Tizard himself knew his own weakness – 'you might not think it now', he once said to his assistant, half in mitigation and stroking his head thoughtfully, 'but I once had red hair.'

From now onwards he was to be deeply involved in the difficulties of exchanging secret information with the United States. These difficulties had been experienced before the end of 1940 and began to subside only with the entry of the United States into the war in December 1941. They arose largely from the success of the Tizard Mission and from the mutual trust which it had created. That there were difficulties at all was due neither to the scientists nor, with certain exceptions, to the statesmen of either side. But there was still the constant British fear, unjustified by events but natural enough in the circumstances, that information given to the United States might fall into enemy hands. And there were the occasional suspicions, aroused equally on both sides, that sharp-minded business men might be utilizing the opportunities of war to steal a post-war march upon their industrial competitors across the Atlantic, a subject still veiled not by security but by the laws of defamation. Good-will did much to oil the machinery which ground down such problems. Yet it is certain that the process would have been both slower and less satisfactory without Tizard's activities, without his personal knowledge of the men involved – and without the universal belief that he would, whatever the consequences, give an honest opinion. His unwillingness to abandon his chosen standards of conduct might have served him ill in the past; it was now beginning to reap dividends for the country. For anyone could come to him – dozens did – quite confident that he would be grinding no private axe, making no personal balancing for the future, never wondering whether, apart from the needs of the job, it might be expedient if events were toppled this way or that.

His authority for much of the delicate negotiations in which he became involved was, of course, remarkably insubstantial. As early as 20 November 1940, he had noted in his diary: 'Saw Colonel Llewellin [Parliamentary Secretary M.A.P.] again about the American situation, and explained to him my difficulty with regard to telegrams, which were now coming in marked to me for action, namely that I had no authority to take action, nor could I reply to telegrams or letters knowing that my views differ from those in executive authority.' The following day it was decided that a committee of the Supply Ministers, acting in consultation with the Service Ministers, should meet to advise what information should be disclosed to the United States, or to selected firms, and that their advice should then be submitted to the Prime Minister as Minister of Defence. Tidy in theory, in practice this arrangement left a large number of loose ends; and it was natural that Tizard should eventually take upon himself the task of tying them up. On 1 January 1941, he sent a note to the Directors of Scientific Research at the Admiralty, Ministry of Supply, and Ministry of Aircraft Production. 'I propose to have, if possible, regular fortnightly meetings of a small committee consisting of the Directors of Scientific Research of the Admiralty, Ministry of Supply and Ministry of Aircraft Production, Controller of Tele-communications Equipment, M.A.P., or his representative, and Dr. Cockcroft, with myself as Chairman and Woodward Nutt as Secretary', this said. 'The object of holding these meetings is to keep in touch with action taken on reports and information gained by the British Technical Mission to U.S.A., and to advise the Ministers concerned on future scientific collaboration with North America.'

Tizard's note aroused considerable opposition. Sir Frank Smith, Controller of Telecommunications Equipment, wrote to say that he discussed such matters direct with the Minister, Lord Beaverbrook, Chairman of the committee handling such matters, and added that he did not propose to be represented on the committee. Dr Gough wrote from the Ministry of Supply to say that his Minister already received advice, and that if he attended 'it must be entirely without commitment on our part to the terms of reference you suggest.' At the Admiralty, Dr Wright had apparently felt it necessary to act with somewhat similar care, since Admiral Fraser, Third Sea Lord and Controller, now wrote to Tizard. His D.S.R. would attend the first meeting. 'I feel, however', he added 'that it would be inadvisable to set up a body which might have the effect of restricting the present freedom of Departments to deal directly with the United States authorities on matters with which they are concerned.' Tizard was quick to reassure everyone that his group would be purely advisory, and smoothed ruffled feathers with all the skill that he could exercise as second nature. The D.S.R.'s met on a number of occasions, but by the summer their labours were being thrown into shadow by American activity.

This began early in January when Vannevar Bush wrote to Tizard asking whether he could set up, in London an office of the National Defense Research Committee. 'I hope his suggestion will be welcomed', Tizard commented to Beaverbrook. It was, indeed, the obvious sequel to the Tizard Mission but it raised a number of delicate points. There was, according to the official U.S. historian 'a renewal of hesitation in London, and it was not until January 29 that the hoped-for invitation was cabled.'[8] Finally, in March, Dr James B. Conant, then President of Harvard, arrived in London. The nature of his brief can be judged by the tone of his comment today. 'Although this was before the entry of the United States into the war', he says 'the President felt we were authorised to establish such exchange by implication at least of the Lend Lease legislation which was just then being passed by Congress'.[9] One of his first actions was to arrange a meeting with Tizard, to whom he proposed that the United States should help Britain by selecting U.S. scientists to work in British research establishments. There is something intriguing in this when one remembers that Tizard was merely the personal, unpaid and unofficial, adviser to Lord Beaverbrook.

> I said [he explained to Beaverbrook on April 2], I felt quite certain this offer would be greatly appreciated, but that there might possibly be difficulties in the way . . . . The difficulties, in my view, are two-fold (a) If we have the American staff in our Experimental Establishments they would have normal access to most if not all of our secret developments (b) Patent difficulties may arise. Of these the first difficulty is the most important from the point of view of the war: the second may be serious when the war is over. Nevertheless, I strongly urge that the offer should be welcomed in principle. Risks cannot be avoided in war, and I feel that the advantage we should gain by having our staff strengthened by first-class young scientists and engineers from the United States would far more than outweigh the risks of premature disclosure. I feel too that we must treat the Americans in this respect as wholehearted allies. Whatever else has been said, or may be said, of the

motives of our American cousins, I feel assured of one thing, viz. that the overwhelming majority of American scientists have as their first object a passionate desire to help England to the utmost of their capacity.

That Tizard himself held no doctrinaire view, in spite of his belief in co-operation with the United States, was shown when he wrote to Air Vice-Marshal Baker of the British Air Commission in Washington on 15 May, and noted that he was not 'in favour of giving detailed information about new equipment, especially of armament, that has not yet been used against the enemy but which will probably be the object of operations in the near future. Nor am I in favour of giving detailed information about new experimental developments unless it is quite clear that by doing so we can get such technical co-operation as will hasten practical development. For instance, I am not in favour at present of giving information about the Whittle engine.'

The jet was a tricky matter. From time to time over the previous year various U.S. authorities had sought detailed information about it. Tizard had talked of it to Bush in a general way during his Mission and General Arnold was subsequently given a longer, but still general, statement. To both, as well as to Dr Conant, Tizard had explained why the British authorities were not prepared to do more. The balance against this had altered by June, when the U.S. formally asked for details, and on the 12th Tizard wrote thus to the Minister. 'I now recommend that we should convey full information on the subject to the American authorities through the B.A.C., with a request that they should proceed with parallel development in America under strictly secret conditions.' The advantage, which he felt outweighed the disadvantages, were that the Americans had by this time gained certain knowledge and experience through their development of turbo-superchargers which would be of value in developing the jet. Tizard felt jet propulsion in one form or another likely to be common in the not too distant future; and, perhaps more important, 'Generally I am in favour of a full reciprocal exchange of information with America.'*

* Full information on the progress of the jet was given later in 1941, after the signature in October of an Anglo-U.S. agreement 'to assist the joint defence plans of our respective Governments.'

This position was underlined the following month when the National Defense Research Committee asked for the latest night fighter specification. Tizard short-circuited the usual machinery, and obtained from Portal approval to pass on the highly secret details. 'Broadly speaking', he wrote to Portal on 30 July, 'I take the line that we should give the properly accredited representatives of the United States Government, whether they belong to the N.D.R.C., the War Department, or the Navy Department, the fullest help and information, and that if there are any subjects about which for reasons of high policy we are told to withhold information, we should explain particularly why we are withholding it. That is the way to avoid misconceptions which are harmful to our cause. I know of some misconceptions now which are doing harm, and which I am doing my best to remove.'

It was not only questions of high policy, and the bedevilling problem of post-war patent complications, that could create misconceptions. Tizard, as well as others, was more than once distressed by the farcical situations which differences in the security regulations of the two countries could produce. Typical of these was the occasion when an article was extracted from the open technical press in the United States and reprinted for a British technical Committee. It was reprinted, however, as a secret paper; and when this was, in due course, sent for information to the United States it was accompanied by instructions that it be kept under lock and key.

To these minor irritations as well as to the major problems, Tizard brought a particular flair. He was, Portal has stated, 'a good lubricator'. And now he was employed, in multitudinous ways, in eliminating the friction which inevitably arose as the British and American industrial machines rubbed together in closer contact. The Americans were in no doubt about his value. Bennett Archambault, for more than three years in charge of activities in the European Theatre of Operations for the Office of Scientific Research and Development, has bluntly stated his own view of Tizard's contribution. 'My associates and I found Sir Henry to possess one of the most capable minds in England in his approach to these complex problems', he says.

U

He had extraordinary ability to foresee problems, and to specify the means by which they could be met. Further, he had remarkable competence in convincing both his civilian and military associates to undertake the programme which he recommended. I consider that Sir Henry represented one of the United Kingdom's greatest assets, whose contributions to the entire Allied effort were immeasurable.[10]

By the time the United States entered the war in December 1941, her scientists, nursed through the difficulties of co-operation with a country already fighting desperately, had already taken back information which enabled them 'to catch up quickly and to save long months of trial and experiment'. Tizard's part in this is clear.

With the Minister's authority [he wrote on 19 June to Pye, Director of Scientific Research], I am retaining the authority to decide what scientific information should be given to the N.D.R.C. of the U.S.A.

He remained, so far as the Minister of Aircraft Production was concerned, an unofficial, unpaid adviser; but during the summer he had, despite considerable opposition, been brought on to the Air Council as an additional member. The events which brought about this change began towards the end of February, when Tizard fell ill with erysipelas, and was taken to the Woolavington Wing of the Middlesex Hospital. Three days later he wrote to the Minister.

Dear Lord Beaverbrook [he said]. It was very kind of you to telephone. I had already written to you, but the letter had not gone – so this is a substitute.

I have been very ill for three days, but am a good deal better now. I hope to get out of here within a week, but am told that at least another three weeks must elapse before I go back to strenuous work. This is a sad confession of weakness, but there it is. In the circumstances it seems to me wise, from all points of view, that I should sever my connection with the Department at once. The work that I have been trying to do for you is too important to be left undone, even for a few weeks in these critical times. What is more, as I have said before, it should be done by someone who enjoys not only your own confidence, but also that of the Air Ministry, and of the Prime Minister. It has been made very clear that that does not apply to me. I have nevertheless hung on, doing what I could, and consoling myself with the thought that I was after all doing *some* good for the war,

and that therefore private feelings must be suppressed, and all difficulties faced. But I no longer have that happy delusion; and I strongly
advise you to select someone more acceptable, and to give him the
authority and status that are appropriate to the post. I feel sure
that this will be in the best interests of the country. I am so glad
that you yourself are fit again and have lost none of your infectious
energy.'

To Tizard's friends, his decision was a straight one of resignation. It was also this to Beaverbrook who replied by return. 'I have
not the slightest intention of accepting your resignation. You must
just be patient and wait until complete health is given to you once
more. And when you come back, you will be welcomed with enthusiasm.'[11] Tizard, however, merely regarded himself as suggesting that someone should be appointed to a post which he had
never really held. He travelled up to Oxford early in March for
recuperation. And here, late on the evening of 11 March he was,
as he noted in his diary, rung up 'by the Press Association who
asked if I had any statement to make about the debate in the
House. I said "No", not knowing what it was. They then gave me
a garbled version of it. Today (the 12th) I find a lot was said about
my alleged "resignation" '.

Curiously enough, the specific claim that Tizard had 'resigned'
from the Ministry was never explicitly made by anyone, although
it was clearly inferred by A. V. Hill, now a Member of Parliament
for Cambridge University. The occasion was the debate on the Air
Estimates, part of which developed into an attack on the manner
in which scientific research and development was being handled
within the Ministry of Aircraft Production. The whole matter
remained as unclear at the end of the debate as it had been at the
beginning. However, Tizard had, Hill pointed out, 'found all sorts
of difficulties in his way. He faced those difficulties', Hill continued, 'with much more patience than I should faced have them. I
know those difficulties and I agree with the decision to which he
has now come. . . . The matter could be put right now if Sir Henry
Tizard could be induced to return by offering him proper facilities and proper authority in his work. He is not like Achilles,
sulking in his tent!'[12]

The attack was continued by Austin Hopkinson who claimed

that Tizard had 'found it – and I make no bones about the matter – quite impossible to work at the Ministry of Aircraft Production.' To all this, Colonel Llewellin, the Parliamentary Secretary, was able to return the bland answer that Sir Henry was merely ill and that he would, it was understood, be returning to the Ministry on his recovery.

Such was in fact to be the case. For the well-intentioned efforts in the House succeeded, where all else might have failed, in pushing Tizard firmly back into the Ministerial arms. His reaction was in character. He wrote to Hill – who replied that 'whether you technically "resigned" doesn't much matter; and if you like you can tell the Beaver that we are a reprehensible lot of people and that you disown us – provided he gives you a proper position & authority.' Tizard wrote, but did not send, a letter to *The Times* which began: 'In *The Times* of March 12 I see a headline "Case of Sir Henry Tizard"; as if I had committed some crime against the State.' And on 12 March he wrote a letter to Beaverbrook which revealed his loyalty and would no doubt have irritated his supporters had they known of its terms.

Dear Lord Beaverbrook [this went]. Many thanks for your letter of March 6th. I ought to have answered it before.

I am very much better, and am becoming more energetic, although I am not quite fit. However, in view of the remarks in the House yesterday I propose to get back to work as soon as I possibly can. I shall either return to London on Monday or Tuesday, or start more gradually by visiting some of the experimental stations and works from here.

I must say that the talk about my resignation affords me some sarcastic amusement. I could not 'resign' because I have nothing to resign. All I have done is to advise you that it would be better, in all the circumstances, to make a normal appointment of someone else in my stead. You say you want me to come back and are prepared to wait. In that case I shall certainly come back, as the thing that interests me is to do the best work I can for the war, whatever the difficulties.

I appreciate very much your kind remarks, and see no reason why I should not work happily with you as my Minister. But your reluctance to make the position clear to the outside world concerned does indeed puzzle me. In particular I still attach importance to being a member of the Air Council, for two reasons: first, because it will help by giving me the right status in the Royal Air Force; and secondly because it should make easier the close collaboration between MAP and the Air Ministry, which is so essential.

Who objects to this? Is it the Prime Minister, acting on private advice? I think I am entitled to know. However, let me make it clear that I am not making anything a condition of returning to work.

Tizard did return. But within a few weeks it was clear that the situation might be changed. For Beaverbrook was now to become Minister of State and to be replaced by Colonel Moore-Brabazon, a former President of the Royal Aeronautical Society and an old friend of Tizard.

Within a few days of taking over, the new Minister of Aircraft Production had proposed two major changes in the organization. Air Vice-Marshal Sir Roderic Hill, the Director-General of Research and Development who was now going to Washington as the British Air Commission's Controller of Technical Services, should be replaced by Air Marshal Linnell, who would occupy a new post as Controller of Research and Development. Simultaneously, Tizard should become Chief Scientific Adviser to the Ministry, and both he and Linnell should become ex-officio members of the Air Council – a necessary move if the link between operations and science was to be strengthened, as it needed to be. Moore-Brabazon's reasons for what might have been considered a radical change were more than sufficient. 'When I arrived at the Ministry of Aircraft Production, for some reason, no doubt tied up with personalities, etc. things were not going too well', he says. 'The Air Ministry and the M.A.P. were scarcely on speaking terms, so to speak, and as our sole reason for existing was to supply the R.A.F. with 'planes, this struck me as rather ridiculous. . . . We were there to try to express the desires of the Air Ministry, and it was a great help to be given a full technical appraisement by Tizard of what was required, as he was now in both camps.'[13] The gulf, it should be stressed, had been betweeen the politicians – and possibly the permanent Civil Servants – rather than the Service Officers attached to the two Ministries; and, perhaps more importantly, between the 'old hands' of both Ministries and the new men of both. At Air Vice-Marshal-level all was well, and it was at this level that Tizard was strongest.

However, Sinclair now interpreted Moore-Brabazon's proposals

as giving Tizard purely advisory functions, and Linnell full executive authority. In addition, when direct contact was to be made
at high level with R.A.F. units, it would be made by Linnell.
Thus while Moore-Brabazon's proposal would have greatly
strengthened Tizard's position, Sinclair's interpretation of it
would do the exact reverse.

'I should be quite content to do what I could for the Ministry
of Aircraft Production and for the Royal Air Force by acting as
an adviser', Tizard informed Moore-Brabazon. But he insisted
that he be allowed to retain his close personal contact with the
Commands, with Research Establishments and with the staff. And
he considered it essential that he should become a member of the
Air Council – a point on which Sinclair had already implied that
there might be difficulties. He outlined how such a system could
be made to work, and in a memorandum to Moore-Brabazon
dated 12 May, concluded by saying: 'If such an arrangement is
accepted by the Minister concerned I should ask for a small but
expert staff to act directly under me. This is a matter of detail
which can be left until the principle is settled. . . . I should like to
make it clear that if it is not considered desirable to put me in this
kind of position I feel I must relinquish all responsibilities *vis-à-vis*
the Royal Air Force. Half-measures don't work – they cause confusion without producing results.'

Ten days later he stated his position in a note to the Minister
which he drafted but did not send.

> I do not know whether you realise that I have now been working in
> the department since the beginning of November without any kind
> of appointment [this went] – that is to say, no notice of any kind has
> been issued within the Department or to the Departmental stations,
> let alone a public notice, that I was in charge of research and devel-
> opment. What happened was that Beaverbrook asked me to come in
> for a short time to fill Freeman's place when he went to the Air Staff,
> and then asked me to go on, and certainly told me on one or two
> occasions that he was very happy with me in charge of research. But
> he did not, in fact, at any time make the position clear to the staff of
> the Department as a whole. It is, as you will imagine, not easy to
> carry out important duties with any handicap of that kind; but
> I fully recognise that the last Minister acted in an unconventional
> way, and I admired his energy and the way he got on with the job;
> and I also wanted to do anything that I could to help in the war. But

just before he left I was rather pressing him to regularise the whole position.

This was indeed becoming more necessary than ever. For Tizard was now, with Hill preparing to leave for Washington, carrying out much of the routine executive work.

I am not giving the right study to the important broad problems, and I find myself more and more tied to the office. Therefore I ask that I shall be relieved of these duties as soon as possible [his note continued]. I also hear that the Secretary of State has considerable doubt of the wisdom of appointing me a member of the Air Council. Now do let me say that I should regard this as a vote of no confidence; but I do so, I hope, without any sense of grievance, at any rate without any quarrel.

I ask for the earliest possible decision, and I hope that Air Vice-Marshal Linnell will be established in my place very soon. I will give him all the help I can until he is well settled in the job. But if the Secretary of State does not want me on the Air Council I should like to take a short holiday and then go to other work which I have been asked to do.

Nearly a fortnight later the position was officially still the same and on 3 June Tizard wrote to the Permanent Secretary.

Officially I know nothing of the impending moves. Unofficially I understand (a) that Linnell is taking over my responsibilities soon, (b) that I must turn out my room for him. Mrs. Ainge told me on Saturday on the telephone that I was expected to clear out today. I said this was quite impossible. I must have 24 hours' notice now of the time of handing over to Linnell. Is it, however, too much to ask that these things should be done with as little inconvenience as possible to myself, and with some of the normal courtesies. [He added a P.S. on a typical Tizard note]: Thank God for a sense of humour, not yet entirely destroyed but sometimes, I fear, rapidly diminishing.

Tizard was now about to go, an event which would have been regretted as much by his Minister as by the Chief of Air Staff and most senior R.A.F. officers. Such a calamity was averted at the eleventh hour. On 5 June he received a cordial letter from Sinclair, stating that the Ministry of Aircraft Production was to be represented at meetings of the Air Council, and inviting Tizard to serve on it as an additional member. He had already been brought on to the M.A.P. Council by Beaverbrook, and a few weeks later he was able to write to General Arnold saying that he was now 'acting as Scientific Adviser to the Ministry of Aircraft Production as well as the Air Ministry in my capacity as member of both Councils', a description used by Moore-Brabazon when he referred to Tizard in a memo to the War Cabinet's North American Supply Committee.

Yet the Ministry of Aircraft Production never had a formal Scientific Adviser and the Air Ministry only appointed one – on Tizard's advice – in 1943. In practice, the outcome of the six months' negotiations had altered his position only slightly. He would remain, for more than two years, the indispensible adviser; but he was still unpaid and unofficial. When he asked to be put on the distribution list of the Air Staff's Daily Operational Summary he received a courteous but significant reply. Unless he pressed the point, Freeman wrote, the answer was 'No'; he could always look at Linnell's copy.

CHAPTER THIRTEEN

Semi-Official Adviser

The summer of 1941 thus saw Tizard firmly established at the Ministry of Aircraft Production, although the position which he occupied was both more unorthodox and more powerful than was usual even in that eyrie of unorthodox eagles. There is no indication, in the official records or outside them, that he ever received a farthing for his services. He was still chairman of the Aeronautical Research Committee. He was, like some Trade Union leaders and M.P.'s, a member of the Minister's Aircraft Supply Council, although most of his real influence sprang rather from his unique position as the Minister's scientific right arm. Years later – when in 1947 he was coaxed into the Ministry of Defence – it was pointed out that he had not been a Government servant since his resignation from the Department of Scientific and Industrial Research in 1929.

He remained Rector of Imperial College but had so arranged matters with deputies and substitutes that little more was needed than an occasional firm touch on the helm. All thought and energy was now concentrated even more acutely than before on winning the war, and concentrated with an abnegation only rarely found among those who rise high. At times, virtue brought its own reward. When, for instance, Churchill wrote that he intended to propose that Tizard should be made a Knight Grand Cross of the Order of the British Empire in the coming Birthday Honours, Tizard declined. 'Wrote thanking him', he noted at the foot of Churchill's letter, 'but saying that I would prefer no public recognition during the war.' He was thus saved from what might have appeared an invidious comparison. In the same Honours List Lindemann was created a Baron, becoming Lord Cherwell of Oxford. Tizard, a self-denying man, made only one comment – 'Anyway, the Cherwell is a small and rather muddy stream.'

He bore no ill-will. He rarely complained. He knew his activities were worthwhile, that word which comes so frequently into his notes and comments. He showed a continuing surprise that the meek did not inherit the earth, but accepted the fact without grudge. His personal optimism continually shone through, kept alight by the background of a happy family life, and a philosophic sense of proportion. This was well shown in a note which he prepared for his wife and sons after a sister had been killed in an air raid, and which was to be sent if he suffered the same fate.

My dear family [it went], it is all a matter of luck in London of course. What I want to say is don't be too upset and distressed. All good things come to an end sometime. One has got to die, and I would rather be killed by a bomb while doing a worthwhile job, than die of some nasty disease in a helpless old age. It is not as if I were young with most of my life in front of me – and after all I have had more than the average share of happiness and success. I should hate to think of you all being downhearted. I should like to feel that you took it quite philosophically, and very soon were your own cheerful selves again, having a good laugh about *something*.

Tizard himself witnessed his full quota of air raids. When these took place while he was sleeping at Imperial College he would usually make a round of the fire guard posts with Dr Ellingham, chatting with the staff on the exposed roofs and helping to keep up morale. In the summer of 1941 he found that he had been put on the list of those due for regular fire-watching at Westminster Abbey. He wrote back explaining that although for sentimental reasons he would do what he could to protect the Abbey, he would not be available every night. 'The spirit is willing but the circumstances are difficult', he added, noting that he would, if possible, come as a stop-gap when required. 'I am taking steps to get thoroughly familiar with Westminster Abbey roofs and the methods of watching, so that I shall not be a passenger if I am called upon suddenly', he added.

From mid-1941 onwards his activities increased. As the personal adviser to the Minister of Aircraft Production he could affect the fortunes of a wide sector of British industry and the work of numerous research organizations. But he also served on, and later led, the Radio Policy Committee, an influential offshoot of the Chiefs of Staff Committee whose decisions almost directly controlled the wartime activities of the radio industry. He was a member of the Engineering Advisory Committee of the Cabinet, 'really set up', he noted, 'because the engineers felt that their nose had been put out of joint because of the formation of the S.A.C.' There was also the Aeronautical Research Committee, of which he was still Chairman. Here his touch on the reins was inevitably a light one, since the bulk of the Council's work was done by subsidiary bodies. Yet their extent is shown by the fact that in the spring of 1941 they included separate sub-committees dealing with aerodynamics, alloys, elasticity and fatigue, engines, Fleet Air Arm research, meteorology, oscillation, seaplanes, stability and control, and structures, the more important of the committees meeting about every six weeks. If this were not enough, Tizard was also technically responsible for panels of experts who dealt with airscrews, fluid motion, free flight, kite balloons, lubrication, navigation, and the high-speed wind tunnel at Farnborough.

In addition, there was his work as an additional member of the Air Council, although this was less onerous than might be thought. Tizard's account of how the main item at one meeting was inspection of competing designs for W.A.A.F. underwear does not tell the whole story; but it correctly infers that throughout the war the Council tended to discuss administrative matters, while the operational decisions were made elsewhere, by the Chiefs of Staff, the Chief of Air Staff, or those at Command level.

There was, moreover, the impression that permeated both the Civil Service and the Royal Air Force, that if advice were needed on a delicate scientific issue, having a word with Tizard would probably be the best investment of time. Pye, D.S.R. at the Ministry of Aircraft Production, leant heavily on Tizard's advice. His successor, Lockspeiser, sought it frequently. There was also, quite apart from the wide experience that made Tizard's advice so useful, his flair for appreciating how ideas put forward in the office or the laboratory would work out in the air, on operations. Pilots still remember the meeting which he called at Imperial College early in 1941 to discuss what the current problems of night interception really were. His attitude on such occasions is shown by the minutes of a conference of some forty photographic experts

which he convened later in the year to 'enable the technical people
to find out by personal contact with those on the job what troubles
were being experienced, so that they might study how to overcome them'. The report of the conference is studded with 'Sir
Henry Tizard enquired . . .'; '. . . in reply to a question by Sir
Henry Tizard . . .'. He finally wound up the meeting by 'extending to the Photographic Reconnaissance Units the warm congratulations and good wishes of those on the ground'. Only Tizard, one
feels, would have got so much over in those three words, 'on the
ground'.

On a different level, the members of the Scientific Advisory
Committee of the Cabinet were in close and regular touch with
him, both as friends and as working colleagues. In 1940 he had
been elected Foreign Secretary of the Royal Society, an appointment whose significance was of course affected by the war but
which gave its holder a link, tenuous though this might be, with the
Advisory Committee itself. At this level it seemed, in any case,
natural to turn to Tizard, whatever his official status or lack of it.
Thus when three scientific advisers were appointed to the newly-
formed Ministry of Production in August 1942, it was suggested
that one of their first meetings should be with him. And when the
Army Council at last agreed that it would tolerate a Scientific
Adviser, it was Tizard who was asked to mull over the matter
during lunch with Sir James Grigg, then Permanent Under-
Secretary, and General Sir Ronald Weeks, Director-General of
Army Equipment. 'We discussed possible scientific representation
on the Army Council and generally the troubles they had in certain War Office departments', he wrote in his diary. 'I promised
to look over possible names and send suggestions later on.'

*   *   *

Tizard had reinforced his position at the Ministry of Aircraft
Production only a short while when he found himself faced with
the report of the Maud Committee, set up some fifteen months
earlier to investigate the possibilities of a nuclear weapon. Its work
had been carried out in British universities, aided since the fall of
France by two members of the Joliot-Curie team from the Collège
de France, and since the start of 1941 by advice from the technical

staff of Imperial Chemical Industries. Tizard himself had remained sceptical of success and had discussed the work with
Thomson, the chairman of the committee, on his return from the
United States in November 1940. 'I said I quite agreed that some
uranium work should go on but could not regard it of such importance that he should spend his whole time on it', he noted. A
few months later, in a letter to Fowler in Washington he had
asked to be informed of any practical application of uranium
research, adding: 'At present I am bound to say it occupies none
of my thought'. Fowler, in reply, reflected the general feeling in
the United States – as well as that of many if not most British
scientists. 'No one that I know of has suggested any war use of
uranium', he wrote. 'If the uranium reaction does go on a reasonable scale it looks like being a source of power of indefinite life,
but certainly not an explosive.'

In Britain, meanwhile, the work of the Maud Committee was
pointing towards very different conclusions. In Cambridge, the
French team had virtually proved that a nuclear chain reaction
could be achieved. In Liverpool and Birmingham, Chadwick,
Frisch and Peierls had managed to confirm the awful power of
the explosion that could probably be created. And at more than
one ICI works a start had been made in probing the immense
problems of chemical engineering which would be involved in
production of a nuclear explosive. The result was that the Maud
Committee – Tizard's small committee which 'ought to sit soon
and advise what ought to be done' – was able to report optimistically in July 1941. With Blackett the sole dissentient, its members
forecast that a uranium bomb could be built within two years at
a cost of £5,000,000. However, much work remained to be done
in Britain before the remaining doubts could be removed, while
it was suggested that the bomb itself should be built in Canada.
A further query was raised a fortnight later by Lord Hankey,
Chairman of the Scientific Advisory Committee of the Cabinet,
who wrote privately to Charles Darwin querying whether, if the
bomb were made, any Government would really sanction its use.[1]

Hankey was not the first to get the report of the Maud Committee. With the extinction of the Committee for the Scientific
Study of Air Warfare, its labours had been pushed beneath the

umbrella of the M.A.P., and it was to Colonel Moore-Brabazon that Professor Thomson addressed its findings. Moore-Brabazon passed on to David Pye, his Director of Scientific Research, what has not too inaccurately been called this blue-print for the world's first nuclear weapon. Pye duly wrote to Linnell, suggesting that the next obvious step was to ask Tizard's opinion. Tizard however, had already given an opinion, since he had been visited earlier in July by Sir Charles Ellis, Wheatstone Professor of Physics at King's College London, and later Scientific Adviser to the Army Council. 'He is confident that the uranium bomb might be successful if the very considerable and expensive development work can be accelerated', Tizard noted in his diary.

> I said I was not at all optimistic about the scheme. In fact, I was prepared to take a bet that there would be certainly no military application in this war. But I promised to look through the Maud Report carefully and with an open mind. On the whole I thought that the wisest thing would be to transfer the work to America. He agreed. He also spoke about the desirability of getting more accurate intelligence on what the Germans were doing. I explained what I thought to be the difficulties in this.

Shortly afterwards, Tizard received a copy of the report from Linnell, and on 5 August, wrote to Lord Hankey.

> I hear [he said], that you have been discussing 'MAUD' in the highly optimistic atmosphere created by the enthusiasm of three well-known Peers.*
>
> I think I ought to tell you that I am still a sceptic. In the first place I don't think the physics of the problem are at all settled, and in the second place, even if the optimism of the physicists is justified, the time and money needed to produce a practical success will be far greater than that indicated in the report.
>
> I should, myself, think it is absurd to embark on this very big and highly speculative industrial undertaking in this country with all we have to do in other ways, and I think the only sensible thing to do is to send Chadwick and Thomson to America to discuss all the results with the Americans who have been doing similar work, and on the basis of that decide whether a plant should be put up somewhere in North America.
>
> The suggestion is being made that the report should go formally to your Scientific Advisory Committee.

* Presumably Cherwell, McGowan and Melchett.

Before replying to Linnell, Tizard sought the advice of Philip Dee, then Superintendent at the Telecommunications Research Establishment, into which Bawdsey had by this time blossomed. Dee also was cautious, and Tizard remained so when he replied to Linnell on 21 August. 'Broadly speaking', he said, 'when this work started I expressed the view that it was extremely improbable that an effect of military importance could be obtained during the war, and that one could not exclude the possibility. The position now is that the probability has increased but is still very small. As for the suggestion made in the report that success on a large scale could be achieved by the end of 1943, I entirely disagree with it. Even if we accepted all the conclusions of the optimists, based as they are on insufficient evidence, it would, in my opinion, be out of the question to expect large-scale success in so short a time.'

Now, on 27 August, while Moore-Brabazon was considering the situation, Cherwell gave Churchill his own opinion of the Maud Report. 'People who are working on these problems consider the odds are 10 to 1 on success within two years', he concluded. 'I would not bet more than 2 to 1 against or even money. But I am quite clear that we must go forward. It would be unforgiveable if we let the Germans develop a process ahead of us by means of which they could defeat us in war or reverse the verdict after they had been defeated.'[2] Cherwell sent a copy of this note to Hankey, with whom he had discussed the matter a few days earlier, and who had by this time been requested, by Moore-Brabazon, to put the matter before the Scientific Advisory Committee. This Hankey now did. 'We . . . set up a special panel under my chairmanship', he has stated, 'heard the evidence of many famous scientists and before the end of September we presented a report, clearing up some of the doubts and endorsing the feasibility of the project.'[3] This was as well. Three days after receiving Cherwell's comments, Churchill had sent his famous note to the Chiefs of Staff Committee, saying that although he was 'content with existing explosives, I feel we ought not to stand in the path of improvement, and I therefore think that action should be taken in the sense proposed by Lord Cherwell . . .'

The result was Tube Alloys, which carried on research in

Britain; the formation of the American organization for building
the bomb; and the movement of the British teams to the United
States in August 1943. Tizard remained cautious of success, as
did Cherwell, but he was even more sceptical; in the circles where
such things could be discussed, he spoke with less reserve than
Cherwell, and 'hedged his bets' with less care. In addition his day-
by-day contact with the physical problems of war-production
possibly gave him a greater insight into the diversion of men and
materials that was involved. It certainly gave him more opportunity for over-statement. In May 1942, for instance, he deplored
the fact that jet-development at Metropolitan-Vickers appeared
to be hampered by work for Tube Alloys, and noted: 'If this is
true, we are running a serious risk of losing the substance for
the shadow'. Six months later he still regarded the project as 'a
waste of time', and deplored the transfer to it of men from other
work.

Cherwell, with his more deeply-based fear of what Germany
might achieve, was more anxious than Tizard about the possibilities of defeat in the nuclear race. Yet in essentials the two men
were less separated here than can be argued by pointed selection
of the facts. Both were sceptical of the Maud Committee's target-
date of mid-1943. Both felt that the major effort should be made
on the far side of the Atlantic. And Cherwell would have agreed
with Tizard's post-war comment that: 'It was indeed fortunate
that the atomic bomb and the long-range rocket were publicly
demonstrated before the end of the war, although they had very
little effect on its outcome. They opened wide the eyes of the
people of the world who otherwise might have gone happily to
sleep again while such weapons were developed in secret.' He
would also, no doubt, have agreed with Tizard's wish that the
demonstration of the bomb's existence and power 'could have
been made in a way less shocking to the civilized world.'

Even more important, Tizard and Cherwell were united
throughout the war years in the hope that the thing would not
work. They had a common repugnance of the idea, which
savoured too much of things undreamt of in their philosophy.
Thus 'the idea of such destructive power being available in human
hands', wrote R. V. Jones of Lord Cherwell, 'seemed to repel him

so much that he could scarcely believe that the universe was constructed in this way'.[4] And of Jones Tizard merely asked: 'Do you
really think that the Universe was made in this way?'[5]

Tizard's doubts about the bomb-project in the summer of 1941
were based partly on his judgement that its development was a bad
gamble so far as the war in hand was concerned. The opposite
side of the coin was shown by his vigorous support for the other
scientific device which was significantly pushed towards practical
use during this period – and which, after the uranium bomb and
radar, was probably the most important developed during the
war. This was the jet, of whose significance Tizard seems to have
been uncannily aware.

When news of the first jet flight came into his office in Thames
House in the spring of 1941, he exclaimed: 'History has been
made', stretched for a piece of paper on his desk, and immediately
began to rough out the future of the gas turbine. 'It was amazing
to watch him', says Adamson, his Scientific Assistant at the time.
'He was at once predicting the possibility of sharing out energy
between the propeller turbines, and even hinting at the by-pass
principle.' Outside the small hard core of enthusiasts working
with Whittle himself, Tizard appears to have been one of the few
who foresaw that the 1960's might well be known as 'the jet age' –
although, like many others, he had been sceptical as to whether
its development would affect the war.

It will be remembered that he had supported Power Jets in
1936 at a time when support was badly needed. However, as the
prospects of war loomed larger he became more impressed by
the need to concentrate on essentials. Thus when Whyte expressed
his fear, in the summer of 1939, that Whittle might be called back
into regular service, Tizard commented that 'if war broke out in
the next few months it was unlikely that the Whittle scheme could
possibly be developed to have any material effect on a war, and
that therefore Whittle ought to go back to other duties'.

However, he rarely minded trimming his opinion to the new
facts of life, and early in 1940 he altered his view about the chance
of the jet-engine's utility in the war. The cause was apparently a
visit to Whittle's works in January when he watched a demonstration run on the experimental engine. 'A demonstration which does

x

not break down in my presence is a production job' he commented
dryly; and before leaving he assured Whittle that more progress
had been made with the combustion problem than he had expected. From now onwards he had faith in the need to push ahead
with the engine and it was unfortunate, but perhaps inevitable,
that relations between the two men should become strained.

Whittle had two grounds for suspecting Tizard's support. The
first was his discovery in July 1940 that Beaverbrook had been
shielded from information of jet development and had heard of it
only indirectly. 'It was not until a long time afterwards', he wrote
later, 'that I heard that knowledge of our work had been with-
held from him because it was feared that he might consider it to
be an interference with immediately urgent requirements, and
that having heard of it indirectly, he sent for me to find out what
was going on. However, the axe did not fall, and indeed Lord
Beaverbrook's parting words to me were to the effect that as soon
as we were ready for a prototype fighter to take the engine we
should have it.'[6]

In this particular case it was perhaps – in view of earlier Air
Ministry action – natural enough that Tizard should have been
suspected. It is not so easy to understand the suspicion felt for him
by some of the jet's supporters as plans for research and development went ahead from the latter half of 1940. One of Tizard's
first conclusions, once he believed that the jet might be developed
during the war, was that work should be pressed ahead by a
number of firms, including Rolls-Royce, BTH, Rovers, Vaux-
halls, and de Havilland's, with Whittle and his colleagues acting
as advisers. This would bring a larger number of brains to bear on
the questions involved, would spread the load of what was still
speculative research among a number of firms and, with the prospect of air raids still growing, would divide the research eggs
among a number of well-spaced baskets. Whittle felt, however,
that if he and his team were to act only as advisers then Rolls-
Royce was the only company equipped to handle the work.
Tizard's attitude is shown by his comment when Vauxhall's
wanted, against official advice, to start work on a new test house
for the jet-engine before it was certain that they would be involved
in the scheme. 'This engine is still a gamble, but may be a war-

winning gamble if it comes off', he wrote. 'It is so important not
to waste a week unnecessarily that I think the possible waste of a
few hundred pounds extra may be faced without qualms. A large
sum of money has already been spent on the development of the
engine.'

This was early in 1941. In April the first jet aircraft left the
ground during taxiing trials, and on 15 May the first real flight
was made. It was followed by others. By the early summer it became necessary for a major decision to be taken, and late in May
Lindemann, as he still was, appears to have written to Tizard
enquiring about the exact position.

> My dear Lindemann [Tizard replied], the experimental aircraft with
> the experimental Whittle engine has done some very satisfactory
> flights; quite enough to establish the soundness of the principles,
> silence some of the sceptics, and to encourage everyone to go full
> steam ahead. At the same time we have a long way to go yet. We are
> gambling, I think rightly, on the production of an aircraft with
> engines the design of which is not yet settled. We have not yet had
> anything like a type test, even of an experimental engine approxi-
> mating in size and power to the project engine for which the aircraft
> has been designed. So we must not be too optimistic. I am sure that
> the outstanding problems can be solved – the great thing is to solve
> them in time. I have just been making arrangements for still further
> extension of the development work. . . . Yours very sincerely,
> H. T. Tizard.

On this occasion Lindemann – about to become Lord Cherwell
– appears to have agreed with Tizard's advice, since on 13 July,
the Minister of Aircraft Production received the following 'Action
this Day' minute from Churchill. 'Will you convene this week a
meeting of the necessary authorities, including the S. of S. for
Air and C.A.S. and Lord Cherwell, and report to me whether in
the circumstances we ought not to proceed forthwith in the production of the Whittle aircraft without waiting for a pilot model
of Mark II. If this latter course is adopted we shall be delayed till
January or February, and very high level German bombers may
well appear over Britain in the interval. I am assured that the
production of say 1,000 WHITTLES would not cut in upon the
existing types of aircraft to any serious extent.'[7] Five days later
Tizard, Cherwell, and Moore-Brabazon were among those who

met at the Ministry of Aircraft Production. The entire question was thrashed out in detail. And it was decided that Gloster's, already planning to build a plane to carry the first Mark of jet engines, should speed up their plans. The Whittle engine was 'over the hump'.

Tizard was in a strong position when it came to the potential use of a new technical development, the problems that might arise when it was introduced to the Services, the best ways of ironing out the troubles that so frequently arose within the eternal triangle of scientist, production manager, and Service user. His position was weaker when it came to operations, although he was certainly linked with one of the most spectacular of them. On 16 January 1942 Robert Cockburn, working at the Telecommunications Research Establishment on methods of deceiving enemy radar, suggested to Rowe that samples of the latest German equipment might be captured by a Commando raid. Rowe passed on the idea to Tizard, who minuted Portal on the 21st, saying: 'If any more Commando raids are being planned is it possible to include as one of the objectives the capture of enemy RDF equipment. The raid would have to be planned in detail and it would be highly desirable for scientific personnel to form part of the landing forces. The Cherbourg Peninsula is the obvious choice, but I suppose that this may be thought to entail too big an operation at present. There are, however, other more vulnerable places where RDF installations exist.'

One such place had already been noted by R. V. Jones, by now Director of Scientific Intelligence in the Air Ministry, and plans were already being prepared for an attack on the radar site at Bruneval.

Tizard's interventions of this sort were rare. For when it came to questions of strategy, long-term policy, the best way of winning the war, he could fight only on less certain ground. For here he was handicapped by three circumstances. He was attempting to achieve political ends even though he distrusted political means. His whole attitude to the waging of war was both more scientific and more cautious, less emotional and less amenable to moving presentation, than those of the men in command. And he was perpetually to find, on the other side of the table, as it were, exactly those who had watched his discomfiture in June 1940 – Churchill, Sinclair, Cherwell, and Portal. Thus it is possible to trace, through the correspondence files and the minutes, many such minor engagements where the attitudes both of Tizard and of his opponents can be correctly prophesied before turning the page. All shrink beneath the argument as to the part that the bombing of Germans should play in Allied strategy.

*   *   *

The disagreement between Tizard and the Air Ministry on the strategic bomber offensive was not, as we shall see, the direct cause of his final retirement in the summer of 1943. It was an argument, however, which spluttered continuously from the autumn of 1940 onwards, which formed the background to many minor conflicts of opinion, and which cut him off from the majority of those who were guiding the course of the war. This disagreement on a basic policy has been represented as a personal disagreement between Tizard and Cherwell, and even as a disagreement between their allegedly different moral concepts of how war should be waged. This was not so. The argument, which was on strategic and not humanitarian grounds, went far deeper than personalities; it had begun long before Cherwell's much-publicized paper of 1942 advocating the 'de-housing' of the German population; and it continued long after the suppositions of that paper had been resolved.

Before recounting the progress of the argument, and its effect on Tizard's life, it is necessary to clear away two illusions. The first of these is that the policy of attacking German civilians was the result of Cherwell's paper of 1942. This policy had in fact been inherent in the Chiefs of Staff recommendation of autumn 1940, that Britain's immediate action should be to destroy the basis of the German war machine – 'the economy which feeds it, the civilian morale which sustains it, the supplies which nourish it and hopes of victory which give it courage'.[8] And it had become explicit when, in the following year, the C.-in-C. Bomber Command was instructed that, with the exception of diversionary attacks, he was to 'direct the main effort of the bomber force, until further instructions, towards dislocating the German trans-

portation system and to destroying the morale of the civil population as a whole and of the industrial workers in particular'.[9]
Finally, on 14 February 1942, it was decided that Royal Air
Force attacks were 'to be focussed on the morale of the enemy's
civil population and, in particular, of the industrial workers' in
cities within range of the new navigational aid known as Gee.[10]

The second illusion is that Tizard himself shrank from the fact
that in an industrial society war is indivisible – that he believed
there was some point along the bicycle path from the factory to
the home where the morals of killing civilians suddenly changed.
Three weeks before the outbreak of war he wrote to Ludlow-
Hewitt saying: 'I believe it to be possible to "area-bomb" an industrial district blind with the use of the latest R.D.F. equipment.'
And his attitude is further suggested by a note which he sent to
the Controller of Research and Development on 11 August 1941
on the re-designing of bombs so that more of them could be carried
in any one plane. 'For bombing urban areas', he wrote, 'it is not
necessary to go for extreme ballistic efficiency.'

Tizard's argument was simply that the enormous cost, human
and industrial, involved in any major bombing offensive, must be
expended to produce the maximum result. And he became convinced that this could only be brought about by Britain directing
a smaller proportion of her growing bombing effort to attacks on
Germany and a larger proportion to attacks on German U-boats,
in port or at sea. In this strategic choice he was supported by much,
and possibly by the bulk, of informed scientific opinion – notably
by Blackett, Director of Naval Operational Research at the
Admiralty whose attitude had been formed after he had carried
out a detailed statistical analysis of the situation. This objective
approach to the use of the bomber force made little headway,
largely because Churchill, Cherwell, the Air Staff led by Portal,
as well as the Chiefs of Staff in general, were convinced that an
essential preliminary to victory was a massive and sustained
bombing offensive against Germany itself.

In support of the strategic choice advocated by Tizard and his
supporters, it can be claimed that the Battle of the Atlantic was
won by too dangerously narrow a margin. This, without doubt,
is a more tenable argument than any claim that the strategic

bomber offensive achieved the results expected. Yet this is but a partial – if not a partisan – comparison. For the polarization of the argument around the destruction of Germany and success or failure in the Battle of the Atlantic has overshadowed one decisive outcome of the bomber offensive – the winning of air supremacy. This outcome may well have been, as the proponents of the offensive claim, an inevitable result of implementing the Trenchard doctrine that an enemy should be hit as hard, and as near home, as possible; it may, on the contrary, have been both fortuitous and too dearly-won. Yet whichever view lies nearer the truth, it is unwise to overlook the fact that the offensive moulded the Luftwaffe into an unbalanced weapon, steadily eroded its value, and by forcing the Germans to use it almost exclusively for the defence of the Reich, forbade its use in the only way in which, after the end of 1941, it would have been militarily viable – as a successful deterrent to Allied invasion of the Continent. For without air supremacy, however achieved, the troops would neither have got ashore in Normandy nor been able, when that was done, to fight up the long road to Berlin. However, this aspect of the bomber offensive was not openly raised in the argument as it developed early in 1942.

Tizard's attitude was scientifically-based, but it is difficult not to believe that it was strengthened by factors of a different kind. He felt deeply what he considered to be the failure of his Committee for the Scientific Survey of Air Offence. He knew that this failure was not of his making, and he no doubt realized that with the need for putting first things first, it had been inevitable that the problems of Bomber Command should have been given scant consideration. This meant, however, that men went into battle less well equipped than they had any right to expect. Tizard never reconciled himself to this fact and it heightened his horror that the bomber crews – 'la crème de la crème de la crème' as his old friend Colonel Cooper called them – should be expended on targets which were, objectively speaking, not worth the cost of their lives. The feeling remained, and if 'haunting' were a word which his mind would not have ridiculed, Tizard might well have used it here. Only a few months before his death he received a cutting from *The Times* in which a letter suggested that for stretches of the war the average life of a bomber crew was about three months. Tizard replied, saying that he was surprised that it was as long and concluded by quoting Southey on Blenheim –

> '*And everybody praised the Duke,*
> *Who this great fight did win.*'
> '*But what good came of it at last?*'
> *Quoth little Peterkin.*
> '*Why, that I cannot tell*', *said he,*
> '*But 'twas a famous victory* '.[11]

It is against this background that one must consider Tizard's assessment of the bombing situation that began to develop during the late summer of 1941. The M.A.P. was 'under continuous and heavy pressure from the Air Council and the Prime Minister' to increase bomber supplies,[12] and on 7 September Churchill gave instructions that a plan should be drawn up for a further increase in deliveries. Tizard was involved in implementing this plan and his attitude hardened against it as he realized its implications. 'The war', he wrote to Freeman on 24 December, 'is not going to be won by night bombing. This programme assumes that it is.' The reasons for his scepticism were indicated in a note he had sent to Air Chief Marshal Sir Charles Medhurst, Assistant Chief of Air Staff, a few weeks earlier, after talks with Professor Bernal who had been helping to analyse the German bombing of Britain.* 'Who', he asked, 'has the responsibility of examining and advising on the destructive efficiency of particular types of bombs and thereby guiding technical policy?' His views are further revealed by a diary entry for 17 February.

> Wrote a note urging use of long-range bombers for anti-ship work rather than night bombing of Germany [this went]. The latter is ineffective unless done on a scale very much larger than at present. It will only be really effective when American production gets into

---

* The idea for the bombing analysis arose during a conversation between Lord Cherwell and Professor Zuckerman when both were members of the High Table at Christ Church, and a request that one should be carried out was made to Sir Reginald Stradling. Professors Zuckerman and Bernal were then given the task of directing the enquiry and were jointly responsible for the report, which was used by Lord Cherwell to support his own shorter paper.

full swing. Lyster sent me a similar note he had written, with a memorandum for the First Sea Lord. Blackett came to see me with his note about civilian deaths in Germany. He makes out a good case for these not being much higher than our own losses of trained crews of bombers. Bernal left his summary of the results of German bombing of England. Taken as a whole the effect on production and morale has been surprisingly small.

The following day Tizard sent a note to the Minister.

I say emphatically as a conclusion [this ended], that a calm dispassionate review of the facts will reveal that the present policy of bombing Germany is wrong; that we must put our maximum effort first into destroying the enemy's sea communications and preserving our own; that we can only do so by operating aircraft over the sea on a very much larger scale than we have done hitherto, and that we shall be forced to use much longer range aircraft.

The only advantage that I see in bombing Germany is that it does force the enemy to lock up a good deal of his effort on home defence. This end could be achieved by steady bombing on a much smaller scale than is at present contemplated by the Air Staff, as is obvious from our own action in this country. The heavy scale will only be justified and economic at the concluding stages of the war when (or if) we are fortunate enough to have defeated the enemy at sea and to have command of it. Until that time is ripe, everything is to be lost by concentrating on this bombing offensive instead of by concentrating on the sea problem.

Shortly afterwards he wrote an additional memorandum to the Minister admitting that the last two paragraphs of his previous note were 'perhaps too provocative'. He wanted, he said, 'to start from the standpoint that the difference of opinion is not so much one of object but one of timing, and that where you put your available bombing force at any period of the war depends on the changing conditions of the war. At one period the policy of bombing land objectives may be right, and at another it may be entirely wrong.'

His position, and that of his opponents during these first few weeks of 1942 can finally be fixed by a letter which he wrote to Freeman on 20 February, and by Freeman's brief reply. Tizard first pointed out that during the previous thirty-four weeks Bomber Command had lost 728 planes, and had probably suffered as many casualties in trained bomber crews as the number of

Germans killed. 'You and others on the Air Staff may say, while admitting the truth of all this, (that) we are now approaching a period when we shall get real results', he continued. 'I say that you are deceiving yourselves because you don't really grasp yet the size of the effort necessary to get a real result, and you are going to give away a new method to the enemy* before you can put it into operation on such a scale that it will be worth while.' Freeman replied with a short note three days later. 'My dear HT', he said, 'I have read your personal letter to me about bombing, and my first reaction is that you have been seeing too much of Professor Blackett, but I hope to let you have some more detailed criticisms in the near future. Is not Blackett biting the hand that fed him.'[13]

Thus was the stage set for the internal battle of the next two months. It was to be a battle, it must be stressed, waged about the best use of the bomber forces which would be available during the next year or so – not about the morals or long-term expediency of bombing German cities. The Air Ministry was to be ranged against the Admiralty; those guided both by the Trenchard doctrine and the public wish to kill Germans, against those who supported the cooler statistical approach of Blackett and Tizard. It was also, although to a more limited extent, to be a battle in which Tizard was ranged against Cherwell, although the correspondence of both reveals that Tizard's initial attitude was later so qualified that he could write to Cherwell saying: 'I don't really disagree with you fundamentally, but only as a matter of timing.'

The operations opened in March, when the Chiefs of Staff instructed the Joint Intelligence Sub-Committee to prepare a report assessing the effect on the German war effort of air attack on Germany and German-occupied territory, with particular reference to assistance to Russia that summer. On 30 March Cherwell, who had by this time studied the analysis of what had been achieved by the bombing of Birmingham and Hull in 1940, prepared a paper implying that Bomber Command could turn out of house and home a majority of the inhabitants then living in Germany's fifty-eight largest cities. The paper was circulated for comment, which came within a fortnight. Sinclair discussed it with

---

* The new navigational aid, Gee.

Portal, and prepared a minute dated 6 April which stated that both found Lord Cherwell's calculations simple and convincing. Certain very important conditions would have to be fulfilled. However, both agreed that the start that had been made in recent attacks was a promising one, and they saw no reason to doubt that within eighteen months, and with American help, the degree of destruction which Lord Cherwell suggested was possible could, in fact, be achieved.

Tizard had other views.

He had seen the paper, he wrote to Cherwell on the 15th.

I am afraid that I think that the way you put the facts as they appear to you is extremely misleading and may lead to entirely wrong decisions being reached, with a consequent disastrous effect on the war [he said]. I think, too, that you have got your facts wrong. I have written to Sinclair suggesting that if the War Cabinet are going to reach a strategical decision on this paper I should be given an opportunity to comment officially on it; but I do feel that it is most unfortunate that you and I should be completely at cross purposes on a matter of such importance. Is it not possible to try to resolve our difference of opinion together?

Cherwell replied immediately and amicably.

My dear Tizard [he wrote on the same day]. Many thanks for your note. I would be interested to hear what you think wrong with my simple calculation, which seemed to me fairly self-evident. I had no idea you took a different view, and I should be very glad to try and come to agreement. Please excuse this hasty note, and believe me, as ever, Yours Cherwell.[14]

Blackett submitted a detailed criticism of the Cherwell paper the following day, the nub of his comments being the statement that 'Lord Cherwell's estimate of what can be achieved is at least six hundred per cent too high'. This straight contradiction of Sinclair's optimistic view was utilized in a minute which Tizard sent to Cherwell and Sinclair on the 30th and which ended by concluding '(a) that a policy of bombing German towns wholesale in order to destroy dwellings cannot have a decisive effect by the middle of 1943, even if all heavy bombers and the great majority of Wellingtons produced are used primarily for this purpose (b) that such a policy can only have a decisive effect if carried out on a much bigger scale than is envisaged in (the Cherwell paper).'

Thus Tizard disagreed. But he felt it fair and proper to point out that he was disagreeing only with the claim that the results forecast could be attained within the stated time, with the forces that he expected to be available. He made this clear in the letters which he sent with his comments to Sinclair and to Cherwell on 20 April. Both covered similar ground, but the letter to Cherwell is particularly revealing.

> I don't really disagree with you fundamentally, but only as a matter of timing [this went on]. I enclose a little note from which you will see that I cannot quite make out from where you get your figure of 10,000 heavy bombers and Wellingtons. My figures are taken from the latest M.A.P. programme. I also think that you always tend to over-estimate the capacity of the average crew when operating at night. I believe that roughly 50% of the total bombs cast do reach the built-up area of Cologne. Cologne is a large place, and it should certainly not apply to smaller towns at a greater distance than Cologne, even after more experience.
>
> My trouble is that I don't see a decisive effect being caused by this wholesale bombing before the middle of 1943. In the meantime, we must preserve command of the seas, and it is difficult for me to see how we are going to do this without strong support of the Navy by long-range bombers. However, I may be wrong here. You certainly have more access to the right information than I have.
>
> Having said that your calculations are wrong, I hope that my arithmetic is right; but as I was caught out doing a little wrong arithmetic a few weeks ago I am not too sanguine.

In some ways the letter was curious, a tribute to Tizard's political innocence as well as his integrity. Quite possibly he had made a mistake. Men do. But on the figures at issue he was right and Cherwell was wrong, as events were to prove. It is, of course, easy to make too much of what was a small incident in a long campaign. And it is quite clear from the evidence that Cherwell, with all the heavy artillery at his disposal, would have won this particular battle whatever Tizard had written. Yet the letter is revealing; and it is not difficult to imagine Cherwell smiling as he read it.

The plans for the bomber offensive, however developed, were buttressed now by the estimates of the Prime Minister's Scientific Adviser, and on the 30th Sinclair replied to Tizard's previous letter. Sir Henry had intended this partly as a letter of protest;

he now found, however, that he was being thanked by the Secretary of State for the reassurance that he 'did not disagree fundamentally with our bombing policy'. Freeman was not so sure of this. Tizard realized this when he discovered on his desk one morning the transcript of a monitored enemy radio broadcast; attached to it was a note from the Vice-Chief of Air Staff: 'To see attached where marked', it said, '. . . like you, the Germans are very anxious for us to stop raiding their towns.'[15]

The fallacies in Cherwell's paper were to be revealed only by time – and fallacies there were, however disarmingly it is argued that the paper contained but rounded-out figures of little significance. The immediate result of the engagement was to underline not only that Cherwell, in the words of the historians of the strategic air offensive, 'exerted much greater influence upon the Prime Minister than did Sir Henry Tizard',[16] but that his influence extended, also, over Sinclair and Portal. At this level, Tizard's stock was falling; elsewhere it was as high as ever.

*   *   *

In February 1942, Moore-Brabazon was replaced at the Ministry of Aircraft Production by Colonel Llewellin, whom Tizard met on the 24th. 'Told him I had better go, but he wants me to stop, so I said we would say nothing more about it for a month', he noted in his diary. Llewellin's plea was reinforced by Brabazon who a week later wrote: 'I do implore you to hang on doing the best you can at a difficult time'. Tizard hung on. He continued to hang on, as we shall see. But in the spring there took place an event that was to affect his whole future.

On 12 March, Professor George Gordon, the President of Magdalen College, died after a lingering illness; in the early informal discussions that followed, Tizard's name was put forward as a successor. The Fellows who supported him included not only scientists but also non-scientists, some of whom warmly welcomed the idea that Magdalen should become the first Oxford College to have a scientist as head. Tizard was, moreover, known as a very distinguished scientist-administrator, but there were objections. There were rumours that he had been somewhat tyrannical at Imperial College and since he was well-known to only a few

Fellows, some reliance was placed on such hearsay evidence. There was also a fear that he might be too narrowly scientific and thus not interested in the College as a great historical foundation, hitherto ruled over exclusively by men such as Gordon of whom it could be said that his 'profession was English letters from Chaucer'. The doubts were not entirely removed when Tizard dined at Magdalen late in April. He was lively and amusing. But he may have been nervous and to some of the Fellows who were regarding him as a possible President he appeared slightly self-important and inclined to show off.

However, his name went forward, and during the early summer it seemed likely that there might be a close election, with strong runners in the persons of Tizard, Sir Alexander Carr-Saunders, and a third internal candidate. It then became known that Carr-Saunders was bound to remain as head of the London School of Economics until the end of the war, and Tizard's prospects therefore grew. From the latter part of May he knew that he was being considered seriously for election, and on 7 June was informed of the fact by Paul Benecke, the Senior Fellow. Benecke spoke, however, with considerable circumlocution and qualification; so much so, in fact, that Tizard did not think it necessary to consider the intricacies of combining his duties in London with those of President. During June he discussed the possibilities of election with a number of Fellows, stressing that he wanted Oxford to gain more influence in affairs and that he wanted to help create the scientifically-minded administrator. He had other worries, including financial ones, but it appears that one of the things which he did fail to explain with sufficient clarity was the extent of his work for the Ministry of Aircraft Production and the Air Ministry. This explanation could, in the nature of things, have come only from Tizard himself. He was naturally limited by security in what he could say, even in the strictest confidence. And the cold-shouldering to which he had been persistently subjected no doubt tended to make him under-estimate his own value. It was thus perhaps natural that one of his friends should emphasize, at an informal meeting of Fellows on 18 July, that Tizard had no administrative, but merely advisory, duties; that he had refused to take on any more official work as he wished to give more time to

Imperial College; and that he would be able to give it, instead, to Magdalen. There was some measure of accuracy in this. But that it represented only part of the picture was shown by the reaction a week later.

On 23 July, Tizard dined at Magdalen as Benecke's guest. Two days later, on Saturday, 25 July, he was elected President – the BBC pronouncing his name incorrectly and making him fume. The Secretary of State for Air wrote to him immediately, hoping 'that this does not involve your retirement from the Air Council'. The Minister of Aircraft Production, Colonel Llewellin, congratulated him, 'so long as it does not mean any lessening of the great help which you are to us here and more particularly to me personally'. There was some suggestion that 'tenure of the new office be *de facto* postponed until the end of the war', and many queries as to how he could take up the appointment. 'I do hope, however, that it does not mean giving up your present war work', wrote Lord Hankey. 'That would be an absolute disaster . . .'

Yet the offer of the Presidency must have been difficult to resist. Oxford itself had continued to exercise its own peculiar charm on Tizard. He liked the place; he liked the life; and he was not oblivious to the personal honour involved. More important, perhaps, was the accolade which he felt the appointment would give to science itself, an appointment which brought the first scientist to the head of Wood's 'most noble and rich structure in the learned world'. There was, of course, his war work. But there is little indication that at the time of his appointment Tizard felt it would be necessary to relinquish much of this; and, as we shall see, he was to run in double harness for more than eight months. It is not, after all, so surprising that he would think this would be possible. He had been able to divest himself of many Imperial College duties as the war pressed in more closely about him, and to cope satisfactorily with his other duties. He no doubt retained, at least at the back of his mind, a memory of his predecessor there, Sir Thomas Holland, who used to claim that he had reduced the running of the College to twenty minutes work a day. And he may even have felt that some such feat of delegation might now be possible at Oxford. He was, after all, still personal Scientific Adviser to the Minister of Aircraft Production, a member of the

Aircraft Advisory Council and of the Radio Policy Committee. He was a member not only of the Air Council but of the Air Interception Committee, of the Air/Sea Interception Committee, the Bombing Committee, the Air Fighting Committee, the Torpedo Attack Committee, and the Operational Research Committee. He was now to become, in addition, President of Magdalen.

As a footnote to the election it is perhaps necessary to deal with the rumour that Cherwell played some part in bringing it about. So far as the College is concerned this rumour is totally untrue, since Cherwell made no approach, direct or indirect, to any of the Fellows; the likelihood is that it gained credence only some years later when the relationships between Sir Henry and Lord Cherwell became less obscured by the secrecy of war.

*   *   *

From the summer of 1942 onwards it was thus clear that Tizard's influence, if not diminished, would from the autum be exercised from Oxford rather than from Millbank. Yet this fact appears in no way to have affected either his current activities or his plans for future work, and throughout the summer his diary is filled with the customary concentrated round of committee meetings. Two things, perhaps more than any others, engaged him throughout 1942. One was his battle for a greater and more orderly utilization of scientific advice in the running of the war. The other was the organization and better operational use of the growing armoury of radio and radar weapons now being fashioned by the Allies.

As we have seen, the widespread discontent with the way in which scientific advice was being used by the Government had been brought almost to the boil by Tizard's resignation two years previously. But the threat of invasion, the rigours of the blitz, the changed circumstances brought about first by the German invasion of Russia and then by the entry of the United States into the war, had in succession served to prevent criticism reaching too dangerous a temperature. Nevertheless dismay remained. It was openly expressed by Tizard when he spoke at the annual lunch of the Parliamentary and Scientific Committee on 3 February. 'There is no doubt that many experienced scientific men are suffering from a sense of frustration', he said. 'They feel that they are not pulling their weight in the war, and do not know why. This feeling is perhaps not confined to scientists. There have been many mistakes and shortcomings due to non-application of science, or to its mis-application; nevertheless, no-one can deny that the influence of science is now greater than it has ever been, and that the present Government and Parliament attach a value to the help and guidance of scientists that no previous Parliament have ever done.' He paid a courageously fair tribute to Churchill, asking 'What previous Prime Minister of England ever had a scientific adviser continually at his elbow?' But he made it quite clear that no-one had yet worked out who was 'to decide the strategy of scientific war, to settle what are the things that really matter, where we are to devote our scientific strength to get the greatest results in the shortest possible time'.

Even at Departmental level much scientific collaboration was still on a purely hit-and-miss basis and it was to obviate this that Tizard called the first 'Informal meetings of Scientific Advisers' in June 1942. 'All of us who are engaged in the scientific study of problems which confront the Service Departments know how much these problems overlap, and how important it is for us to keep in as close a touch with each other's work as we can', he had written to Blackett on 26 May. 'I think it would be a very useful idea at this stage if we had an informal meeting to take stock of the present position to see whether we can help each other more than we are doing at present.' Darwin, Cockcroft, Fowler, and Bernal were some of those who agreed with the proposal and who from June onwards met in Tizard's office at the M.A.P. at roughly three-weekly intervals.

Elsewhere the system was apt to be chaotic. Individually the Chiefs of Staff took personal, private, and sometimes conflicting advice from their own Service advisers or from whomsoever they thought fit; collectively, they were advised on specific subjects by organizations such as the Radio Board, and on others by no-one. Luck, personal acquaintance, and the vagaries of circumstance therefore played a large part in both the quantity and the quality of the scientific advice taken before Chiefs of Staff decisions were passed to Cabinet level. Here the Scientific Advisory Committee,

Y

or one of its sub-committees, might or might not be asked to give an opinion. And here, of course, much would depend on the weight which the Prime Minister would give to the opinions of Cherwell. In a rough-and-ready way the system did work. The argument of Tizard, and of many others, was that it worked badly and expensively, not only in scientific capital but also in men and materials.

This criticism rose to its climax in the summer of 1942. The occasion was the defeat of the Eighth Army in North Africa and the fall, for the second time, of the great fortress of Tobruk. A deputation from the Parliamentary and Scientific Committee saw Mr R. A. Butler – who had become chairman of the S.A.C. in succession to Lord Hankey – and appealed that a more workmanlike organization should be set up. A. V. Hill thundered in *The Times* that the inferiority of British tanks, prime cause of the defeat in the desert, was due 'to a system which has failed to anticipate future tactical requirements in guns, projectiles, armour, and performance; failed to collect, analyse, and profit by previous operational experience; failed sometimes even to obey the elementary rule that production must follow, not precede, development.' Appleton, Secretary of the D.S.I.R. as well as adviser on numerous Boards and Committees, produced his own remedies. Tizard wrapped up the whole argument in a lengthy note to Sir Arthur Street, Permanent Secretary, and Secretary of the Air Council, after a meeting at which they considered the problem as it affected the Air Ministry.

'I can well sympathize with the Ministers and Chiefs of Staffs and other highly placed officers concerned, who must regard the scientific people as a temperamental lot who are often a great nuisance, though they have their nuisance value', said Tizard's covering note. 'But I do think we want more farsighted action in this war, and that many mistakes could have been avoided.'

His enclosure was headed: 'Note on Use of Scientific and Technical Resources in War'. It outlined various possible methods of re-organization, supported Appleton's proposal for a Board of scientists to be attached to the Defence Committee of the Cabinet, and concluded by saying that if the Board had more authority than the existing Scientific Advisory Committee, 'it would be a step in the right direction'.*

The 'step in the right direction' was never taken. The nearest approach to it was the proposal to appoint to the staff of the Minister of Production, in the following September, three full-time scientific advisers. 'The proposal irritated the Prime Minister who wrongly thought that I was trying to expand my "empire" and invade some of his', Lord Chandos, then Oliver Lyttelton, Minister of Production, has written. 'Here's Oliver', said Churchill on being reminded of the proposed appointments, 'always avid of power: now wanting to run the scientific side of the war: he's going to take it over from me . . .'[17] Lyttelton had been appointed the previous spring with general responsibility for overseeing war production but without a separate Ministry, and when Tizard was asked by his own Minister to comment on the terms of reference of 'the Three Blind Mice' as he called the three advisers, he replied that he did not know what field was really covered by the Ministry of Production. 'I am not sure that the terms of reference will help them very much, and I can imagine an enterprising Member of the House of Commons asking quite a lot of nasty questions', he added.

*   *   *

The move to Oxford was now imminent, and it might have been natural if Tizard had begun to shed his responsibilities. Yet it was now, early in August 1942 that he inaugurated a series of meetings which were to buttress the growing importance of Operational Research, not only in the Air Ministry but in all three Services. Held in Tizard's office on 5 August, the first was one of many to be attended by Pye, Bullard or Blackett from the Admiralty, Cockcroft from Supply, and many others who had helped to develop the new method.

Tizard himself had really laid the foundations of Operational Research during the Biggin Hill experiment. Rowe at the Telecommunications Research Establishment had appreciated the value of this and had sent a number of scientists from Bawdsey to Fighter Command on the outbreak of war – the R.D.F. (later

* Tizard's memorandum is given in full in Appendix 2.

Stanmore) Research Section. Nine months later the Committee for the Scientific Study of Air Warfare had recommended that a scientist should be posted to Bomber Command to study bomber losses – a proposal from which the Command's vitally important Operational Research Section grew. In the following month, August 1940, it was Tizard who had visited General Pile at Anti-Aircraft Command Headquarters, where the first primitive radar gun-laying sets were about to come into operation. Only by scientific appraisals, he said, could the best results be got from them – a comment which resulted in the appointment of Blackett as Pile's Scientific Adviser, the establishment of 'Blackett's Circus' as it came to be known, and the later introduction, by Blackett, of Operational Research techniques first to Coastal Command and later to the Admiralty. In October 1941 he had taken the chair at informal discussions during which the separate units by this time working at Fighter, Coastal, and Bomber Commands had been brought under central control. And almost exactly a year later he suggested to the Air Staff that statistical methods should be used to discover the effect of Allied bombing in the Middle East – a task subsequently carried out by Professor Zuckerman, then of the Research and Experiments Department, Ministry of Home Security.

However, as his scheme for the inter-Service discussion of Operational Research techniques got under way, a fresh crisis was arising in his relations with the authorities. The occasion was a change in the mechanism which controlled the strategy of the radio war, and to understand its significance it is necessary to re-call the steps which had been taken in the preceding four years.

Shortly after the Munich crisis of 1938 an Air Ministry Inter-Services R.D.F. Committee had been set up under the chairman-ship of Air Vice-Marshal Sholto Douglas. Both the operational and the scientific sides of all three Services had been represented, and for nearly three years Tizard himself had helped its members in the process of recommending how available supplies could best be allocated, advising on *ad hoc* problems of operational use, and grappling successfully with the increasingly complicated develop-ments of R.D.F. as radar was still called. In November 1939, Tizard's re-constituted Committee for the Scientific Study of Air

Warfare had recommended the setting-up of a special Radio Research Committee under Appleton, briefed to advise and initiate research on Service applications of R.D.F. and to advise on research to meet any other radio requirements of the R.A.F. which might be referred to it. However, no action had been taken, and by the summer of 1941 it had become clear that a body with backing stronger than that of a single Ministry was needed. For by this time all three Services were demanding radar equipment in vast quantities; new proliferations of the special sets used in the 'battle of the beams' were being designed to deceive the enemy's own detection chain, now known to be more advanced than had at first been realized; radar and other radio devices of chilling complexity were being developed as bombing aids, and yet others would be needed in the war of measure and counter-measure which the bombing offensive would nourish. In June 1941, therefore, Lord Hankey recommended to the Chiefs of Staff that the existing system should be replaced by a sub-committee of their own organization, to deal with R.D.F. policy.*

The first chairman of the new Policy Committee was Air Marshal Joubert, who had held the post for only a short while when he was appointed A.O.C.-in-C. Coastal Command. It became clear that the twin burdens were too much for one man, and Tizard was picked by the Chiefs of Staff as Joubert's successor. An illustration of the way in which Tizard was consulted when advice was needed on delicate matters soon came when he was asked to straighten out an awkward situation which arose from the proposal to drop Watson-Watt from both the Policy Committee itself and from a technical group which was to handle specialist matters. Watson-Watt had then protested to Portal on the grounds that he must interpret this as a vote of no confidence.

* In order to be correct as well as comprehensible, it is necessary to mention here the various ways in which this new organization was to be described. Technically, it was the R.D.F. Policy Sub-Committee of the Chiefs of Staff Committee. This latter, however, was frequently referred to merely as the Chiefs of Staff; its various sub-committees were as frequently known as Committees. This shortening to 'R.D.F. Policy Committee' was often further shortened in letters and documents to 'Policy Committee', a form continued when its scope was enlarged and it formally became the Radio Policy-Sub-Committee – a title given to conceal the fact that it still dealt with radar. Here it will be called plainly the Policy Committee.

Portal wrote to Tizard. His wisdom was soon shown, since Tizard was capable of doing what would have been beyond the bounds of most men. On 21 July he wrote a letter of disarming frankness to Appleton. 'I agree with Watson-Watt and his general contention', this said. 'It may possibly be that certain members of the Service Departments have lost confidence in Watson-Watt as an adviser, but I do feel that in that case the position should be made clear, and that it is a mistake to try to sidetrack him in a rather weak . . . . manner. We all know that in many ways he is his own worst enemy; at the same time a great deal of use can be made of him if he is handled properly.

'I have said as much to the C.A.S. I have also said that I thought it was a mistake in the circumstances to put you on originally as a member of the Policy Committee (incidentally it had got Smith's back up also). It is a great pity that the war is so affected by these human considerations, but there it is . . .'

Having smoothed this matter out, Tizard became Chairman of the Policy Committee itself in succession to Joubert in September 1941. He was still not happy about the organization, which he had earlier described to Portal as 'somewhat ill-conceived', and it appears that when plans were mooted to extend its activities to radio as well as radar, he considered relinquishing his chairmanship. Yet he was, quite simply, considered irreplaceable.

'Portal and I both feel that it is of paramount importance that you should remain as Chairman of the Committee, and hold the balance between the three Services and the conflicting claims of R.D.F., jamming and radio', Freeman wrote to him personally on 11 November. 'It is difficult enough when the Service interests alone compete, but when the workers of Radio of the three Services are likely to compete with the workers on Jamming, then the need for an independent Chairman who knows the subject and interests at stake seems to us to be most essential. We can think of no-one else who can fill this post so well as yourself, and I would rather the proposal was dropped than that you should fall out.'[18]

Early in 1942 the membership of the extended organization was finally settled. Under Tizard's chairmanship it was to include two representatives from each of the Services: Sir Frank Smith; Sir

Edward Appleton; and, as Tizard had insisted, Watson-Watt. The terms of reference of this strong body included inter-Service radio policy, and the recommendation both of priorities and of disclosure of information to Allied authorities. And as it reported to the Chiefs of Staff it could explain the scientific exigencies of the radio war direct to the body best equipped to deal with them.

However, the fact that Tizard was heading a group which had all the authority of a Chiefs of Staff subcommittee represents only a part of the story. His position still retained that anomalism to which he seemed bound, throughout the war, as surely as Prometheus to his rock. One example of this came very soon for in February Tizard wrote to Freeman pointing out that he had heard only unofficially that H₂S, the new bombing aid, was now being developed – even though he was chairman of the committee which was supposed to plot the course of such events.

> I have never been asked to give my advice on the subject by the Air Ministry or anyone else [he wrote]. I made a remark to the Secretary of State some little time ago when I asked to see him, which led, I think, to my being invited to attend one meeting under his Chairmanship recently. This meeting was actually a waste of time. It had previously been decided that this particular development should be higher priority than anything else. I don't agree with this point of view; nor would, I think, the RDF Policy Sub-Committee. But I have not been asked for my opinion nor have they. The matter was settled apparently on recommendations of or pressure from Lord Cherwell. . . . I do feel quite seriously, in exactly the same mood as I have felt for the past 18 months, that it is up to C.A.S. and yourself, not to mention the Secretary of State, to decide whose advice they really want. It is no good having two chief advisers who differ very considerably in their views. If you want to run the scientific war from Downing Street, then I find it extremely difficult to help you, and should, indeed, not be here at all unless I felt that occasionally I am effective by acting on my own initiative. The technical developments which have been sponsored and pushed from Downing Street have, taken as a whole, proved, as I expected, to have wasted time, money and energy on a large scale.

However, the problems were more complicated than those which would have been provided simply by a straight conflict of advice from two scientists. In practice, decisions were the result of numerous and frequently contradictory arguments at assorted meetings which involved also the operational heads of the Royal Air Force, the staff of the Telecommunications Research Establishment, Lord Cherwell, and the Chiefs of Staff. This is well illustrated by the fortunes of the 'Window' controversy, which began early in 1942. In many ways it provides a text-book example of how scientific decisions are taken in war, one for which Tizard's papers produce the evidence for the first time, and one which is complicated by the fact that he changed his views in mid-argument although remaining for some six months – contrary to popular belief – on the same side as Cherwell.

The suggestion that radar could be confused by dropping tin-foil strips had been proposed long before the outbreak of the war, and experiments had been made soon after it. It was felt, however, that the use of this device, subsequently code-named 'Window', should be held as a 'shot in the locker', and it was only in January 1942, that the suggestion of operational use hardened up before the Policy Committee. On Tizard's advice it was proposed that further trials should be made before any decision was taken – for the very sound reason that the effect of German use of comparable material would have to be studied carefully. Early in April, however, he was informed that the Chief of Air Staff had, independently authorized the use of Window. Alarmed, he tried to see Portal but succeeded only in seeing Freeman who he asked 'to hold up action so as to give the Policy Committee a chance to express their view'. At a special meeting of this, held on 11 April, it became clear that the Air Staff was anxious to use 'Window' as soon as possible to cut down casualties in Bomber Command. 'I pointed out', Tizard later wrote in a private note, 'that the casualty rate had not shown any sign of real increase over the last six months . . .'

On 17 April he elaborated the views of the Policy Committee in a special note to the Chiefs of Staff. If the Germans became aware of the potentialities of 'Window', they could, this pointed out, make use of it in the invasion of Malta, of Gibraltar, or even of Britain. The Committee was not as well informed as the Chiefs of Staff on the possibilities of such German attack and its members therefore felt unable to make a definite recommendation about

13A: Sir Henry Tizard (*right*) with members of the Ministry of Defence delegation which visited Canada in 1947. Sir Owen Wansbrough-Jones third from right and Sir Ben Lockspeiser third from left.

13B: Sir Henry Tizard during a visit to India.

14A: Sir Henry Tizard with Alfred L. Loomis (*left*) and Lee A. DuBridge (*right*) examining at the Massachusetts Institute of Technology the cavity magnetron whose development was so vital to the radar war of 1939-1945.

14B: Sir Henry Tizard (*right*) and Marshal of the Royal Air Force Lord Douglas at London Airport.

15: Queen Elizabeth the Queen Mother, Chancellor of the University of London, conferring an Honorary D.Sc. on Sir Henry Tizard, 1956

16: Sir Henry Tizard

the use of 'Window'. However, if German action against any of these three targets within the next few months was highly probable, then it was suggested that Bomber Command should not use 'Window' until the casualty rate showed a marked tendency to rise. This was much the view of Cherwell, who wrote to Freeman a month later saying that the Germans had so far not thought of radio-jamming and proposing that 'Window' should not be used until (1) the Bomber Command casualty rate rose, (2) there was an exceptionally difficult operation suited to the use of 'Window' or (3) satisfactory counter-measures to the German use of 'Window' had been completed.[19] It was then decided at a special meeting called by Sinclair and attended by the heads of Bomber and Fighter Commands, and by Cherwell, that the new device would not be used until further experiments had been made. It was, perhaps, typical of the existing state of affairs that Tizard himself should hear of the meeting only by accident since, as he noted, he 'was not invited to attend', even though as Chairman of the Policy Committee he was vitally affected.

The 'further experiments' were carried out during the summer by Flight-Lt. Derek Jackson, in peacetime a brilliant physicist who had worked with Cherwell at Oxford. The results were discussed on 10 September at the Telecommunications Research Establishment by an august body which included Cherwell, Watson-Watt, A. P. Rowe, the Chief Superintendent, and Robert Cockburn, then playing an important part in the radio-campaign to deceive the enemy. Strangely enough, the Policy Committee does not seem to have been represented. This meeting agreed in general that 'the latest type of enemy ground R.D.F. gear is less vulnerable to the combined effects of Window and of radio jamming' than the British equipment, and it therefore concluded that 'known effects of Window and of radio jamming on British R.D.F. gear for fighter and A.A. control are much greater than the probable effects on German R.D.F.' It avoided a direct decision on whether or not Window should be used, wisely tossing this baby up to an even higher level, but it recommended that whatever decision was taken, this should be reconsidered at intervals. This was in fact Tizard's view also, although in a note to Air Vice-Marshal Tait, the Director of Signals, he went even farther. 'I think the report (discussed during the T.R.E. conference) strongly supports the view that Window should not be used, and this suggested decision should be reviewed in six month's time.'

Thus the position at the end of September 1942 was that Tizard, Cherwell, and most radar experts believed that the revelation to the Germans of Window might well produce more benefit for them than it would for the Allies. Only Bomber Command continued to call, naturally enough, for something that would reduce casualties. This situation was disrupted late in October when R. V. Jones, produced from Europe evidence that the Germans did, in fact, already know what clouds of aluminium foil would do. Therefore, he argued, they were holding back from its use on the assumption that in the balance and loss account they, and not the British, would suffer. This, it might have seemed, cleared the way for its use. Tizard certainly thought so, and on 30 October minuted both Portal and Freeman, saying that he had now altered his views and suggesting that Window should now be used by Bomber Command, on a large scale, as soon as this was possible.

Cherwell, however, was not convinced by the Intelligence Report, and made this clear to Jones who called on him to discuss the meeting to be held by Portal to consider the new situation. But Cherwell had not, as it happened, seen Tizard's note to Portal and Freeman. 'If you go into the meeting and try to get Window used, you'll find me and Tizard united against you', he commented. 'Well, if I've achieved that, by God, I've achieved something', Jones replied.[20]

Events proved to be less spectacular. At the meeting held the following day, 4 November, Tizard was absent owing to illness. More important to the argument, Bomber Command now withdrew its plea for the use of Window, believing that other radio counter-measures would be sufficient. Thus the issue was not pressed; Cherwell continued to oppose its use, Tizard to advocate it. And not until 15 July 1943, with bomber losses rising steeply, was permission finally given – by Churchill – to 'open the Window'.

The disagreements, changes of decision, and misconceptions which bestrew the story of Window were but extreme examples of the internal battles which accompanied the radio war. The personal clash between Tizard and Cherwell was only one of the factors involved, and during the summer of 1942 it became clear that some machinery was needed which would provide a better link between the growing complexity of the operational requirements of radio and radar and the factories which were called upon to satisfy them. Lord Justice du Parcq was called upon to enquire into the position and on 2 July Tizard gave evidence before him in a room in the Palace of Westminster. One point which subsequently became clear, and which Tizard no doubt stressed, was that even a committee reporting to the Chiefs of Staff might not carry enough heavy guns when it came to ensuring that their recommendations were carried out. The results of the only feasible alternative, however, were to be very different from what Tizard must have anticipated.

In mid-August he left London for a short leave at Mullion Cove. Some days later Lyttelton, the Minister of Production, met Llewellin, the Minister of Aircraft Production; the three Service Ministers; a representative from the Ministry of Supply; and Lord Cherwell. Together they decided that the Policy Committee should be re-constituted with more power.

Tizard returned to London on 1 September, unaware of what had been agreed in his absence. He found awaiting him a cable from Dr Karl Compton, who told him that a new Radar Development Planning Committee had been set up in Washington. 'I would be very glad to have your views concerning interchange between our two respective groups to consider at the first meeting of my Committee', he said.

Tizard met the Secretary of the Policy Committee a few days later to discuss the matter. He found that it had, in effect, been spirited away over-night, or at least during his leave in Cornwall. He was told, he wrote indignantly to Portal,

> that the organisation of a new Radio Board under the Ministry of Production had been decided upon, that the Radio Policy Sub-Committee was moribund, if not dead, and therefore that it could hardly act. I was informed from another source that the new Radio Board is to absorb all the functions of the Radio Policy Sub-Committee, that the membership of the new sub-committee appointed to deal

with this will be much the same as the old Radio Policy Sub-Committee, with the exception that another individual has been approached to act as chairman. All this discussion about reorganisation has to my knowledge been taking place for many weeks; but my views on it have not been sought officially in any way.

He concluded by telling Portal that his reply to the Americans would not be unhelpful to them 'and not so crudely informative as I might make it'.

All this was true but it was only a part of the story. For the new organization was to be, as the Radio Board, a Committee of the War Cabinet itself – not a body 'under the Ministry of Production' at all – and would therefore rank equal in the hierarchy to the Chiefs of Staff Committee to which it had formerly reported. The other side of this coin was that the chairmanship of the new Board would have to be held by a Minister of the Crown. The reformed organization would therefore have the increased status which Tizard no doubt agreed that it badly needed, but in the process he would have to step down.

On 7 September, he discussed the situation with Llewellin and on the following day drafted a reply to Sinclair's earlier letter.

You always address one so very formally, but I feel moved at last to take the liberty of addressing you as a friend [he began]. Your letter arrived when I was away on leave and I postponed answering it until I had got abreast of happenings during my absence. I did hope, in fact, that any lengthy answer would be unnecessary, but I have evidently made myself so far from clear in my recent conversations with you, that I must now attempt to make myself clearer.

You remind me of the Air Ministry committees of which I am a member. I thought that I had gone out of my way to speak of these Committees myself and to say that I never had any difficulty in obtaining information from the less highly placed officers of the Air Staff when I wanted it and when it was within their authority to give it. It does not therefore solve my difficulties when you say that C.A.S. is reminding principal officers of the Air Staff that I should receive 'all appropriate papers and minutes', and that I should be asked to attend Air Staff conferences, at the A.C.A.S. level 'on matters of scientific equipment'.

My difficulty is rather this. We never discuss the conduct of the war in the air at meetings of the Air Council. The nearest we get to it is in discussions of supply – and of accidents. The Air Council mainly deals with matters of detail administration to which as a scientific man I can contribute nothing; it is a waste of time for me to be present at most meetings, and at the best part of every meeting.* But you will agree that the efficiency of the R.A.F. in the war, and the best way it can be used, depends largely on the evolution of scientific equipment, and of scientific methods of operation. In fact not only does the right scientific policy to pursue depend on strategical decisions, but strategy itself at any time may, and ought to be, influenced by technical developments. Hence if there are good reasons, and I expect there are, why the conduct of the war should not be discussed at meetings of the Council, I should naturally expect that as the scientific member of the Council who tries, and is expected, to advise on scientific policy, some other way would be found for keeping me informed on strategy and the reasons for it, and of seeking my advice at the highest level before important decisions are made. In actual fact, it is only extremely rarely that you have sought my advice on any point. There have been many occasions on which I have proffered it, and you were kind enough to say that you always treat it with respect. But when do you ask for it? Further, I hardly ever see the Chief of Air Staff, nor indeed the Vice Chief; and is it not natural for me to draw the conclusion that they feel they can get on very well without my advice? They are very busy men, and so are you; but I observe that this does not prevent you from seeking and taking other scientific advice.

Before the war, when high officers of the Air Staff had more time at their disposal, I was Chairman of a *small* active Committee consisting of a few scientists and staff officers, which had the duty of advising on scientific research and development. In that capacity I had frequent discussions not only with Sir Wilfrid Freeman and Commanders in Chief, but with the then Chief of Staff, and the Secretary of State (Lord Swinton). As a result things happened, and it was a very good thing for the country that they did. It is not a good substitute for this to make me a member of Air Ministry Committees on a lower level which have restricted terms of reference, which are much too large to be effective, and which meet only seldom.

Don't you want this kind of forward thinking and planning now,

* Sir Arthur Street, Permanent Under-Secretary of State for Air, would presumably have agreed with Tizard. Writing of the Air Council's functions in *Flying* (September 1942), he says: 'The Air Council may be likened to the board of directors of an industrial undertaking. Its main job is to keep the R.A.F. in the air, well-trained, well-equipped, fighting fit and punching the enemy all the time where it hurts most. Its chief functions are therefore administrative and executive but it also acts in a judicial capacity. Thus, it reviews the sentences of courts-martial which it can reduce but not increase; and it is the High Court of Appeal to which persons subject to the R.A.F. code of discipline can apply for redress of grievances, real or imagined'.

just as much as in peacetime? I feel strongly that it is wanted now,
more than ever. No-one can feel happy about our conduct of the war
up-to-date; no one can say with confidence how many years will
elapse before the enemy collapses. Even at the highest level – and
perhaps especially at the highest level – serving officers are so pressed
with immediate problems that they cannot have time to think ahead
properly. Who is doing the thinking and whose scientific advice are
they seeking and taking in the process? Not mine.

My position as a member of the Air Council seems therefore quite
untenable, and I wish to resign. As this is quite a serious step to take,
I have asked to see the Prime Minister before doing so. I may say that
I had practically made up my mind to do this after reading your
letter, but the news I got on my return to work finally decided me.
I hear that a Radio Board is to be formed to absorb *inter alia* the
functions of the Radio Policy Committee, and that I am deliberately
excluded from the new organisation. As Chairman of the R.P.C. my
views have not been sought officially about the new organisation; but
I have only heard of the developments unofficially except when I
asked Llewellin what was happening. I have been connected with
RDF from the beginning, so this final insult is hard to bear with
equanimity, and has confirmed me in the view that it is no longer
necessary for me, for patriotic reasons, to work so hard, with such
little support, and with negligible result. I am not of course conceited
enough to think that the war cannot be won without my help; we
shall get through somehow, I know, with the assistance of the
Russians and the Americans. But I am conceited enough to say that
I should not be ashamed to have all the advice, positive or negative,
that I have given for the last seven years, published, with notes on
when it was accepted (mainly before the war), and when it was
rejected (mainly after the war) and what was the result in each case!

The crux of the matter was simple. While Tizard had, as he
says, heard unofficially about various plans for reorganization,
these only crystallized into the scheme for a Board, requiring a
Minister of the Crown as chairman, while he was on leave in
Cornwall. On his return, the shock of the news that he was to be
unseated tended to unbalance his judgement; for there were, in
fact, no plans for him to be 'deliberately excluded from the new
organization', and his name was among those put forward to
Lyttelton. His initial exclusion may well have sprung from this
resignation letter of 8 September.

The outcome seemed certain. The re-constituted Radio Board
gave him, as he imagined, a fair enough cause for resignation. In

Magdalen, he had a place to resign to. Yet events shaped differently; what by this time seemed to be an almost constitutional link between the Air Ministry and Sir Henry Tizard was still to remain unbroken.

On hearing from Tizard that he intended resigning from the Aircraft Supply Council, the Air Council and chairmanship of the A.R.C., Llewellin wrote that '. . . quite honestly you are of real value to me here, and I do not see why disagreements with Lord Cherwell should prevent your still giving your helpful advice in a Ministry where it is appreciated and valued.' But it was Churchill who was the great persuader. Earlier in the month he had asked Tizard for an up-to-date report on action being taken to meet enemy jamming of the night Air Defence radio system.

Now he thanked him cordially for it and passed the report to Cherwell, who appears to have agreed with most of it. Shortly afterwards Tizard met Churchill in Downing Street and the Prime Minister assured him that resignation at that critical juncture of the war, when the whole Middle East situation hung in the balance and criticism poured in from all sides, would be held as a mark of no confidence. Tizard decided to stay.

He was, moreover, to serve on the new Radio Board which met under Llewellin on 30 September. One of its first actions was to co-opt as members both Tizard and Cherwell.

CHAPTER FOURTEEN

The Move to Magdalen

It is one of the ironies of history that Tizard became President of Magdalen as the turn of the war was approaching. In the desert the last of the long retreats was ending. In Britain men were already devising methods for the leap back into Europe. In the skies above the Channel, and above ever more distant factories of Fortress Europe, there began to be seen what were, for the Germans, the ominous and unmistakable signs of coming defeat. The light at the end of the tunnel was growing brighter. Yet as the months passed Tizard did continue to exercise his influence on current affairs. His position is indicated by a letter which he wrote to Rowe on 18 September, shortly before moving to Oxford and shortly after he had swallowed his annoyance over the new Radio Board. 'The recent reorganization of radio administration, which involves the disappearance of the Radio Policy Sub-Committee, will not, I am glad to say from my own point of view, prevent my keeping close touch with the work of T.R.E.', he wrote. 'Indeed, as I shall have to centre my work largely on Oxford in the future, I hope to make my visits to you more frequent than they have been in the past – that is to say, assuming they will be welcome. The reorganization has put me in a most difficult position. However, one has to put up with these things during the war so long as it is still possible to do work of value.'

It appears that he considered the Presidency as a 'permanency'. 'Magdalen should be quite nice after the war if I am not too old then, even for fishing', he had written at the end of August to his friend Richard Threlfall. He spoke with satisfaction of the quiet lawns. And it seems likely that he regarded the Presidency as a step which would lead him, after the war, to complete disengagement from the Service world. He was asked by an interviewer in the summer of 1943 whether he was in Magdalen 'for good'. 'Yes', he replied, adding with that slow shy smile which split his face neatly in half, 'whatever "good" may mean'. He appears to have regarded matters thus until he came up once again, cheek to cheek, with the academic world whose isolation he had almost forgotten in the brisk rush of the last decade.

Years later Tizard said that when he was a Civil Servant he had always been impressed by the wisdom and competence of business men but that when he became a business man he changed his views. Some such change of stance appears to have taken place during his years at Magdalen. It is possible that he had only half-deceived himself into believing that he wished to retire from the battle. It is certain that the transition from the wartime world to the secluded world in which some members of the University still tried to live affected him deeply. And there came, in growing measure during 1943 and 1944, the realization that he was in fact still needed. He had decided to 'build his house in the woods', but he now found, with a certain gratified surprise, that the world was making a beaten path to his door. The President's Lodgings took the place of the veneered room in Thames House and these in their turn became 'rather like a bus-stop', with a stream of visiting scientists, Air Marshals, politicians and assorted V.I.P.'s. Their insistence in consulting with Tizard quickly began to impress him. It seems likely that he started, early on, to have doubts as to the wisdom of the step he had taken. And although he addressed himself diligently, and with his customary calm appraisal, to the survey and reform of College affairs, he did this at times, one feels, with a certain abstracted annoyance.

When Tizard began his Presidency he realized that three specific difficulties might soon be worrying Oxford Colleges.[1] There was the problem of financial inflation – a problem unlikely to be so pressing at Magdalen as at other Colleges, but certainly one which would have to be considered in any plans for the future. There was the problem which he saw would arrive immediately after the end of the war, when demobilization produced a greatly increased number of potential graduates. And there was the problem of satisfactorily adapting the administration to the expansion of university education which he foresaw. Tizard

z

grappled courageously with these and many similar matters as they arose during the four years which followed.

He impressed the Fellows as a man of many ideas. He knew how to organize, had in some respects a very tidy mind, and wanted the College run as a smooth, orderly machine. However, he disliked having to work out the detailed consequences of his ideas, possibly because he had previously had a staff who could do such work. At Magdalen he had a full-time Bursar and three part-time officers – a Vice-President, a Clerk and a Senior Tutor. They helped him loyally but were unable to drop everything else in order to work out details for him.

This difference between Oxford and Whitehall was underlined when it came to Committee work where, in spite of his previous reputation, he appeared to have developed limitations. 'He let discussion become too diffuse and ranging', it has been said. 'Indeed, he sometimes made it so by having new ideas in the middle of a meeting. This was exciting and great fun, but not a good way of reaching definite conclusions in complex matters.' As chairman of many inter-departmental bodies he had often been able to wield an authority which other members lacked, and as Rector of Imperial College he had for most practical purposes been the Commanding Officer; as President he was merely *primus inter pares*. This was unlikely to have been the case in President Warren's day, and Tizard remembered the College as it had been a third of a century earlier. He may well have been surprised at the change which had been brought about, partly by the fact that in the thirties a very able group of Fellows had been recruited. They had powers of both constructive and destructive criticism which surprised Tizard; and, above all, they had independence of mind.

Again, in the machinery of Government service there had invariably been a higher body to which he could appeal in the case of serious diagreement; at College Meetings, defeat was final. Moreover there was, in even the most objectionable of Civil Service situations, the continuing possibility that departmental reorganization, a shuffling of appointments, or some similar happy event, would deal the cards differently and that the membership of any particular committee would be reconstituted so that it was possible to try again. At Magdalen this possibility was present, but less significant than it had been in Whitehall.

Thus it was, no doubt, that Tizard appeared to one colleague as lacking 'the peculiar techniques and finesse required to pilot controversial business through a very varied and independent-thinking body of Fellows'. He appeared to others to be nervous during his term as President. 'On ceremonial occasions', one of them has written, 'I have seen his hands shake and heard his voice quaver. At College meetings he tended to get his papers muddled and to get a bit confused. He was not altogether happy here; and after leaving he seemed to have few regrets at having gone. It may well be that he had been so much in the wider world that College affairs seemed rather trivial. Some of us suspect that he was right.'

Yet Tizard succeeded in piloting through a number of lasting reforms, in spite of his constitutional handicaps and in spite of the fact that he continued for nine months to shoulder enough Government work for two normal men. Its demands would have been enough to distract attention from College reforms even had this official work been centred on Oxford rather than London.

The most important of these reforms was his reorganization of the Bursary. This had been considered before his arrival, but nothing had been decided. Tizard supplied the impetus which started effective action, and so supplied some of the ideas. When he arrived at Magdalen in the autumn of 1942 there was a full-time Estates Bursar who was an Official Fellow, and a part-time Home Bursar chosen from among the Fellows, the two Bursaries being independent and isolated. In June 1943 Tizard made his first proposals for reorganization. They were altered and amended after discussion with the Bursarial Committee and with individual Fellows, and as a result the two Bursaries were made into one. A Senior Bursar, an Official Fellow, was made generally responsible to the College for all financial matters, external and internal, while a Junior Bursar, not a Fellow, was made responsible for the domestic organization. 'I think the system is working very well', Tizard wrote in 1946, 'and every year has confirmed me in the view that the change was a good one, and also that the election was a good one.'

He was worried about the wide gap between internal expenditure and income, and contemplated methods of reducing it. He turned his attention to the Junior Common Room, noting later that 'it is useful for a President to keep a fatherly eye on the . . . accounts.' He discovered that past members owed £1,500 to the Common Room – probably due to imperfect accounting rather than to the slackness of members – and started a system under which no-one was allowed to be presented for a degree without a certificate that he had discharged his debts to the J.C.R. as well as to the College. That his interest in such matters went considerably beyond the short-term one of putting on an even keel as many aspects of College finances as possible, is shown by one of the many notes which he left for his successor.

> The capital value of Magdalen College and its estates and property must be something of the order of three millions [he pointed out.] No income tax is paid on its revenue. No death duties are paid. A Labour Chancellor of the Exchequer is bound to look on College revenues with an envious eye and possibly to take the line that there is no reason for allowing such riches to be managed by a body of amateurs, however clever. The only real answer to such a criticism is to show that the property and revenues are in fact managed with a high degree of efficiency. I wonder if there is any College that can bear to have its finances, and its financial policy in the past, exposed to really expert examination? With our present Bursarial arrangements I feel that there is a good chance of getting the finances and management of what is one of the richest private institutions in the country in such a form that it would be beyond criticism. But there is a lot of work yet to be done.

Tizard also raised the question of a post-war building programme to cope with the expected expansion. No definite programme was agreed and at one point the College was surprised – and displeased – to learn that designs for extensions which had not been agreed were being exhibited at the Royal Academy. He took an interest in the multitudinous details of College administration, partly because he felt it his duty to do so, partly because he was intellectually exercised with the need for a compromise between the traditional framework of College existence and the new structure required to meet the different conditions of the years ahead.

The changes in the law brought about by the new Education Act, and the change in social conditions, favoured a reduction by the College of its responsibility for secondary education. As a result the school in Brackley became a controlled grammar school under the Northamptonshire County Council, and that in Oxford a direct grant school. Tizard's attitude to the new arrangements started during his Presidency but completed only after he had left, is shown in the notes which he left for his successor. The reorganization would, he pointed out 'relieve the President of a great deal of detailed responsibility for which he may not be any more fitted or inclined than I have been'.

Here, as in other aspects of his life and work at Magdalen, it is difficult not to feel that while one part of his mind was dealing adequately with the minutiae of College matters, another part was infinitely more concerned with the great struggles of the war that were now rising to their climax. It has been suggested, perhaps incorrectly, that he did not really get to know or to understand the undergraduates. So far as scholarships were concerned he made two suggestions. The first arose from informal discussions during which Tizard suggested that an intelligence test might form part of any scholarship examination. 'We are apt to scoff at intelligence tests in Oxford', he wrote, 'but I think that the scoffing is no more justified than the extreme confidence placed in them elsewhere. There is a good deal to be said for a ten years' experiment which would take the form of giving all candidates the same type of intelligence tests, telling the scholarship examiners that we did not wish them to be influenced by them, and keeping the records in order to see if there is any close correlation between the performance of undergraduates in their intelligence tests and their subsequent performance in Schools.' However, the proposal was not adopted.

His second innovation was to sit in on a number of scholarship interviews. Here the first scientist to become President received some surprises. Thus one history candidate who had been studying the latter half of the seventeenth century, was asked by Tizard to name one scientist from his period. When this failed to produce an answer, he asked more forcefully: 'Can you name any scientists at all?' When 'Isaac Newton' came as the reply, Tizard suggested that he might have come from the late seventeenth century. The candidate, rather surprised, suggested that this would, as he put it, 'only be of interest to scientists'. On another occasion, the interview provided an illuminating glimpse of Tizard's attitude. The occasion was a clear and frosty winter evening, and after the candidate had been put through his paces Tizard asked him the distance and – failing to get a reply – the name of the nearest star. The lack of answers might mean nothing. Yet if ability to store up factual information is no measure of a scientist's worth, curiosity and observation are essential.

'Weren't the stars shining when you came in?' Tizard asked, with a quiver of irritation. The wretched candidate did not know. 'Don't you ever look up at the sky and wonder what it's all about?' he continued. 'Well, if you don't, you may know all about the quantum theory but you'll never make a scientist.'

Whatever the stresses and strains produced by the contrast between the work at Oxford and that at Thames House, Tizard's Presidency was handicapped by the combination of wartime austerity and the fact that he was not a rich man in the days when the President was still expected to be rich. Even the simple matter of furnishing the Lodgings raised its problems, since in the autumn of 1942 these lacked both carpets and curtains. In a move that was to benefit Tizard's successor more than himself, the College agreed on 17 October 1945 that the President should be author-ized to spend up to £5,000 for the purchase of furniture, carpets and hangings, and Tizard's later comment on this underlines both the predicament he had had to face, and his inability to make decisions on some matters of detail. 'I have spent less than £500', he noted, 'most of this being the cost of a dining room carpet. I have not been able to bring myself to pay the ridiculous prices asked for secondhand curtains. The only curtains that we have seen that we considered would be suitable for the dining room were priced at £500.' He was unable to use the State drawing room due to lack of a carpet, the only suitable one being priced at £900, and there were other problems of an austerity that, in wartime, was only partly off-set by his entertainment allowance. One, for instance, was the difficulty of dealing with the constant stream of guests on food obtained only on the ration-books of

Tizard, his wife and their one servant, plus parcels of food from several kind friends in the Commonwealth and the United States. 'On one occasion, towards the end of the week', says Lady Tizard, 'I added up the "additional meals" we had provided since the Sunday. It was more than 70.' Not that all of these visitors were 'College guests'. Most were concerned with the business of the war, a business in which Tizard continued to be intimately concerned.

*   *   *

From now onwards his day-by-day concern with the war in the air decreased. Yet he maintained his office in the Ministry of Aircraft Production and worked there for a day or so on most weeks. His Scientific Assistant brought papers to Oxford and returned to London replete with instructions. And throughout the autumn of 1942 he was sought, at Magdalen rather than at Thames House, by officers, airmen, and scientists involved in matters as varied as the great raid on the German dams – forced through with Tizard's support in the face of Cherwell's opposition – the growing complications of the radio war, and the progress of the first jet aircraft.

In December 1942, Sir Stafford Cripps, who had succeeded Llewellin as Minister of Aircraft Production and who had become Chairman of the Radio Board at the same time, asked Tizard to advise him on the priorities which should be followed by the Ministry's entire Research and Development programme. Before doing so, Tizard felt that it was necessary to get from Churchill some indication of how long the war was expected to last. The meeting took place on New Year's Day 1943, and the Prime Minister, Cripps was told, had suggested that Tizard should send him a note on the matter. This note emphasized yet again the point that Tizard had tried to make to the Air Ministry three years earlier – that work should be concentrated on essentials.

'Research and experimental work to meet the needs and anticipate needs of the Services is now on a very large scale', he wrote on 5 January.

> If you were to examine the departmental programme you would probably find that there was a good deal to be said in favour of all the included items, but the trouble is that in this, as in many other

directions, there is a constant temptation to dissipate skill and energy so much that nothing important is done in time.

Every successful 'research' has to be followed by intensive technical development, then by production, and then by training in the use of the new equipment. Many researches now completed, or nearing completion, will not affect the war to any extent before 1945. Nevertheless, new ideas are constantly propounded, and fresh items added to the programmes, many of which are of small importance.

Is it possible for you to give a ruling on the probable duration of the European war? If so, those who are responsible for directing and advising on research and experiment, would have a clear lead, and would be much better able to concentrate on work which is going to yield practical results within a reasonable time. I realise that any ruling from now would have to be revised from time to time; but that would not seriously diminish its value.

I am thinking more particularly of work which is the responsibility of the Ministry of Aircraft Production; but the ruling for which I am asking will affect all departments.

Another point. When Germany and Italy are defeated we shall still have the Pacific war to settle. To me, writing without full knowledge, it would seem that the technical problems of the Navy, particularly of the use of aircraft in co-operation with naval units, will then take precedence over all other technical problems of war. Is this view correct? If so, it must be taken into account in settling priorities now.

I should perhaps add that I do not mean to suggest that we should neglect altogether work which may lead to revolutionary advance in the science of war; but the list of items of this kind would be very short.

It was not only the duration of the war which had been discussed on New Year's Day. Churchill had asked Tizard whether he believed in the 'Flying Porcupine' – the bomber so heavily armed that it would be able to attack by day without suffering unbearable casualties – and the result was a final effort by Tizard to switch the emphasis away from night bombing. 'Decoy fires, searchlight dazzle, smoke clouds, and other confusion devices all contribute to the great difficulties of the night bomber, and average crews do not live long enough to get sufficient experience to overcome them . . .' he wrote to the Prime Minister. 'As time goes on, technical equipment for the night bomber gets more and more intricate, while the average crew gets less and less competent because we are now calling up young men who have not had the education that their brothers had. In consequence you never get the results from the equipment that the optimists (scientific and Service) who sit on departmental committees think you will.'

His policy was summed up in one sentence. 'I do not suggest that we should neglect the night bomber altogether, the great thing is to do both; but I do feel, subject to further discussions that are now taking place, that the emphasis should be transferred to day bombing, and the night bombing should be conducted by a smaller force of highly trained expert crews.'

Churchill, about to leave Britain for the Casablanca Conference at which the shape of the strategic bombing offensive was to be laid down, replied on 12 January. He was obviously unconvinced, but added 'It is all a question of figures, and I shall look forward with great interst to seeing the arguments in quantitive form when they have been produced.' Cherwell, to whom Tizard's note was passed, agreed that it was 'all a question of figures', and added: 'Tizard's quantitative appreciation which he promises should be very interesting.'

By this time Tizard was using all his influence in support of the most famous of all air attacks 'conducted by a smaller force of highly trained expert crews'. This was the 'dam-busters' operation, the basic idea of which he had favoured more than two years previously when it had been proposed by Dr Barnes Wallis of Vickers. He had been one of the first to encourage Wallis, whose comment on Tizard's part in the long-drawn-out preparatory arguments and experiments is that 'it is certainly true that without him the raid would never have taken place.'

His connexion with Wallis's proposals began in the summer of 1940 when he supported a scheme for manufacture of a massive 10-ton bomb and a plane to carry it. Despite considerable work on the project by Vickers, and subsequent support by Beaverbrook, the idea was eventually rejected – on the grounds that no Air Staff requirement for the weapon existed. Some months later there dropped on to Tizard's desk a copy of 'A Note on a Method of Attacking the Axis Powers', the document in which Wallis had put forward his original ideas. Attack on the enemy's hydro-electric power formed an important element in 'The Method', Wallis believing that Italy could be swung out of the war and Germany decisively crippled by this alone. Tizard, who had always stressed the overwhelming importance of power supply in war, immediately saw the significance of the suggestion. Within a few days he had formed the Air Attack on Dams Committee, under the chairmanship of David Pye; within a few weeks experiments were taking place at the Road Research Laboratory in which concrete models of the Mohne Dam, built to one-fiftieth scale, were attacked by various charges.

In spite of Wallis's optimism, in spite of Tizard's enthusiasm, the problem appeared to be intractable. All the evidence indicated that the German dams involved could not be breached by any practicable method. The massive bomb, exploding deep down, would not apparently shake their foundations; and there appeared to be no method of exploding a powerful enough charge sufficiently close up against the inner side of the dams, protected as these were by extensive booms. It was at this point that Wallis began to think again.

The story of how he conceived the idea of the 'bouncing bomb', which would skim the water in a series of gigantic leaps and explode against the concrete dam-wall, is well-known. Less appreciated is the story of how the scheme was eventually pushed along the necessary official channels. By this time, early in 1942, Wallis had received the impression that the Air Attack on Dams Committee would probably report adversely on the idea. He confided this to Group-Captain Winterbotham, an R.A.F. officer with various and interesting duties. Why not, Winterbotham asked, put up the idea to the Admiralty? The following day Wallis was taken to see Blackett, Director of Naval Operational Research. Blackett was impressed, and said that the Navy had been looking for something of this kind for years. Shortly afterwards he mentioned the idea to Tizard who a few days later arrived at Burhill, to which Wallis and others from Vickers had been evacuated after the bombing of the works at Weybridge.

'I got hold of Wallis at once and was much interested in his proposals, which I encouraged', Tizard wrote later. 'I put him in touch with G. I. Taylor to discuss the proposed model tests and arranged through Lockspeiser for Wallis to get all facilities at the N.P.L.' For one of the things which Wallis required first was facilities for testing models of the small circular bouncing bombs which he believed would solve the problem. By mid-June Wallis was bouncing two-inch spheres down the Yarrow Ship Tank at the National Physical Laboratory. 'I saw Wallis's model experiments today in the tank at the N.P.L. this afternoon', Tizard noted on the 12th to Pye. 'It looked very promising. . . . I certainly think now that a full-scale test is desirable with a Wellington. In order to get on with this Wallis would like authority to put in hand some drawing office work for the bomb and the necessary modifications in order to fit a carrier. Can you arrange for him to have authority to do this?'

By the following month the need for a different sort of test had arisen and Tizard was instrumental in persuading Birmingham Corporation to permit the use of a small dam at Nant-y-Gro near Rhayader in mid-Wales. In July, experimental charges were fired against it and suggested that, although much work remained to be done, the bursting of a major dam by air attack was now a technical possibility. There was also, however, the operational problem, and it was here that Tizard's unique combination as scientist and airman came into full play. 'As early as the time of the N.P.L. experiments' says Wallis, 'Tizard was thinking out the problem of how low a pilot could dive over the water of a dam'.[2] As always, he was concerned not only with the technical possibility of a weapon but with the practicability of its use on operations, against determined defence, under conditions which, he appreciated better than many of his colleagues, would be basically different from those of calm experiment.

There was, he later wrote, 'a good deal of shilly-shallying. . . . I was in favour of giving Wallis his head', and on 30 September 1942 he noted: 'I sent for the file on bombing attacks on Dams yesterday. I am rather horrified to see that although the Nant-y-Gro experiment was done in July and a report issued in August, nothing much has happened since . . . if we accept the conclusion that a contact charge of 7,500-lb. would breach the Mohne Dam to a depth of about 50 ft., it is not at all outside the range of possibility that the Wallis method might work. Meanwhile nothing has been done. I should myself be inclined to advise that Wallis be instructed straight away to submit an opinion as to whether a bouncing bomb of this size could be fitted to a Stirling or a

Lancaster.' The cause of the delay, as might be expected, was the familiar lack of co-ordination between the Government's right hand and its left; for while the M.A.P. had been encouraging the Wallis experiments, Wallis himself had been informed by Lord Cherwell that the dams were no longer considered important targets.[3] The Air Staff subsequently thought differently, raising the matter with Tizard early in February.

> Let us make it clear [he wrote on 11 February 1943], that neither of us is guaranteeing technical success. We do, however, feel that Mr Wallace's (sic) predictions, as a result of mathematical analysis and model experiments, have been largely substantiated by the full-scale experiments hitherto conducted, and we are convinced that the experimental work should be taken further and is potentially of great importance.

Fifteen days later Wallis was informed that the raid had been approved and every effort should be made to complete the weapon for use in the early spring. Three months later, after the Mohne Dam raid had succeeded, Tizard was able to write to Wallis that he had 'no hesitation in saying that yours is the finest individual technical achievement of the war.

*   *   *

By this time, early in 1943, Tizard was deeply engaged in preparations to lead what might, but for the chances of history, have been a Mission quite as important as that of 1940. This was nothing less than a Mission to Moscow which would have passed over to the Russians much of Britain's most closely-guarded technical information.

There was a good reason, other than the purely scientific one, for giving leadership of the Mission to Tizard. He had never subscribed to the theory that it would be right to allow the Russians and the Germans to batter themselves into mutual extinction on the Eastern front, and on more than one occasion he had pressed for the release of information to Britain's Eastern Allies. 'Would it not be wise', he had written to Freeman, 'to let the Russians have information about what we know the Germans are doing in the way of R.D.F. and beam navigation? It seems to me that if we give them the information we have on beam navigation we need not at the same time tell them anything about the ways we have of dealing with it. There are perfectly good radio technicians in Russia and they can devise their own methods. I do not see that it could do much harm to give them this information, and it might be of great use to them.' The question arose again seven months later when the Radio Policy Sub-Committee was informed that the U.S.S.R. Military Mission wanted certain radar sets and also A.S.V. equipment. Tizard was in favour of handing over the equipment so long as it could be used properly, and in a letter to the Chief of Air Staff on 2 March, wrote: 'We have to try to put ourselves in the position of the Russians. They may justly claim that they are doing all the fighting, and that, with the necessary support, would go a long way to winning the war for us. It is surely then a serious matter to refuse to give them information about up-to-date equipment for which they have asked, when we know that such equipment has great operational value.' However, Tizard failed to win more than half his point. When the matter was considered by the Chiefs of Staff committee on 22 June, it was agreed that the policy of disclosure should be altered; but it was also agreed that the specific equipment referred to in this par-ticular Russian request, should not be revealed. Sir Alexander Cadogan, Permanent Under-Secretary at the Foreign Office, queried the decision; the Chiefs of Staff refused to budge.

This caution in giving information to a hard-pressed Ally was the result of something more practical than a hatred of Commun-ism. It was, of course, partly due to the fact that between Septem-ber 1939 and June 1941 the Russians had stood on the touchlines of the conflict, benevolently cheering on the German forces; and there was also the long persistent suspicion of Russia herself. There was, however, another circumstance which tended to limit inter-change of information, and this was on at least some occasions fully understood and appreciated by the Russians. The battles of the Eastern Front were being waged across vast areas in which the fighting surged back and forth across distances measured not in hundreds of yards but in hundreds of miles. The prospects of the enemy capturing new and secret equipment, valuable not only in itself but as giving important clues to Allied technical thought and development, were therefore considerable.

These points were all relevant to an agreement between Russia and Britain which was reached on 29 September 1942. Under this, both countries were to 'furnish to each other on request all information including any necessary specifications, plans, etc. relating to weapons, devices, or processes which at present are, or in future may be, employed by them for the prosecution of the war against the common enemy. They will also furnish such information spontaneously as regards new weapons, devices, or processes which they may employ and which they consider would be of interest to the other Government. If either Government considers that in the common interest there would be disadvantage in giving such information in a particular case, they shall be entitled to withhold the information in question, but in that event they will indicate the reasons which led them to take this view.' Both sides made use of the proviso contained in the last sentence. There was, from the first, some reluctance to present Russia with more information than could nicely be construed into the agreement, and Tizard noted that in some quarters the general impression 'was much that predicted by Blackett, namely that the Agreement was a diplomatic one which need not be taken seriously'.

There was certainly no undue haste in devising special machinery for exchange of information.[4] The Ministry of Aircraft Production was advised of the agreement on 9 October, ten days after it was signed. It 'was never mentioned at the Aircraft Supply Council and although I was a member of the Council who was immediately concerned with such matters I was not informed of it at all, and only heard of it by accident in the middle of December, 1942', Tizard later noted.

The Allied Supply Executive now asked the Ministry of Production to implement the agreement and on 30 December it was agreed that a Mission, comparable to that which Tizard had led to the United States, should be sent to Russia. On 19 January it was decided that Tizard should be asked to lead the Mission and a few days later he met Lyttelton, the Minister concerned. 'After reflection', Tizard subsequently noted, 'I wrote to him on the 29th Jan to say that I would undertake this duty if the Prime Minister were willing to give me the same directions, and the same measure of discretion, as he did when he sent me on a similar mission to the U.S.A. in 1940.' It would only encourage suspicions, he felt, if the Mission were to go armed with a list of devices on which it could give information; far better would be the disclosure of anything the Russians wished to know – with the exception of specific items whose particular problems could be explained. This attitude, Tizard was informed, was approved, and on 20 February it was agreed that he should lead the Mission.

Now, however, there came an unexpected hitch.

On 21 February the Joint Staffs Mission in Washington were informed by telegram of the proposed Mission to Moscow and told that it would be supplied with three things – a list of devices on which information would be disclosed, a list of devices about which information should not be disclosed, and a list of information required from the Russians. 'This telegram therefore', Tizard subsequently noted with a certain understandable terseness, 'did not give the correct information to J.S.M.' This was not, however, the cause of the trouble which now arose. On 20 March the J.S.M. replied to say that the U.S. Chiefs of Staff had apparently never heard of the Anglo-Russian agreement and felt that they could not become party to it. The explanation was finally unravelled by Tizard.

> I understand [he wrote in one of his private summaries of the events], that the original agreement was communicated to Mr Harriman* with a request that he should communicate it to the right official quarters in America, but in fact it appears that this was not done, so that the American Chiefs of Staff did not hear about it until very much later, and then only by accident, thus having much the same experience as I had myself in this country. Hence, it is not surprising that there has been considerable obstruction from America to the exchange of information as a whole and to the specific authority given to the mission. It might be remarked at this stage that the confusion in our relationship with the United States on this matter of exchange of information appears to be extreme. On the one hand telegrams have been going backwards and forwards dealing with the details of what the Tizard Mission should or should not disclose. On the other hand 30 Mission in fulfilment of the agreement have been handing to the Russians most

---

* Averell Harriman, former head of President Roosevelt's Special Mission to the U.S.S.R., a member of the London Combined Production and Resources Board, and subsequently U.S. Ambassador to the U.S.S.R.

detailed information on a variety of secret British equipment, including Radar equipment, without any reference to the Americans themselves.

This contretemps was eventually overcome, partly with the help of Tizard himself who suggested that Bennett Archambault, his friend in the U.S. Embassy in London, should write to Vannevar Bush. 'I said that I understood the American difficulties and hesitations', he later wrote 'but that I hoped that they would feel that the scientific members co-operated so closely with the American Scientific Organization that they were unlikely to give information to the Russians in such a way that the American effort would be handicapped'.

Throughout April he busied himself with preparations for the coming journey. As for the American Mission, he picked his own specialists – Blackett from the Admiralty; Alexander King who had been a Senior Lecturer at Imperial College before the war and who now worked in the Ministry of Production; Cockcroft, Sir Robert Robertson, and Captain Oliver-Bellasis – who at the outbreak of the war had been charge of experimental mine-sweeping at H.M.S. *Vernon* – from the Ministry of Supply; and Major-General Eldridge from the War Office. The R.A.F. was to be represented by Joubert who completed a strong and business-like team. Tizard himself was not over-optimistic, but he retained hopes, and his attitude was summed up in a note which he wrote to the Air Ministry on 1 April – 'there is a chance, probably a slender one, that my Mission will lead to a much closer co-operation and a more willing exchange of information'.

He now began to collect the equipment which would be sent with the Mission, and late in May decided that he personally would take an account of the R.A.F.'s Battle of Essen, illustrated by photographs; and, if possible, photographs of the Mohne Dam raid. He received a slightly unctuous memorandum from the Foreign Office on how members of the Mission should comport themselves in Russia; heard that he was to carry a personal letter to Stalin; and prepared a speech which he hoped to make to the soldiers of the Red Army. 'I speak to you', this began, 'as Foreign Secretary of the Royal Society of London which for nearly 200 years has steadfastly pursued its aim of advancing knowledge for the good of mankind'. It was a good speech, concluding with the assertion that 'when better times come, which you have brought so noticeably nearer, we mean to work with you still, and to do all that science can do to restore your country that you love so much, so that you may feel that your courage and endurance have not been in vain.' The Red Army, one feels, would have taken to Tizard much as the Royal Air Force had taken to him.

One point which caused great argument was the uniform which should be worn. The members of the Mission were to fly to Moscow, and if their plane were forced down, either by enemy action or by other hazards, the occupants should not be in civilian clothes. At one stage it was therefore arranged that Tizard should fly in general's uniform, and that the other civilian members of the Mission should have ranks, and uniforms, at suitable positions down the scale.

Meanwhile pressure for a 'Second Front now' was increasing, and so was suspicion of Anglo-U.S. ardour. On 16 June Tizard wrote to Lyttelton, pointing out that 'the position now is that no cable welcoming the Mission has arrived from Russia, the United States appears to be increasingly restive about the general authority given to the Mission, and finally, so I am told, no transport can be made available for several weeks because a number of other people, including Citrine's party, must have preference. The indefinite postponement of the Mission completely upsets my plans, and the work of other members. In the circumstances I think it should be abandoned; it will certainly fail if it goes with grudging permission of the Soviet authorities, and without the fullest support of the British Government. In any case, whether it goes or not later, I should like to be excused from the responsibility of taking charge of it.'

The disappointment helped Tizard make up his mind.

He havered for another four weeks. Then, learning that the Mission was to be indefinitely postponed, wrote to Lyttelton on 14 July agreeing that this was the right decision. 'We should not do much good if we went now', he added. 'If it is decided to send it later on I should be glad to discuss with you the possibility of my going, but naturally it is difficult to give a promise now.'

AA

The following day he wrote to Churchill, recalling the events of the previous September and continuing:

> My experience since then, particularly during the last few months, convinces me that in the present circumstances my work is of very little value to the war effort, and I am not in a position to discharge the responsibilities that ought to attach to members of the Councils. The Aircraft Supply Council now meets very seldom and is an ineffective body. Policy is determined by a smaller body which meets daily which I have never been invited to attend and even if I were invited I could not now attend regularly . . . There is no complaint about this, I am merely stating the facts. I am not really in touch with decisions of policy and in many respects do not know what is going on. So far as the Air Council is concerned, matters on which I might be able to give useful advice are not discussed on the Council and I am not now in touch with them outside the Council.

This time the resignation was accepted, both by Churchill and by Sir Stafford Cripps, the Minister of Aircraft Production. Before he finally severed his links with the Air Ministry Tizard suggested that the Air Council might well appoint its own official Scientific Adviser. The Army Council had at last been induced to accept one, and with Blackett at the Admiralty, this left the Air Ministry as a third Service operating without benefit of scientific knowledge at the highest level. Portal, to whom Tizard wrote late in July, was inclined to agree with the idea and discussed it with Tizard the following month. Eventually, in November, Professor Thomson of the Maud Committee was appointed. That he was not a member of the Air Council, as Tizard had been, was of relatively little importance since it was through the Vice-Chief of Air Staff, to whom he was responsible, that advice could most easily be given. However, in the words of the Air Ministry, 'The Air Staff emphasized that the scientific adviser would be concerned primarily with the scientific aspect of their operations, obviating any necessity for him to be the channel of communications with the M.A.P. on any question of operational requirement, development or supply.'[5] This was, of course, just the essential function that Tizard had performed.

He now prepared to relinquish the last of his unofficial but valuable links with the Air Ministry, just eight years after he had begun to coax radar into useful existence. Before he did so he sent one more minute to Churchill. Today it has a slightly prophetic ring.

1. The remarks in this Minute [it began], arise from a conversation with a colleague. His point of view was new to me, and as it is just possible that it may be new to you I thought it worth while bringing it to your notice.

2. Our present offensive plans include a wholesale attack on Hamburg which is a much easier target than Berlin, and probably easier than such places as Hanover and Brunswick. But is it wise to eliminate Hamburg.

3. We look forward to an occupation of Germany in the not very distant future. Doubtless the Russians have the same hope. From what town are we to administer the occupied territories? If Germany were to surrender with Berlin practically intact, while all the leading cities South and West of it were reduced to the condition of Cologne and Dusseldorf, it would be impossible to base the administration of Germany anywhere except in Berlin.

4. Hamburg is anti-Russian, anti-Prussian and anti-Nazi. It may well be soon, if not already, anti-war. Apart from submarine construction and shipping generally, it is not industrially important. It is a centre of commerce rather than of production. It is a very important port and might therefore be much more useful to us alive than dead. To destroy it before Berlin would make it much harder to eliminate the Prussian hegemony in post-war Germany. To destroy it after Berlin would deprive us of a valuable port and administrative centre without causing any great industrial damage apart from submarine construction. It might be also true to say that the rate of submarine construction at Hamburg is much more affected by the bombing of Hamburg itself. If we administer occupied territories from Hamburg we should be less likely to get into difficulties with our Russian allies than if we tried to administer from Berlin or even from Munich, Dresden or Vienna.

5. The practical conclusion therefore is that Hamburg should be left alone and that it is much more important to attack Hanover, Magdeburg, Brunswick and especially Berlin.

It might be thought that with this parting comment Tizard was finally leaving the problems of the war for the quiet of Magdalen. This was far from so. At the conclusion of his resignation letter to Churchill he casually reported an invitation to make a three-month tour of Service and other defence installations which he had received from the Australian Government 'I am sure that such a visit would be of real use and I advise you to accept it', Churchill replied a fortnight later.

This invitation was no unexpected bolt from the blue. Tizard's relations with scientists in Australia had been extensive and cordial, and he had actually helped in the birth of more than one organization which was to become integrated into the Australian war effort. As early as 1936 a thick wad of papers had arrived on his desk at Imperial College with a note from A. C. D. Rivett, then Deputy Chairman of the Commonwealth Council for Scientific and Industrial Research. The gist of the whole matter, explained Rivett, whom Tizard had known at Oxford, was that for defence reasons the Australian Government was trying to encourage a big venture into the engine building industry in Australia, and it looked as though the C.S.I.R. would now, after ten years abstinence from work relating to secondary industries, be obliged to turn seriously to the question of establishing for Australia the beginnings of a National Physical Laboratory and much else besides. 'Both Julius* and I decided that there was no-one to whom we could go for advice with more confidence than you . . .'[6] Three years later, when Dr David Martyn had come to Britain to study radar he had visited Tizard – the one man who would, he had been told, 'be of great value in helping to start off such Australian research on the right lines'.

In the winter of 1940, when the war had made even closer collaboration necessary, Richard Casey, the Australian Minister for Supply and Development then in Britain, cabled Robert Menzies, Minister for Co-ordination of Defence, stating that a first-class Australian research scientist should come to England and that 'Tizard would undertake to place appropriately any such man or men personally recommended by Rivett, good radio men in particular'. Rivett subsequently wrote to tell Tizard that Dr Madsen, chairman of the Radio-Physics Board, would be arriving in Britain soon, and added, 'I expect you are being driven pretty hard, but we out here simply must make a success of this job and I know perfectly well that there is no one who can help Madsen to take the right track more effectively than you can.' Tizard duly responded. Six months later, on 10 June 1940, as he was about to be pushed from the Air Ministry, he was officially informed by the Australian Prime Minister that the 'Madsen

* Sir George Julius, Chairman of the C.S.I.R.

scheme' was being rapidly developed, and that the Radio-Physics Laboratory had been completed and staff installed.

Thus by the summer of 1943, the Australians had good cause for thinking that they could make use of a man such as Tizard. Two years previously they had denuded their own defences to support the Middle East; they had seen the much-prophesied threat from Japan suddenly emerge dark and looming over their heads; and they were more and more dependent for protection on the United States whose Pacific forces overwhelmingly outnumbered their own, on the ground, on the seas, and in the air. One result was an uneasy lack of satisfactory inter-Service cooperation and a feeling that neither information nor help came from London as frequently as it should come. Much of this was to be expected. Britain herself had had little time to iron out the problems of waging war by combined operations; Australia, where the need was greater, had had even less. The situation was therefore one in which Tizard's advice would be of particular value. He himself welcomed the opportunity of giving it – not least because there had always been something about the outspoken honesty of the Dominions that he not only understood but thought necessary.

As usual his status was a peculiar one. His brief was, he later wrote to Admiral Sir Guy Royle, First Naval Member, Commonwealth Naval Board, 'to advise the Council for Scientific and Industrial Research generally on scientific development in Australia and particularly on their scientific work in relation in the Pacific war. I have a general remit to be of any help that I can to the Australian fighting Services while I am here, but I have no specific authority to deal with any matter other than in an advisory capacity.' He now had no official status whatsoever in Britain – with the exception of membership of the Radio Board; he was merely the President of Magdalen, come to advise the Australians. He was, however, assigned J. E. Adamson, his Scientific Assistant who now accompanied him. He was treated by members of the Australian Government, and by the Australian Service chiefs, much as a Scientific Adviser to the Ministry of Defence would be treated today. And to many Australians he appeared to be the man with the magic wand who could conjure results from very little indeed.

A series of delays interfered with Tizard's departure. At first it was arranged that he and Adamson should fly by a commercial plane, and at short notice he packed and travelled to Poole, whence a flying boat was to take them to Foynes. 'After a long wait I was taken into a kind of Gestapo cell where two people, one in a Home Guard uniform, glared at me like American detectives on the cinema screen', he later recorded indignantly in his diary. 'No. 1 looked at my passport, and at me, with the greatest suspicion. I showed him my official papers, certifying that I am to be given every facility on my passage, but that made no difference to his behaviour. He asked me where I was going. I said "Australia". No. 2, with a strong man's gimlet eye on me, asked me what was my business there. I asked him what authority he had to ask me such a question. He said he had full authority. I asked him to show me his authority. He made no answer, and did not press me further.'

Eventually Tizard reached the flying boat. The window-blinds were drawn down for security purposes and the ship took off. His trained ear soon distinguished something wrong and shortly afterwards the ship turned back for Poole with a faulty engine. Tizard and Adamson, together with the other passengers, were taken to Bournemouth – and told soon afterwards that the Pan-American plane had left Foynes, that there would not be another for a week, and that they would have to return to London. Then, resigned to another week's wait, they were informed that space had been found on a Liberator, which would be taking ferry pilots back to the United States within a few days. 'At last' wrote Tizard, almost in despair, 'we got off; and the final result was that counting from the time I first left Oxford to the time I arrived at Montreal, I took 142 hours to cross the Atlantic, at an average speed of say 20 m.p.h. Give me a nice fast ship for comfort, security, certainty and absence of annoyance. And what, I may add, is the use of scientists and engineers spending so much time, skill and energy in endeavouring to increase the economic speed of air transport when the really important thing is to stop the waste of time on the ground.'

The journey was uncomfortable and cold, in spite of the flying suit, boots, Mae West, and parachute harness. They sat on the floor munching sandwiches and oranges, and then tried to sleep on mattresses hitched across the bomb bay. 'For most of the way we flew in calm weather and bright moonlight, above a continuous cloud layer – a beautiful sight', Tizard noted. From Montreal they flew on to New York and then to Washington, where Tizard found the Shoreham much the same centre of pro-British activity as it had been almost exactly three years previously. Here was Charles Lindemann, as helpful as ever; Air Vice-Marshal McNeece Foster, now Deputy Head of the R.A.F. Delegation in Washington, who by telephoning Portal in London 'cleared' useful information for Tizard; and the members of other British missions, some of them the direct outcome of Tizard's visit in 1940.

In Washington he saw Vannevar Bush once again, and the two men discussed the work on nuclear research which had sprung from the Maud Committee. Thus the following month he was able to explain to the Australians something of the tortuous Anglo-U.S. negotiations which were accompanying development of the uranium bomb. In a letter to Rivett he said on 25 September that when American work had increased, the flow of information to the British had ceased for a number of reasons. Among them, he said was this.

Our British representative in Washington enquiring into the subject was an employee of I.C.I. The N.D.R.C. had not given information in full to any single firm or corporation in America, but had divided the work for the large-scale trials among a large number of firms, so that none of the firms knew the whole story. It was, perhaps not unnaturally, felt that it was unwise to give an employee of I.C.I. the whole story.

(2) At that time, and, I believe, now also, Dr Bush felt that there might be a great post-war development, but that results of the work during the war would not affect the war itself. His relations with Congress are very different from the relations of a man of his position in Great Britain with the House of Commons. Congress could criticise and cross-question him publicly on his actions. He took the line, therefore, probably advised by others, that he was entitled to withhold information unless it was definitely of value to the war effort.

(3) However, this position had been cleared up by the time I saw Dr Bush in Washington on my way to Australia, and I understood from him that interchange of information had been resumed and that there had been a reasonable agreement about the control of stocks,

if the commercial value was confirmed by further experiment. However, I am not sure that things were quite so straight-forward as he implied, because when I suggested that I should see some of the experimental work on my way through the States, he told me that he would rather I did not. . . .

This note appears to have given the Australians a considerably more detailed account of the position than they had received from anyone else, and it is significant that it should have come from Tizard, who had been apprised of it not through any official status but solely through his own personal private contact with Bush. The two men trusted one another. They both also acted, as Tizard would have put it, 'in the best scientific tradition.' They were at times – as in 1940 – limited in their confidences only by their official instructions. And it is difficult not to feel that they both relished the intellectual sparring match that sometimes took place when they met. Tizard's attitude was revealed to an old friend, whom he met during the war outside the Boscombe Down experimental station on Salisbury Plain. With Tizard was Bush. 'Both' claims the friend, who went up to them, 'were extremely dishevelled, and Tizard said that they were going fishing. A day or so later I saw Tizard in London and asked him how the fishing had gone. "Very well" he replied. I asked him if he had caught much. "Caught nothing", he said smilingly, " – but the fishing went very well!" ' [7]

On his way to Australia in the summer of 1943, Tizard's contact with Bush was a relatively brief one, and he was soon on his way to San Francisco and Honolulu. On this second leg of the journey he travelled in a U.S. Naval Air Transport Boeing Clipper, suffered from altitude as he frequently did from 1918 onwards, and at one point turned to his companion to remark that: 'There are only two people who are enjoying this war; one of them's Hitler and the other's Churchill.'

At Honolulu there was a further hitch in the travel arrangements and Tizard utilized the time to visit Admiral Nimitz's headquarters at Pearl Harbour. Two of the naval officers on the Staff had known him in Washington in 1940, a third had met him in London, and the Admiral 'did me proud, took me to lunch, and showed me the latest radar equipment afterwards' Tizard recorded in his diary. 'We discussed at some length the war against our enemies and our prospects at the time' says Nimitz today. 'Our conversation was primarily an exchange of information – he bringing me up to date on affairs in Europe and the Atlantic and I reciprocating with the situation in the Pacific. . . . I was pleased and gratified to have him visit me and to bring me up-to-date on his thinking.'[8]

Tizard now turned to the last lap of his journey. This was made in a U.S. Naval Air Transport Services Martin 'Mariner', a twin-engined flying-boat not unlike the Catalina. It carried five passengers as well as considerable equipment and at a cruising speed of 130 knots it island-hopped from one U.S. base to another across the Pacific, dropping off *en route* such items as a fresh supply of baseball bats.

Tizard eventually arrived in Brisbane on 28 August, was subsequently met by Julius and Rivett, and was soon afterwards rushed into the first of a series of interviews, visits, consultations, and meetings with politicians and Service chiefs.

It is no discredit to the Australians to say that within a few days Tizard had untangled a minor mystery of non-co-ordination that was becoming troublesome – he had after all developed a sixth sense for such things from frustrating experience. This one concerned the radio and radar counter-measures which were assuming more importance as the Allies developed their offensive against the Japanese. One of Tizard's first appointments was with the unit handling these, and he soon found that its members were receiving no technical or operational information from Britain on how the subject was being tackled there. It looked, at first, as though Australia was being left in the dark – either by design or by accident. Within a few days Tizard discovered that full reports were in fact coming to Australia. But they were going to the Radiophysics Laboratory of the C.S.I.R. – an organization which those in Britain no doubt compared to Rowe's Telecommunications Research Establishment. However, while information from T.R.E. was automatically channelled to the Services, the organization in Australia was different and a mass of useful data was languishing in the Radiophysics Laboratory whose staff did not appreciate its value to operational units. 'I remedied this before I left', Tizard briefly noted.

This was typical of the matters in which his experience of Government machinery, his personal knowledge of people in key positions, and of the methods by which the machinery itself could best be made to work, were all of help to the Australians. From the day of his arrival he was sending back to London requests for information – on the special paint used for the variable wind tunnel, on the status of aerodynamic development in Britain, on the towing of gliders below aircraft, on gridded oblique photography and on numerous similar subjects. It was two-way traffic, for Tizard was at the same time receiving requests from the Air Ministry for the latest information on research in Australia, the Ministry adding on one occasion that its latest on the subject in question was a year old.

These day-to-day problems formed the background to many formal meetings and discussions. Tizard visited the National Standards Laboratory and the Munitions Supply Laboratories; he also again met Essington Lewis, now Director-General of Munitions, who had greeted him at Broken Hill on the British Associations visit twenty-nine years previously. He lectured to Royal Australian Air Force officers, asking searching operational questions and impressing them by the fact that he had the business of war at his finger-tips. He inspected captured Japanese planes and visited the Ionospheric Group in Brisbane University. At the Radiophysics Laboratory in Sydney University he laid down the best lines for carrying out inter-Service radio counter-measures, recommending that operational flights with flying laboratories should be made over such strongly defended areas as Truk Island and Rabaul. Only thus, by probing the most strongly defended Japanese areas, by watching for new frequencies, and tying-in the results with a research organization, would it be possible to keep one step ahead in the evolving radio war. On 20 September he addressed the Australian Advisory Committee on Aeronautics and three days later, at a meeting with Senior Officers of the Royal Australian Air Force at Victoria Barracks, he hammered out the most efficient way in which an Operational Research Group could be set up within the Force.

All this was of immense help to the Australians. Almost equally important was the report which Tizard prepared for the Secretary of the Australian War Cabinet, Sir Frederick Shedden, on the

Australian Programme of Aircraft Production, a matter into which he had been especially asked to enquire by the Prime Minister, Mr Curtin. Six different types of aircraft were being produced in the country and Tizard proposed that these should be reduced to three – with, if possible, the same basic engine for all of them. His brief, direct report reflected his main beliefs as to how the war should be fought. There was his emphasis of liaison between the technical man and the fighting man – 'I feel that any original Australian design is doomed to failure unless it is greatly influenced by men who have had the fighting to do.' There was his emphasis on quality rather than on quantity – 'Too much that is being built today is second-rate, and will have little influence on the defeat of the enemy. To give first-class human material second-rate equipment merely lengthens the war at the cost of valuable life.' And there was a return to his old argument, more clearly visible in terms of the Pacific War than of the European, no doubt. 'Is it not obvious that the wholesale destruction of enemy shipping is the best way to shorten the war? Up to now the destruction of shipping has been the secondary, and not the primary object of Allied Air Forces.'

Tizard's work in Australia had been a success, as was his post-war work there, partly because he worked at the Australians' own level of innocence and honesty. No-one could claim that they lacked at this period their own fair quota of personal and political intrigue. But it was bred less surely into the system than it was in Britain, it was less inevitable, and in spite of it there was an atmosphere about high-level negotiations to which Tizard warmed.

*   *   *

He returned to Magdalen for the start of the Michaelmas Term. From now onwards it was clear that while he might have his own views about the way the struggle was going, he was no longer fully informed of events. He retained his membership of the Radio Board, although his attendances appear to have been sporadic. He was consulted from time to time by those who felt that only Tizard could give the advice that was needed. And there was the suggestion that he might become, once again, a fully-fledged scientific adviser. His reaction is shown in his letter to

Rivett, written on 5 July 1944. 'India is very anxious to get scientific people' this went. 'I was asked to go out there for six months to advise the All Highest. I said that I would go if anyone in real authority would persuade me that he honestly thought that the Japanese war would be over a month, or even a week, sooner if I did go than if I stayed in England. As the powers that be could not commit themselves to this view, I said that I had something better to do in England. . . .' He had, in fact, cut as completely loose as was possible from those tasks which, tiresome and demanding as they were, had yet enabled him really to know how the war was going.

One result was an uncharacteristic mood of pessimism. Habitually, Tizard was the man 'on top of the world', brimming over with good plans for the future. Now he appeared to feel differently not only about post-war prospects, but even about the date when victory itself could be achieved. On 16 April General Montgomery, commander-designate of the forces preparing for the invasion of the Continent, visited Oxford. He toured the Colleges, was shown around Magdalen by the President, and in his usual jaunty fashion gave the impression of inevitable victory. His confidence must have appeared somewhat strange to Tizard who almost exactly a month earlier had laid a bet which threw into relief the current hope that the war might be over before the year was out. For Tizard not only believed that the Allies would be unable to reach Berlin during 1944; he also believed that if troops were launched on an invasion across the channel by mid-June they would be thrown back into the sea. It is difficult to know whether this attitude was the result of faulty information; of despondency bred by the fact that Tizard, who felt that his place was in the centre, was now on the outer rim; or whether it was yet another example of the Devil's advocacy which he was to employ throughout the remaining months of the war.

In many fields Tizard's constant prodding did a great deal of good; he was, after all, a good prodder, he had few inhibitions when it came to reporting unpleasant facts, and he was a man who could never be accused of paddling his canoe into the easier waters of the post-war world. His comments and criticisms during the last year of the war ranged across industry, research, and education, and they more than once brought him hard work which he cheer-fully undertook – on the grounds that it was 'worthwhile'.

One such case arose from a speech at the Royal Society Club in February 1944, and in which he criticized Imperial Chemical Industries. Among those present was Lord Melchett, deputy chairman of I.C.I. He complained that Tizard's speech implied a general attack on the administration of I.C.I. and that at the time he, Melchett, was not properly equipped to deal with it as seriously as it deserved. Tizard, replying to Melchett on 21 February, was quite unrepentant, re-iterating that much depended on the calibre of directors of research and good technical direction from above. 'There certainly is a feeling in the scientific world, which I frankly share, that the technical judgement of the board of I.C.I. is not so good as it might be and ought to be,' he con-tinued. 'You spend a lot of money on scientific and technical developments, I know, and you propose to spend more. You do a great deal in the support of science at Universities and elsewhere. All this is to the good, yet the results on the whole, over the last twenty years, have not been strikingly good. Why is it?' Melchett took up the fight with a slightly defensive document which was approved by the I.C.I. board and sent to Tizard. The latter re-mained unconvinced, and replied by inviting Melchett and the directors to luncheon at Magdalen where, on 17 July, they had a two-hour discussion on the points involved.

Tizard believed that in the post-war world much industry and many universities would have to be spurred into taking the oppor-tunities which science would offer, but he had no illusions about the probable position of Britain herself. He firmly believed that much would devolve upon the Dominions – for whom he persistently argued a major immigration plan; he believed that in the early stages the production of nuclear power, both for war and for peace, should be primarily a matter for the United States. And he be-lieved that whatever Britain's position was to be in the future she would be able to make the best of it only if she began now while the war was still going on, to plan for the post-war years. This was of course a commonplace, but Tizard saw certain aspects of it which had so far escaped attention.

One of these lay in the dangerous drain on British physicists which the war in general, and the United States work on the atomic bomb in particular, was continuing to inflict. Tizard had belittled the chance of nuclear success in the early war years, and had felt that both geography and industrial strength favoured research on the far side of the Atlantic. But now, as success began to look possible, he realized that America's gain might have been Britain's loss. In September he had a long meeting with Chadwick, now the head of the British team in the United States, who was making a short visit to Birtain. And on 30 September 1944, he addressed a lengthy memorandum on the subject to Sir John Anderson, now Chancellor of the Exchequer but still the Minister responsible for British nuclear research. This memorandum stressed the numbers of British physicists who were working abroad and outlined the dangers of the situation to Britain during the next few years.

'Now let me recapitulate my own views', it concluded.

(a) No new research is going to affect materially the outcome of this war. (b) There are most important, and indeed alarming, developments which must not be neglected in the interests of national defence in the future. (c) We must take a long view of these developments, and realise that the form will be very different in twenty years' time than appears now, and that success will depend, not so much on the present, as on the future generation of scientists. (d) That, therefore, it is of vital importance to revive education and research at Universities, especially in physics which has been so long neglected. (e) That industrial supremacy, with all that this implies to the nation, also depends essentially on the revival of University work.

Only my strong feelings, which make me fear that in the present policy we may be grasping at the shadow, and losing the substance, have induced me to write at such length. I hope that I have not exhausted your patience.

Tizard, as the Foreign Secretary of the Royal Society, could write with authority while his knowledge of the country's University needs was better than most. However, his long scepticism of what nuclear energy might produce limited the effect of his appeal; and he was – as was everyone else in Britain with the exception of the Prime Minister, Lord Cherwell, Sir John Anderson, and Anthony Eden – lacking a reasonably full knowledge of the progress which had been made towards production of an atomic bomb.

So far as aeronautical research was concerned, his position was radically different, and proposals for drastic post-war reorganization which he made in an address to the Parliamentary and Scientific Committee in October 1944, were seriously studied. He outlined the problems and opportunities for civil aviation, stressed that Britain's position would rest basically on the success or failure of research, and called for a reconstruction of the Aeronautical Research Committee which would free it from Service control. 'There is no more reason for putting fundamental research in aeronautics under the control of the Air Ministry, or any Supply Ministry, than there is for putting fundamental research in Universities under the control of the Service Departments', he pointed out. His suggestion was that there should be an executive – as compared to the existing purely advisory – Aeronautical Research body attached to the Lord President of the Council in much the same way as the Medical Research Council, and provided with a block grant by Parliament, which would be at least £1,000,000 a year.

> The Council should be empowered to create and manage an experimental establishment to which would be transferred much of the work now carried out at the Royal Aircraft Establishment, leaving the latter to concentrate on scientific work of preponderating military importance [he continued]. The Council should also not only be authorised, but expected and encouraged to spend money on experimental work elsewhere, e.g. at Universities and in industry. In fact it should spend its money where brains and ability can be found. *It should be expected also to direct and finance the development work that is necessary before the value of new ideas can be fully demonstrated in practice.*

Tizard's proposals represented a clean break with the existing system and it was perhaps too much to hope that they would survive the British facility for compromise. Yet it was already clear that the future of flight, civilian as well as Service, would have little resemblance to the past. Whittle's jets – as well as their German counterparts – were already flying. Supersonic flight was already being discussed. The pilotless planes of the V-weapons bombardment had already presented Fighter Command with a new problem, while the rockets of the same campaign had in a single step given an old-fashioned look to both fighters and the Early Warning radar chain. The Services were the first to realize that these developments called for a complete re-appraisal of possibilities, and in December 1944, the Chiefs of Staff Joint Technical Warfare Committee decided that only scientists could assess the probable effect of new weapon development on Imperial Defence Policy; its members also decided that Tizard was the only man capable of handling such an enquiry. Thus, a few days before Christmas, he began, once again, to work on a new Service project. There had been slightly more than a year during which he had reduced such interests to a minimum. Now, through no seeking of his own, they had begun to grow once again – as they were to do through the next six years.

Tizard quickly formed a committee which included Blackett, Charles Ellis, G. P. Thomson, and Professor Bernal. He wrote to Cripps saying that in view of his new commitments he would have to give up membership of the Radio Board, and within a few weeks was tackling the job in his usual experienced way – enquiring whether any pilots had yet broken through the sound barrier accidentally; what the extension of rocket-range was likely to be within so many years; and whether submarines would be likely to add considerably to their submerged range within the foreseeable future. He and the other members of the committee probed deeply down into the mysterious ways in which science might affect the Armed Forces of the future, and they were given every facility to do so. At least, they were given almost every facility; yet in one respect they were forced to work in blinkers. For although work on the atomic bomb was by this time coming to its climax in the United States, it was decided that information on its possibilities must remain hidden from the committee enquiring into the weapons of the future.

Early in April Tizard drafted a letter on the subject to the Prime Minister, sending it first to Sir John Anderson, who in turn passed it over to General Ismay.

Personally [Tizard was told by Ismay on 6 April], he (Anderson) would see no objection to your putting questions to the British physicists engaged on the special project, some of whom happen to be in this country for a short time now. He thinks, however, that you would be well advised to make it clear to the Prime Minister that you do not intend to make any allusion to the topic in your main report; and that your best line would be to indicate that at this stage you are only seeking background.[9]

Tizard persevered, but without success. 'Pray see my previous minute' [Churchill minuted to Ismay on 19 April in referring to his initial response to Tizard's letter].

and reply in that sense on my behalf to Sir Henry Tizard. He surely has lots of things to get on with without plunging into this exceptionally secret matter. It may be that in a few years or even months this secret can no longer be kept. One must always realise that for every one of these scientists who is informed there is a little group around him who also hear the news.[10]

The main argument advanced for maintaining the utmost secrecy was that it was essential to fulfil the terms of the Quebec and Hyde Park Agreements, made between Roosevelt and Churchill after a good deal of hard bargaining. And it was not Tizard and his fellow-scientists who had been singled out for special treatment. The same had been given to a suggestion by Anderson, roughly a year earlier, that the Service and a few other Ministers, as well as the Chiefs of Staff, should be informed of the progress being made on the bomb.

When the report of Tizard's committee was finally presented in June, the future of nuclear energy was put high on the list of new scientific and technical developments within sight. But the committee members had been prognosticating in the dark, a fact which became apparent when the first atomic bombs were dropped on Japan early in August. The new Labour Government, recently hoisted into the saddle, set up a new Committee on Atomic Energy under Sir John Anderson. The Chiefs of Staff were, according to a private letter from Ismay to Tizard on 22 August 'in process of considering the best and quickest way of ensuring that you were given the fullest information on the subject, with a view to the revision of your report on the future development in weapons and methods of war, when the announcement of the setting-up of the new Committee burst upon them.'[11] And the Chiefs of Staff appear to have been 'most disappointed' that Tizard was not a member of the committee.

BB

This is perhaps not as surprising as it seems. For as the war in Europe had ground to an end on the plains of northern Germany, demands for Tizard's services had increased; with few exceptions, they had been rebuffed. On 3 May Sir Alan Barlow of the Treasury asked whether he would become chairman of a committee to examine existing arrangements for radio and radar research, and to advise on any changes considered necessary. Tizard declined briefly. But he first drafted a longer letter which was not sent but which clearly reveals his feelings.

My Dear Barlow [this went], I'm sorry to give you the trouble of finding someone else, but the answer is No, thank you!

During the last few months I have been asked to be chairman, or member, of the G.B. (Governing Body) of the new College of Aeronautics, Chairman of the Advisory Committee of the Min. of E, to look after, or rather advise on, the outlook of education other than University education, Chairman of the Research Committee of the Ministry of Works, and to undertake other minor responsibilities, all, I need hardly say, unpaid, as I am a scientist! These I have refused. I have also been formally approached to be Chairman of a Committee 'in connection with a new weapon', and have refused. I accepted the Chairmanship of a special committee of the War Cabinet, but that job, I hope, will be finished by the end of June; I have told Havelock that I do not want to be reappointed a Development Commissioner and have suggested a better man. In short, now that the national danger has passed, I hope that I shall be able to avoid, with a clear conscience, all time-consuming and indirectly expensive Govt. Committees, with the exception of the University Grants Committee, which I suppose I must continue, reluctantly for a time.

You will guess that my reasons for refusing your invitation are complex and not entirely due to these duties and 'preoccupations'. For over ten years I have devoted all my spare time, and during most of the war my full time, to work of national importance. I have lost a lot of money in consequence. I have been treated with great discourtesy by some Ministers and others, and have had to contend with great personal difficulties and intrigue. I want to get back to work of real interest, in co-operation with friends rather than self-seekers, and, if possible, to do something to avoid a poverty-stricken old age, particularly for my wife if she survives me.

Lest you should think that I am one of the crowd looking for 'honours', I add that I hold that men in my position should do what they can for the nation during war without that kind of public recognition – when other men are getting killed, maimed, or losing their all.

What an outburst! The fact is I am feeling Bolshevistic. I may feel differently six months after the war, when I have had something of a rest; but that is my mood now.

It was his mood a few days later when the end of the European war was formally announced. 'I do not feel elated' he wrote in his diary that night. 'I feel rather sad, as I did on November 11th 1918. Nor is there much excitement in the street or in College. The tower was flood-lit this evening – looking beautiful. The night is clear and warm. Undergraduates are wandering over the roofs but are very quiet. Perhaps they will be noisier tomorrow.' His mood the following night was the same. 'Celebrations were livelier today', he noted.

Shops and factories were closed, and the streets filled with cheerful crowds. Plenty of flags, and bell-ringing. Little disorder, no 'mafficking'. We had a special dinner in Hall on 8th – free port for all, but no speeches. Afterwards we had a bonfire in the Meadows. Well, it certainly is a great day: a great historic day. It is hard to realise now, but we shall know better later on. I feel rather like a patient coming round after a severe but successful operation. Deep down there is a feeling that all is well, and that a great oppression has been lifted, but other feelings are not so pleasant, and the nurse who pats one on the arm and shouts that all is over is excessively exasperating. All is not over by any means. There is a secondary and still serious operation to follow, after which will come a long period of convalescence and slow recovery for the nations of the world and everyone knows how fretful patients are in convalescence. We shall want all our stock of courage, forbearance, and hope for many years. Memories crowd in on me; memories of acute anxieties and tragedies – memories too of absent friends – and of the dismal prophecies of utter destruction of the cities of England which proved in the event so greatly exaggerated. I wonder if the part that scientists have played will ever be faithfully and fairly recorded. Probably not.

CHAPTER FIFTEEN

Ministry of Defence

When the first atomic bombs to be used in anger exploded over Japan early in August 1945, Tizard was within a few weeks of his sixtieth birthday. He had been for nearly three years deeply engrossed in the work of an academic appointment which if only partially satisfying during wartime was at least pleasant, stimulating and mentally rewarding. He had decent quarters at a time when decent quarters were not easy to secure, and although their upkeep had been hampered by war-time restrictions, things would no doubt now turn for the better. His salary, if not excessive, was at least sufficient, and it seemed possible that it might now be supplemented by those *honoraria* and other good things which come the way of academic men. Moreover, he was secure, since, as his friend Charles Lindemann had written to him on hearing of his election to the Presidency, it was an appointment which 'nobody can deprive you of except for immorality and even that must, I understand, be of the grossest and most notorious variety.'

There seemed, indeed, little reason to move. Even the national need for Tizard's particular form of expertise, for his unique understanding of scientific-cum-operational possibility, was no longer there with its constant reminder that he might be working in a larger field. Britain's post-war problems would be economic rather than military, and Tizard had been one of the first to realize this; flying over a huge industrial area of the United States during his journey to Australia in 1943, he had turned to his companion and reflected: 'You know, after the war we're going to be a second-rate power'. Now, two years later, he could see that his ominous prediction had been correct; that behind the enthusiasm of the new Government there lay the need to restore the basis of the economy, to make the country as self-supporting as the facts of life would allow, and only then to consider, within a realistic framework, the size of the military forces and the tasks to which it was practicable to direct them. Such work could benefit from the advice of a man with Tizard's experience, but in these matters he was now merely one among a small number; in war, he had been unique.

During the first months of peace it was therefore on the use of scientists in the post-war period, on the country's resources, and on similar matters that his advice was sought. He declined an invitation from Herbert Morrison, Lord President of the Council, to serve on a committee which would 'consider the policies which should govern the use and development of our scientific manpower and resources in the next ten years' because he was already involved in much additional work and never liked 'joining a Committee and then being a passenger.' He was still, in Newall's words, one of the prickly scientists rather than one of the smooth ones, and had replied without inhibitions when, soon after the end of the war in Europe, his advice had again been sought by Sir Alan Barlow of the Treasury. Tizard's draft answer summed up the lessons learned during the five and a half years of war; it throws direct light on his attitude to science and Government; and it is therefore worth quoting in full.

Dear Barlow [he wrote], You have asked me to give you my views on the problem of fitting the scientists into the Government machine.

I have read a good many proposals, all of which in one way or another purport to give the scientists greater freedom, better status, better prospects, better salary and better conditions of service. All this sounds like a move in the right direction, but I do not believe that scientists will ever fit comfortably into the machine unless and until they feel that they are regarded as equal partners. All these proposals are palliatives which stand no real chance of providing a solution of the problem; I believe in fact that they will aggravate the position by putting the scientists at a level somewhere between the administrative and executive classes in the Civil Service.

Before the year 1936 the academic scientists lived in a little world of their own, with their own hierarchy, their own levels and even their own honours list, which took the form of elections to the Royal Society, medals and special lectures, and as a closed community the system worked pretty smoothly.

The scientists who were in the Government service were, with rare exceptions, second rate. The state of national emergency which culminated in the war brought practically every scientist who was any good into the Government service in one way or another. No-one I think will question the value of the contribution which these scientists have made to the war effort, but the time has now come when the Government must decide whether it is desirable to retain a fraction of the first-class men in the service of the State and, if so, what steps are necessary to achieve this result.

The semi-totalitarian conditions which have, during the war, reduced the scientist to a pawn which could be moved at will by politicians, civil servants, and the fighting services, will not be a practical proposition in time of peace, and I do not believe that it will be possible to exploit the patriotism of the scientists when the state of national emergency has passed.

I think that the root of the trouble lies in the fact that, with some exceptions, there is a tendency for the politicians, the civil servants, and to some extent the Service chiefs, to dislike the scientists, and this dislike, again with exceptions, is reciprocated. Many of the civil servants regard the scientist as an uncultured barbarian who may perhaps, in a restricted field, know 'more and more about less and less', but who is not a man of affairs, who has little capacity for administration, who is constantly trying to interfere and who is nearly always difficult to deal with. There will always be people answering to this specification and I should be the last to maintain that they are in short supply amongst scientists, but if you take a man of over forty years of age who has been running a team of a dozen or so researchers and expect him not only to show scientific originality and good judgement, but also to administer a large organisation efficiently, without friction and with an understanding of his fellow men which his previous experience and education have not provided, you are yourself making a serious administrative blunder – and you aggravate that blunder tenfold by not treating him as an equal. You give him a salary which bears no relation to the importance of his responsibilities and you add insult to injury by the kind of public recognition he is given. Such phrases as 'back-room-boys' are deplorable.

It is, therefore, not surprising that many scientists feel that they are looked down on as belonging to a lower stratum – strange creatures who are fetched out in times of emergency (just as you go to a dentist when you have a hollow tooth, or to a plumber when the pipes have burst) and cast back into the obscurity to which they properly belong when the emergency has passed. So long as this state of affairs obtains, I am convinced that the best of the scientists will prefer either the 'splendid isolation' of academic life or the material rewards which industry is prepared to offer.

I think that the experience of the war has shown that fundamental scientific research on the one hand and the applied science that is needed in the service of the State are very different.

If you take a first-class scientific researcher with originality and energy and turn him loose in a suitable environment, something will come out but you cannot say what. In fundamental science everything must be understood, nothing can be ignored, all knowledge is of value and every phenomenon must be pursued relentlessly and logically to the end. The researcher in fundamental science tends to confine himself to a restricted field and to know 'more and more about less and less', and the peculiar qualities which are needed to yield fruitful results in fundamental science have usually passed their zenith before a man has reached the age of 40. The laboratory which is devoted to fundamental research is no place for the production efficiency expert. Many acorns must fall to the ground for every oak which reaches maturity.

Most of the scientists who have made important contributions to the war effort have done so in fields far removed from their pre-war activities. It would be astonishing if in time of peace a biologist were to submit a paper on radio for publication by the Royal Society, but in war time we find, for example, a biologist working with outstanding success on radiolocation; a specialist on electron diffraction designing incendiary bombs, and so forth.

Applied science is different from fundamental research and is essentially not self-fertilizing. It is no good shutting a man up in a laboratory and telling him to find out something that will win the war. He must be constantly confronted with new problems, new needs and new projects, and in this field I think that there is no reason to suppose that his originality and versatility will decline at an early age, but rather that they will be fortified by the judgement which comes from experience. Applied science, which has a definite object in view, is more in the nature of an art and, like the art of painting a portrait, it is the recognition and isolation of the essential that really counts, though, of course, this art must be backed by sound scientific knowledge and understanding. Fundamental research is the ultimate source of all applied science.

Scientific men with first-class judgement and originality, who are also good administrators and men of the world, with political wisdom and with a sympathetic understanding of their fellow men, are, if they exist at all, so rare that for practical purposes they may be ruled out of account. (Some of my scientific colleagues will no doubt think that I am unduly pessimistic, though their natural modesty would preclude them from suggesting the name of one such paragon.) It is unfortunate that whilst there are few who would fancy themselves as experts on, say, cosmic rays, there are certain human activities, which include administration (and chicken farming), which everyone thinks they can take up successfully at any time of their life. All this has led me to a series of conclusions which sound terribly like platitudes.

Scientific men are usually indifferent administrators and seldom men of the world. They should not be expected to undertake tasks for which their experience and training have not fitted them. It is wasteful to turn a first-class scientist into a second-rate administrator.

Administration is a job for people who have been trained to administrate, but if they are to administrate scientific activities they must have had a broad general scientific education. I cannot see that this is impossible, though I admit that it is a long-term policy.

The function of the scientist is to give scientific advice and to guide the strategy and tactics of scientific research and development. He cannot do this effectively unless he sits with the planners.

The administrator and the scientist have complementary and equally important functions to fulfil. They must sit together at the same level. One must not be the master and the other the servant, but they must work together as partners and equals. (The relation between the Permanent Secretary and the Chief Executive of a Ministry is an example of such a partnership.)

There are many questions relating to the existing organization on which I have not touched in this letter, which is already too long, but I believe that these questions are relatively unimportant in comparison with what I regard as the fundamental principles.

I have written this letter with some misgiving, since there is something for everyone to disagree with. Indeed, I should not have done so were it not that, after more than two and a half years as a chartered privateer, following some four years as a privateer without marque, I feel that I can, with a clear conscience, retire from a task which nothing but the national emergency would have induced me to endure for so long. Yours sincerely.

Yet it was only the direct, official, task, from which he wanted to retire. In others, he was as active as ever. His position in the Royal Society drew him into the early negotiations from which grew Unesco, of which he wrote that 'we are trying to do these things too hurriedly after a war. We may get an elaborate organisation which is of very little value. Nevertheless, if we are going to have a Uneco, science must take a very important part.' He was [sic] a Managing Trustee of the Nuffield Foundation, a post for which he refused the annual honorarium of £250 since, as he put it, Lord Nuffield had already done so much for Oxford. 'In the event of acute signs of bankruptcy appearing in a year or two, which seems not at present improbable', he had written, 'I may return to you: but I hope not'.

He took considerable interest in the work of the Goldsmiths' Company to which he had been admitted in 1940 in recognition of his services at Imperial College and on the Aeronautical Research Committee, and of which he became Prime Warden in 1955. He served on the Company's Education Committee and here had a habit of disconcerting with a single question any young man who had been working his way from grant to grant for an undue time. 'Tell me, Mr So-and-So', he would ask quietly, but with just a trace of irony, 'have you ever thought of taking a job?' He was a Governor of Rugby and of Westminster. He busied himself with the affairs of the British Museum of which he was a Trustee, with the work of the University Grants Committee of which he had been a member since 1943, with the Regional Conference for Further Education, the Hansard Society and a thick gathering of similar bodies. At times it must have seemed difficult to believe that the rancour and unpleasantness of the war had ever existed.

Even before it had ended he had shown an almost unhuman reluctance to maintain ill-will. Offered a directorship of the Bank of England by Lord Catto, he replied that he was unable to make up his mind quickly, had better refuse, and had then added; 'You have probably already thought of Lord Cherwell, and ruled him out because of his present position, but I don't think he is going on with politics after the war . . .' Cherwell had, in fact, returned to Christ Church after the fall of Churchill's Coalition Government. His path once again crossed Tizard's. They dined together occasionally. And it was to Cherwell that Tizard wrote in 1946 on taking up the scientific editorship of the Home University Library. 'Is it possible', he said, 'that you could find time to write a book in the series on Physics and Philosophy? I think it ought to be one of the best sellers. The difficulty is to find someone to do it. Philosophers do not know any physics, and very few physicists have taken a real interest in philosophy. In fact, you are the only man who could do it well. It does not pay to do it. I shall be much surprised if such a book would bring in more than £200 in royalties. But nevertheless I hope you won't turn the idea down offhand. It might prove the starting point for a larger work, which eventually

those who study Greats might read.' Cherwell appears to have
asked for a specimen book in the series and when Tizard sent him
Whitehead's *Introduction to Mathematics* a few days later he added:
'I do hope you will write a book, and that it may be a prelude to a
more ambitious work.'

There seems little doubt that education, the wider post-war
problems of applying science, and the search for a solution to
Britain's economic and industrial difficulties, were the spheres in
which Tizard now felt that his future lay. He felt that they presented the most important issues for a country in Britain's economic
plight. He knew that his training qualified him. And he believed
that here he would be less worried by the political intrigue which
he detested, and which he must have felt would always bedevil
matters of defence.

Yet in all this Tizard was fighting a losing battle. The atomic
bomb and the rocket had between them cut the ground from
beaneath all pre-conceived ideas of war. The Service chiefs therefore had to wipe the slate clean and start again – writing their new
military equations with more regard to the scientists than ever
before. It was natural that they should turn to Tizard, natural that
they should brush aside his protests, natural that they should
prevent him from abdicating. Thus the process which had begun
at the end of 1944 when the Chiefs of Staff had asked him to investigate new weapons now quickened – in spite of all his efforts.

He had presented the report on new weapons to the Chiefs of
Staff in June 1945. Shortly afterwards he was asked by Sir William
Douglas, Permanent Secretary to the Ministry of Supply, to accept
the chairmanship of a Central Co-Ordinating Committee which
would have 'wide powers of guidance and review over the whole
field of guided missiles and projectiles.' Tizard declined – bearing
in mind, no doubt, the refusal to allow his earlier committee access
to information on the atomic bomb. The refusal had come from
Churchill, who was at this date still Prime Minister. He did, however, accept a 'rather formidable' bundle of papers from Air
Marshal Sir John Slessor, recently brought back from the
Mediterranean to become the Air Council's Member for Air
Personnel, and agreed to give him advice. He became first chairman of the Advisory Committee on Airborne Research Facilities,

set up to consider proposals for the use of naval and R.A.F. air-craft and facilities for assisting scientific research, and to make recommendations to the Council of the Royal Society, the Lords Commissioners of the Admiralty, and the Air Council.

Far more important than any of these activities, were the recom-mendations for a basic reorganization of the ways in which scien-tific advice should be given to the Services, a re-organization which Tizard outlined in the autumn of 1945. Since he had left Whitehall in the summer of 1943, there had been changes. First the Chiefs of Staff had set up a Joint Committee on Research and Development Priorities on which scientists from the three Services, the D.S.I.R. and the Radio Board were represented. Then a Deputy Chiefs of Staff Committee had been set up to over-see scientific questions of Service interest. Finally, in March 1945, this work had been taken over by a special committee under Lord Cherwell's chairmanship. Now, following Cherwell's disappearance from Whitehall with the Churchill Government, there were doubts as to whether the Deputy Chiefs of Staff Committee would be the best organization to carry on with the task.

Tizard was asked to advise, and attended a Chiefs of Staff meet-ing on 20 September, apparently at the invitation of Field-Marshal Lord Alanbrooke, Chief of the Imperial General Staff. 'I had to try and induce him to carry out another review of the implications of science on strategy in the next few years', the Field-Marshal wrote in his diary. 'He would not take it on but pressed for the formation of a scientific organisation under the Committee of Imperial Defence or Defence Ministry to keep scientific develop-ment continually under review and to direct research and develop-ment to the best advantage of the country. I asked him to submit a paper on his proposals, which he will do. I think he is quite right and that a development of this kind is highly desirable. . . .'[1]

Tizard's paper, on the Central Direction of the Scientific Effort, was presented on 12 October. It wrapped up the lessons of the previous decade, incorporated the recommendations which he had made in one form or another to many Ministers, and laid the foundations for the system which is still in operation today. The nub of his proposals which, he was informed a fortnight later, were 'in principle acceptable to the Chiefs of Staff', was the appointment of a Scientific Adviser who would act as chairman of a reconstituted Deputy Chiefs of Staff Committee, and who would also serve on a new body which would consider civilian matters. The Government could – and presumably would – thus be presented with one comprehensive scheme for cutting up the country's scientific cake instead of having to consider one plan from the Services and another from their civilian advisers.

This was at least a step towards the idea which he outlined in a lecture on 'Science and the Services' given to the Royal United Services Institution the following year. 'What is needed', he then said, 'is a scientific staff attached to the central Chiefs of Staff organisation that will have no executive duties, nor be over-burdened by administration, but will devote its whole time to the study of the influence of advancing scientific knowledge on the problems of defence. This is a branch of strategic study that needs just as much attention and forethought as any other branch of military strategy; indeed, it requires more. If we neglect it I see no chance whatsoever that our great country will survive another world war.'[2] Such study, he pointed out in a letter to the *Daily Telegraph* of 1 April 1946, would involve 'planning on the basis of things to come, taking into account developments in science that are only in their infancy. Such planning can be done only by a scientific staff, continuously studying the changing world. It is not enough to enlist the part-time help of independent scientists from universities whenever this is deemed necessary.'

The plan which he presented to the Chiefs of Staff went some way towards this ideal and after certain minor modifications had been agreed on 1 November, the proposals were sent upwards, with due blessing, for consideration by the Cabinet. By the winter of 1945 Tizard was therefore being drawn once again, without much enthusiasm and with some reluctance, into the complexities of defence politics from which he had apparently escaped. The pressure did not come only from those in England. In the summer he had been consulted by Rivett in Australia about the German V-weapons and had replied: 'I think it would be a good thing to do some experimental work in Australia. I had already suggested, before receiving your letter, that Australia should be encouraged to organise a research station. You have, as you say, the desert country, you have very good engineers, a high-class steel industry, and I have no doubt we could reinforce you if necessary with young scientific men from England. Also Australia is a good place to do experiments involving radio communications that we don't want other people to listen to. I am not in a position to influence these things very much now, but I hope that the suggestion has fallen on fruitful land. . . .' It had indeed; the rocket range of Woomera was to grow from it.

By many Australians Tizard was now regarded as the one man in Britain from whom advice should be sought on defence matters, and in April 1946 Sir Frederick Shedden, Secretary of the Australian Department of Defence, sent him a draft of the Memorandum on Defence Scientific Advisory Committee, Constitution and Functions which had recently been drawn up. Tizard's reply shows the way his mind was working. 'Many thanks for your letter and enclosure of April 11th', this read.

> I already knew something of your plans, but was very glad to have the full document. You are giving the mother country a lead, but I am not sure that she will follow it. I know that some people are content with things as they are. I suppose that much depends on the discussions going on, or soon to go on, in London.
>
> I do not know how we are going to get security unless some scientific men are going to give continuous thought, on the highest plane, to the problems of future defence. And the problems are very serious, and are going to become more so. They do not only include ways and means of dealing with atomic energy in war and peace: what is more important is that we should get the fullest scientific co-operation throughout the Empire, and a much better balance than exists at present of human and material resources.
>
> Australia is in a special position, I feel, and has a great part to play. In fact I think that the strength of the British Commonwealth (as I had better call it!) is going to depend crucially on the prosperity and scientific progress of Australia; and when I say strength, I do not mean aggressive but moral strength. So your chief Scientific Adviser, and your Scientific Advisory Committee, must not have a horizon limited to the coast of Australia or even to the Pacific. And it does seem to me that he, the Adviser, must have an opposite number here.
>
> However, I can't teach you anything about this, I know. You must regard this little outburst as an indication of my anxiety, shared by many others.

Some years later, Tizard was to serve the Australians in a

slightly different way, encouraging Professor Oliphant's efforts to found an Australian Academy of Science, and pleading that it should not become so 'pure' that it was sterile. 'He urged that we include engineers and other users of science in the Fellowship from the very beginning' says Oliphant, 'as they were an essential part of the spectrum of scientific activity, whose work influenced basic discovery both by uncovering needs, and by the feed-back of technique. He was a realist about the development of Australia, saying that investment should be confined to areas yielding greatest and most immediate return.' An enormous debt was owed to him, says Oliphant, for his wisdom and guidance. 'This was always given in such a way as to earn the affectionate regard of men of science, if not of opportunists or politicians.'³

Meanwhile, the British Government had been thinking about Commonwealth co-operation on defence, and the way in which it should be tied in with the massive reorganization which was seen to be necessary. Mr Attlee, the new Prime Minister, had for the time being retained the additional role of Minister of Defence and in the spring of 1946 decided that an informal Commonwealth Conference on Defence Science should be held in London before the shape of a new British defence structure was settled. Canada, Australia, South Africa, New Zealand, and India were all invited to send delegates, and it was hoped that the conference would make recommendations for collaboration in research and development which would form a basis for discussion at Government level. Tizard was the obvious choice to head such a conference – 'you are, whether you know it or not, the apostle of Empire team-work', Rivett later wrote to him – and to Tizard Attlee wrote on 3 May.

He received the answer that the President was really rather reluctant to add to his labours.

On the 16th Tizard wrote to Tedder, now Chief of the Air Staff, noting that he had heard no more about the conference

except through Watson-Watt, whom I saw yesterday in London and who showed me the proposed agenda. The fortnight in question is right in the middle of term [he continued], and of course all this extra work gets rather tiresome, although I am quite prepared to do it if it is really of value and importance. But I very much doubt whether this is. I do not like the word 'informal' because it seems to me to imply that people are going to talk a lot and then no particular notice will be taken of their conclusions; and in the second place I do not see how one can give really good advice on the development of science in the Empire in the interests of defence without being instructed and guided in future strategy. Finally, on my glance through the agenda I had the kind of impression that everybody is going to be interested in fighting the last war over again.

Is all this too critical, and do you really want me to do it? As you know, I think that the proper direction of scientific effort in the interests of defence, both in this country and in the overseas Dominions, is of immense importance but that it wants continuous study, and cannot be achieved by occasional meetings rather amateur in character.

Before Tedder could reply, Attlee had renewed his appeal, stressing that he was 'clear – and the Chiefs of Staff entirely agree with me – that there is no-one with comparable qualifications to yourself for the Chairmanship of the Conference.' Ismay, writing from the Cabinet Offices, added that the Chiefs of Staff 'feel that you are head and shoulders above anyone else for this particular purpose'. Tizard inevitably assented.

However, he was still not happy. 'But why is atomic energy neglected?' he asked Tedder in a letter on 30 May.

It seems to me that the delegates are bound to try to get information on that. What am I to do if they ask if they can be kept in touch with results in England? Am I to say no? Surely not.

I do not yet know how serious our rulers at home are about close co-operation. Personally, I think that we must disperse the scientific effort throughout the Empire and encourage the building up of first-class organisations in places like Australia. The old argument that scientists were too isolated in Australia to do first-class work has lost much of its point, now that we approach the time of quick, safe air travel. Canada clearly does not want a formal connection, or any kind of suggestion that the scientific work in Canada may be directed by a central body. But personally I think Australia would like to be told what we want her to do, and would then gladly do it if we could encourage the movement of really first-class young scientific men.

I am very much inclined at the opening of the Conference to give my own views on broad lines, guarding you and others by emphasising that they are personal views. Am I permitted to do this?

He was permitted. And when he addressed the conference at its opening session the following month he spoke with more freedom than would otherwise have been possible – 'with the warning that what I think is not necessarily what the British Government or the British Chiefs of Staff think.' He made three main points – that the primary aim must now be to prevent wars rather than to win them; that if war did come once again, scientific strength would be as important as military strength; and that Commonwealth co-operation was an essential of the scientific dispersal which should be encouraged.

With the first of these points he staked a claim for science itself. 'Let us start from the broadest possible standpoint', runs the paper from which he read.

What is the ultimate aim, even if it can only be reached after many years? It is surely to sweep away all fear of war between civilised nations. To all intelligent educated men, national boundaries that restrict the freedom of trade and hamper the movement of individuals are fundamentally silly, and will in time disappear as completely as the boundary between Scotland and England disappeared many years ago. If they do not, civilisation itself may disappear. But human nature being what it is, this view is only now taken by a small minority of the population of the world. Indeed, nationalism and national boundaries have become more accentuated in this century rather than less; witness, for example, the boundary between Northern and Southern Ireland.

But there is a hopeful sign. Science is doing what statesmen, philosophers, economists, and leaders of the church have failed to do. The atomic bomb may prove to be a blessing in disguise. It has already forced some, although not all, nations out of extreme isolation and into a modicum of common sense. In fact, just as the threat of hell after death curbed the evil passions of individuals for centuries before the spread of education brought about a better society, so the more immediate threat of a hell on earth may curb the worst impulses of nationalism until national boundaries and prejudices are swept away by a rising tide of education and prosperity. But that may be a long way off.

Meanwhile, his paper continued, one thing was clear.

The outcome of a future world war, if it ever comes, will depend far more on the scientific strength of the warring nations than on any other single factor. Courage, discipline, and numbers will avail little if we fall behind in science. It is no good breeding Winston Churchills unless we also breed Rutherfords.

This was where the Commonwealth could help. For 'the defence of the U.K. against a determined aggressor becomes more formidable with time and the advantages of concentration become less as communications improve.' Moreover, there were, beyond the seas, those great lands of opportunity to which he had so often looked before. 'We must encourage dispersal of scientific effort. And that means that we must encourage the development in the Dominions of great centres of scientific education and research. It is easy to say, not so easy to do. But if the Dominions decide to accept the responsibility for the study of special scientific problems of defence, the development of industry and of great centres of scientific research, all naturally follows.'

In these words it is not difficult to see a rough outline of what was to come. It was sketched more clearly in the recommendations of the conference which were approved a few days later after those attending had discussed such subjects as the development and location of facilities for testing guided missiles, for testing supersonic aircraft and for investigating underwater acoustics and problems of chemical and biological warfare. A Commonwealth Advisory Committee on Defence Science was to be formed with a permanent office in the United Kingdom and its first meeting held in Canada the following year. Facilities for the study of guided missiles and similar weapons should be set up in Australia. And although collaboration with the United States was at present informal, 'all results of research in the Commonwealth should nevertheless be made freely available to the U.S. without bargaining or restriction.' The report, as a member of Tizard's secretariat described it, was 'a reasonable compromise between the original nicety of wording and the vagueness which tended to be introduced for political ends.'

Now, the conference over, it became possible for the Government to see, in the summer of 1946, how their new machinery for defence might be constructed and set in motion. The previous system had shown both the benefits and the disadvantages of a qualified dictatorship. Churchill as Prime Minister and Minister of Defence had controlled the supreme strategic direction of the war effort through the Defence (Operations) Committee of the War Cabinet; the three Supply departments – the Admiralty, the Ministry of Supply, and the Ministry of Aircraft Production – were
cc

co-ordinated by a Minister of Production who in turn worked under the dominating influence of the Minister of Defence. This existing organization had been handled more gingerly by the new Socialist Government than some had expected. The Ministry of Production had been abolished and the Ministry of Aircraft Production merged with the Ministry of Supply; the Service Ministers had regained their old importance with the abolition of the small War Cabinet in May 1945; but only now, more than a year after the new Government had come to power, did a small committee set up by the Prime Minister produce its plans for a separate Ministry of Defence.

There was good reason for hurrying slowly. It was not yet clear how soon it would be before the atomic bomb and the rocket were married up to make Britain the most vulnerable target in the world; but it was quite clear that the whole defence structure, if it were to have any credibility at all, demanded a reorganization which would give scientists more influence with the Services than they had ever before wielded. Here was the rub. For great debate continued on the way in which this influence could be exercised – much of it based on Tizard's paper of the previous autumn on the Central Direction of the Scientific Effort. However, it had become clear by the summer of 1946 that Tizard alone would be acceptable to both Services and scientists as the head of whatever scientific body was finally set up. 'It seems impossible to get agreement among the scientists about their Chairman', stated a minute from one high Service officer in June. 'They will accept Sir Henry Tizard but nobody else. On the other hand they submit in complete amiability to a Service Chairman since he does not offend their *amour propre*. However, if it was appreciated in Whitehall that Tizard's experience in science and Government gave him a unique qualification, it was known also that his opinion of the Civil Service machine, and the rough handling which he had received during the previous decade, had by this time made him a prickly character.

The first tentative approach was made by Sir Alan Barlow, on 24 July 1946, Barlow recalled that he had discussed with Tizard the central government organization for dealing with science that was to be set up.

The Services, he went on, were most anxious that he should head the reconstituted Research Committee that was then in process of gestation. Everyone had refrained from approaching him since they knew his need for a rest. But it was sincerely hoped that he would not be taking up any further commitments.

Tizard replied a few days later from Magdalen, stating his position in three pungent paragraphs. 'I have no intention of "taking up commitments" ', he said.

Indeed I am getting out of them. In particular I am busy collecting all confidential papers for return to various Government departments. I am sure that I cannot now satisfactorily combine my College and University duties with part-time work for the Government of the type I have been doing so long. Whatever may have been the position in the happy days before the wars, the Presidency of Magdalen is not a sinecure in these days. In other words, far from looking for more work, I am hoping to do less, and better!

I should only leave the comparative peace and freedom of Magdalen if I were convinced that there was work of real national importance that I could and ought to do. I should not leave just to be Chairman of the Defence Committee, because I think that to be effective I should have wider responsibilities.

If the Government wish me to take on wider responsibilities I should like to have these defined before the end of August. If I thought seriously of accepting I should have to consult my colleagues here in the autumn. I should not even mention the possibility to them unless I were persuaded (a) that there was no younger man available and acceptable, (b) that the conditions were satisfactory.

Almost exactly a month later Barlow wrote to inform Tizard that the existing Scientific Advisory Committee of the Cabinet was to be replaced by a Scientific Advisory Council. Would he be willing to take up the chairmanship of this as well as of the Service committee – 'there is universal agreement that you possess unique qualifications for the combined posts' – at a salary of £3,000 a year.

Tizard's reaction was immediate. 'I am afraid that the whole thing is impossible so far as I am concerned' he wrote.

I am asked to give up my house in Oxford, which I occupy rent and rates free, to move to London at a time when, if one can get a house or suitable flat at all, the prices are prohibitive, to give up, in addition, my special pension rights as President of Magdalen, and the comparative freedom of that office, and to accept by way of compensation a net salary, when income tax has been deducted, rather less than I have at present. It is true that I should be relieved of certain necessary expenses that I incur in Oxford, but that would be insufficient.

I lost all pension rights when I left the Civil Service at the age of 44; I cannot afford to lose them again at the age of 61.

This was not all. Even had there been no financial difficulties he would have had little wish to leave Magdalen in a hurry. He was, he put it, 'well dug in there now'.

This was the letter he wrote. He had no wish to suffer financially, while the battle for the sake of the battle had never attracted him.

And yet he stopped to think again. He considered, no doubt, the fact that he could do the job better than most men. He may well have considered the occasion, more than twenty years previously, when he had declined to become first Director of Research in the Air Ministry. He would have been superhuman had he not considered what Cherwell would say if he heard that Tizard had become the Government's chief scientific adviser. Whatever the exact combination of motives, he decided not to send the letter. Instead, he wrote Barlow a short note. There were difficulties in accepting the dual posts, he said; but he would be willing to talk about them.

Conversations spread out across weeks and then months, and only on 10 October did Tizard write to say that he was willing to become chairman of the new defence committee and to serve as a part-time member of the body which would deal with civilian science. 'To accept both (posts) would certainly involve my resignation as President', he said. 'On the whole I think it would be best to accept the offer, and resign; but the College Officers, whom I have consulted, have asked me to explore the possibility of combining one Chairmanship with the Presidency. This I have done, and will gladly try it if there is a strongly held opinion among my colleagues that this would be best for the College. I should not like to go away feeling that I had done the College any harm by coming or going.'

The matter now depended on how 'strongly' any opinion about his future was held. This was shown when at a College meeting a substantial majority of the Fellows decided that he should be asked to continue as President. To Tizard, who of all men wished to be fair to both sides in any argument, the position was awkward – made even more difficult, no doubt, by the fact that while his inclinations had now begun to pull him back to Whitehall his duty to Magdalen appeared to pull in the other direction. There were two points of view, and more than one friend advised him that he would be able to exert more influence if he stayed outside Whitehall. 'I have no quarrel at all with the minority; in fact I think they are right', he wrote to the Visitor, the Bishop of Winchester. 'What I personally fear is the risk of doing two things badly, instead of one well. Both responsibilities have their own special difficulties, very different in nature. On the other hand I don't like going against the wishes of a large majority.'

Nevertheless, a minority of the Fellows had decided that he should not be asked to stay as President. He hesitated for a few more days. Then, at an Extraordinary General Meeting on 6 November, he gave formal notice, as he reported to the Visitor 'of my intention to request you to permit me to retire from my office at the end of this calendar year'. The same evening he wrote to Barlow accepting the Chairmanship of both the Defence Research Policy Committee and the Advisory Council on Scientific Policy at a combined salary of £4,500 a year.

The impression that he left on his contemporaries was that he was coming back reluctantly, with some misgivings, honoured of course, but certain that he would be poorer because of it, hoping that he would do all that was expected of him, and still doubtful as to whether he had done the right thing. 'He was not altogether happy here', says one of his Oxford colleagues. 'Perhaps from temperament, but more likely from later development and from pressure of time, he did not relish the attention to detail which was expected of him. Much College business probably seemed too trivial to him. He felt also that some of the criticisms of his proposals were factious. In some respects, therefore, his reign was disappointing to him and to us, but looking back one is impressed by how much he did while he was here. The changes which he initiated were fundamental, and they have proved to be of lasting value. The College has good reason to be grateful to him for guiding it through some of the most difficult years of transition.'

For Tizard, it had probably been a mistake to accept the Presidency but now it was something of a wrench to go. There were, of course, compensations. Almost exactly twelve years after he had met Lindemann at the Royal Society and discussed the problems of air defence he had become, officially, and in no hole-and-corner way, the country's open adviser on the implications of science, both military and civilian.

In his diary for 7 November, the day after he had accepted the dual post in Whitehall, there is a single entry – 'Cherwell to dinner'.

*   *   *

Tizard now busied himself with preparations for his new work, deciding with the Service chiefs exactly what functions should be taken over from the Deputy Chiefs of Staff Committee by his Defence Research Policy Committee, and agreeing with the Treasury on the details of his secretariat. He left his rooms in Oxford at the end of December – the Hon. Secretary of the Oxford Society of Change-Ringers having written that 'we thought it would be a nice gesture on our part if we could ring a farewell peal for you on Magdalen Bells (5,000 changes) as a mark of our appreciation for the kindness you have extended to us in the past'.

He arranged to stay at the Athenaeum for about a month after Christmas, while he worked himself into his new post during the first weeks of 1947, and this now became his second home. Here, as in the days of the Tizard Committee a decade earlier, he would take a colleague by the arm, lead him up the central staircase and, guiding him to the long central bench where the stairs branch, would say: 'Come and sit here: no-one will be able to hear us'.

On 1 January, he moved into the offices of the newly-created Ministry of Defence in Storey's Gate. His Minister was A. V. Alexander, First Lord of the Admiralty through most of the war and a man with whom he already had friendly if only passing contacts. His colleagues on the Defence Research Policy Committee were mostly those with whom he had already worked – Frederick Brundrett, Chief of the Royal Naval Scientific Service; Owen Wansborough-Jones, Scientific Adviser to the Army Council; John Carroll, Scientific Adviser to the Admiralty. At this level all was well. All was well with the Services who sent their representatives to the meetings of the Defence Committee which were held every other Tuesday.

But neither here, nor in the work of the Defence Committee's civilian counter-part, the Advisory Council on Scientific Policy, was Tizard happy about what he called 'the domestic arrangements'. He worried about the small things, about the points of protocol, and even before he arrived at Storey's Gate, he found that in some respects these had altered little in two decades. When negotiating the final details of the appointment he had stipulated – 'remembering the fine limousines in which Ministers were accustomed to drive' – that he should be given adequate transport. He would have to do much travelling, and it was science as much as Sir Henry Tizard who would be down-graded by having to use anything less than the best. But he was not a good stipulator. When he arrived at Paddington from Oxford one morning soon after his appointment he found, waiting to take him to the Ministry, a slightly embarrassed young naval officer who conducted him to a car of little dignity and considerable age. It is claimed that Tizard took one look at it and exclaimed: 'Call a cab.'

At Storey's Gate, Ismay had arranged that his own personal secretary should become Tizard's. As a personal aide and assistant he was given the services of Captain Thorold, an officer with a fine war record then serving as Naval Assistant Secretary in the Cabinet Offices. These things helped, but there is some evidence that Tizard was unable to settle down in harness, and that he felt himself cabined, cribbed, confined by Civil Servants. It was, after all, nearly twenty years since he had left the D.S.I.R. and he now began to appreciate the freedom of those years when, unestablished, he had provided Britain with the radar warning chain; and, dis-established, had advised four successive Ministers of Aircraft Production. Now, like those who had so irritated him, he was forced to work through the proper channels.

However, this was only a minor handicap in the task to which Tizard was now to devote himself for five years. Its formidable size was emphasized in the *Statement relating to Defence* issued by the Government the following month. The new Committee 'will be continuously aware of the latest concepts of strategic and operational thought', this pointed out, 'and will itself be able to influence those concepts by reason of its knowledge of future trends in the field of defence science. From this collaboration will emerge a unified and comprehensive view of the probable nature and methods of future warfare . . .' And, it was added, Tizard's additional appointment as Chairman of the Advisory Council 'will ensure that knowledge of developments over the whole field of science will be pooled to the benefit both of the civilian community and of national defence'.

At first glance the machinery to hand appeared excellent. So far as the Services were concerned, the Defence Research Policy Committee would help the Chiefs of Staff to decide what was necessary. Its chairman, metaphorically changing Service cap for bowler, would then preside over the Advisory Committee, on which such civilian bodies as the Department of Scientific and Industrial Research, and the Medical and Agricultural Research Councils were represented. Competition for specially valuable men, for facilities at research stations, or for money to expand them, would therefore be cut to a minimum. In addition, the University Grants Committee, whose recommendations affected the amount of research carried on in the Universities, was represented on the Advisory Council. To Tizard, who had been campaigning for some such system for a quarter of a century, the prospects must have looked encouraging.

At least, they looked encouraging at first glance.

On closer inspection there was seen to be a worm within the apple. For the Defence Research Policy Committee did not directly concern itself with the development of nuclear weapons, a situation which was curious if not ludicrous. This situation was the result of historical circumstances. By the end of the war the United States had achieved, for most practical purposes, a monopoly of nuclear research. Then, during the second half of 1945, the new Socialist Government decided that this should be resumed in Britain. At this date it was not known how nuclear energy could be practically applied to social ends; and it was felt by some that there was a need to equip Britain with nuclear weapons. It therefore seemed inappropriate that any Ministry concerned with peaceful power should be responsible: but no separate Ministry of Defence yet existed. The result was that the Minister whose duty it became, under the Atomic Energy Act of 1946, 'to promote and control the development of atomic energy' was the man responsible for the provision of weapons, the Minister of Supply. This was not all. The latest and most detailed information on what nuclear development was going to mean for Britain went direct to the Prime Minister from Sir John Anderson's Advisory Council on Atomic Energy set up in August 1945. This went out of existence in January, 1948 but Attlee, 'who had kept the general supervision of atomic energy matters in his own hands (in 1946) continued to do so throughout his tenure as Prime Minister.'[4]

The reason for the Prime Minister's insistence that he should retain a dominant, if somewhat lonely, position of control were compounded of politics, personalities, and the belief in some circles that nuclear power, as distinct from nuclear explosives, was a will-o'-the-wisp on whose pursuit it would be unwise to expend too much time or money. It was also expedient, in the delicate state of Anglo-U.S. nuclear relations, to keep nuclear research free from any direct link with the new Ministry of Defence, since the Government had not yet spelt out in plain words the implications behind the Atomic Energy Act. In addition, there perhaps remained in the Prime Minister's mind a memory of those hot summer days at Potsdam two years earlier when the Allies had finally agreed to drop atomic bombs on a country already – although Attlee himself was not aware of the fact – negotiating for peace; in future, he may well have thought, he would keep as much control as possible in his own hands.

Tizard's feelings cannot have been unaffected when he saw two familiar figures a step ahead of him. One was Portal, who just a year earlier had been made Controller of Atomic Energy in the Ministry of Supply – the head of the organization which was, in Mr Attlee's equivocal words, to produce the fissile material for such 'use of atomic energy as circumstances may require'.* The

---

* According to Sir Leonard Owen, deputy to Sir Christopher Hinton, in charge of the field work, 'the remit given to the new organisation (in 1946) was the production of plutonium for military purposes' (*Nuclear Engineering in the United Kingdom – the First Ten Years*, Journal of the British Nuclear Energy Society, January, 1963).

other was Lord Cherwell, Consultant to the Ministry on atomic energy matters and a member of Portal's Technical Committee.

There were numerous points of which he was critical, and his achievements between 1947 and 1951 were made against the background of a Government uncertain of itself in Service matters and, since the advent of the bomb, profoundly worried about what the scientists might next put on the agenda. These achievements were considerable, and the greatest of them was that under Tizard's direction the new machinery was made to work. It allowed scientists to give the Chiefs of Staff clear, balanced, information, and it enabled the Chiefs of Staff in turn to ask for scientific advice on any particular problem or situation, and to get it. The advice was not always understood and it was not always acted upon, either by the Chiefs of Staff or by the Cabinet. Their instincts, their prejudices, or their ignorance might drive them the other way. But over the years Tizard and the members of the committee persuaded them that to consider such advice was not unreasonable, a waste of time, or mere pandering to that music-hall character, the absent-minded professor. The difference from pre-war days was startling, as Tizard noted after he attended an Army Exercise on the problems of Civil Defence, held at the Staff College, Camberley, in the summer of 1949. The various situations 'had been minutely analysed by the scientific Staffs of the War Office and Home Office . . . and their conclusions submitted to the searching criticism of the audience', he later said. 'As I listened, I could not but feel what suffering and what mistakes might have been avoided if we had had such a system and such a spirit of co-operation in the years before the last war.'

A new war was avoided, although by a hair's-breadth, when at the height of the Berlin blockade, after the destruction of the British Viking over Gatow Airport, it was decided not to provide armed escorts for civilian flights into Berlin. And nuclear war was avoided when the Prime Minister flew to Washington and dissuaded the Americans from nuclear attack in Korea. It would be wrong to claim that the scientists played a decisive part on either occasion; yet the climate which they had encouraged, a climate in which there was a cool calm appraisal of facts, made decisions easier. Blackett's words of a few years earlier had been that you could not run a war on gusts of emotion. Neither, it was now being stressed, should you start them that way. However, it was not only an indirect influence which Tizard was now able to exercise. As he himself said in describing the position of the chairman of the Defence Research Policy Committee, 'no major recommendation on defence policy is made by the Chiefs of Staff without his knowledge and assistance'.[5]

His work touched foreign affairs at a number of points and it was as well that he developed a strong – and, to some of his friends, surprising – admiration for Ernest Bevin. Their relationship had got off to a poor start when, in November 1945, Bevin had made some comments on British scientists that had roused Tizard's anger. There had followed a prickly exchange of letters. But mutual understanding emerged, and in later years Tizard was fond of describing an incident round a conference table at which the technical pros and cons of Britain starting her own nuclear power industry were being debated. It appeared that the cons were winning when Bevin suddenly intervened: 'What!' he said. 'Do you mean to say that our kids are going to have to grow up without the benefits of nuclear energy?' Tizard, explaining that no-one could really avoid answering such blunt questions, would add: 'Fine man, Bevin.'

He was not, rather strangely perhaps, a member of the Scientific Committee for Germany which had been set up by the Foreign Office. He was, however, invited to one or two of the Committee's meetings and received copies of the minutes and scientific papers produced by its members. In 1948, moreover, Dr Blount, then Director of the Research Branch, Control Commission for Germany, proposed that Tizard should visit that country.

His journey was exceptional for its catalogue of misfortunes and, by Tizard at least, was long remembered. He spent the preceding night at the Athenaeum where he now stayed regularly, and was driven down in the early morning to Northolt where he expected to find a private plane waiting. It was soon clear that this was not to be provided and he then attempted, without success, to telephone the Chief of Air Staff. Eventually, after a delay of more than an hour, there rolled on to the tarmac one of those part-worn and ominous Dakotas so familiar to those in lowly positions who travelled by air during this period. As Tizard entered the plane he saw that it was, as he had by this time expected, a conversion in which passengers sat, or tried to sit, knee by knee, on metal benches fitted to the fuselage. Sir Henry Tizard, tightly packed in with the aircraftmen who formed the bulk of the passengers, might well have regarded this as part of the rough that in the natural order of things comes with the smooth: the Scientific Adviser to the British Government summed it up in one word – 'Shameful!' His attitude was hardly altered when a some-what grubby-looking aircraftman arrived with a pail of warm tea, dipped a metal mug into the unprepossessing liquid, and offered it to Britain's Scientific Adviser, who viewed it with intense disgust.

This, however, was only the beginning. By the time the Dakota had reached Germany, circled over the Teutoburgerwald and dropped down on to the airfield at Buckeburg it was more than an hour late. At the headquarters where Tizard was expected it was assumed that his journey had been postponed. The special luncheon prepared for him was finished before he arrived, thus providing the last incident in a journey against which he made a formal and bitter protest to the Foreign Office.

The Allied authorities were helping to re-establish German science, and to ensure that it was rebuilt free of any pro-Nazi leading strings. Tizard had his own comment for the grotesquerie involved: 'How funny that we should be trying to teach them this', he said. 'If they'd only done it during the war, they'd have beaten us.' His visit of some ten days did more than make up for the chaos of its start. He met German scientists then working with the British Navy. He visited German research institutes in the British Zone, and in Berlin where he stayed with Sir Cecil Weir, President of the Economic Sub-Commission, Control Commission for Germany, he spent a day touring the city in a huge Horsch – possibly Goering's. He was deeply moved by the damage. He then crossed into the Russian sector and drove to the drab laboratory in East Berlin where, just forty years earlier, he had studied under Professor Nernst. He went in, discovered the bench where he had worked, and tried to find out what had happened to those whom he had known there. The quest was not as wild as it might seem. A few days later, in the University town of Göttingen, Tizard met two men. One was Otto Hahn, whose work in December 1938 had pointed the way to the Maud Committee; the other was a former student who had worked under Nernst at the next bench to Tizard in 1908.

This visit was only one of many journeys which Tizard managed to squeeze in during his five years at the Ministry of Defence, and one of his main personal contributions during these years consisted of strengthening the links with Canada and Australia which he had done so much to forge. In July 1947 it was suggested by Dr O. M. Solandt, then Chairman of the Canadian Defence Research Board, that he should visit Canada with members of the Defence Research Policy Committee. Two months later Tizard sailed with Ben Lockspeiser, Wansbrough-Jones, and John Carroll. Their brief was to discuss Canada's programme for the future, the prevention of overlapping in research programmes, and the possible dispersal of British research in any future war. They also exchanged views on the strategic aspects of atomic energy, biological warfare, operational research, and research on Arctic warfare. Tizard addressed the Canadian National Research Council, and the British party attended a meeting of the Defence Research Board at which a general discussion took place after an outline of Canada's defence problems had been given by the Chief of General Staff. They also visited Fort Churchill on Hudson Bay where the problems of Arctic warfare were being investigated, and a number of stations such as the Naval Research Establishment at Ottawa. It was clear that the effects of Tizard's visit seven years previously had been deep and permanent, and in the tour of defence establishments which followed, there was an interchange of views that was free, blunt, and informal.

Tizard managed, as usual, to squeeze one day's fishing into the journey. Colonel Carrie had arranged a visit to a famous salmon river. 'I thought they would let him fish from the water', he says. 'I had probably overdone it in describing who this visitor was, because they put him in a canoe with cushions and a guide front and rear to paddle him to the choice spots. He got fish all right but was utterly disgusted at that method of fishing and never let me forget it.'

Tizard had the true sportsman's belief that the rules must not be made too easy, and when he again visited Canada a few years later, and was once more given special-person treatment at one of the country's most exclusive fishing clubs, he left his own cryptic note as a comment. 'The fishing', this went, 'is suited to the elderly. One sits comfortably in a chair in the middle of a broad canoe, with one guide in the bows, and the other in the stern looking after a 20 h.p. outboard motor, and steering. The river runs fast, and one goes along to a suitable spot chosen by the guides, drops anchor, and then stands up to cast. When a fish comes on, one sits down again, and holds on while the guides help the boat to drift near the bank, where one of them can get out in shallow water and net the fish when it is tired.'

The journey to Canada in 1947 was followed the next year by a visit to Australia. This time Tizard was charged not only with discussing the scientific aspects of defence with the Australian Prime Minister, Mr Chifley, but with removing a source of irritation which had arisen between Britain and the Dominion, concerning the passing-on of information by Britain to Australia. There had been cases where this had been clearly avoided and the feeling had arisen in Australia that distrust of some Australian scientists was the cause. Tizard was able to untangle this skein to the satisfaction of everyone, publicly stating that there had been no case where Australians had been distrusted, and privately explaining to Mr Chifley that while this was true the problem was more complicated: that Britain had signed an agreement with the United States under which some information coming from the United States to Britain could not be made available to third parties – any Dominion being, for this purpose, a third party.

He visited with an almost fatherly interest both the Radio-Physics Laboratory about which he had advised the Government during the early days of the war, and the rocket range which was by this time being built at Woomera. That the range was completed at all was largely due to Tizard's intervention at a critical stage in its history. This came when W. A. S. Butement, Chief Superintendent of the Long-Range Weapons Establishment of which Woomera formed a part, learned in London in 1948 that the weapons project was about to be abandoned. General Sir

John Evetts, head of the British Ministry of Supply staff in Australia, was also in London, and his reaction has been described by the historian of the Woomera range, Ivan Southall.

Evetts, together with Butement and Professor L. H. Martin, the Defence Scientific Adviser to the Australian Government, took the problem to Tizard , he says. 'Sir Henry came through on their side, and his verdict was final. He sent them back to Australia to build a general-purpose range, not 3,000 miles long but 30 miles long, to test purely defensive weapons. "If the range is there", he said, "it will attract the work as a magnet attracts iron filings." ' Years later, not long before Sir Henry's death, Butement met him in London and reminded him of his prophetic words. 'Did I really say that', he said. 'It was very appropriate wasn't it'.[6]

During 1948 he visited shipyards, conferred with the Service authorities and succeeded, as usual, in leaving behind him the impression that whatever the politicians might be doing, matters would be quite safe in his own capable hands. This was no less than true, and with Tizard presiding over the periodical meetings of the Commonwealth Committee on Defence Science, there was the minimum chance of misunderstanding – either with Australia or with Canada, which he visited again in 1951.

In London, he took a personal interest in the development of the Joint Intelligence Bureau, whose members were able to draw on him for advice on the multiplying scientific aspects of their work. He stimulated the growth of operational research. And when, early in his chairmanship of the Defence Research Policy Committee, the general shortage of scientific staff and of materials made cuts in defence projects inevitable, the cuts were made so that damage was kept to a minimum. Thus Tizard and the other scientists helped. That they were not able to help more, that the safety of the country continued to remain ever a few hundred million pounds away, was due not only to the destruction of all existing conceptions which nuclear weapons had brought about, which was now being understood and even more slowly admitted. It was due also to the Government's belief that Jerusalem could be built, if not overnight at least very quickly, in England's green and post-war land. For the erection of the Welfare State was intimately linked – in terms of the available resources of men, materials, and money – with the military defence of the country in the nuclear age. This was of course a prime reason for having a chairman common to both the scientific committees. And it was emphasized by one of the first and one of the last of Tizard's actions in the joint role.

Within a few days of going to the Ministry of Defence he had asked for figures showing the proportion of their national incomes which the United Kingdom and the Commonwealth Governments had spent on defence during the preceding ten years. Much, he felt, could be learned not only by studying the size of the various national cakes, but also the ways in which they were cut up between civilian and Service needs. Four years later, as he was about to retire, he called for the detailed study of a policy of large-scale emigration from Britain to the Dominions and Colonies, since 'it would be extremely dangerous in my opinion to base a long-term policy on the belief that food supplies will become ample and cheap before many years have passed'. He contemplated figures of five million emigrants within ten to fifteen years and called for three main enquiries – 'a considered statement of the future of agriculture in this country . . . a study of the prospect of greatly increasing the food production in the countries within the sterling area', and the examination, on the assumption that Britain could not hope to recover and maintain a stable condition or prosperity with its present population, of 'the probable effects of large-scale emigration'.

Interlocking of the civilian and the Service problems dominated much of Tizard's thought during the immediate post-war years. So did the need to increase productivity, a matter which runs through a majority of the civilian Advisory Council's activities. This body made informed technical reports on subjects as varied as standard of nutrition and the quality of coal supplied by the National Coal Board. When the Chancellor of the Exchequer, Sir Stafford Cripps, recommended a lowering of food rations, the Council pointed out that this would lower production and by reducing exports would affect the balance of payments adversely. And at the end of 1947, it set up the Committee on Industrial Productivity under Tizard's chairmanship.*

* The Council died in 1951, with the exception of the Panel on Import

He himself was in no doubt as to what this could achieve. 'The Prime Minister', he said when addressing the annual meeting of the Parliamentary and Scientific Committee in February 1948, 'has said that the economic problems of the country would be largely solved by an all-round 10 per cent increase in productivity. Speaking as a scientist, I think this target is too low, and that we should aim at getting a 50 per cent increase as soon as we possibly can. That is perfectly practicable with good will all round.' To help achieve it, four groups were established under his main committee. They dealt with operational research, import substitutes, the provision of technical information, and human relations. Their work and their reports laid the foundation for the massive 'productivity movement' which within the next few years was sweeping the Continent. Britain alone, Tizard must have contemplated ruefully, appeared neither anxious nor willing to learn the lesson.

He was essentially the practical man, and he appears to have felt that much of the Advisory Council's work was passed on only to be bedevilled by good intentions. One sentence in the memorandum he signed in 1949 and which gave the Council's observations on the report of the United Nations Secretary-General to the Economic and Social Council was a good indication of his attitude. The report, he noted, 'set out in general terms a great many aspirations which are obviously worthy of support but which would have been of greater value if accompanied by clearer indications of the means by which they could be put into practice.'

Trying to get things 'put into practice' was a constant preoccupation with Tizard throughout these years as head of the two scientific advisory committees – and there was much to be said for Ian Mikardo's comment in *The New Statesman* that the civilian committee had 'no powerful channel to get its views accepted; and . . . operates only through the painful process of one-sided negotiations with vested interests'. This civilian committee, on which Professor Zuckerman played the part of an increasingly strong right hand, advised on a vast range of subjects – from coast erosion to State scholarships at Provincial universities; from the

---

Substitution which became the Natural Resources (Technical) Committee in its own right.

DD

possible re-opening of Cornish tin mines to the collection of medical statistics by the National Health Service and the increased use of nitrogenous fertilizers. It also, in 1950, reported in favour of Britain developing her own nuclear power. Until this date one of the main objects of Britain's nuclear research had been to discover the best way of building a nuclear weapon – although discretion had tended to conceal the details from friend and potential foe alike. Now, it was suggested by the Atomic Energy Committee, Britain should turn her sights towards nuclear power. Its report went to the Lord President with a covering note giving the scientific policy committee's comments. There was first the warning that Ministers should not be led to expect an abundance of cheap power. However, this consideration was balanced by two others. Both the Americans and the Russians would possibly develop nuclear power for industrial use; if Britain failed to do so, there would probably be two results. She would be left behind in the acquisition of technical knowledge, and she would be left behind economically, particularly when it came to the supply of equipment to overseas customers. The result, after some discussion, was the nuclear power programme whose current version continues today.

However, it would be unwise to stress this one example too strongly. For the Advisory Council on Scientific Policy could only advise. And its effects can be seen rather in a changing attitude in Whitehall – slowly-changing is perhaps more accurate – than in any spectacular record of success. Here the main result of Tizard's personal efforts, as in the Service Committee, was the movement of opinion at the top towards always considering, if not always accepting, serious scientific advice.

That no-one could have done better was due mainly to Tizard's three-fold reputation – with the Services, in Whitehall, and in organized science. In 1948 he became better known to a yet wider audience with his election as President of the British Association and his Presidential Address on 'The Passing World'. When it came to putting a point of view to the Service chiefs, arguing with Civil Servants or scientists, or explaining to the general public just why such and such an action was necessary, Tizard could show the gleam of genius. It would be wrong, however, to suppose that his return to Whitehall aroused no opposition or that he fulfilled all the hopes either of himself or of his friends. The comment of one high Service friend that he was 'disappointed and disappointing' may be harsh but contains a seed of truth. He had come to power too late and the power, when it came to the crunch, was too slight. For the Service Committee on which all depended had practically no executive power in the period during which Tizard chaired it and could therefore make little more than isolated raids against the entrenched positions held by vested interests in the Civil Service and the three military Services. Tizard accepted the position and it is possible that with the forces he could muster he had no alternative. He may well have thought, as well as hoped, that things would be different. He had expected the going to be uphill but he had no reason to expect that it would be vertical. He had, moreover, little faith that the machinery of Government would be efficiently oiled by the milk of Socialist kindness. He had begun to develop a technique of 'running' his committee-colleagues that was often justified, always efficient, and sometimes resented.

All these things made his job more difficult than it would otherwise have been. A yet more significant handicap was his lack of interest in the mechanism of power. For most of his life he had held himself aloof from politics, and had therefore failed to develop the sensitive tactile antennae which men who govern thrust out around themselves to discover how events are moving. Yet the scientific adviser to any of the Services, let alone to the Minister of Defence, – Tizard's real post, even though in theory he was merely chairman of the D.R.P.C. – now had to be more than a first-class scientist who was trusted by the men in uniform. The scientist had, at least in certain respects, been hoisted to the level which he had eyed for so long; he could at last not merely advise but might be able to exert pressure to get his advice accepted, thus he needed to use the somewhat contradictory qualities of scientist and politician. This, however, was an exercise for which he had little sympathy – 'I am inclined', he said in 1951, 'to agree with Professor Blackett's remark that if scientists became politicians they would act like politicians.'[7]

There was, moreover, that deft and almost dangerous facility for pulling officialdom's tail which he could never entirely subdue. 'Tizard loved to put the cat among the pigeons', says Lockspeiser, one of his colleagues for years, 'and with a brain like Tizard's it was some cat'. There was, for instance, a 'Rag Report' from the Advisory Council, the product of a colleague in Tizard's secretariat which Tizard duly had circulated on official paper – with a great deal of glee. At first this suspends disbelief; and it is only on reading later pages that one begins to doubt the authenticity of a report which concludes: 'Neither do we at this stage recommend the abolition of the National Health Service; but if (contrary to our expectation) it should result in an improvement in the nation's health and length of life, we consider that the desirability of retaining it should be reconsidered. Defence research and development should be actively encouraged since it is to be hoped that it will ultimately lead to a reduction if not of the population of this country, at least to that of others. Finally the Council recommend that, when all the foregoing steps have been carried out, they themselves should be dissolved.'

He had, too, his own way of lampooning what he considered to be the foolishness of some aspects of defence policy, and shortly before leaving for Canada in 1951 circulated, as a Top Secret paper, a document purporting to give the latest thought of the Kremlin on the future of strategy. It had, he said in a covering note, been discovered among loose papers in a neglected drawer. The result was that while Tizard was peacefully touring the Canadian defence establishments, a considerable though private row sprang up in Britain. Intelligence authorities protested vigorously that the document was too secret to have been circulated. Lockspeiser, at first taken in, was one of the first to reflect that the paper was what he later called 'gorgeous satire'. Only after Tizard's return to Britain was it discovered that he had written it at Keston on odd bits of paper, and subsequently typed it himself.

Beneath his slightly professorial exterior there lurked a sense of the ridiculous. It was unfortunate that when in 1949 he was announced into the Presence to receive the insignia of the Knight Grand Cross of the Bath he should be announced with a long 'i' to his name. It was natural that he should whisper a correction: 'Tizard – rhymes with gizzard'. This ability to cut through the flummery created almost as many enemies as gusts of appreciative laughter, and there was more than one sigh of relief when it became known that he was considering retirement. He had agreed with Barlow that his appointment would be for five years, but by the end of 1949 he was beginning to show signs of overwork. On 18 October he wrote to his Minister, now Emanuel Shinwell, suggesting that Cockcroft should succeed him on the Defence Committee and that Brundrett should act as deputy for the next year or so while the change-over of responsibilities was taking place. This, it should be noted, was five months before the Socialist majority in the House fell to eight, and two years before the 1951 election brought Churchill and Cherwell back to Downing Street.

Tizard now began to ease himself out of his official responsibilities, to clear up his official papers for the last time, and to provide what help he could to his successor. Shortly before he left the Ministry he put down what he described as 'a few parting thoughts'. Some of them, he said, were unpleasant; many of them showed that his ideas had been modified under the pressure of events. In 1945, when he had prepared 'Some Thoughts on the Problems of British Security', he had remained optimistic. Although air power had profoundly altered the situation, he could say that

> to talk as if we would be an easy prey to our enemy in the next war, to speak of annihilation of the British Isles by air attack, seems to me to be taking a very gloomy view of the picture. New weapons are never so efficacious as is feared, or hoped, as the case may be. No unanswerable weapon or method of warfare has yet been devised. I sometimes think that this is a pity; if there were an unanswerable weapon perhaps civilised nations would not think war worth while, because both sides would be annihilated. If the laws of duelling had compelled opponents to stand a yard apart, with pistols at each others hearts, there would have been no duels.

Now the facts of war were moving to create just such a situation. However, it was still the economic threat to which Tizard drew primary attention. 'Two exhausting wars', he pointed out, 'have reduced us from a first-class Power, and prosperous nation, to a second-class Power on the verge of bankruptcy. I use the words "first-class" and "second-class" in the quantitative sense; the quality is still high.' He pointed out that the United States and Russia could both grow enough food and also had ample sources of raw material under their control. 'That is why they can stand the shock of war, and we cannot, even when victorious', he went on.

> If we become involved in another great war before our industry is restored to health and vigour, and before we can pay our way year by year with confidence, we shall be ruined, win or lose. Widespread distress and starvation will follow. Nothing is gained by reluctance to face this ugly probability. The conclusion I draw [he added], is that our own present strategy should be to create the maximum insurance against war rather than the maximum contribution to a possible major conflict between the United States and the U.S.S.R.

To Tizard, this was the reasonable, logical, conclusion, and as a man of integrity he felt compelled to put it down in black and white. As he left Whitehall for the last time he must have wondered what the politicians would make of it.

CHAPTER SIXTEEN

Final Years

Tizard had now withdrawn from the official arena, and it is tempting to ask whether during the previous three decades he had revealed the qualities of a 'great man'. Tizard himself might very well have answered 'No – thank Heavens!' In the early 1940's he had explained his pessimism by saying that during the First World War he had not known the men at the top; this time he did – hence his fears. He was dubious about the way the mechanics of politics worked. And he would probably have agreed that there were only a few exceptions to Acton's second and lesser-known sentence on power – that 'great men are always bad men'. He was suspicious of the roads that took many men to the top, but even had he wished to follow one of them he would have held back from the venture, wondering for a long while whether it was the proper course to take. 'Greatness', says Humbert Wolfe, 'is to hear the bugles and not to doubt.' With Tizard, a thought for the consequences of action, sweet reason, and a consideration for the other side kept creeping in. At times the necessary iron was lacking. Thus he was good rather than great; his influence more lasting than spectacular. Yet overhanging all, there is the blunt fact that without the Biggin Hill Experiment the Battle of Britain would have been lost.

Men like Tizard do not retire. They continue to pursue the same ends by different means, merely diverting their energies into other channels. It was natural, therefore, that from 1952 onwards, he should continue to press his beliefs – above all that of the value to the nation of the scientific approach – not only in a succession of masterly lectures but also in an entirely fresh field, that of business and finance. For more than one reason he was glad to enter the commercial world, which he had for so long regarded from the other side of the fence. He had given up his pension rights on leaving the D.S.I.R. in 1929; he had done the same thing again when he retired from the Presidency of Magdalen in 1947. And the terms which he had been able to wring from the Treasury on joining the Ministry of Defence bore no relation to his work for the country since 1935. Thus the man who had done so much to save 'the Few', who had laid the foundations both of Anglo-U.S. scientific co-operation during the war and of British defence science after it, was now left with an income of a few pounds a week that was fitting, fair, and just according to Government accountancy, but nevertheless derisory.

Two motives therefore lay behind the bids that were made for Tizard's services in the early 1950's. His knowledge of that country where the frontiers of industry, science, and administration all meet was unrivalled; and it was no doubt shrewdly estimated that during a period of growing Government intervention a man with Tizard's knowledge of Whitehall would be of special use. But it was also felt that industry should play its part in redressing the balance of the Treasury. If Tizard had done no more than sit complacently on the Boards of half-a-dozen companies for half-a-dozen fat fees, many would have felt that he was getting no more than his due. However, any feeling that he was to be acquired as a figurehead was quickly dispelled. Between 1952 and 1958 he served as director or adviser with some half-dozen firms; all found he had retained his peculiar and sometimes disconcerting ability to note the one badly-fitting piece of the jig-saw, to ask the one dangerously leading and possibly unanswerable question. The simple explanation was the breadth of his experience, but the result was sometimes uncanny.

The first approach came from Glaxo, whose board he joined early in 1952. He agreed 'to watch the progress of research and development and to advise . . . on policy' and in his usual manner, he added in a letter of acceptance to Sir Harry Jephcott 'I want to repeat that if you should find at any time that the arrangement is not of such value as you hoped, it shall be terminated without the smallest trace of ill-feeling on my part.' He began, as usual, by closely scrutinizing the economic background of the company, followed it up by the first of a regular series of visits to the research stations, and was soon busy making suggestions for improvement

– including the revolutionary one that 'Directors of Research should be allowed to spend 10 per cent of their budgets on research of their own choosing provided it fell within the normal activities of the Company.'

He was nearly seventy now, but he still produced results that resembled those of the Biggin Hill days. After one visit to a Glaxo laboratory he wrote expressing doubts as to his value to the company. 'In so far as I am one part of Glaxo you certainly do me good', replied one of the senior research staff, 'I always have at least one jolt during questioning either of myself or others . . . You may reasonably say, I suppose, that I oughtn't to require this treatment and that we oughtn't to expect someone like yourself to spend time in this way: but however this may be, you certainly help me a great deal and I'm very warmly appreciative.' So were many others.

In 1953 he was drawn into a wider industrial circle, being brought onto the Board of Solway Chemicals of Whitehaven to which he now made a monthly journey. He would inspect progress in the works, attend the Board meeting, and sometimes walk the five miles to St Bees across St Bees Head, intently interested in the masses of sea-birds which he saw at close quarters for the first time.

His use to Solway Chemicals lay not only in his advice on the multitudinous technological problems that had to be overcome. He also revealed his practical common-sense on less scientific matters. There was, for instance, the problem of sulphuric acid mist at the Whitehaven works. The troubles that this was alleged to cause were much in dispute. In particular there seemed no forseeable end to the litigation which had dragged on between the firm and one former employee who claimed that the mist prevented him from growing dahlias in his small nursery garden. It was difficult to prove whether this was true – until Tizard came up with the proposal that finally settled the problem. 'Buy the next garden and try to grow dahlias there', he advised.

In 1951 Tizard joined the Board of Albright & Wilson and later became consultant to Humphreys & Glasgow. In both cases there was one expected result – 'his greatest value to us', says one fellow-director, 'was that he was perpetually asking awkward questions.'

But there was also another result, for Tizard showed a grasp of company accounts, and a facility for assessing them, which suggested that he might have flourished as well in the business as in the scientific world.

These regular interests now formed much of the background to his life. But he was still interested in a multitude of separate projects. After hearing a broadcast by the Minister of Transport on road accidents, he proposed that the Insurance companies might well finance an investigation into their causes, since they had a mass of statistics which might throw fresh light on the problem. He was invited with A. V. Hill to attend the Fourth Pakistan Science Conference in Peshawar and four years later was sought out by the State of Oklahoma to speak at their Centenary celebrations. The latter was Tizard's first visit to the United States as a private citizen for more than forty years, and he was forced by the immigration authorities to fill in a lengthy questionnaire which asked, among other things, for his occupation. In view of his past, and the fact that he was now virtually retired, he found difficulty in saying anything worth while in the space provided. He made some attempt of a formal kind, gave it up, and entered the words 'domestic drudge.'

At the time of the Suez crisis there was a revival of his wartime scheme for the underwater movement of petrol to Malta, and he was co-opted on an unofficial basis to bring together two separate groups working on a plan to tow petrol supplies around the Cape. He served as Consultant to the Atomic Energy Authority for a number of years, and was asked to advise on, among other things, the growth of Harwell and its satellites – an ironic task in view of his earlier views about nuclear energy.

For six years, he was a member of the National Research Development Corporation which had been formed in 1948 to exploit British inventions and processes. It was not altogether a happy experience, partly no doubt because of Tizard's own attitude. 'I am one of the people appointed to help the Corporation to succeed in its task', he said, 'but I must admit that I do not altogether like it in principle. I do not like to feel that British leaders of industry are becoming less adventurous, and that a Government Committee has to be appointed to manage the adventure for them.'[1] He also thought, as he wrote to an economist friend, that the Corporation suffered 'under the difficulty of all bodies which spend taxpayers' money. It cannot be so adventurous as a well conducted private company or even finance house.' There was more than one letter in his old contentious style to Lord Halsbury, then the Corporation's Managing Director, and misunderstandings occurred. Other members of the Corporation, gathering for their monthly three-hour meeting to discuss policy, would find Tizard anxious to leave on time for a meeting somewhere else. They would feel that he was attempting too much, giving his best to those companies on whose Boards he sat, and not always in touch with what had been going on. Tizard sometimes felt that he had been wasting three hours.

He also became a member of the North Thames Gas Board, and immediately set about studying the statistics. Any hope that he might be a mere passenger was dispersed two months after his appointment. 'Your productivity figures are depressing', he wrote. 'How this country is going to get over its economic troubles when large capital sums have to be spent in order to regain pre-war productivity, I don't know. The coal industry, the dockers, the railways, road transport, the building industry . . . all have the same story to tell. . . . Has anyone on your staff ever considered the layout of a works for the generation of gas *and* electricity? In other words, have you ever indulged in the academic exercise of forgetting that two antipathetic nationalised industries exist, and considering what you would do if they were sympathetic and free from prejudice? From what I read and hear it would be useless to put this question to the present leaders of the Electricity Board.' But, it was claimed, it was not the leaders who were at fault. The real difficulty, he was informed, was that 'labour has got to be treated so carefully these days, particularly in a nationalized industry, that one is forced to go very slowly and not introduce too many reforms all at the same time.' Tizard left the Board after his initial one-year appointment.

He remained as outspoken as ever. In his Messel Memorial Lecture to the Society of Chemical Industry he added a postscript to his own efforts on advising the Government when he said that 'in this year of 1952, seven years after the Second World War ended, we still depend on charity from overseas to avoid bankruptcy. Shortage of raw materials, high taxation, controls and restrictions hamper enterprise and adventure. I do not think that the serious state of the country is sufficiently realised; certainly not by the average working man, who is more politically intelligent than the average working man of any other country. Can one blame him for not being able to see the dangerous condition of the economic structure of this country, when it is hidden by a false facade of full employment and of record output, and profits of the manufacturing industry; and when no political leader tells him the truth in plain language.'

He was sceptical of many things – of the dangers of nuclear radiation, of the time needed to 'make democracy conscious of Christianity or anything really worth-while', and of most politicians who, he noted, 'gradually form the opinions which seem to me to have stuck out for years'. To a correspondent asking him to support abolition of the death penalty, he replied that he was not in favour of unqualified abolition, adding that he was 'more interested in the expectation of life of policemen than in the expectation of life of murderers'. Of the business world which he had glimpsed at close quarters for a short while, he remained questioning and slightly aghast. Writing to his old friend Colonel Cooper only a few weeks before his death, he noted of a mutual acquaintance in the Royal Air Force that he 'didn't get a peerage which was bad luck; so he missed the chance of £30,000 tax free for getting kicked out of one chairmanship, and being promptly appointed to another at £10,000. Can you wonder at the attitude of the working man when such things happen in the City?'

When he returned to Whitehall in 1947, he may have hoped that the Socialist Government was at last to put the country's defences on a planned, orderly, basis. He may have hoped that the same would be done with the country's scientific resources. But he seems, in his later years, to have reacted to the lassitude which he felt was being induced throughout Britain by increased Government control, whichever party was in power. 'We like to fancy we are at the beginning of a new and glorious Elizabethan age', he said in the Messel lecture. 'The first Elizabethan age was glorious because it was adventurous. It was adventurous in war,

in exploration, in literature and in the arts. We must encourage
the spirit of adventure in all walks of life, particularly industry,
without which British influence will become negligible.'

Two things stand out from his records of the 1950's. One is the
influence which he still wielded in Government circles. On one
occasion, as he wrote to a friend, 'the directors of a certain large
firm came to me and told me that they had been refused sanction
to spend capital on the development of a new process. They had
the money, they had the steel, they had the bricks, they had the
labour – they had everything except the permission of Civil Servants, and that they could not get. I thought the development was
of importance and they freely gave me their confidential information and allowed me to cross-examine the witnesses concerned. As
a result I wrote a private letter to the head of the Government
department concerned, and said I was not expressing any opinion
but I wished he would look into the matter personally and satisfy
himself that the refusal was justified.' The firm got its sanction
within a week. Secondly, there was his attitude to money, distinctive if not quixotic. When he received a cheque for 300 dollars
for his help in organizing an Executive Conference at Queen's
University, Ontario, and for speaking there, he insisted on returning the cheque. After a business visit to the United States he
attempted to repay a trifling difference in his expense allowance,
only to be informed by the company that 'the difference is too
small to bother about'. On another occasion he was offered
£5,000 – in notes if he preferred it that way – by a rich business
colleague who felt that Tizard had more than earned that amount
by his help and advice. Tizard refused; the business man insisted;
eventually there was evolved a compromise by which the money
was presented 'by an unknown donor' to a cause which Tizard
had much at heart.

He could usually be persuaded to find time for work which he
thought worth-while, and in the autumn of 1950 succeeded
Oliphant as Chairman of the Royal Society's Rutherford Memorial Committee. He took immense trouble over the Society's
obituary memoir of his old tutor, Sidgwick, who died in 1952,
and once again noted, as he had noted with his D.N.B. memoir
of Rutherford, that facts, figures, and dates given by scientists were

as variable as those given by other mortal men. 'I have resolved never to write another obituary except my own, to save other people trouble', he wrote to his friend Rivett. 'It will be rather a nasty one.'

Those who required his help had to be prepared for the Tizard technique. Thus when he was asked to become chairman of the Southern Regional Council for Further Education, he replied by asking for reasons. The persuader, Mr Brewer of Oxford University's Inorganic Chemistry Laboratory, replied by explaining how the southern region was mainly an agricultural area and how necessary it was for people in the area to appreciate the needs for, and the possibilities of, technical education. They must have someone who would be more than a figurehead. There came a brief note saying: 'Dear Brewer, Blast you, I've accepted.'

He had been a Governor of Westminster School since the early days of the war, and was now able to give more time to its affairs. He opposed too conservative a policy. He felt very deeply about the way in which the needs of the School had been neglected before the Governing Body had been set up in 1869, and he was a powerful advocate for the better teaching of science and for the planned use of the money which had now become available from the Industrial Fund, set up to provide new laboratories for schools throughout the country. The number of his Honorary Degrees and Honorary Fellowships multiplied, and in 1952 he became a Pro-Chancellor of the newly-created Southampton University – when he stressed the need for literate technologists and liberal scientists.*

He was never under the delusion that science provided more than one of many roads to a useful human existence and in a letter to the 'Daily Telegraph' little more than a year before his death, he asked whether it was not about time that the 'absurd and historically unjustified distinction between humanists and

* Tizard's Honorary Degrees were D.C.L. Durham University, 1943; Ll.D. Queensland University, 1943; D.Sc. Leeds University, 1945; D.Sc. Cambridge University, 1946; Ll.D. Edinburgh University, 1946; Ll.D. Sheffield University, 1948; D.Sc. Reading University, 1951; D.Sc. Manchester University, 1952; D.Sc. University of London, 1956. He was made an Honorary Fellow of Oriel (1933), Imperial College (1942), Magdalen (1947), and University College, London (1954).

scientists was dropped? A humanist has come to mean a man who has had a higher education which had completely neglected science. How do you define a humanist? Not as one, I hope, "who has his studies behind him". Is a doctor, who spends his life studying human beings, a humanist? No, because he has had a scientific education. Is a philosopher a humanist? Yes, so long as he is not a natural philosopher. Is a man who devotes himself to the study of a narrow branch of the Classics a humanist? Yes, but I doubt if he would be considered eligible for the highest positions in industry. Is a chartered accountant a humanist? I suppose the answer must be "Yes" because (a) he usually knows nothing about science and (b) he is often highly successful in business.'[2]

He had always staked a large claim for science, but there had always been common-sense about it, and when he became the Vice-Chairman of the Parliamentary and Scientific Committee in 1952, he commented that 'the proper application of science to the needs of the nation cannot be determined by scientists alone, any more than it can be determined except on the basis of the best scientific advice available'.

Such views were being accepted. Of that he felt certain. But the pace was too slow. More prodding was needed. More energetic, thought-provoking questioning. With, from time to time, a fair-sized cat let loose among the Whitehall pigeons. This attitude, a young man's adventuring attitude, stands clear-cut, although in various guises, from the five or six major lectures and addresses which he gave in the 1950's.

In 1951 he had been asked to give the Arthur Dehon Little Memorial Lecture during the Massachusetts Institute of Technology's Centenary celebrations. His Lecture discussed 'Science and Democracy' and Tizard was later chosen to speak during a panel discussion on population problems. Two of the four speakers tended to be prophets of doom. Tizard and his old friend Vannevar Bush, were, as Bush puts it, 'added as a sort of counter-irritant'. After the opening moves, the discussion was thrown open to questions from the floor. 'Two Indians, apparently not students, sat in the front row and proceeded to direct at Tizard some questions, supposed to be embarrassing I think, about the Indian population problem', says Bush. 'Tizard answered courteously and said, among other things that during Britain's involvement in Indian affairs the population there had increased by some fifty million, and that this had intensified the problem for the Indian Government. He then turned to the Moderator and commented: "You do not have this problem with your American Indians, do you?"[3]

More important than the M.I.T. paper was the Messel Memorial Lecture on 'The Strategy of Science'. In this he argued for the place that science should hold in national life, once again made his plea for industrial adventure and enterprise, and challenged the existing system under which 'the responsibility for deciding whether any branch of industry shall spend anything on new ventures rests largely with civil servants in government departments.' The following year his lecture on 'Government and Science' read at the University of Belfast provided a leading illustration of his belief that the sinews of a nation sprang from research. It was typical that he should start his detailed enquiries by writing to a former colleague in the Civil Service and asking: 'Can you help me by getting someone to dig out the total Government expenditure on scientific research in the years 1900, 1910, 1920, 1930, 1940 and 1950. I want the information for a lecture I have to give in Belfast.

'Omit Defence research, but include all grants given to independent bodies, e.g. the Royal Society. It would save me trouble if you could also give me the total grants to universities and university colleges for the same years . . .'

He was ambivalent about the Civil Service itself, as is shown by his Haldane lecture, 'A Scientist In and Out of the Civil Service', and to the end of his life he concerned himself with the problem of marrying up Treasury control with the uncertainty of producing viable results from defence research. That he was still the master of defence science was shown by his Lees-Knowles lectures on the impact which war had made on science, while during the 1950's his assessment of the impact of nuclear weapons became surer and clearer. From the first he had felt that their use had on balance been a gain, although he wished 'that they could have been used in a way less shocking to the civilised world'. His report to the Chiefs of Staff, written before the dropping of the bombs had, as he said in a letter to Blackett on 18 September 1958, 'emphasised that in future it might well be said that the atomic bomb was the greatest contribution to peace that science had ever offered.' He had believed for years that the prospects of a major nuclear war were remote, although local wars would still have to be dealt with, and in mid-1950 he summed up his beliefs in a letter which he drafted to Wansbrough-Jones. 'I cannot myself envisage a war on a global scale between advanced nations', this said.

If for instance Russia went to war with the United States, dragging the U.K. and other western countries in, the only effect would be that countries like China would win, unless the radio-activity dissipated over the earth was too much even for them.

In the present state of the world, I feel it is necessary to keep building up stocks of modern atomic bombs and methods of delivering them, merely to make the prospect of war still more absurd than it is now. Any agreement to limit or abolish nuclear warfare would merely make the chance of another world war greater, and it would in the end involve nuclear warfare.

The only way to stop war on the large scale definitely is to reach agreement for the virtual abolition of all fighting forces and to reduce them to something like a police force. The prospect of such an agreement seems at present rather remote, but that it will eventually come I am sure.

Tizard had no doubt of what some of the repercussions would be.

Have you ever considered what would happen if the Prince of Peace really descended on the earth and abolished all war, all fighting Services, and all Defence Research and Development? [he wrote to a friend in Canada at Christmas 1953]. I fancy that Canada would stand the shock as well as most countries, but the U.S.A. would have to throw out the Republicans & develop a Newer Deal of colossal proportions.

He had taken part in the conference on limiting warfare out of which had grown the Institute for Strategic Studies and became an original member of its Council. He was sought by the Air Ministry when advice was needed about the scientists best able to guide the destinies of the Royal Air Force through the perplexities of the 1960's. The Canadians still felt that when they wanted advice on science and defence they should ask for Tizard, and in

1954 they invited him to Ottawa to discuss the implications of atomic and hydrogen weapons on the future of war; and on the growing complexity of weapons systems with all that these involved. Tizard accepted, toured Canadian defence and research laboratories, visited Washington where he was 'mainly engaged in trying to collect records of my 1940 mission, which are hard to get at in London,' and attended a seminar at Queen's University where some forty Presidents and Vice-Presidents of companies listened 'for a week to Professors and others, most of whom had had no experience of business.' On his return to Britain he prepared for his Canadian friends a 4,000-word report covering research in their country which is a remarkable document – cool, impartial and questioning.

His papers of this period are full of letters requesting facts and figures for lectures which he was committed to give, or might be giving. He would 'work them up' at various stages, write short summaries of the points he wished to make, and on occasion type a fuller set of notes. One such double-page, apparently written some three years before his death, and dealing with the outlook for the human race, sums up some of the lessons of his life.

Tizard starts by noting that for the first time mankind was able 'to get within measurable distance of extinguishing human life altogether'. He suggested that the chances of survival were no better than even. And he noted that 'for centuries now the real division has been between those who believe in a revealed, absolute dogma (no matter what form it may take), which invariably leads to intolerance and repression, and those who believe in what is in fact the scientific method, i.e. the search for truth based strictly on the evidence, no matter where it may lead.' He found it difficult not to be pessimistic, noted how vital it was 'that there should be a sufficient background of general education if we are not to become a community of philistines with a high material standard of living', and summed up the chances for the future with a paragraph on human behaviour.

Finally [he asks in this], what are the prospects of man becoming a more moral, less anti-social animal than he is at present. That depends, to my mind, not on any resurgence of faith in mystical beliefs or divine laws, but on the hope that the ordinary man will learn to think more clearly for himself. So long as he is told that moral principles are based on arbitrary laws handed down from some supernatural source, he will always be apt to kick over the traces, if only as a protest against arbitrary authority. Once he learns to look upon them as resting on plain commonsense and enlightened self-interest, and to see that it is much cleverer to take a long rather than a short view of his true interests, then I believe there is a real hope of raising standards of human behaviour. For some reason, the organised religions have always gone to great lengths to deny that moral behaviour was based on reasonable principles, and have asked us to believe that to act unreasonably was in some ways better than to act from sound practical motives. No wonder human manners leave a great deal to be desired.

It was natural that Tizard should thus be still speculating, asking himself in the words of his question to the Magdalen candidate, 'what it is all about'. He still bore that hall-mark of the first-class mind, an interest in everything new that he saw. And that he still had a good deal of energy is suggested by a letter to his old friend Threlfall in August 1958, after returning from a fishing holiday in Ireland. '. . . I had a good Friday morning in Dublin', he said. 'Saw Swift's grave & dropped a tear on Stella's. Went to T.C.D. which I think is a magnificent place. The library is worth a much longer visit that I could give it. I then went to see the Irish antiquities at the Museum. By the time I had finished with them it was time I went to the Airport, so I took a taxi, went out of the way round Phoenix Park, & arrived at the airport about ½ hour before the plane left, a long enough interval to get a sandwich & a Guinness!'

He was still mentally crisp, but the effect of the hard years was beginning to tell. He spent more time working in his study at Keston, less at the Athenaeum, and less still making those seemingly endless journeys to conferences or meetings, or interviews with individuals who wanted his advice, and his alone, on some problem of importance.

He looked back with more impartiality than most men would have been able to summon up, and his comments on Churchill provide a perfect example of how, to the end, he was intent on doing 'the right scientific thing'. In April 1959 he was asked by the editor of 'Engineering' for his views on Sir Winston's influence on science and engineering. 'The fact is', he replied, 'that in my experience Sir Winston Churchill has had neither a great influence on science and engineering, nor indeed has he displayed any real interest in science. For instance, he was elected a Fellow of the Royal Society in 1941. He has not displayed the slightest interest in the Society ever since, and did not even come to the Society to sign the Charter Book. As for his interest in applied science, I think I can truthfully say that when I was quite intimately concerned with his doings in this respect, before and during the first two years of the war, Mr Churchill as he was then, was always pressing for the wrong developments against the advice of most scientists concerned. This does not mean that he had no influence on applied science and engineering; the very fact that he was enthusiastic about everything that in his opinion could help to win the war, was of great value.' Many might have left it at that. But Tizard continued: 'I think he is such a great man that it is a pity to exaggerate his doings in every direction. He has surely done enough for his reputation to be established for ever. Personally I think the great motto in referring to him is "Be to his virtues ever kind and to his faults a little blind". I am not sure that I have this quotation right, but it conveys what I mean.'

The rift with Cherwell was never completely closed. Tizard's attitude was revealed a few years before his death when a relative implied that it was he, rather than Cherwell, who had taken the famous notes during the spinning incident of forty years earlier. 'Oh, no, it was Lindemann', he answered. 'Give the devil his due.'

Towards Watson-Watt he adopted much the same attitude. A few years earlier, when Sir Robert, as he had become in 1942, brought his claim for the development of radar before the Royal Commission on Awards to Inventors, Tizard was about to leave for the United States. But he provided a generous and lengthy statement, supporting Watson-Watt's claim and thus helping to bring about the substantial award to the scientists concerned. When, seven years later, he was asked to review Watson-Watt's autobiographical account of radar, he politely declined.

My review would not be of a kind to give him pleasure and I should dislike writing anything for publication which would give him pain [he wrote], especially as I had a high opinion of his work before and during the war. Perhaps this view is reinforced by his description of me as a *Cambridge* physical chemist.

He held strong personal views about accepting either money or honours, but these were offset by what he regarded as the shabby treatment accorded to many of the men who had won the radar or radio-war – men to whom, as he put it, the country owed 'an immeasurable debt, which has been recognised, in one or two cases, by the award of the O.B.E.'

He saw little hope of the full story of the scientists' war ever being told, and he feared that his long conflict with Cherwell might be portrayed with more bitterness than he felt was warranted. He completed his 'personal record' for the Royal Society, omitting the most contentious facts but noting that his two pre-war Scientific Committees had been 'ended as a result of political intrigue'. He began to put his papers and reports in order, and he started work on the draft of an autobiography. He had toyed with the idea of writing a short book on his American Mission of 1940 but appears to have been discouraged by the difficulty of obtaining access to records; and he decided that to write his own story of how defence science had developed between 1934 and 1945 would, as he put it, 'cause too much distress to those still living'. The autobiography on which he had started was an altogether gentler affair, designed solely for the information of his relatives, affectionately recalling the past, spiced with distant kindly gossip, and describing a world which to a younger generation had the remote quality of the early Middle Ages.

By the autumn of 1959 Tizard had taken his first draft only to the mid-1920's. During the previous months he had shed a number of business responsibilities. He was beginning to 'take things carefully', and there are some indications that he felt more than normal concern for his health. Yet there was little specific warning when he collapsed suddenly at Keston on the evening of 8 October. The cause was a cerebral haemorrhage, and he died early the following morning.

It was probably as he would have wished. When his old friend Sir Frank Heath died in 1946, Tizard wrote to Heath's son. His father, Tizard pointed out, had 'lived a long life and did great

work, and never lost interest in men and things, and I gather that
he died suddenly and without any suffering. So what more can
one ask for?'

His ashes were buried in the floor of the Oriel College Ante-
chapel, below a stone bearing his initials and the dates 1885–
1959. On 19 November, a Memorial Service was held in the
Henry VII Chapel, Westminster Abbey. It was a Service whose
setting Tizard would have appreciated and about whose congregation he would no doubt have had perceptive comments to make.
It included a fair cross-section of those among whom his life had
been spent – not only relations and representatives from the
various bodies he had helped to direct. It included, also, such
people as Bill Carpenter, the former head-porter from Imperial
College, now very old himself and racked with arthritis, who had
come from his home in south-east London. Tizard would have
liked that.

He had been one of those men of ability and charm who can do
most of the things they wish to do. They are limited only by their
self-imposed objectives and by the price which they are willing to
pay for success. Tizard's personal objectives had been modest. He
wished to see science used as he felt it should be used to help the
nation – and other nations for that matter; he wished to leave the
world a better place than he found it. But for himself he wanted
little more than did his old friend Sir Richard Threlfall, whose
'ambitions were of the homely friendly sort', as Tizard himself
put it. The wonder is not that he failed to reach the Lords or to
become Britain's first Minister of Science, but that his own aims
carried him so far, reined in as they were by his own rigid principles. For no man was quicker to pounce on any attempt to
smudge the line between right and wrong; no man more suspicious that when science or scientists entered the political arena the
fight would rarely be on equal terms. Thus in his attempts to
achieve what were really political ends he was handicapped by
an unwillingness to use anything that fell within his own clear
definition of intrigue, a definition including much that passes as
the common coin of political life. There is not the slightest indication that he ever regretted this; indeed, there was no reason why
he should. He had gone far. He was much loved. He knew that

with the passage of the years it would become ever clearer that the battle of 'the Few' had been won with the weapon of radar, handed to that bright company almost as the chocks were pulled away. He had, moreover, walked not merely with crowds but also with politicians and yet kept his virtue; in itself, perhaps, a considerable enough achievement for any man.

List of Sir Henry Tizard's publications, papers and lectures

Sir Henry Tizard's Papers, Lectures and Addresses, based on the bibliography compiled by Sir William Farren for his Royal Society Memoir (Biographical Memoirs of Fellows of the Royal Society, Volume 7, November, 1961).

PAPERS

1908 (With N. V. Sidgwick) 'The initial change of the radium emanation.' *Proc. Chem. Soc.*, **24**, 64.

1908 (With N. V. Sidgwick) 'The colour of cupric salts in aqueous solution.' *Trans. Chem. Soc.*, **93**, 187.

1910 'Mechanism of tautomeric change.' *Proc. Chem. Soc.*, **26**, 125.

1910 (With N. V. Sidgwick) 'The colour and ionization of cupric salts.' *Trans. Chem. Soc.*, **97**, 957.

1910 'The colour changes of methyl orange and methyl red in acid solution.' *Trans. Chem. Soc.*, **97**, 2477.

1910 'The hydrolysis of aniline salts measured colorimetrically.' *Trans. Chem. Soc.*, **97**, 2490.

1911 'The sensitiveness of indicators.' *Rep. Brit. Ass.*, p. 268.

1912 (With R. T. Lattey) 'The velocities of ions in dried gases.' *Proc. Roy. Soc. (A)*, 86, 349.

1912 (With J. S. Townsend) 'Effect of a magnetic force on the motion of negative ions in gas.' *Proc. Roy. Soc. (A)*, **87**, 337.

1913 (With J. S. Townsend) 'The motion of electrons in gases.' *Proc. Roy. Soc. (A)*, **88**, 33.

1917 'Methods of measuring aircraft performances.' *The Aeronautical Journal*, **21**, 108, 122.

1920 (With J. R. H. Whiston) 'The effect of a change in temperature on the colour changes of methyl orange, etc.' *Trans. Chem. Soc.*, **117**, 150.

1921 (With A. R. Roeree) 'The volumetric estimation of mixtures of acids and of bases, etc.' *Trans. Chem. Soc.*, **119**, 132.

1921 (With A. G. Marshall) 'The determination of aromatic hydrocarbons in mixtures of hydrocarbons.' *J. Soc. Chem. Ind.*, **40**, 20T.

1921 'The causes of detonation in internal combustion engines.' *Proc. N.E. Coast Inst. of Engrs. Shipbuilders*, May.

1922 (With A. G. Marshall) 'Method for the determination of the vapour pressure of hydrocarbon fuels and the estimation of dissolved air.' *J. Instn. Petroleum Tech.*, **8**, 217–223.

1922 (With D. R. Pye) 'Experiments on the ignition of gases for sudden compression.' *Phil. Mag.*, **44**, 79.

1924 (With D. R. Pye) 'The character of various fuels for internal combustion engines.' *Auto. Engr.*, **11**, 55, 98, 134. Also printed in the *Report of the Empire Fuels Committee*.

1924 'Fuel economy in flight.' *J. Roy. Aero. Soc.*, **28**, 604.

1926 (With D. R. Pye) 'Ignition of gases by sudden compression.' *Phil. Mag.* **1**, 1094.

1926 'Explosions in petrol engines.' *Trans. Faraday Soc.*, **22**, 352.

1927 (With R. W. Fenning) 'The dissociation of carbon dioxide at high temperatures.' *Proc. Roy. Soc. (A)*, **115**, 318.

BOOKS

1911 Revised and largely retranslated 6th German edition of Nernst's *Theoretical Chemistry*, for third English edition (Macmillan).

1938 Co-Editor: *Science of Petroleum* (O.U.P.).

SPECIAL LECTURES

1929 The Mather Lecture: 'Science and the new Industrial revolution.' *J. Textile Inst.*, **4**.

1932 First Hinchley Memorial Lecture: 'Chemical engineering and the aircraft industry.' *Trans. Inst. of Chem. Engrg.*, **10**, 87.

1934   Presidential Address to the Science Masters' Association:
        'Science and the industrial depression.' *School Sci. Rev.*,
        No. 59, p. 257.

1934   Presidential Address to Section L., British Association:
        'Science at the nniversities.' *Brit.Ass. Reports.*

1938   First Perin Memorial Lecture: 'Industrial research,
        present and future.' Publ. by the Tata Iron and Steel
        Co., January.

1939   Rutherford Memorial Lecture to the Chemical Society.
        Delivered March 29, Publ. *J. Chem. Soc.*, October 1946.

1948   Presidential Address to the British Association: 'The
        passing world.'

1950   Lees-Knowle Lectures, Cambridge: 'The influence of war
        on science.'

1951   Arthur Dehon Little Memorial Lecture at Mass. Inst.
        Technology: 'Science and democracy.' Publ. by M.I.T.

1952   Messel Memorial Lecture: 'The strategy of science'. *Chem.
        & Ind.*, p. 788.

1955   Haldane Memorial Lecture: 'A scientist in and out of the
        Civil Service.' Birkbeck College.

OTHER (SELECTED) ADDRESSES

1924   'Commonsense and aeronautics.' *J. Roy. Aero. Soc.*, **28**,
        632.

1928   'Scientific and industrial research.' *Roy. Colonial Inst. J.*,
        19, 186.

1931   'The British fuel problem: future possibilities.' *Chemistry
        at the Centenary Meeting. Brit. Ass.*

1944   'Problems of Aeronautical Research.' Parliamentary &
        Scientific Committee.

1946   'Science and the Services.' *Roy. United Services Instn. J.*,
        March.

1946   'Teamwork in research.' The Franklin Institute. 17, April
        1946.

1949   Address to the Annual Conference of the Institution of
        Professional Civil Servants.

1957   Address to the Frontiers of Science Foundation of
        Oklahoma.

OBITUARY NOTICES

1931 (With Sir Richard Threlfall) Sir William McCormick, *Proc. Roy. Soc. (A)*, **130**, xv.

1935 (With W. S. Farren) Hermann Glauert. *Obit. Not. Roy. Soc.*, **1**, 607.

1937 Sir R. Threlfall. *J. Chem. Soc.*, p. 186.

1946 Sir Frank Heath. *Nature*, **158**, 823, Dec. 7th, 1946.

1954 N. V. Sidgwick. *Obit. Not. Roy. Soc.*, **9**, 237.

Life of Lord Rutherford. *Dict. National Biography*.

Life of Sir Frank Heath. *Dict. National Biography*.

Life of Sir R. Threlfall. *Dict. National Biography*.

BROADCASTS

'Bertram Hopkinson': 5 March, 1937.

'Airships': 9 May, 1937.

'What More Do You Want From the Scientists?': 15 December, 1937.

'Lord Rutherford': 16 December, 1945.

'High Altitude Flying': 18 December, 1946.

Appendices

APPENDIX ONE

Letter sent from Sir Frank Heath to Henry Tizard on 5 May 1926, in reply to Tizard's request for further details of the new Co-Ordinating Committees of the Department of Scientific and Industrial Research.

Dear Tizard . . . you begin with a general statement of what you understand the policy to be so far as research for the fighting services is concerned and I think it accurately represents the position, though I should like to add one or two guarding statements.

You say these Committees 'will examine the proposals critically, will endeavour to co-ordinate the research work of the three departments and will provide such work as *they* decide should be carried out'. That is the intention, but obviously it will be necessary to make sure that the decision of the Board for undertaking the special piece of work themselves could safely be acted upon. It could not, at any rate in the early days, without our satisfying ourselves that their decision would not be opposed by any of the Departments represented upon the Board. It would fall to the Assistant Secretary in charge to satisfy himself that the supreme authorities in the fighting Departments or other Departments represented, were in agreement with the proposals put forward before action was actually taken. This, you will realise, would be one of the important duties of the high official in question.

In a later sentence you go on to say that 'investigations will be carried out either at existing Government experimental establishments or at the Universities, private firms, etc. whichever is most suitable'. I agree that we cannot safely exclude the possibility of research for the fighting services by private firms, but the actual arrangements are not easy, and will need to be carefully considered in the light of the general attitude of the Department to private firms – a delicate problem, which is not by any means solved at the present moment.

I now come to the definite points which you put to me;

(1) The Assistant Secretary will be responsible for seeing that the decisions of the Committee, so far as they fall within the approved

programme of research, are put into action. Our idea is that each of the more important Boards or Committees will have a Technical Officer of the Department attached to them, whose duty it will be to prepare the technical material for the Committee under the general directions of the Assistant Secretary, and also to act under him if he thinks desirable in visiting laboratories and the like. The Assistant Secretary will also have a small staff, which will be used as the Secretariat of the Boards in drafting minutes and in seeing that the finance and more purely administrative work is put through in accordance with the practice of the Department. In these senses the Assistant Secretary will be executive, but naturally keen members of a Board may sometimes themselves take a more or less active part on the scientific side of the Board's work.

(2) It is not contemplated that the Assistant Secretary should be a member of each Board, but he will always of course be able to attend when he thinks it desirable, and it will sometimes be important that he should be present in order to explain the policy of the Department and keep the Boards for which he is responsible in line with each other. The Committees or the Boards will be kept as small as is consistent with a due representation upon them of each Government Department directly concerned and of the inclusion amongst them of independent men of science appointed by the Department through the Advisory Council.

(3) We contemplate that the Assistant Secretary and the Boards will have direct access to all experimental establishments in which any work is proceeding under their direct scientific control but, as you say, the administration of these Stations will be unchanged, and the control on our side will be confined to the work for which one of our Boards is responsible and will be scientific rather than administrative. The cost of this work, estimates of which will be submitted to and approved by the appropriate Board, will be met by periodical accounts sent by the Departments doing the work to us and discharged by our Finance Branch in due course, on the certification of the Assistant Secretary or one of his Officers.

Your reference to the research work at Farnborough which is of importance to industry in general, touches upon a part of the field where there is likely to be difficulty, because, as you know, before the co-ordination policy of the Government was adopted, the cabinet had decided that the Air Ministry was to remain responsible for all research work dealing with civil aviation, except in so far as it might be undertaken by a Research Association under this Department or as part of the general policy of the Department for aiding research in pure science.

If you will look at Page 11 of *The Times* for today you will notice that there are three clauses defining the respective spheres of the Air

Ministry and this Department. Clause C contemplates the establishment of permanent machinery for general co-ordination of Government research, and so far as the Air Ministry is concerned this general co-ordination has to be worked out. The devising of a workable arrangement will fall largely upon the new Assistant Secretary, and that is one reason, I may say, why I should like to see you in this Office; but if we may take as an example some other research establishment for the fighting services, such as Woolwich, where the particular complication that exists in the case of the Air Ministry is absent, your assumption that the whole of their scientific investigations should be submitted to the appropriate Board is right. I have no doubt that we shall find a certain unwillingness to place all cards on the table – indeed there is some evidence of it already – but with patience and tact I believe this can be squared, for we have the Treasury firmly behind us in this policy, and if any Department is unwilling to play the game it will soon find that its means are cut off at the source. It is quite true that in practice research work is likely to be initiated by Officers of the different Departments, and the money difficulties are insufficient to ensure that the Department concerned will keep the Boards informed, but, as you rightly say, it is an important part of the work of the new Assistant Secretary to see as tactfully as he can that everything possible is referred to the co-ordinating Boards.

(4) As you will have gathered from what I have already said, the Aeronautical Research Council is just the most difficult part of the whole problem. The trouble is, it does not fit in to the new policy of the Government, and it ought, as you said, to be a committee of this Department; but we shall have to be slow in this matter, and begin by a working agreement which may lead to a tidy organisation later. The new Admiralty experimental Station at Teddington ought to be much easier to deal with because that Station will be confined to doing work of a secret nature for purely Admiralty purposes. All work of wider interest and the preliminary investigations upon which these secret applications will be built up is to be done at the National Physical Laboratory buildings, and I have no doubt whatever that the amount of work done in their own Laboratory will form a very small proportion of the total amount which they will wish to see done.

Turning next to your personal difficulties, I think you must recognise that the post is primarily administrative, but it is administration of a kind which deals throughout with scientific work and research. It would be almost impossible for anyone to fill the office effectively who was not a man of scientific standing. The amount of scientific initiative which the new Assistant Secretary can undertake will depend almost entirely upon himself. I am quite certain that he will not be discouraged, and if it were not exerted it would be at the least unfortunate. On the other hand, the initiation must, I think, be personal rather than official, just because of the doubts which might arise in the minds of other Departments if an officer in the powerful executive position of the Assistant Secretary had also the means of initiating research on behalf of this Department in his official capacity.

This sort of illogical position is, as you know, very common in this country. If scientific initiation were definitely stated as one of the Assistant Secretary's functions, it might lead to suspicion, while if he is the right man he will have ample opportunity in fact of exercising it. It would be absolutely essential that the Assistant Secretary should, as you say, 'Try to get and keep the confidence of the scientific, as well as the military, world', and to this end his connexion with Scientific Societies would be vital. I also agree that the more direct contact you could have with the investigations for which the Department and the Boards would be responsible the better, so that, as we agree, your work would by no means be confined to the Office, though in the early days I am afraid you would find it necessary to be on the spot a good deal.

APPENDIX TWO

Note from Sir Henry Tizard to Sir Arthur Street, Permanent Secretary at the Air Ministry and Secretary of the Air Council in June 1942, on suggested reorganization of Scientific and Technical Resources in War.

Note on Use of Scientific and Technical Resources in War

(1) There is undoubtedly a number of men of standing in the world of science and engineering who are unhappy about the use of the scientific and technical resources of the country. It must be admitted, however, that many of these have not sufficient inside knowledge to give a really informed opinion. At the same time the people, of whom I am one, who have inside knowledge are also unhappy although much has been done.

(2) The immediate reason for this rather sudden public agitation and for the action of the President of the Royal Society, and others, must be attributed to the defeats in Libya and Russia. I always think it is unfortunate that people should get very excited about organisation whenever there is a defeat. At the same time the Government may well feel impelled to do something now to allay public anxiety.

My anxiety is that they should not do the wrong thing and get the last state of things no better or worse than the first.

(3) Perhaps I had better state why I am anxious. On paper the position is much better than it was at the beginning of the war, and very much better than it was in the last war. There are now scientific advisers in each of the Service Departments in very close contact with the operational staff. In the Air Ministry, which has gone further than any other Department within my knowledge, committees which discuss matters of technical importance to the Air Force are seldom without scientific advice. The Research Establishments working for the three Services are on the whole very good. They might, of course, be better. I should be surprised if the standard of the personnel, in corresponding German Stations was higher than in ours. So what I call the tactical strength of science in this war is good. In other words, once it is decided what to do, the technical job is, as a rule, done well. I am, however still concerned with what I call the strategy of science applied to war. This is to say, broadly the problem of deciding what to do and particularly the problem of preparing for the future, because research and development and production take a long time.

(4) This is or ought to be the main work of the Chief Scientific Advisers. The trouble is that they all feel that their advice is not sufficiently taken, or not taken in time. A good many instances of this could be given. There is, in fact, only one Scientific Adviser who is in a position to get something done quickly even if the Fighting Service staffs do not altogether agree with him, and he is Lord Cherwell. The feeling, which a good many of us share, is that this power to get some decision made quickly, and some action to follow, should not be altogether confined to Lord Cherwell.

(5) In America there is a Joint Weapons Committee under the Chairmanship of Dr Bush, who was at one time Head of the Massachusetts Institute of Technology and who is very well known by scientists and engineers. This Joint Weapons Committee has direct authority from the President to initiate developments which in their opinion are likely to be of importance in the war. Professor A. V. Hill and others have urged that there should be a corresponding body in this country. I think it would be difficult to achieve this because our constitution is different. Ministers in this country have far more responsibility than Ministers in the United States, and they might well claim that the existence of a body corresponding to the Joint Weapons Committee would interfere unduly with their responsibilities.

(6) Professor A. V. Hill's suggestion is to form a Technical Chiefs of Staff Committee corresponding to the Chiefs of Staff Committee and on the same kind of level. The broad duty of such a committee would be to determine the strategy of science and technology applied

to war, just as the Chiefs of Staff Committee determine the strategy of operations. I very much doubt, however, whether this would work unless there was in existence a man who could be appointed Chairman and who would have the full confidence of all the Service Departments, the two Production Departments, and the independent scientists and engineers. I do not think such a paragon exists; and if the wrong chairman were put in only confusion would result. He would have too great executive powers.

(7) Sir Edward Appleton has suggested to me an alternative which has a good deal to be said for it. I think I should be right in interpreting his suggestion as implying the abolition of the Scientific and Engineering Advisory Committees of the Cabinet and the appointment in their place of a Board of Advisers of about six people and not more than ten, which would be attached to the Defence Committee of the Cabinet. Such a Board might include the present Chief Scientific Advisers of the Prime Minister, and the other Ministries, strengthened by some really prominent representatives of engineering. Such a reconstituted Board should have, in Appleton's opinion (which I share) much greater powers than the present Scientific and Engineering Advisory Committees. The Board as a whole through its individual members would be empowered to initiate any enquiry which was thought to be of value to the war effort and to report direct to the Defence Committee. It would not be executive. I do not see how it could be executive, unless the whole present departmental machinery is changed. In fact, it would be no more executive than Lord Cherwell; but as a Board in a corresponding position it would have equal power to get something done if the Defence Committee accepted its advice.

(8) I must confess that when I try to think of concrete terms of reference I find myself a little at a loss. My view is that if scientists who are trying to determine technical policy do not work in the closest collaboration with the staffs of the Service Departments and of other Government Departments concerned, they will not be of great value. The trouble now, however, is that most of the highly placed officers on the staffs of the Service Departments are so pressed with urgent matters and day-to-day problems, that they have not the time to put the right amount of thought to the more distant problems, and broadly speaking people in my position can help far more on the more distant problems than they can on the immediate ones which are well looked after by other people. So we are in this difficulty, namely the Chiefs of Staff and the highly placed officers serving under them must trust someone to form a good judgement on these more distant problems, or we shall go on throughout the war taking hurried and even panic action to get over difficulties as they arise, which not only might have been but often have been foreseen. I

FF

think that the kind of body envisaged by Appleton would really help in giving the Scientific Advisers rather more authority in fact, although not on paper. If this was so I think it would be a step in the right direction.

References

References to Sir Henry Tizard's writings are given when the quotation is from his unfinished and unpublished autobiography, his addresses or, as in a few cases, from material in the Cherwell Papers. Most of his letters, notes, and summaries of events are, however, in the Tizard Papers, and references to these are only given where special circumstances appear to warrant them.

Abbreviations: Tizard Papers T.P.; Cherwell Papers Ch. P.

CHAPTER ONE

1. Autobiography.
2. Autobiography.
3. Information on Westminster in earlier years from Lawrence Tanner.
4. Autobiography.
5. Autobiography.
6. Address to Belfast University, 1953.
7. *Oxford Mail*, 22 July 1943.
8. T.P.
9. N. V. Sidgwick, *Obit. Not. Royal Soc.*, 9.
10. N. V. Sidgwick, *Obit. Not. Royal Soc.*, 9.
11. Autobiography.
12. Address, Frontiers of Science Foundation, Oklahoma, June 1957.
13. Autobiography.
14. Personal Record, Royal Society.
15. Statement by Lord Hankey to author.
16. Broadcast, *I Knew A Man*, 16 December 1945.
17. Autobiography.

CHAPTER TWO

1. Autobiography.
2. *The Aeroplane.*
3. Talk to H.M.S. Collingwood, 9 September 1944.
4. Letter from R. B. Bourdillon to Sir Harold Hartley.
5. Autobiography.
6. Autobiography
7. Autobiography.
8. Letter to Sir Harold Hartley in T.P.
9. 100 *Years of Phosphorus Making*, R. E. Threlfall.
10. 'Science in the Air Force', written for *R.A.F. Review.*

11. *Spectator*, 8 November 1963.
12. Broadcast, *Bertram Hopkinson*, 5 March 1937.
13. Autobiography, notes compiled by Tizard from log-book, and cuttings in T.P.
14. '*A Scientist In and Out of the Civil Service*', Haldane Memorial Lecture, 1955.
15. Autobiography.
16. Autobiography.
17. Autobiography.

CHAPTER THREE

1. T.P.
2. Autobiography.
3. Statement to author.
4. Ch. P.
5. Autobiography.
6. Letter to Sir Harold Hartley.
7. Letter to Sir Harold Hartley.
8. Letter to Sir Harold Hartley.
9. D.S.I.R. Annual Report.
10. T.P.
11. Autobiography.
12. Letter from Sir Cyril Hinshelwood to Sir Harold Hartley.
13. T.P.
14. *The Department of Scientific and Industrial Research*, Sir Harry Melville, p. 34.
15. T.P.
16. T.P.
17. T.P.
18. Autobiography.
19. T.P.
20. T.P.
21. Letter from R. E. Threlfall.

CHAPTER FOUR

1. Letter to author from Dr. H. J. T. Ellingham.
2. T.P.
3. *Science at the Universities*, Aberdeen, 1934.
4. Letter to author.
5. Letter to author.
6. Letter to Sir Harold Hartley.
7. T.P.
8. *Focus and Diversions*, L. L. Whyte, p. 144.
9. T.P.
10. Autobiography.
11. *The Gentle Art*, R. E. Threlfall.

CHAPTER FIVE

1. *The New Cambridge Modern History*, Vol. XII, p. 283.
2. *The Battle of Britain*, Basil Collier, p. 18.
3. *One Story of Radar*, A. P. Rowe, pp. 4–5.

4. The main documentary sources for the setting-up of the Tizard Committee are the Tizard and Cherwell Papers, and Wimperis's diaries.
5. Statement to author.
6. Statement to author.
7. *Proceedings of the Institute of Radio Engineers*, 1922, 10.
8. *Proceedings of the Royal Society*, A, 1925, 109.
9. *Nature*, 1925, 115.
10. *Army Radar*, Brigadier A. P. Sayer, pp. 301–2.
11. Post Office Radio Report, *No*. 223.
12. *Proceedings of the Institute of Radio Engineers*, 1933, 21.
13. Statement to author.
14. T.P.
15. Quoted in *Three Steps to Victory*, Sir Robert Watson-Watt, p. 109.
16. Wimperis diary.
17. Ch. P.
18. Ch. P.
19. Ch. P.
20. T.P.
21. T.P.
22. *The Second World War*, Winston Churchill, Vol. I, p. 117.
23. T.P.
24. T.P.
25. Ch. P.
26. Information from Mrs. John Watson, daughter of H. E. Wimperis.

CHAPTER SIX

1. Talk to H.M.S. Collingwood, 9 September 1944.
2. Memorandum by Mr. Justice du Parcq, quoted in *Design and Development of Weapons: Studies in Government and Industrial Organisation*, M. M. Postan, D. Hay and J. D. Scott.
3. 'Infrared Detection in British Air Defence, 1935–38', R. V. Jones, *Infrared Physics*, 1961 Vol. I, p. 154.
4. Ch. P.
5. Sir Robert Watson-Watt, *Discovery*, June, 1961.
6. T.P. and Ch. P.
7. Ch. P.
8. Ch. P.
9. Ch. P.
10. T. P.
11. T.P.
12. T.P.
13. Ch. P.
14. T.P.

CHAPTER SEVEN

1. The main sources drawn upon for the account of the Biggin Hill Experiment are the Tizard Papers and interviews with those concerned.
2. *Three Steps to Victory*, Sir Robert Watson-Watt, p. 173.
3. T.P.

4. T.P.
5. T.P.
6. Letter to author.
7. Letter to Dr Noble Frankland.
8. T.P.
9. T.P.
10. 'Science in the Air Force', written for *R.A.F. Review*.

CHAPTER EIGHT

1. T.P.
2. *Old Men Forget*, Duff Cooper, p. 220.
3. *Deep River Review*, October, 1946.
4. *The Battle of Britain*, Basil Collier, p. 162.
5. T.P.
6. T.P.
7. Letter to author.
8. *Now It Can Be Told*, Leslie R. Groves, p. 33.
9. *ALSOS: The Failure in German Science*, Samuel A. Goudsmit, p. 71.
10. T.P.
11. T.P.
12. *The Second World War*, Winston Churchill, Vol. I, p. 301.
13. T.P.

CHAPTER NINE

1. *The Strategic Air Offensive Against Germany*, 1939–45, Vol. I, p. 80n.
2. Statement to author.
3. Statement to author.
4. Letter to author.
5. 'Science in the Air Force', written for *R.A.F. Review*.
6. Letter to author.
7. Letter to author.
8. T.P.
9. T.P.
10. T.P.
11. T.P.
12. Letter from M. Allier to author.
13. T.P.

CHAPTER TEN

1. Sources for the account of the German navigational beams, of their discovery, and of the manner in which their importance was recognized
include the Tizard Papers, the Cherwell Papers, other documents, and
interviews with a number of those most closely involved.
2. Ch. P.
3. T.P.
4. Quoted in *The Prof. in Two Worlds*, Birkenhead, p. 195.
5. Ch. P.
6. *The Second World War*, Winston Churchill, Vol. II, p. 342.
7. Statement and letter to author.

8. T.P.
9. T.P.
10. T.P.
11. T.P.
12. T.P.
13. T.P.

CHAPTER ELEVEN

1. *North American Supply*, Duncan Hall, p. 46.
2. Main sources for the account of the Tizard Mission and of the events leading up to it, are Tizard's diaries and the material which he began to collect when contemplating a history of the Mission.
3. T.P.
4. T.P.
5. T.P.
6. T.P.
7. T.P.
8. T.P.
9. Ch.P.
10. T.P.
11. T.P.
12. Letter to Sir Harold Hartley.
13. Letter to author.
14. *Scientists Against Time*, J. P. Baxter, p. 255.
15. *Deep River Review*, October, 1946.
16. *Five Years at the Radiation Laboratory*, p. 12.

CHAPTER TWELVE

1. *The Second World War*, Winston Churchill, Vol. II, p. 407.
2. Royal Society Archives.
3. *Grand Strategy*, Vol. II, J. R. M. Butler, p. 354.
4. *The Memoirs of Lord Chandos*, Lord Chandos, p. 170.
5. *The Battle of Britain*, Basil Collier, pp. 27 and 54.
6. *Leader of the Few*, Basil Collier, p. 226.
7. *The Prof. in Two Worlds*, Birkenhead, p. 215.
8. *Scientists Against Time*, J. P. Baxter, p. 121.
9. Letter to author.
10. Letter to author.
11. T.P.
12. Hansard.
13. Letter to author.

CHAPTER THIRTEEN

1. Ch. P.
2. Ch. P.
3. *The Times*, August 7, 1945.
4. *Nature*, Vol. 180, 1957, p. 581.
5. Statement to author.
6. *Jet*, Air Commodore Sir Frank Whittle, p. 112.

7. Ch. P.
8. Quoted in *British War Production*, Michael Postan, p. 122.
9. *The Strategic Air Offensive Against Germany*, 1939–45, Vol. IV., Sir Charles Webster and Noble Frankland, p. 136.
10. *Victory in the West, Vol. I, The Battle of Normandy*, Major L. F. Ellis. p. 23.
11. Letter to Colonel Cooper.
12. T.P.
13. T.P.
14. T.P.
15. T.P.
16. *The Strategic Air Offensive Against Germany*, 1939-45, Vol. IP336, Sir Charles Webster and Noble Frankland.
17. *The Memoirs of Lord Chandos*, Lord Chandos, p. 169.
18. T.P.
19. Ch. P.
20. *Oxford Magazine*, May, 1963.

CHAPTER FOURTEEN

1. Tizard compiled a series of notes for his successor which give a good idea of what he regarded as the present and future problems of the College.
2. Statement to author.
3. *Vickers*, J. D. Scott, p. 280.
4. Main source for the account of the projected Russian Mission is the series of summaries made by Tizard of the events leading up to its final cancellation.
5. *The Origins and Development of Operational Research in the Royal Air Force*, pp. 34–35.
6. T.P.
7. Statement to author.
8. Letter to author.
9. T.P.
10. Ch. P.
11. T.P.

CHAPTER FIFTEEN

1. *Triumph in the West*, 1943–46, Sir Arthur Bryant, p. 487.
2. 'Science and the Services', *Journal of the Royal United Service Institution*, August, 1946.
3. Letter to author.
4. *The Atomic Origins of the British Nuclear Deterrent*, Alfred Goldberg, *International Affairs*, July, 1964.
5. *A Scientist in and out of the Civil Service*, Haldane Memorial Lecture, 1955.
6. *Woomera*, Ivan Southall.
7. *Science and Democracy*, Arthur Dehon Little Memorial Lecture, M.I.T., 1951.

CHAPTER SIXTEEN

1. *The Strategy of Science*, Messel Memorial Lecture, 1952.
2. *The Daily Telegraph*.
3. Letter to author.

Bibliography

The Tizard Papers and the Cherwell Papers are the main sources on which I have drawn in the writing of this book. The diaries of the late H. E. Wimperis have been of very great help in dealing with certain periods, and other manuscript material has also been made available to me. Much information, as will be clear from the references, has also come direct from Sir Henry's friends. In addition, I have been helped by the following published material:

Baxter, James Phinney, *Scientists Against Time*, (1946)
Birkenhead, the Earl of, *The Prof. in Two Worlds*, (1961)
Blackett, Professor P. M. S., *Tizard and the Science of War* (Tizard Memorial Lecture), (1960)
Butler, Professor J. R. M., *Grand Strategy*, Vol. II, (1957)
Bryant, Sir Arthur, *Triumph in the West*, 1943–1946, (1959)
Chandos, Lord, *Memoirs*, (1961)
Churchill, Winston, *The Second World War*, (1948–1954)
Collier, Basil, *Leader of the Few*, (1957)
Collier, Basil, *The Defence of the United Kingdom*, (1957)
Collier, Basil, *The Battle of Britain*, (1962)
Crowther, J. G., and Whiddington, R., *Science at War*, (1947)
Ellis, Major L. F., *Victory in the West.*, *Vol. I, The Battle of Normandy*, (1962)
Farren, Sir W. S. and Jones Professor R. V., *Henry Thomas Tizard* graphical Memoirs of Fellows of The Royal Society), (1961)
Goudsmit, Samuel A., *ALSOS: The Failure in German Science*, (1947)
Grey, C. G., *A History of The Air Ministry*, (1940)
Hall, Duncan, *North American Supply*, (1955)
Hill, A. V., *The Ethical Dilemma of Science*, (1960)
Melville, Sir Harry, *The Department of Scientific and Industrial Research*, (1962)
Pile, Sir Frederick, *Ack-Ack*, (1956)
Postan, Michael, *British War Production*, (1952)

Rowe, A. P., *One Story of Radar*, (1948)
Sayer, Brigadier, A. P., *Army Radar* (1950)
Scott, J. D., *Vickers*, (1962)
Snow, Sir Charles, *Science and Government*, (1961)
Southall, Ivan, *Woomera*, (1962)
Watson-Watt, Sir Robert, *Three Steps to Victory*, (1958)
Webster, Sir Charles, and Frankland, Noble, *The Strategic Air Offensive against Germany*, 1939–45, (1961)
Whittle, Air Commodore Sir Frank, *Jet*, (1953)
Willson, F. M. G., *The Organization of British Central Government*, (1957)

Index